Mitchell Smith

SIMON & SCHUSTER

DUE
NORTH

A Novel

NEW YORK LONDON TORONTO SYDNEY TOKYO SINGAPORE

SIMON & SCHUSTER
SIMON & SCHUSTER BUILDING
ROCKEFELLER CENTER
1230 AVENUE OF THE AMERICAS
NEW YORK, NEW YORK 10020

1   3   5   7   9   10   8   6   4   2

LIBRARY OF CONGRESS CATALOGING-IN-PUBLICATION DATA
SMITH, MITCHELL, date.
DUE NORTH : A NOVEL / MITCHELL SMITH.
P.   CM.
I. TITLE.
PS3569.M537834D8   1992
813'.54—DC20   92-17875
                                                              CIP

ISBN: 0-671-73877-1

To my friends—treasure irreplaceable

One cannot, I believe, look deeply into Nature, regarding her with any degree of penetration, without discovering one's self in her depths—by reflection sinister, but most perfectly placed . . . and wonderfully at ease.

REV. HENRY NORRIS NASHE

GRAMPIAN RAMBLES

STENNOCH & MILES

NEW COTTERS' LANE

EDINBURGH 1883

1

Sara stood on the fox until it died.

It had hissed at her, shown its neat white teeth, skipped around the number four leg-hold first one way, then the other, until she'd hit it hard on the muzzle with the hickory club. At that it collapsed, rich red as an autumn leaf, and stretched and trembled on the snow.

Sara stood on it until it died—felt the faint motion through her boot-pacs' thick soles as it tried to breathe, then no motion as it failed.

Alan had believed in skinning warm when possible—thought the pelt often tufted otherwise. Sara tugged her gloves off, pushed her snow-goggles up onto her forehead, then took the folding knife, a Clipit, from her parka pocket, thumbed the blade open and slit the fox's belly-skin from throat to vent. And on up the inside of each leg—working right-handed, holding, turning the warm carcass with her left.

The dogs, downslope, yelped and shifted in their harness, smelling blood, staring with light-blue eyes up through the spruce scrub where she was skinning.

The pelt, reversed as it came off, was difficult around the head, and Sara picked it loose with little nicks under the ears, then tugged and pulled it steadily off to the muzzle, where lips and nose caught and were cut free.

She finished, wiped the blade on her wool trouser-leg, closed the knife, and put it in her parka pocket. Then she snapped the hide like a small bath towel to pop some shreds of meat and fat off it, stretched it in her hands, and laid it flat on the snow to stiffen. Her hands, covered crinkled with bright freezing blood, were woody from the cold. She snow-scrubbed them fairly clean, put her gloves on, then picked the bare carcass up—already cool—and slid downslope.

The dogs were tied off on their gangline stretched straight from the sled to a small white spruce. Sara, holding the fox's body high out of their clamoring reach (yelps, ululations), slid the camp ax out from under the sled's bungees. She laid the fox along a root risen out of the snow, and chopping with her hand held almost up to the ax's head, cut the animal into seven roughly even portions, then tossed these to the dogs, an accurate piece for each—the first out to Dutchy, her lead; the second and third to Cherry and Kickapoo (swings); fourth and fifth to Dipsy and Doodle (team haulers); and the last two pieces to Fatso and Smiley (wheelers). Fatso's piece never hit the snow; he was an always-starving dog.

All the meat and bone was gone in a bite or two, and Sara kicked through snow with a remnant of the fox's guts in her gloved hand, and fed that to Dutchy. "Oh, there's a dog," she said. ". . . There's a *strong* dog."

And so he was. Finished eating, he sat smiling, red tongue lolling (steaming in frigid air), his eyes, a movie star's bright and vacant blue, squinted with pleasure while she scratched behind his ears and praised him—a freighter malamute at almost a hundred pounds, and the grandson of an all-state weight-pull winner, Ping-Pong. Heir to that dog's great strength and rough, short, black-and-white coat— heir to his short temper as well. Sara never touched Dutchy while he was eating; he hadn't been able to stand that, even as a pup.

"Have you been good?" Sara said. "—Have you? Have you been good?" She hugged him; felt through her parka the softness of his fur . . . felt, beneath that, muscle smooth and dense as oak. He smelled only of snow. "—Yes. Dutchy is a *very* good dog."

Sara stroked him, then left him to climb the short slope to the trap and pelt. She unclipped the trap's short chain, retrieved the small sheet of white waxed butcher's paper that had protected and concealed it amid the snow, then shook snow from the fox skin, and slid down to the sled. She tucked the jingling trap and chain away in the big canvas trap-bag with the others, corded the rich red fur on top of the bundle of hides—mostly marten, smoky brown—then packed both trap-bag and pelts away into the sled sack, and zipped its long zipper closed.

"Last line, now. Last sets," Sara said to the dogs, stepped over to lift Kickapoo where he'd tangled tug-lines with Cherry, then walked up the team to slip the gangline tie from its sapling spruce.

"A straight gangline from sled to lead, tied-off lead and anchored sled— that's parked. That, or take the gang around the sled, tie off the first tug-line to the sled. That's also parked. Anything else," Alan had said, *"—is*

bullshit for dog-whippers, Natives, or that bunch down on the river. In the mountains, let's do it right."

That had been after their first few months in the range, when they'd felt it was very important to do things right—before they'd learned just how important it was.

"Make one mistake too many, and this mountain'll roll over in its sleep and pop us like ticks. . . ."

That was their first winter. Sara'd seen wolves—the only time in three years she was to see them so close. She saw wolves lying in the sun-struck snow fallen on their garden ground out beside the cabin. Stretched out on bright snow as if there were no small cabin beside them, as if they hadn't noticed Sara's face through the single side window's thick plastic sheeting. As if they heard no uproar from the dog yard farther out, above the creek.

The wolves had rolled in the snow, the soft stuff caking in their gray coats, then showering free as they rose and shook themselves. They didn't look like dogs—too big and big-headed, long-legged, low-tailed.

An older female, Sara'd thought, and three younger males—maybe her pups of two years before.

The wolves had stretched and rolled, paying no attention to the dogs' noises, to Sara watching. They'd dug in the snow here and there. Then—the female deciding and suddenly leading out—they'd left, quartered the slope over deep drifts, reached the woods and filed away.

Alan said it was the dog salmon, hauled up rotten for the garden, that had drawn them. Said he'd been in the country eight years, and had never seen wolves that close. Envied her. . . .

Sara walked back to the sled, bent behind the runners to haul the snow-hook up and hang it at the sled's right-side stanchion, said "Whoa . . . whoa," as she felt the dogs stand out of the snow, set to their harness, eager to go. *"Whoa,* goddamn it!"—then hopped onto the runners and gripped the drive bow as Dutchy lined out, led the team snaking through the last of the stand of spruce . . . and their harness faintly jingling, on at a run along the open slope toward evening. A twilight, soon to end the afternoon, was settling shadowed from the west, where a wall of black clouds leaned over the peaks.

Sara, gliding fast, looked up to study the storm, and saw it would bring down too much wind and weather to travel through to home.

*   *   *

She'd set the last snares and traps of the line along a brushy creek-bed breaking below a two-mile reach of open ground, snowed-over tundra. The team was happy with that stretch, even after four days out, pleased with the chance to run without bucking brush and rocks, without hitting steeps where they had to drag the sled up almost on end (Sara shoving behind).

Dutchy led them in a long descending curve across the mountain's flank—Sara riding all the way, standing balanced on birch runners, the wind of their passage stinging her face, making her cheekbones ache. There was still enough sunlight glittering off the snow to hurt her eyes, even through the goggles. First morning out, she'd left her snow-goggles off through late winter's short daylight hours—and the morning after, she'd been blind to fine detail, her eyes painful enough to make her cry.

The storm wind came down the mountain just before they reached the willows along the creek—combed the running dogs' fur in swift patterns of gray, black, and white, and shoved the sled skidding downslope until Sara, hauling on the bow, wrestled it back on line.

"Hey, *haw. Haw* you Dutchy!" And that fine lead—so much better in the mountains than Flyer had been, much better at working through brush, past granite outcrops—swung the team left and into the creek bed's rough tunnel under bent alder and dwarf willow. The wind blew hard behind them, pushed them farther in, the dogs scurrying, leaping through snow, wind blowing the plumes of their tails.

The daylight was almost gone under weather, and Sara—riding the left runner, scooter-kicking with her right boot—jockeyed the sled along, bumped over roots beneath the snow, and felt the strength of the storm shove at her back, then lessen as the willows took the brunt.

In this shelter of frozen wickerwork, wind and snow hissing hard through tangled brush, Sara ran the team along the creek edge to find overflow under bare arching branches. The sled's left runner rode high over a sudden willow root, and the sled slewed—the team still galloping—struck a small alder's trunk along the left rail, and knocked Sara off the runner. She held onto the bow and was dragged along, struggled to get her feet under her, screamed *"Whoa!"* into the wind's noise—and as the sled struck something else and bucked harder, was thrown forward and hit her face on the drive-bow so hard she thought she'd broken a front tooth. "Whoa, fuck you god *damn* you!" and the team slowed—slowed as well by the deepening thicket—so she was able to pull herself back up on the runners and stomp the brake to slow the sled, then *gee*'d Dutchy right along the creek side, yelled "Whoa!" again, and slid where snow lay folded down through the willows to border shallow overflow. Here, the water ran over crumbled glittering edge-ice, and the dogs, panting, their deep fur frosted with their breath's condensation, drank in harness—a long drink while they high-stepped like cats as their paws got wet.

Sara, behind the sled, took her right glove off and felt gingerly at her mouth, touched her front teeth gently with her fingertips—feeling less and less as her fingers grew colder, but felt no broken bit, no sharp edge. Her upper lip was numb from the blow; her gums ached there. . . . When the dogs were finished, she put her glove back on, called for their attention, and *haw*'d Dutchy back upslope a few yards, clear of the closest of the brush. She dropped her snow-hook, stamped to set it in, and ran up the right side of the team with the coil of tie-off—interrupting Dutchy as he was stepping a bed-circle in the snow—and knotted the end of the gangline to a stunted willow.

Then she kicked back through wind-streaming drifts, lifted the strap running diagonally over her right shoulder, swung the sheathed shotgun off her back and set it by the sled. The darkening air grew heavy with cold; ten below, she felt, and dropping.

Sara unzipped the big sled sack, and reached in to tug her pack-board and heavy parka out. She ran her tongue along her front teeth—they seemed to be all right; there was some feeling in her lip, now. She took off her light parka, tucked the snow-goggles and gloves into its pockets, and stuffed it down into the sack. Then she struggled into the heavy parka, a thick down pullover reaching below her knees, lifted the pack-board to her back and adjusted its wide straps. She put on the mittens that hung from the parka's sleeves, and from its right pocket pulled her miner's headlamp—the strap heavy with four small batteries clipped along it—then pushed her parka hood back to fit the headband on tight enough not to slip, tight enough to give her a headache as long as she needed light.

Sara unhooked the bungee cords holding the chuck box to the sled's frame, slid it from behind the sled sack, lifted the lid, and took out seven pieces of frozen caribou, tossed them out to the team—Dutchy's piece first—then closed the box and shoved it back into place. She pulled the hickory billy from beneath its lashing, then went to the sled's drive bow, dug in the possibles-sack hanging there for the small white-plastic box of spare .22 ammunition, and slid it down into her right parka pocket.

She picked up the sheathed shotgun, swung it to her back to lie alongside the pack-board, and settled its shoulder strap—then trudged past the team and turned down toward the creek and first set, a number two leg-hold. The snares and traps, last of winter's last line, had been set alternately upslope and down along the creek's course through the drift of dwarf trees and scrub. Here, two years before, Alan had taken three wolverines—each succeeding drawn by the animal trapped before.

The snow was coming in fast, deeper as she walked it. By morning, she'd have to snowshoe out before the team, break trail so the dogs could haul without sinking.

Bending her head to keep ice-sheathed twigs from her eyes, Sara pushed her way through frigid willows to the creek. There, under a low roof of dark, bending branches, the stream lay frozen to its pebbles, only an occasional shallow streak of overflow still glimmering liquid in failing light. She knelt carefully by one of these, and bent to drink as her dogs had drunk, the water numbing her mouth, making her teeth ache. She saw in black ice-water faint reflected shadows of her dark eyes, her face, long-nosed, long-jawed within the parka's wolverine ruff. . . . She stood, stepped carefully across the creek, and followed the edge of that bank, her boot-pacs silent through frangible ice and stricken brush, their noise lost in the wind's hissing through branches, the dry pouring sound of more snow blowing in.

The first set, a cubby with a lure stick just downslope, was sprung and empty.

Sara unclipped the trap's chain from a willow root, reached over her left shoulder to stuff trap and chain down into her pack-board's sack, and walked on.

The second and third sets—snares—were empty, and she crossed back over the creek, coiling the snare wires, tucking them over her shoulder into the pack.

The fourth set—a pole trap baited with a spruce-hen's wing—held a small marten, a female, by the left foreleg. The marten dangled frozen to death, smiling in uncertain light, its slight body swinging in wind gusts to nudge the leaning pole it hung from.

Sara forced the trap—felt the carcass stiff as wood—slipped her mittens to unclip the trap's chain, then swung the pack-board off her back and slid trap, chain, and marten into its large sack. She lifted the pack onto her back again, settled it into place . . . then pulled on her mittens and walked along, ducking her head under branches, shoving her way through dense willows to the creek.

It was getting too dark to see through blowing snow. She reached up, switched her headlamp on, and found the modest light made darkness more definite beyond its small circle.

The next two sets—snares—were empty.

The seventh (a number one), held a muskrat's paw, right fore.

The next, a snare a long way out, had been set over a snowshoe-rabbit run along the creek, and fronted a stick smeared with lure, Pacific Call. —It held a mature lynx, a very big lynx in prime pelt. The cat, caught with its neck and left foreleg through the wire noose, was alive.

It stared into the soft tangerine of Sara's headlamp—the beam wavering as if the wind were blowing it—with eyes much more lambent than the light, and slit each center with a slice of black. Its rich pelt, soft and silver, was speckled, spotted, streaked with various grays seeming to flow up into its eyes, where those cool shades heated at once to molten gold.

The big cat's deep fur was divided, its sleek muscle dented beneath, where the snare's fine wire held it, forcing its left foreleg out at an awkward angle.

"I'm sorry," Sara said—not, she thought, over the noise of the wind, the snow's sifting sound—but the lynx jumped slightly in the snare, its glare more furiously yellow. The fluffy fur at its shoulders ruffled as a harder gust blew past and down the frozen creek, rattling willow branches to sound like caribou bucks fencing their antlers in the spring.

Sara stepped back a little for room to aim, and for that much more distance from the cat's stare—took off her mittens, tugged up her parka's fat bottom hem, and reached up into the warmth along her belt for the holstered Ruger .22. She drew the revolver, cocked it, raised the weapon . . . and saw a flurry of snow obscure her lamp's light as the lynx leaped and spun in the snare loop, bounded this way and that—and Sara thought right at her, so she stumbled back with a vision of the animal free, ripping through her parka, setting its claws into her breasts.

She almost fired at it from fear, fear's shame—then seeing it still caught firm, aimed the Single-Six with both hands, sighting first for the animal's left eye, then, that being too beautiful to spoil, a black-tufted ear. But the lynx wouldn't stay still. It twisted and leaped to the snare's limit—left, then right—hysterical at her closeness.

By the headlamp's light—hazed near with her frosting breath, hazed beyond by swirls of snow—Sara saw only shifting gray-and-cream fur, savage eyes, the faintest strand of black wire still mottled camouflage-white with chalk. The snare wire swung and creaked softly (within the wind's larger sound) as the cat struggled. The lynx's soft, furred, outsized paws—the three free—patted and thudded lightly in the snow while it struggled, whirling, spinning half around in the noose to kick and spin again the other way, as if it were performing for Sara some rehearsed and intricate dance, presented in her lamp's mild beam.

She could draw no bead on an ear, be certain of no single shot where two or three might spoil the pelt past mending. Sara carefully eased the Ruger's hammer down, then lifted her parka's hem to reholster the pistol. She thought of killing the lynx with the hickory club (as Alan certainly would have), just as she'd hit the near-frozen fox—but imagined at once what a battle that would be with this animal, saw herself stooping to strike at the cat through low tangling brush, swinging the club in swaying light into a mask of toothed rage and fencing paws batting . . . claws reaching and reaching for her as she grunted with effort, stepping awkwardly in the snow, hitting.

It seemed too direct and embarrassing a thing to do, to try to kill it with the club. She wished for a poison dart. She wished the lynx had been caught fairly around the neck and hung already dead. Even better if it had passed the set by—and now slept miles away, a last clump of ptarmigan feathers, pink-white, blood-spattered, drifting away in the wind before its tree-root den.

Sara heard the dogs barking behind her, down the creek bed. The storm gusts blowing from this quarter had brought them the lynx's scent—or perhaps another's. She reached back over her right shoulder to find the sheathed shotgun's pistol grip, and drew the piece up and out, levering the weapon's weight off her shoulder so its short muzzle described a quick half-circle forward and down, its forestock smacking into her left hand as she snapped the safety off.

Sara turned, staring through driven snow and frozen willow, looking along the headlamp's beam for a more definite darkness than the storm had brought, some sizable dimness moving against the wind. . . . But saw nothing like that, nothing to have disturbed the dogs more than the scent of cat.

She stood watching a few moments longer, then turned—the headlamp's narrow beam, the shotgun's muzzle both turning with her—to look the other way, staring past the trapped lynx through latticed willow branches obscured by blowing snow.

Nothing there—and probably many weeks before there might be.

She watched a little longer, waited to see if the dogs began barking again . . . and when they didn't, set the safety, reversed the shotgun, and with both hands held high for an instant as if she were combing her hair, slid it back over her right shoulder and down into its sheath beside the pack.

The storm's wind, more and more tumultuous, sounded like surf among the willows. The snow rose up around her, whirling in her light. Out of this, only the cat's face, its full attention.

Sara shrugged out of her pack-board, swung it down, and bent to search among the traps, chain, and wire in the big sack for a snare. She tugged out a nine-foot Thompson, wound the tie-off end of the wire three times around her left wrist, shook out the snare's loop, and stepped up through snow to circle the lynx as it stood still for a moment—bound, held half-reared, watching her.

She got upslope of it, shouldered low willow branches aside, set herself, then tossed the loop out over the cat underhand, out into the lamp's soft light. The lynx reached up with its free right fore—so apparently casually that Sara saw out of downy fur, five horn-brown curved claws come springing, that very quickly hooked, snagged, and yanked on the wire, hauling hard for an instant so she was tugged sharply and slid a little in the snow, then recovered as the noose wire twanged softly free.

The lynx spun half around—and even trussed so, held reared in the air, batted out at her again with its free right front paw, as if the very sight of her were an enemy worth a blow. It struck out, the broad handsome face a mask of fear or rage or both, the fine eyes bright coins—and made a sound like a house cat's purr, but deeper, harsher, thick with vibration.

Sara retrieved her noose, set herself, threw again, and missed. The cat squalled and convulsed in its tether with such an explosive effort she stepped back into brush, afraid it would break free. Then, panting as if from great effort, she pulled the snare wire in again—and while the cat hung still for an instant, staring not quite at her, but as if at something just beyond, she lofted the loop out and knew it would catch before it did.

The wire settled, barely visible, over the tufted ears, the bulky tomcat's head—and Sara yanked back hard as she was able, felt her boot-pacs slipping in the snow, dug in her heels and hauled again. It occurred to her she hadn't put her mittens back on.

With her headlamp steady, she saw the lynx watching her, surprised, the foam of fur at its throat now disturbed by a second fine encircling line. Its masked face held a kitten's expression, so familiar when the little animals were held up by tender napes, the look startled, oriental, undignified, curious as to what might happen next.

Sara set her boot heels, dug them deep into the snow, and heaved back on the snare as suddenly, as forcefully as she could. She felt an instant shudder and twisting through the wire, then a shock and another as the cat yanked back, thrashing—struck back like a great hooked fish, slammed itself back so Sara slipped, tripped, fell on her back in the snow, and was dragged nearer the lynx. Its forepaw, the yearning claws, reached out as if to save her from further sliding.

Sara heard herself squeal in panic, and was ashamed as she sat scrabbling, lamplight swinging wildly, the heels of her boot-pacs digging in to kick and kick her away from the cat so she could scramble to her feet—imagining what Alan would have said if he'd seen her set herself to strangle an animal in blowing snow, with no thought of slipping.

The lynx hung still in the snare, watching her. It had bared its teeth, glistening white and perfect, teeth seeming too small for that wide great-eyed head.

Sara stamped deep into the snow, forced her heels down, checked that the snare wire was wound tight around her left wrist, got a grip on the wire with her right as well—and threw herself back, hauling with all her strength and weight.

The lynx, in the same instant, snarled coarsely as a starting engine and exploded in a cloud of fur and snow. Sara felt the snare wire bite hard into her wrist—as if the cat held her, not she the cat . . . as if it intended to haul her in, haul her in where it could reach her and rip through her parka in a flurry of white down that an instant after would turn red.

Her heart thumping, thumping, Sara grunted and heaved away, lay almost on her back and pulled as if her wrist were thick rope, insensible. Through the taut wire, she felt tremors . . . strumming harsh and various as if the cat, whirling, doubling, thrashing, were playing a sort of string music with her.

The storm wind blew a stream of snow whipping past them, and as if that wind had whispered the secret to her in the dark, Sara, remembering she'd left her mittens off, found she'd lost the feeling in her hands.

The lynx seemed to twist and twist, frighteningly strong, and dragged her slightly nearer. The cat was staring into the circle of her light, its eyes rich as pirate treasure.

Sara's hands now were only instruments, frost white in lamplight, no longer part of her. She admired them for holding on. —Arched, grunting into the wind's sounds, she pulled with the long muscles of her legs and back . . . and felt along her arms a sort of sinuous rhythm that would have been breathing if it could have been, and realized the lynx was strangling at last. Now, listening, she heard its harsh chain-saw snarl choked to whining as it found a last purchase in the willows it was snared among, and pulled away so violently she was yanked sitting up, and had to dig her heels in deeper.

Storm sounds slackening, Sara heard softer sounds of strain, of trying to breathe, and felt through dead hands a desperate vibration that trembled up her arms and shook tears from her that made her eyes ache, then ran freezing down her face.

The cat's head seemed larger than it had before, gleaming eyes half closed, its throat's fur gathered within the noose. Jaw slightly open, a row of small white teeth showed, and a hint of the dappled roof of its mouth, the tip of its pink tongue. The lynx was shuddering, this traveling down the wire in complicated telegraph—and presented, in desperation as it tried to breathe, what seemed a confiding expression, as if it were a pet, only mistaken for wild. So that now, rough play at an end, exhausted, frightened, it expected from this human human mercy, a different outcome than conflict's end with wolf or wolverine—as if it were requesting from this singular opponent (smelling female, though smelling odd) who had come upon it while it was caught in so strange a way, an armistice.

Sara, embarrassed, hauled harder, her head back, her back arched, until the wind slackened slightly, then blew harder—and as if that gust had taken the lynx's life with it as it went, rattling away through icy willows, Sara felt no more tremors through the wire.

She let the snare wire go, which was difficult to do, her silver fingers slow, very slow to open—and worked her hands up under the hem of her parka, up under her sweater and wool shirt and long-johns undershirt, and was able to hold them against her bare belly. Her hands were so cold they felt hot, and seemed to burn her skin.

Hands held pressed against her, Sara bent closer to see the lynx by lamplight. Obscure through falling snow and seeming smaller than before, it sagged relaxed as if asleep in its cradle of nooses. The perfect eyes were slightly open, its neat jaws agape. Sara, now bold, stepped in to nudge it with her right boot toe. The lynx hung unresponsive—a playmate sick of play, and gone. Sara's hands were hurting a great deal as they warmed, and she stood a while longer in the wind, the swirling snow, waiting until she could feel her fingers as separate, move them freely.

The storm was growing slightly worse, the air a little colder—she felt it near fifteen below.

She touched the cat with the toe of her boot once more, to be certain, then slid her hands quickly from beneath her clothes and bent down to search at its snow-soft throat, find both loops of wire and tug them away, as if it were important that the cat, now dead, be free.

Then Sara fumbled her mittens on, lifted the lynx—surprisingly long, surprisingly heavy—and carried it over to a small driftwood log come down the creek last spring, an alder trunk a half foot thick, its narrow back just showing above the snow. She stretched the cat along the log, displaying fur rich as opal under the headlamp, then took her Clipit out, opened it, and slid the blade, edge up, into the belly skin and sliced it open. It was delicate work, mittened . . . to produce at last, in a haze of blowing snow, the lynx's stiff new carcass, smaller without its rich robe, and roped and threaded through with braids of dark-red muscle.

The last trap, a number one leg-hold set down into a rat run in the bank a hundred yards up-creek, held a frozen muskrat.

. . . Finished dealing with that, traps and chains in her backpack, the lynx's carcass and pelt, the muskrat and marten packed in as well, Sara trudged through darkness in deepening snow back down the long creek grove to the sled.

She unbuckled her pack-board, set it down, unzipped the long sled-sack and wrestled the big pack in, lumpy with gear and dead animals. Then dug for her tent, rations, and sleeping bag, left them in the snow, and untied the bundle of dog chains from the sled's left-side stanchions.

Sara went down the line, calling the team up out of their snow beds, unharnessing, petting and praising, checking pads for cuts and ice balls. She chained each dog to a willow—all except for Dutchy—to form a big uneven six-dog circle around the sled. Then she opened the chuck box and took out the last seven servings of caribou-gut mulligan, frozen into heavy white chunks. She tossed one to Dutchy, then fed the others . . . and stood listening to the wind, her feet cold, toes numb in the boot-pacs, watching to see how eagerly each dog ate, whether it seemed more tired than it should be, whether its tail was held up or down. They'd watered in overflow four times through the day, which should have been enough.

Cherry was a sweet-tempered dog—Siberian cross, though marked Siberian—and the only female in the team, with Vanilla out pupping. She was strong at the start, but liable to run out of gas, let Kickapoo pull for her. Sara stood watching Cherry eat frozen caribou in the headlamp's light. She seemed lively enough—not too weary from four days mushing, with only one good hot meal at the line shed. Lively enough. . . .

Feeling sleepy with the cold, Sara heard echoes in the wind as often when she was very tired, as if people were shouting a distance away. Or had called out a long time before, and now the wind had brought those sounds with it. . . . She thought about what she had to do, and put those things in order in her mind. She stopped watching Cherry (who'd eaten, and was already circling to make her snow bed), stopped watching Cherry and walked back through the snow to the sled, unzipped the tent sack, tugged the small bundle out of it, and began to set the two-man mountain up—hearing herself grunt with effort just from fitting the fiberglass rods together, making sure the red tent-fabric was taut, its metal clips (covered with black plastic so as not to stick to skin in the cold) hooked to the rods. For the clips, she had to take her mittens off—was careful to remember to put them on again when the tent was set up, its snow-fly taut across it.

Sara walked around the mountain tent to be certain it was up right and tight. Wished now for the big wall tent and sheepherders' stove, weight, trouble and all. The snow, hard, fine, and grainy, was blowing in through her parka-hood's ruff so she could see only with eyes squinted almost shut. She went over by the small willow where Fatso lay chained, watching her (his eyes reflecting electric-green circles in the headlamp's light) and hoping for a surprise, a treat, a snack. Dutchy, loose, followed to see what she was doing. Sara kicked a shallow hollow in the snow—could see it filling as wind blew fresh snow in—then took her mittens off, tugged a wad of toilet paper from her parka's left pocket, lifted its hem, and reached under her sweater to unbuckle the pistol belt and her pants belt. She unbuttoned her wool trousers, pulled them down (her two pairs of long-johns pants as well), squatted, and peed.

Dutchy and Fatso sat staring at her, interested.

In those few seconds, crouched in a whirling fabric of blown snow tinted orange by her headlamp, Sara felt her buttocks begin to sting with cold. She reached under to wipe herself, stood up in the slight steam rising from her urine, pulled up her long-johns, her pants, buttoned them, and buckled the belt. She rolled the pistol belt around the holstered .22, tucked it under her left arm, then put her mittens on.

She stepped over to scratch Fatso behind his ears. "You pudgy," she said to him above the wind. "—Did you think I had a treat for you? Did you? Well, I don't." Fatso paid such close attention to this speech, looked up at her through the snow so much like a child by lamplight, that Sara bent and kissed the soft muzzle, felt the dog's nose cold against her cold cheek. Dutchy, annoyed by any display of affection unless to him, turned and trotted off into the dark.

Sara walked back to the sled bow, opened her possibles-sack and put the pistol and belt away, then picked up her bed-roll and un-hooked the bungees from her sleeping bag—very expensive, an Ice-Master mummy with five-inch Fiberfill loft. (This had been Alan's; she used it because it still smelled of him a little.) She shoved the sleeping bag through the small tent's flap entrance, pushed her ra-tion sack in after that, brushed what snow she could from her parka, pants, and boot-pacs, then went to all fours to crawl in, her head-lamp revealing the tent's vaginal reds, its seamed and narrow space.

Inside the fabric's close drumming, in the headlamp's glow, Sara took off her mittens, lifted the shotgun strap over her head and swung the weapon off her back. She slid it out of its sheath, and laid it (muzzle toward the entrance) along the tent's right side, the side the sleeping bag unzipped. Then she dug into the ration sack, took out a spoon and a jar of *kamamik* and two thick sticks of moose jerky. The *kamamik* (this recipe moose-kidney fat and blueberries, all whipped with honey) was frozen stiff as ice cream, and tasted almost sweet as ice cream from her spoon. The spoon was cold enough to stick lightly, momentarily, to her lower lip as she began to eat.

Sara dozed off for a moment as she was eating, and woke (bent over, head drooping) staring at the weave of her wool pants by the headlamp's light. The jar of *kamamik* had rolled away, and she found it beside the sleeping bag . . . discovered she was still holding her spoon, and ate a little more. Then she chewed the moose jerky soft, bite by bite, wishing she had a bacon bar. There wasn't enough salt in the jerky. Needed more salt, or crushed red peppers. —Needed something.

When Sara finished, she put the *kamamik* away, wriggled out of her parka, bundled it for a pillow and stuffed it behind her. She bent forward to unlace her boot-pacs (her fingers stiffened in the cold), wrestled them off, and tugged the thick felt liners out to dry.

Grunting at the effort, murmuring to herself—the lamplight more trouble, with its quick shadows as she moved her head, than simple darkness might have been—she rolled the sleeping bag out (its bulk nearly filling the tent), and unzipped it down the right side. Still wearing her wool socks, long-johns and trousers, her wool shirt and sweater, she wriggled halfway down into the bag's icy softness, unfastened the headlamp's heavy band, switched the lamp off and stuffed it behind her, under a fold of the parka. She reached out with her right hand to touch the shotgun's chill receiver, its checkered pistol grip. Then whistled for Dutchy.

The big dog came bustling, wriggling through the tent flap, bringing a flurry of wind and cold and powdered snow in with him. He filled the small tent, thumped and shouldered at its sides, and walked over Sara with pads heavy, hard, and dense.

He leaned on her left side in darkness as she sat up and bent forward to find the flap's zipper, fasten the tent's entrance—sniffed and nosed at her, snuffled, then nibbled at her hair.

"No! Lie down and go to sleep!"

Dutchy breathed out noisily at this command, stepped on her twice more—tried to turn around and found too little room for it— breathed noisily again, and suddenly collapsed against her, heavy as a sack of cement. She had to thump and shove a thick-furred flank before he shifted slightly, so she could slide deeper into the sleeping bag and zip it up from inside—as safe from weather as she could be without a shelter and stove. And wedged beside by a masculine presence, simple, warm, and strong enough for comfort.

2

She dreamed the lynx was walking down Lacey Street in Fairbanks, past a saloon called Easy's. The lynx had its fur back on, and was dressed in jeans, a blue work shirt, and brown down vest. It was walking on its hind legs (furred pads shoeless), and looked like a child out of school, wearing a lynx costume for Halloween.

Sara hoped it wouldn't notice her as she walked past. No one else (and there were several people on the street) was paying it any attention.

But the lynx did notice, and recognized her. It was looking into a camping-store window as she passed, and she saw its mask in dark reflection, saw its wonderful eyes as they saw her. She kept walking, afraid the cat would call after her, or follow. But it didn't. She went to Montana to prevent that, out to the ranch in a rented pickup. . . .

Her trembling woke her.

She was shaking with cold, cold too severe for late in the season. It seemed to be pouring out of the dark, flowing into the sleeping bag, so frigid the long bones in her legs and arms ached with it. It was frightening, felt forty or forty-five below at least—the wind punching and striking at the tent's material as if it were trying to tear it, come rushing in. Sara thought she might have to get up, go outside and gather dead willow to make a fire. She wished there were something she could bargain with—perhaps agree to die a year early at the end of her life—so it would become warmer, and she wouldn't have to get up and try to make a fire out in arctic wind.

Dutchy lay beside her as still as if dead, and for a moment, so savage the cold, Sara thought he might have died—thought perhaps all the dogs were dead outside, curled frozen in the snow—no protection now from a winter bear, which might come out of darkness as if born to the storm, padding softly down the frigid creek through frosted willows, thick sheets of overflow frozen in its fur . . . ice armor making soft sliding sounds as it came.

Sara elbowed Dutchy through the sleeping bag's gelid loft, and the husky grunted and shifted in his sleep. Alive, at least.

Then, thinking there might be something wrong with the sleeping bag to allow so much cold in, she lowered the zipper only a little, three or four inches, so her face was exposed—and felt night press on her forehead a cold that seemed to devour her body's heat, freezing the bones of her face so they ached as if she'd been hit.

Sara unzipped the sleeping bag halfway down, and sat up into darkness and heavy air that stirred as the wind struck the tent, shaking the fabric. Her breath crackled softly, freezing unseen into a small snow flurry before her. Her face and hands tingled and began to numb, and she reached behind her for the folded parka, felt the thick coating of frost on it—from her breath, and Dutchy's—shook it out, drew its frigid thickness over her head, and lifted her buttocks in the sleeping bag to tuck the bottom hem under her. She raised the parka's hood, tightened the drawstring of the wolverine ruff, then slid back down into the sleeping bag—fatly crowded now, with the parka's bulk inside—and zipped the bag back up, then fitted on her mittens.

For a long while, she was no warmer . . . and lay cushioned, cocooned in cold, blind, softly smothered and shaking, trying to sleep but unable, hearing through the parka's hood, the sleeping bag's deep loft, only the muffled rattle and thud of wind against the tent.

Still no warmer, she finally slept—for a few minutes, perhaps half an hour—and woke trembling, her legs doubled up, arms wrapped around them, her fingers aching in her mittens, sore as if they'd been stepped on. She thought she was drowning in cold, that perhaps an avalanche had come hissing down the mountain, surfed out along the slope and covered the team and her tent. Had left her buried in ice and snow twenty or thirty feet deep. —But if that were so, there'd be no wind. And there was; she could hear it.

Sara woke to stillness, and was sweating slightly in the parka and sleeping bag; she smelled her body's odors, and stale woodsmoke, and blood. She turned in the bag, pulled her mittens off, found the right-side zipper and slid it down a few inches—enough so she could breathe better—and saw sunlight pale crimson through the tent's material. The air against her face was only chill. Five, ten below, no colder than that.

She turned her head into a gust of carnal breath, and saw Dutchy standing looming over her in the tent's close quarters, staring down with blue-white eyes. He leaned down, poked her cheek hard with a cold black nose.

"All right. . . ." She unzipped the bag halfway, leaned forward to unzip the tent flap, and Dutchy shoved and squirmed out through the close passage, jumped free into heaped snow.

Bathed in filtered scarlet, Sara struggled out of the sleeping bag and parka, then went on all fours to the tent entrance.

The storm had blown itself out, or over the peaks to the river. Late morning flashed into the tent with sunlight off new snow more than two feet deep. —They'd been lucky with snow to run the lines the last four days, a good solid base of old, and powdered four inches more. Now, with last night's fresh fall, she'd have to break trail for the dogs the last nine miles to home—snowshoe out ahead of the team for a mile or two, then snowshoe back to mush them up to the new trail head while she rode the runners for rest. Then strap on the Sherpas again to break out the next mile or two, go back to get the team, and do it all again. Light parka, today. And goggles, for the hours daylight would last.

She heard Fatso muttering off to the left, through the tent's side. He'd be annoyed at Dutchy's running around loose, annoyed at waking hungry. Sara decided to skin out the marten and muskrat in camp, divide those for the dogs—short rations before they mushed out. She dug into her food sack for a stick of moose jerky to thaw in her mouth, bite by bite, while she put her liners back in the boot-pacs, got the boot-pacs on.

Doing this, she noticed how dirty her hands were—grimy, broken-nailed, scarred with skinning cuts, and dark as an animal's paws. A thin animal, wiry and strong, some sort of snow monkey. . . .

In afternoon light—already fading, less flat and bright, lengthening spruce shadows no longer crisp as cut gray paper on the snow—Sara stepped on the sled brake at the crest of East Ridge, pushed her goggles up on her forehead to look the place over, and knew at once someone had been at the cabin . . . and wasn't there now. She smelled only remnant woodsmoke hanging lightly in the air. Seasoned birch, green alder.

Below, downslope through birch and tall sheltered spruce, the log cabin (twelve by fourteen feet) lay squat, snow draped, set on a narrow terrace well up from the bare-branch willows along Casual Creek, the creek frozen hard. A narrow, rough-planked dogtrot porch ran enclosed half across the cabin's front from right corner to its doorway. Against the cabin's near-side wall lay a long stack of split firewood, only a third of what it had been in the fall.

Fifteen yards upslope, an out-house shelter stood almost buried in drift. And across the hillside from that, through small scattered birch, the little cache-cabin stood high on its four tall spruce-pole supports. Above, along the crest of the rise, the low snowy tangle of berry bushes, leafless now, lay where the old bear trail passed through.

The outhouse and cache, like the dogtrot porch, were plank-built, the lumber bucksawed out the first fall after she and Alan had come up—bucksawed while they were starving, their gums bleeding, eyes unable to focus as they staggered, stumbling back and forth on the saw. Then (the snow already blowing in hard) they'd hoisted notched cabin logs, nailed the sawed planks up for roofing—staying alive on snared snowshoe hare, mourning the sacks of rice and corn-meal they'd lost in the river . . . the sack of beans, the lard. Then, when the cabin was almost up, the caribou had come. . . .

A tool-and-puppy shed, farther along the terrace beside the dog yard, was plank built as well, but double walled, with slabs of tundra turf stacked between, and turf paving the roof.

Sara drove the team down the ridge—angling to the left as she came, so as not to run over her wheelers—and soon was close enough to see the shuffling tracks snowshoes made. Only visitors to come up in almost nine months. Three men snowshoeing—the tracks leading away from the cabin and down into thickening willows along the creek. And from there, no doubt, west. West with the flow of the creek, then northwest around the mountain's tundra steeps and broken scree, a day's travel to where they'd cached their snow-machines.

The dogs were hustling, happy to be home, leaping and bucking through deep snow. Sara stepped up on the runners, rode, and let them go. She closed her eyes, gliding, gliding, cold wind in her face, down the last of the slope, then—Dutchy needing no "Gee"—felt the sled angle as the team turned half right to run level along the terrace bank toward the cabin and the dog yard beyond.

The runners hissed on a stretch of packed snow, then went silent through drifts, the sled jerking as the dogs lunged, wading through powder.

If Alan had been waiting for her as they came down—and with her eyes closed, he might have been—if he'd been sitting cross-legged on the cabin steps, mending dog harness, now he'd call, *"Big trip, Bones?"*

Eyes still closed, Sara saw the cabin's sudden shadow darken the sunlight on her eyelids . . . then pass as the dogs ran on to the shed and yard. After that short stretch, she felt the sled falter, slow, and stop, the team standing shifting in their harness, yelping, excited, their noise echoed by Vanilla and Lobo, greeting from inside.

Sara opened her eyes to failing sunlight and the shed's wide rough planking, weathered dark silver to black. The heavy door, hung on three gray galvanized strap hinges, was still crossbarred with an alder pole. There were no snowshoe tracks; nothing had been disturbed out here.

She lifted the snow-hook from the sled's right-side stanchion, set it, and stamped it solidly in—then, so weary she stumbled stepping to the shed door, heaved the crossbar up and out of its catches and swung the door open. Vanilla came trotting heavily out of dogshit-smelling dark, nuzzled and nosed at her as the team grew noisier outside. Lobo, less than a year old and half wolf, stayed back in the dark, staring, shy after five days without being spoken to. —They'd finished the pans of dry rations she'd left them.

"Well, *hello*. . . ." Sara knelt to Vanilla in hay dusted by snow blown in under the door. "Is that a pretty lady? Is it?" and scratched the malamute's ears, combed her fingers through the deep pelt. Vanilla, a very pretty lady in buff and black—a German shepherd's colors—stood broader-chested, stronger than any German shepherd, her coat richer, thick as pile carpeting. She had an Outside dog's dark-brown eyes, almost exotic in this country, where blue-white was usually seen.

Collapsing under caresses, Vanilla stretched on her side, revealing a plump belly, a row of swollen, tender pink teats.

"Are you going to have babies? *Are* you?"

No reply but a groan of pleasure.

Sara unhitched the team one by one (Vanilla greeting them, Lobo still silent in the shed), unsnapped neck and tug lines, and took their harness off. She checked each dog's feet, led it out to its small snow-drifted house, and chained it to its post. Then she went back into the shed to talk to Lobo, and after a while was able to stroke him and lead him out to his place at the edge of the lot, a distance from Dutchy.

Vanilla chained last, Sara forked summer hay down from the shed's small loft, and carried bundles of it out to stuff into their houses for fresh bedding. Done, she went into the shed to shovel Lobo's and Vanilla's frozen crap into the honey pail, and set that back outside. Then she took the ax down from a side wall, and sliding down from a number seven cat he was driving through the summer, ramping a platform for storage tanks. Got off the machine, slid down the bank, and said to her, "If you're the person you look like, I like you." She'd been trailed that afternoon by seven Eskimo second-graders, who'd stood in a line like ducklings to watch their teacher encounter this white man in a faint, whining cloud of mosquitoes, other insects singing in the sunlight. A man, at least—young (younger than she), red-bearded, bandy-legged, sweaty, long-armed and direct, eyes a slightly glassy blue. A pleasure to encounter after months of child handling, children's smells of pee, milk, and cookies . . . their parents' occasional odors of fish and fuel oil, engine oil and seal.

"I know exactly what I look like," Sara had said, and walked past him, her train of children trotting after.

"No, you don't," he'd called. "—You don't have any idea what you look like."

But Sara'd been approached by one or two clever men before, who'd used her plainness as a pivot to swing around and counterpoint to fuck her, and she didn't like it.

It took Alan Maher twelve days of trying—a sample of white wooing affording great amusement to the Eskimos of Inuviak—before she could be made to listen to him, begin to read the messages he left on the classroom blackboard in the morning. Until then, she'd erased them first thing, before the children came into class—hadn't bothered to read them through.

The twelfth day, she arrived a little early—expecting something to have been written—and found he'd left another chalked letter.

DEAR SARA,

I call you dear, because that's what I hope to call you for many years, so why not start now? Love has to start sometime.

You remind me of a slide alder, that bends downslope from the direction the avalanches and mud flows come, all its pretty branches and fine green leaves growing downhill to protect itself from being broken.

You ought to try putting out just one little twig, uphill. Who knows, there may not be another avalanche.

Very truly yours,
ALAN

Sara had felt at last that such effort deserved sensible, gentle, and direct discouragement, and had agreed to walk with Alan out along picked up the bucket yoke and two of the two-gallon buckets stacked in the near corner of the shed. An old barrel stove stood there with firewood—insurance should the cabin burn in winter.

It was a steep walk down through drifted snow to the willows, then along a narrow path through small tangled trees to the creek. In the frozen thicket, several birds, crossbills—very small, with brown bodies and white patches on their wings—came swarming in the branches around her. They sang no song, only the hurried ruffle of their wings accompanying as Sara walked through, brushing willow branches aside. Carrying the yoke over her left shoulder, empty buckets dangling, she walked along the creek to a small pond of refrozen overflow where she'd chopped through the week before. She put the yoke and buckets down, stepped carefully out onto blue ice, set herself, and swung the ax to hack down to running water. The dark ice, a foot thick, fractured as reluctantly as armored glass, splintering into shallow spalls at every stroke.

When overflow finally came bubbling, the water a lighter blue than the ice had been, Sara brought the buckets over and knelt to fill them. Then, crouching to balance the yoke across her shoulders, she slowly stood and started back through the willows, then upslope—misstepping once, so some water sloshed out of the buckets. She stopped in the deepest drifts and went to one knee in the snow to rest, the yoke still balanced on her shoulders.

. . . If Alan had been sitting on the cabin steps to greet her, had said, *"Big trip, Bones?"* she would have seen the cool mountain sunlight reflected in his wire-rim glasses, might have seen the snowy meadows beyond, or herself, reflected very small behind a tiny sled and team.

The glasses had embarrassed him. "—A necessity. But Crockett wore them, and Hickok. We can't be pure new planet, no matter how hard we try. . . ."

Sara shifted the yoke (it was catching her wrong, hurting the back of her neck), slowly stood, and started climbing again.

"Tell me," he'd said to her once. They were lying in the warm bed, caribou skins under them, wolf furs over. "Tell me. . . ." They'd just made love so merrily, as if they were a teamed pair, dog and bitch, drawing a sled of pleasures. He'd said, "Sweetness . . . sweetness." After, she'd rested her head on his bare chest as she listened to his heart's slowing hammer, the resonance of his voice.

"Tell me," Alan had said, "—haven't we found our old earth, that everyone else has lost?"

He had from the beginning approached her very romantically,

the Arctic Ocean (glittering under the six-week summer's sun) to discuss it. Had discovered in that conversation, and many after, that Alan Maher was one of those white men obsessed with distance and wilderness—a trapper, hunter, and cabin builder much of the year, determined to live deep into the country, free at last from crowds of people, their lies, greed, and compromises.

Sara had explained herself very well to Alan Maher—and mentioned the difference in their ages, too. She was four years older. She had explained, strolling with him—and several small Eskimo children, from time to time—and he had talked about the country, and the mountains, and leasing homestead and so forth.

Just before the beginning of the next school year, she'd resigned and flown far south to Fairbanks to marry him. And after they'd spent all their money for a year's supplies, they went upriver in summer with several dogs in a small boat with a small outboard motor—traveled until they reached deep mountains just over the Arctic Circle, walked days up and inland, then higher, and made their home. . . .

Sara had to rest again on the snowbank just below the shed. She lifted the yoke off her shoulders carefully as she could, but still spilled a little water out of the left bucket.

She sat, then lay back in the snow. She could smell herself—odors of sweat, blood, and woodsmoke from four days traplining. Five days, now. She closed her eyes and drifted into almost-sleep, so pleased by the warmer weather, now more than ten above.

It was the swift darkening of the day that roused her, the afternoon sinking toward twilight, the low winter sun already setting. She sat up and fitted the yoke across her shoulders, got to all fours, then to her feet, and climbed to the dog yard without spilling any more water.

Sara filled the dogs' water pails; Fatso, Cherry, and Dipsy were already curled deep in the hay in their houses, asleep. But Dutchy was sitting outside at the limit of his chain, staring, displeased, across the yard at Lobo—annoyed on returning home to find this young half wolf, half MacKenzie River husky, still present . . . and, Sara thought, sensing a someday rival armored in youth's muscle, armed with youth's jaws.

"Not for a long time, sweetheart," she said to Dutchy, and scratched behind his ears. "Boss dog. Boss-dog Dutchy. . . ."

The watering done, Sara dug the lynx out of the sled sack, then walked up across the slope with the carcass over her shoulder—the snow drifted deep here, tiring to wade through—went upslope to the cache (each of its tall spruce-pole supports banded with five feet of tin sheathing to keep parky squirrels, porkies, martens, or wolverines from climbing for food). The ladder was lying alongside, where she'd left it, hadn't been moved by the people who'd been on the place. A fox had strolled a long loop in the snow nearby, its neat prints circling the faint scent of frozen meat drifting on the air.

Sara dragged the ladder out in front of the cache platform, walked its weighty length slowly upright, and set its top rungs against the platform's edge, twelve feet up. She climbed to the platform, unbarred the little tin-sheathed door, crawled into the cache and laid the lynx down, then pulled out a burlap sack of frozen caribou guts, and sat back to swing those out behind her to drop off the platform to the ground. Then she crawled back inside, dug a big chunk of tallow from the tub, and wriggled back out with a half-sack of brown rice as well. Beside dog food—a half-sack of Eukanuba—there was a side of caribou left in the cache, the last of two winter-kill bucks. . . . Climbing down the ladder, Sara looked off to her left, never turned her head to look the other way.

The dog pot—half a blue oil drum, now filled with snow—sat three yards from the cabin's west wall, propped over a shallow fire pit on a circle of big rocks Alan had hauled up from the creek bed. The laundry tub—the oil drum's other half—sat beside on another fire pit, the worn gray handle of its wooden plunger sticking up through snow.

Sara dumped the frozen innards, the tallow, and six double handfuls of rice into the dog pot, and walked over to the cabin to drag splits of firewood, a tie of kindling, and a battered can of Blazo from underneath the porch. She set kindling and wood under the half-drum, splashed Blazo on them, and took her match-safe out of her trouser pocket for a blue-tip to light the fire.

Then she carried the yoke and buckets back down to the creek for cooking water. One trip would do; the snow in the dog pot would melt for a start. . . .

By the creek, Sara looked up from filling the buckets and saw what seemed through dusk a cow moose and calf more than a rifle shot away across West Meadow, the cow grazing, kicking up the snow for small plants. It was too early in the season for calving, and when Sara closed her eyes and opened them to look again, there were no animals there . . . so she supposed she'd been imagining.

At the overflow, with the buckets full, ready to be lifted, she was so tired she stood aside to watch herself struggling with them, hooking them onto the yoke, getting the yoke up onto her shoulders (it slipped down her back the first time, struck the sheathed shotgun's grip). She watched herself, surprised how thin she'd gotten. It hadn't helped her looks.

"Put on a little weight, Sara," her mother'd said, as if it were thinness that made her plain, and not her long face, her definite nose. —At school, Bobby Boetcher had called her "Lassie," and everybody had called her that behind her back for almost three weeks. Including her best friend (her so-called best friend), Gale. In the evenings, alone in her room, Sara had pretended she was a Russian ballerina in Saint Petersburg, and the other girls at the ballet school (admiring that elegant aristocratic profile) called her Borzoi, the wolfhound. . . .

Sara brought the water up to the cook fire without spilling any. She was feeling better now, less tired than she had been, as if labor had worn the weariness out of her. She brought the water up and dumped it into the dog pot. Then she went around to the front of the cabin—the drifts deeper there, so she waded through—and saw, even in fading light, faint yellow staining the snow beside the steps. Two men, at least, had been pissing from the steps this morning, after the storm.

Sara supposed they were Natives, come up to hunt sheep back in the pass.

She went up the cabin steps to the threshold, unbarred the dogtrot door on the left, swung it open, and looked into the narrow porch. The tools and traps and fur bundles there, what goods remained on the shelves, seemed undisturbed. She closed the porch door, stamped snow from her boot-pacs, opened the cabin door and went inside. . . . They'd talked of extending the porch on across the cabin front so they'd have a storm room, have to come through the porch to get to the cabin door. But had decided to stay with less of a cave after all, at the cost of burning more wood for warmth.

The cabin, dimly lit by its single small window, seemed colder than outside. Sara's breath smoked frost, trailed frost as she turned her head.

The men hadn't dirtied it. They hadn't disturbed any of the fresh-tanned furs hanging on stretchers from the loft edge. They'd left everything in place except for the hand-cranked grain mill. They'd unclamped that from the table (for elbow room, perhaps), and set it on a shelf over the stove. . . . And two cans of sardines were missing from the shelf below the window—a south-wall window that still left the cabin shadowed in even the sunniest summer weather.

Otherwise, except for their different odor than hers, only faint, and the smell of tobacco smoke and slightest astringent scent of Everclear, they'd left no trace but Indian-laid wood in the heat stove (the wood-splits and kindling stacked on end), a five-dollar bill (for the sardines, probably) lying beside a long brown envelope on the table. And a picture one of them had whittled into the table-top.

He'd carved the large outline of a bear's head, jaws open, teeth bared. And, below that: NEXT TIME SHE COME FOR YOU.

Sara ran her right forefinger along the outline of the whittling, cut a quarter of an inch deep. Now, the table-top so badly scarred, she'd have to be careful writing on it, not to tear her paper. Have to write with her notepad for backing.

She took out her match-safe, lit the kerosene lamp on the table, and turned the lamp's wick key slightly for more light that bloomed yellow into brightness, revealing the complimentary butterscotch of the cabin's peeled spruce-log walls. Then she picked up the brown envelope—badly wrinkled, stained by something—and tore it open. There were two folded sheets in it—a note on yellow paper, and a letter on white bond.

Sara read the note first.

> Sara—When you come down,
>   you see me.
>   Frank Solokoff

Then, the letter.

Feb 13, 1992
The Porcupine Corp.
1129 W. Fourth Ave.
Anchorage, Alaska

Ms. Sara Elaine Maher
Fort Billy Mitchell
Alaska, 99501

Ms. MAHER:

   *Pursuant to current rulings under the Native Land Claims Set-
tlement Act of 1971, you are hereby given termination notice re:
Remote Parcel Leasing agreement #0040106.*

   *Present holding has by survey been found to be included in the Ft.
Billy Mitchell Village Corporation Area, and as such may not be
homesteaded or inhabited by non-Natives without renewed leasing*

provisions satisfactory to the Village Corporation and to the Porcupine Corporation (as parent body).

If an exception to this ruling is not filed by May 15, 1992, Parcel Leasing Agreement will be terminated forthwith. Termination may be appealed to Alaska Land Claims Settlement Commission no later than Oct 15, 1992.

CARL GRESHAM, ESQ.
Executive Vice President,
Porcupine Corporation

Sara wanted to sit down at the table and read the letter through again, but she was too tired. She folded both sheets, tucked them back into the brown envelope, and put it on the table. She had the notion that when she came back inside after feeding the dogs—or maybe later, when she'd had some food and a bath—that then the letter might have changed to something that wouldn't please her so.

She went to the airtight, took a match from the jar beside it, then bent to light the Indian-laid fire and watched the kindling catch. She added a fat birch round for holding, and saw, as the first flames took hold, the chill mist of her exhaled breath fade away into the fire's swift expansion, its conquest of kindling, the first bright runners licking at split logs.

Then she swung the stove door shut, and left the cabin.

As if the dog-pot's boiling had been instantly scented many miles away, Sara heard wolves howling high in the mountains—higher than they usually ran. Hunting Dall sheep along the ridges.

She tugged the feed pails from under the porch, dipped them to fill in the pot, and—not bothering with the yoke—carried them across to the shed, the caribou-gut stew steaming, slopping as she trudged, stepping high through deep snow, her fading shadow stretched stilting beside her. At the shed, she brought out the stack of food pans to a clamor of yelps and whining, and ladled six of them full. She carried the pans into the yard in order of seniority, Dutchy's first—and hummed to herself, as she often did now when feeding the dogs, to avoid hearing the noises they made, eating.

Sara tramped back across the slope to the dog pot for the last pailful, and brought that over to feed Fatso, Lobo, and Vanilla. She stood for a while, humming "Like a Rolling Stone," while she watched them eat. . . . Then she called goodnight to each dog by name, and walked back to the sled. She carried the dogs' harnesses into the shed to hang in order on nails along the back wall, then went out to unfasten her sheathed rifle, snowshoes, trail-ax, camp saw, club, possibles-sack and ration box from the sled's stanchions . . . unclipped the gangline, coiled it, and carried all but the rifle and snowshoes inside to stow. Went out to the sled again, tugged the bundle of hides, trap-bag, and her pack out of the sled sack, and dragged the long sled into the shed to rest against the near side wall.

Sara picked up the last two water buckets, left the shed, swung its door shut, and barred it—then carried her snowshoes and sheathed rifle across the slope to the cabin steps. She took a small red-plastic sled down from its nail on the cabin's south wall, went back across the slope, and used that to haul her hide bundle and pack, bed-roll, trap-bag and possibles over to the cabin steps. Then she walked around the cabin's corner, past the dog-pot's dying fire, and reached up to take the big zinc washtub down from where it hung beside the washboard.

The afternoon had become evening, cold taking the place of light. Now, east and west, only the highest peaks of unnamed mountains glowed red as if heated in a forge, where late winter sunset shone on granite or fields of ice and snow thousands of feet higher than the homestead.

Only this mountain, their mountain, had been named. Renewal.

Sara took the yoke down to the creek twice more, to fill all four water buckets. She moved much slower her last trip up (buckets swinging unsteadily as she climbed) so it took a considerable while. The light had faded shade by shade to dark when she carried the yoke up the cabin steps and set the last load down. She unbarred the dogtrot's narrow door, then swung the sheathed shotgun off her back, reached in to hang the rig on a high peg beside a wall of narrow shelves, propped the cased rifle in the near corner, then slid her snowshoes in, shut the trot door and barred it. She used the door broom to brush snow off her trouser legs, stamped snow from her boot-pacs, and opened the cabin door to shove the big washtub, her pack, bed-roll, trap-bag, pelts, and possibles inside. Leaving the yoke leaning by the door frame, she picked up the buckets of water two by two, carried them in, and came back to close and bar the door.

Ice fog had come rolling into the warming cabin with her, settled into a foot-deep haze along the plank floor . . . then began to slowly thin and vapor away, first from the stove, then from the flooring around the stove.

Sara'd thought of having Dutchy in for company—or Vanilla, so her pregnancy might be relieved by one warm night—but she was tired of animals, tired of being such an animal herself that she'd had to trudge out back between water-carries, drag the outhouse door open against mounding snow, then crouch in darkness on an icy board to produce her shit and be rid of it. This to avoid the stuff's company in the honey pail through the night.

She pulled the pelts from the trap-bag, and reached up to hang them to thaw from wire loops tacked to a rafter. Then laid kindling and wood in the cookstove—a sheepherders', its narrow rectangular box made of light sheet steel—lit the fire, and set three buckets on along the stove's length.

The cabin was warm enough now for Sara to take her parka off. She hung it on the peg by the door, thought of the men who'd come by, and went to tug the kindling box away from the cabin's back wall. The rat-hole plank didn't seem to have been disturbed. She went to her knees, grunting like an old woman, and pried the plank up. The jar of money was there—seventy-three dollars (eleven dollars of that in change). And a larger jar holding matches and emergency rations—salmon smoked to squaw candy, and six bacon bars. And the .44 Magnum was there, the handsome Redhawk wrapped in a cotton rag. She unwrapped the big revolver by the kerosene lantern's soft egg-yolk light, sprung its cylinder open to check the loads. Then, keeping the Ruger with her, she slid the rat-hole plank to its fit, and dragged the kindling box over to cover it.

Feeling the bloom of warmth from both stoves, Sara foraged at the cabin's shelves, then sat back in the rocking chair (made by Alan out of steam-bent birch, when he was making sled runners) and the pistol shining on the frozen floor beside her, ate thawing peanut butter out of its half-gallon can with a cottonwood spoon, while she waited for the water to heat.

With a pat of peanut butter slowly melting on her tongue, Sara rocked forward, leaned down, and made a clicking sound at the back of her throat, then softly called "Lonnie . . . *Lonnie*. . . ." She waited a while and called again, "Lonnieee . . ." then heard the faintest tissue-paper rustle along the cabin's back wall. She bent down, holding out a forefinger, its tip smeared with peanut butter. Waited, sitting still . . . and saw a flirting shadow from behind the stove. Then the red-back vole, fat and only slightly larger than a mouse, came scurrying halfway across the frozen floor to her. And paused, bright eyes black beads, watching. "Come on, little moochness . . . I won't hurt you. Is he watts? Is a bozz a booz?" Reassured by this accustomed baby talk, the little animal skittered closer quick as a blown leaf, leaving sparrow tracks on the floor's frost, until it rested trembling under Sara's fingertip, and commenced to nibble the smear of peanut butter away.

The vole fed, and scurried off, Sara ate three more spoonfuls, then set the peanut-butter can on the cabin floor, leaned back . . . and slept, still rocking slightly, dreaming of forget-me-nots on a southern slope—the little flowers, brilliant blue, golden-eyed, shifting in a mild summer breeze. . . .

She woke to soft seething from the buckets on the stove—thought at first there was some trouble, someone calling outside the cabin—then realized not, and got up with a groan to drag the big zinc tub nearer the heat stove. Using folded rags to handle the hot metal, she poured the buckets' steaming water out into it, one by one.

Next week, and three or four weeks after, there would have been time to set and run the southern end of the line again. Time after that to fine-finish the martens, rough-tan the last pelts before going down to Fort Billy to leave the dogs—then take the river to Chancy to see Bud LeBeck, and fly from there to Fairbanks. Now, with the letter, with Frank Solokoff's note, she had her excuse, had reason enough to leave sooner, leave in a few days. Pack, and take the last hides only scraped, stretched, and salted. . . .

Warming with the cabin's air, the odor of these hides and permanent odors of alder-cured meat, cut wood, gun oil, dogs and wet wool rose to the low pole-ceiling and drifted there like smoke.

She'd have one of the lynx quarters tomorrow—fried breaded with cornmeal. As good as chicken. Browned in bear grease, better than chicken.

Sara went to close the window's curtains (striped blue, once pillowcases) as she always did at night to shut herself more fully in. Then, standing by the heat stove, she took her clothes off slowly, dreamily as if she were stripping for a lover. First, unlaced the boot-pacs and dragged them off—the floor, frigid, still glittering with frost-spiders, numbed her stockinged feet. She pulled her sweater off over her head, ruffling short dark-brown hair (clumsily cut, and barely dusted above her ears with gray). The sweater was warm from the stove's heat, the wool shirt beneath still chill from outside. She took off her shirt, red long-johns top, and her bra—all grimy from five days hard work, sled-running, and campfire smoke.

Sara glanced down at her breasts once they were bared, a habit from teenage years, when she'd looked down always after undressing in hope they'd grown larger during the day, more beautifully weighty—not just barely adequate, too slight for such forthright nipples.

She balanced herself with a hand on the rocking chair's back, lifting her left leg, then her right to tug the heavy wool pants off . . . then two pairs of red long-johns pants, and her panties (dirty as the bra had been). Took off her two pairs of wool boot-socks last. They were chill, matted, damp and sticky from days of wearing, and smelled like small dogs.

Thank God her legs had been all right. A little slender, but when she was fourteen, already longer than her mother's. Legs had been all she had, except for her skin—very pale, with only a few freckles. Used to play with herself one summer, lying there looking at her own legs held up in the air—lying there naked except for stockings and Mom's maroon heels. Pretending a man was looking at her, at everything. Mister Olsen standing there watching her—dressed, but with his cock sticking out of his pants. Mister Olsen, at least forty years old, tall and tired-looking. . . . There'd been something she'd wanted to know about him, though what it was she couldn't have told. It was as if by showing herself, she might bring him to show that secret to her, of which his cock was only a sign.

Her mother had almost caught her once, walking in one Saturday—had come quietly up the stairs, made just enough incidental noise for Sara to stop, get off the bed and to her closet, pretend to be dressing . . . taking the maroon shoes off in there, saying she'd be right down to do whatever. Help with dinner, make a salad. Her mother—pretty, softly brunette—had stood in the middle of Sara's room, stood relaxed, complaining in her humorous way about Sara's father, due home after almost two weeks 'of being a manufacturer's representative.' This phrase always said as if being that sort of 'representative' was an improbable occupation for a man who'd been a rancher—could still have been a rancher, if he'd been a competent one. The 'representing' seeming an excuse, more than anything, for foolish and aimless behavior—only an excuse, as most men's traveling jobs were, for time away from their wives and children.

"Happiest if they lived in caves," Helen Whaley said on that occasion, as she'd said before, standing in Sara's room. She never commented on the room's neatness as opposed to Annie's—smaller, and always destroyed—but stood talking only of Evan Whaley and men's pleasure in departures. After almost everything she said, Sara's mother smiled, hazel eyes merry, as if recalling another matter she might have mentioned, but decided not to. Sara'd thought this smiling made her father nervous, more likely to take long trips rather than be present when his wife decided to reveal what was so amusing.

Helen Whaley had short legs, soft and curved, and Sara had imagined them, once or twice, bent around her father's lank waist, the ankles hooked to hang on like the girl's in Vivian's brother's magazine, while below the thing went in.

Sara'd thought about that once or twice, but never while she played with herself.

"They haven't done it for years," Anne had said, younger-sister snotty, and looking very much like Sara—favoring their tall and bony father—except that for her those sharp features had softened, eased, smoothed into a face really beautiful, well-boned instead of bony, elegant rather than raw. Aunt Megan said at least twice—twice when Sara was there to hear—"Annie should be a model. She got the looks in this family . . . should go to modeling school."

"When she finishes college," their mother had said, "—then Anne can go to modeling school and make an ass of herself wearing unwearable clothes." Their mother, top of her class in high school, regretted not having gone further, felt she'd been cheated of amusing incidents in the sororities. She also had trouble finding clothes to fit. "I have size eight shoulders, and size ten hips," she said on any shopping trip, no matter what they were shopping for—once, a new refrigerator—even when she was shopping for her daughters. "Look at this damn dress." She'd hold it up to her throat, staring into a store's long mirror at the mall. "I wish they made them for human beings. . . ."

As Helen Whaley grew older, she grew plumper, her face by that staying surprisingly young, looking not much older greeting Sara home from college—or greeting her almost four years later, back from Butte for her father's funeral. Anne had said goodbye to him— Sara missing that—and reported their father had been the same, sentimental and temporary, as he'd been when healthy. Had wept and blessed them, and his mind wandering, had promised no more trips.

Sara's mother had greeted her then looking almost the same except for graying hair. . . . The last time, though, when Sara'd flown down from Fairbanks after her mother's fall, she'd found her sagging at last though still plump, sardonic at the door, leaning on an aluminum cane with the same relaxation she'd shown without it. Her

left hand, faintly freckled, gripped the cane's curved black handle;
her other hand was free to gesture, exercise itself during conversation.

"You look fine, Mom—you really do."

Helen Whaley, lounging on her bright third leg, had watched her
daughter as if hoping for something more, something sensible . . .
then had said, "Looks aren't everything," and gone stilting into the
kitchen to make grilled cheese sandwiches, refusing help.

Sara supposed if her mother had caught her in that ridiculous
posture—naked, feet in the air, imagining Mister Olsen—she would
after all not have made much of it, certainly wouldn't have told
anyone. Only afterward, when her mother smiled as she so often
did, Sara might have supposed she was smiling at that, no matter
what she said at the time. . . .

Sara took a gray cloth and a bar of laundry soap from the wall shelf
above the sheepherders' stove—the soap, streaked white and yellow, worn to shallow curves—walked lightly across icy planking to
the tub, and stepped into it through steam. At first, as she stood
there, the water felt only cold, colder than the floor had been . . .
then grew warm, then quickly hot.

"Oh, God," Sara said at the comfort, dropped the cloth and soap
into the water, then crouched, and holding the sides of the tub
slowly lowered herself, knees up, legs doubled so she'd fit. The
water's heat smacked and spanked her, made her vulva sting as she
settled down.

"Too hot," she said, but stayed in it.

After a minute or two—when she might have dozed a little, her
head bent forward, almost touching her knees—she roused, felt beneath herself for the cloth and soap, found them, and slowly began
to bathe, happy with the laundry soap's harsh odor, the washcloth's
stroking. She held the dripping cloth up, and wrung it over her head
several times, until her hair was soaked. Then she scrubbed her hair
gently with the bar of soap, almost making suds, but never quite.

Finishing soaping her hair, Sara raised the sopping cloth and
wrung it to rinse and rinse again, appreciating the hot water pouring
down so generously, willing to warm the rest of her as it ran. She
scrubbed her hands, her arms and shoulders, then washed her
breasts more gently—the nipples sore from being rubbed by her bra's
fabric as she'd worked the trails, used the ax at the trapline shack.

She lifted up a little in the tub, reached under with the soapy cloth to wash her buttocks and between them, and her groin—then sat back as well as she could while so cramped, lifted her left leg out of the water and washed it, then raised her right leg to wash, taking care to get her feet clean, scrub between her toes. Should shave her legs before she went down to the river. Armpits, too.

Finished soaping, she rinsed, taking all the time she wanted, resting in a haze of steam that slowly faded in the cabin's growing warmth. The heat stove thudded and creaked, its iron expanding.

It had taken them almost a week—and seven borrowed dogs to make a fifteen-dog team—to get the cast-iron stove up from the river. Alan had gotten the stove free, a gift, and was determined to use it, not make do with an altered oil barrel. Determined, too, to try a shortcut up the side of the mountain—straight up the steep Kenana's rocky bank, fair enough on foot, but treacherous mushing. The borrowed dogs, Ralph Murphy's dogs, had fought with their team in a mad tangle at least once every day along the trail—as if that were a rule, that Native dogs had to fight white people's dogs at least once a day. "I dreamed of helicopters last night," Alan had said. "—those big twin-engine mothers that can pick up any goddamn thing, take it anywhere you want. . . ."

Sara hunched deep as she could in the tub's warm water, closed her eyes and sat slack, soaking. The wind had come in as it often did with night, as if darkness were emptiness it had to rush to fill. The cabin trembled slightly as a heavy gust thumped it, then tumbled away down the creek.

Half-asleep, and so tired, Sara couldn't help but hear in the wind the sound like two men running through brush—running side by side, or one behind the other. She'd heard that sound exactly, a soft crashing galloping noise from uphill. And heard Alan, sitting mending dog harness down in the spring grass a few yards away, say, "Oh, shit."

She'd heard that very clearly on her hands and knees half-inside the high cache, cleaning it out, dragging out some dogmeat—boiled once, but already spoiled after only a week, the spring weather was so warm. She remembered that smell, and her knees slightly sore from kneeling on the planks—and the darkness in that miniature cabin, a relief from mountain sunshine's flashing brightness.

Remembered *"Sara."*

Then a pig's squeal, loud as if a musical instrument were imitating a pig. And as if answering it, a tremendous uproar from the dog yard, howling, barking.

She'd backed out of the cache on her hands and knees to look down from its platform, see what was happening below. Blinked a moment in noontime light, then saw Alan running toward her, running through the grass toward the cache ladder. Running like a cartoon creature, his legs moving so quickly. He was frowning, looked very determined. Then a thing came rolling down the slope like a brown-gold carpet, all patched, shedding, roiling along—and ran right past Alan but did something as it passed, so he was lifted into the air, kicking. Then the thing came back uphill as quickly as it had gone down, with a sort of swift swaying gait, and Sara saw it was a grizzly bear.

She screamed as if she could scream the bear away; it was all so surprising that that seemed possible. And Alan got up from where he'd fallen—though she hadn't seen him fall—he got up and came running toward the cache, its tall ladder. He looked strange; his glasses were gone and his scalp was hanging flopping down to his left shoulder, the top of his head a round bright red slick of blood.

Sara's throat already hurt from screaming, and she scrambled back to get to the ladder, saying to herself I must be calm, I must be calm and climb down and go get the rifle. She looked around when she was on the ladder's top rungs, but didn't see the grizzly—thought it had already run away. Alan said something down there and she looked over. He was sitting on the ground; the bear was there with him, biting his shoulder where his scalp and red hair were hanging loose. Sara could see Alan's face very clearly. He looked oddly remote, almost sleepy. He and the grizzly were too close, so she climbed up off the ladder again to the cache platform and looked for something to throw down at the bear. Alan called to her; she was sure she heard that, because it was so quiet, now. She wasn't screaming; she wasn't making any noise.

He called to her, but she couldn't understand him. She didn't want to look over the platform's edge, but she did, and Alan was trying to lie down but the grizzly bit at his arm. The bear looked like a huge gold-brown dog; it had a dog's long, heavy muzzle. And it smelled, but not like a dog—like sour earth, rank as rotting mushrooms. Sara saw it take Alan's right arm and bite it and twist it. When she heard the bone break, she crawled back to the ladder again. The bear wasn't looking at her—wasn't paying any attention to her at all. There was no reason she couldn't take a chance and climb down and run to the cabin, run around to the door and go in. The rifle would be above the door, loaded and ready. And that was all she had to do. The grizzly wasn't paying any attention to her at all.

"*Sara*," Alan said, and he and the bear were so close, if she'd had a rock or anything heavy she could have thrown it down at the bear and hit it. No doubt she could have hit it. The grizzly was pulling at Alan's arm as if it were playing.

"*I'm going for the rifle!*" She yelled that as if the bear would understand and run away. Then she crawled to the ladder again—crawling carefully, afraid she might be clumsy on such a small platform, slip and fall off the cache, and the bear would come.

She heard Alan scream, looked down and saw the grizzly had taken his arm away and left blood spilling there. Alan's head and the bear's head were so bloody now they were the same color, and Alan screamed again, a long shrill scream like a rabbit's.

"*I'm going for the rifle!*" And she was sure he heard her, because he turned onto his stomach and began to crawl with his one arm past a tangle of harness. The bear was sitting up like a huge dog, eating the arm, cracking the bones.

Sara smelled salt in sunny air. She saw a smaller bear—a cub almost full-grown—sitting higher up the slope, watching. Now was the time to go for the rifle. She should have gone before. If she had, now she'd already be at the cabin. She'd be inside and reaching up to take the rifle down. If she'd gone before, now she'd be standing beside the cabin with the rifle's safety off. She'd be putting the sight's thin blade on the bear's shoulder and taking up the trigger, holding her breath.

The grizzly lurched up from the bone it was biting and came over to Alan as if it were finished hurting him, was just curious. The bear's coat was yellow-brown, and it had a long rough streak of fur down its neck over its shoulder, as if the lay of its pelt was reversed there. Its muzzle and neck were red, the long hairs at its throat stuck together in wet clots and spikes.

Now the bear was almost beside the ladder. Now it was impossible to go down.

Sara screamed, "Go *away!*" But it didn't seem to hear her, and went over to Alan and reached out while he was crawling, stopped him and turned him over, as if it was curious. Then put its paw on his stomach and pulled on something, tore something with its paw— and things came out through the shirt. When that happened, Sara heard Alan grunting, or maybe the bear, they were so close together, spattered with bright blood.

Then she sat down, put her hands over her ears and closed her eyes. Now it was over with. It was too late to go down, too late to run for the rifle. Alan wouldn't want her to. She heard him, even through pressing palms, screaming something . . . and supposed it was that, that she should stay where she was. . . .

Sara sat still in cooling water, knowing the expression on her face. She'd seen it several times in the mirror—a mask of fear like a terrified child's. She'd made that face, and then examined it, many times. She thought if Alan had looked up to the cache to see her, that must have been what he'd seen.

It usually took a few minutes, once she'd recalled in such detail, before she could easily move. So Sara sat, patient, looking down at the cabin floor where the big revolver lay gleaming within reach—not like the treacherous rifle, requiring her to come and get it when that was so difficult.

The wind came again as she sat naked; shook the cabin and struck the door.

3

Near the end of their first day traveling—Vanilla, fat with pregnancy, riding the loaded sled—the team had run over ice-crusted granite scree, then snowy tundra belting the mountain's western slope, and around onto the wide tree-line meadows of the lower north face—snow meadows stretching away powdered, sparkling, still blazing under afternoon sunlight, to vanish only with the distant curvature of the mountain's flank.

Here, in still air, in silence troubled only by the dogs' soft panting, an occasional jingle of harness and sled runners' steady hiss, the mountain's peak seemed to Sara to hang over like a granite goblin so huge that only the most desperate actions of living specks here below, their most furious noisemaking, might catch its attention. She'd noticed before how travelers went subdued on the north face of big mountains—Renewal, Kishaldon, Voonerak. . . . Even the dogs pulled silent in these places, none yelping. Even Alan, constant commenter, had been quiet when they'd climbed behind the sled along the mountain's shoulder, coming up from Fort Billy Mitchell, going home.

Riding the runners, Sara pushed her snow-goggles up to her forehead and turned to look back over her right shoulder. Through her breath's trailing haze, she saw how faint the double track they'd left lay in slow curves more and more distant. These minor marks barely sketched across smooth, sloping, scintillant white—a mile, two miles, three miles behind them—then vanished below the horizon of a sky more white than blue. More white than blue except along the rising walls of granite far above, where the blue began to deepen, darkening as it lifted through thousands of feet . . . until, higher than the summit and beyond her depth of vision, past even an eagle's, the sky rose to introduce perfect emptiness, coldness, darkness.

Kickapoo was leading now; Dutchy, very sullen, trotted just behind—the two harnessed in line before the pair of wheelers. Dutchy,
leading, had turned twice in the morning, and the second time had
bitten Kickapoo just below the left ear. Sara had run up the team to
kick Dutchy away, then kick him some more—he standing furious,
unmoved in deep snow as she kicked his stony flank and called him
an asshole.

It had begun with Kickapoo's theft of a caribou chunk that morning in the dog yard, when Dutchy'd been distracted. Dutchy had run
bitter lead for half the day before his temper overtook him. Now,
dethroned, harnessed second on the gangline, he trotted behind
Kickapoo—while that usurper, uncomfortable, led at a strenuous
run to stay well ahead of him.

Young Lobo, pacing with a wolf's scissor stride, was hauling in
Kickapoo's place at right wheel, and keeping his tug-line fairly taut,
only slackening off now and then, puppy-forgetful.

Sara was pleased to be gliding through such vaulted space, unac-
companied, unseen but by the dogs . . . only slipping through still,
icy air, which closed behind her so no trace of her was left. Only
sliding over the snow, only disturbing that crystal powder until the
night's wind, come down the mountain, erased their track. Once
Alan was dead, she'd been able to savor such loneliness, relieved of
any worry and waiting for him—so she'd been ashamed and tried to
call him back to her, had carefully imagined every detail of him she
could. His short-cropped hair, rust red, his short beard . . . the way
he'd had of standing in the tub, bathing, exhibiting such a lean,
wire-muscled body, drifted around its wide back and thick shoulders
with rust-red down—as if practicing life so deep into wilderness had
called from his body all sorts of remembrances of being animal, had
caused that faint residual fur to begin to grow. How he'd splashed
carelessly as a child, stomping in the tub, scrubbing with gritty yellow soap, humming old hard rock numbers—all accents, no steady
rhythms—little shorthand snatches. Then he'd step out in his best
humor to dry with towels (always at least two) that Sara'd sewn
together out of old rags—bending to dry his sturdy legs, slightly
bowed and decorated with the same slight fur as his back and shoulders.

Sara, recalling—remembering her own affection for him on those
occasions more completely than his physical self—could retrieve just
how she felt as she worked some pelt, watched Alan singing so
badly, drying himself by the crowded cabin's stove. He had blue

eyes—she remembered them very well—a brighter, more forthcoming blue than Dutchy's. Eyes direct, unconsidering, that seemed to belong only to a practical man, and so were misleading because he'd been such a dreamer. All his relentless, carefully informed and continuing labor, his gardening, hunting, dog work . . . his harness repair, cabin, shed, and sled repair . . . line clearing, trapping, primitive medicine, woodcraft—and machine-craft, too, gunsmithing when necessary—all at the service of a dream of wildness.

Which dream, it seemed, he'd left most perfectly to her with his absence, his slaughter by the bear. Now, she had what he had dreamed, perfect solitude within great beauty, where lay no reflection of humans except for her reflection in occasional blue overflow risen through the ice. . . .

Four miles farther on, as the afternoon's light began to fail to evening, Sara *haw*'d Kickapoo down to the first thin straggling line of trees—spindly black spruce (martyrs to the mountain's weather) sprouting out of creamy drifted snow, their fading black shadows lying in long combing ranks to the east. At the tree line, she stepped off the runners and trotted along behind the guide bar, keeping up, keeping pace, pushing the dogs as they bucked this deeper snow. Then *haw*'d Kickapoo again, and wrestled the sled to the left to follow down the slope, deeper into the trees' sparse cover. The sled was hard to turn, ponderously heavy with outfit, camp tools, possibles, chuck box, pack, guns, dog rations, and four big bundles of pelts—all together more than six hundred pounds, and Vanilla riding the load with pleasure, bright-eyed, observant, breeze brushing the deep tan fur at her throat.

After camping—tent set up, dogs fed and fed herself (her caribou-rib roasted)—Sara sat beside a spruce-stick fire overshone to paleness by the fading sun, and reread her second-longest story.

Shooksh

One spring, in the Brooks Range mountains or the Alaska Range—wolves don't care what names we give things—a cub was born.

Wolves don't name cubs, either, but we will. This cub, Shooksh, was fat and merry, and gray as a gray cat. But he had a wolf's dark gray mask, a wolf's light gray eyes, and a wolf's sideways way of looking.

At first, he seemed the same as any cub—maybe a little

fatter, a little funnier, a little more curious about why mink and marten climbed trees when wolves could not.

He was hungry to suck milk from his mother; he was happy to play with his brother and two sisters; he was hard to wake up, and easy to put to sleep.

His mother could put him to sleep by licking his fur until it was wet and stood up in little points. She could put him to sleep by letting him drink warm milk from her belly, then curling around him and his brother and sisters until they were cuddled in her soft gray fur. Then he went to sleep every time.

It was when he was older, and growing up, that the other wolves began to notice that Shooksh was different.

"Well," they might have thought (if wolves used words to think with, the way we do), "well, this is a weird wolf."

He wouldn't hunt, and he wouldn't kill.

When he was still a little cub, he played hunting with the other pups. He pretended to hunt his father's tail, and bit it once. He hunted leaves as they blew by. He hunted shadows.

But he never hunted for real—not even little bugs, not even little birds fallen from their nests. He didn't hunt when the spring was over and he grew bigger. He didn't hunt when the summer was over and he was bigger still. He didn't hunt when the winter had begun, and his mother wouldn't let him drink milk from her ever again.

He didn't hunt when the winter was over, and he was almost grown. He would eat when the pack had hunted and killed—but he wouldn't help with the killing.

The rest of the pack—his mother and her mate, his uncle and aunt, his two sisters and his brother—all thought he was very strange, so they began to act like strangers to him. They snarled, showed their teeth, and nipped at him when he came trotting up to share the rabbit or caribou or moose they'd chased and killed.

Once, one of his sisters (the smaller of his sisters) saw him chewing berry leaves when the other wolves wouldn't let him share a caribou they'd run through a long moonlit night. That was such a strange thing to see, a young wolf chewing berry leaves, that Shooksh's sister forgot it right away.

And once, Shooksh's mother saw him trying to eat fireweed blossoms, nibbling at the soft bright pink blooms and trying to swallow them, though making a face at the taste. This was such a strange thing to see that his mother couldn't forget it, not for a day or two, and it upset her.

Finally, when Shooksh was two years old, the pack had had enough of his coming to eat the animals they'd hunted down and killed. They were tired of watching him try to eat tree bark, or spruce root, or mouthfuls of snow.

Besides, he'd gotten so skinny and weak he couldn't keep up when the pack raced for hours over the snow in moonlight, flowing gray-furred, red-tongued, white-toothed along the tracks of some moose or caribou or Dall sheep running before them.

Gasping for breath, their prey would stop to rest for a few moments, then—scenting the pack on the wind, or hearing the swift light padding of their paws—would leap forward, stumble, then gallop desperately away over moonlit snow as white as death.

And there, or a mile away through alder trees shadowed by the moon, or five miles farther on, where the river ran dark, its water slowly freezing into black glass, this moose, or caribou, or Dall sheep would suddenly see before it, as if by magic, the wolf pack waiting. The wolves would be resting in a careless half-circle, the moonlight frosting their rich coats with silver as they rose to greet their prey, so long pursued.

More and more, the pack disliked a wolf who acted unlike a wolf. They were tired of Shooksh behaving like a cub not weaned from its mother's milk. They were weary of so strange a wolf, who wouldn't kill even a parky squirrel or a snowshoe rabbit.

The pack was frightened of a wolf who wouldn't hunt. They were more frightened of Shooksh than they would have been of a foaming fighter, a male wolf with no respect for their mother-leader, with no respect for any of them. They would have preferred that sort of wolf to Shooksh, who seemed not a wolf at all, but something odd.

One night, when he came cautiously to share a meal of sheep—a sheep he had not put a tooth to while it was living, running, trying to escape the pack—Shooksh's own mother snarled him away from the meat, then snapped him away, then bit him on the shoulder.

The pack drove him out. His brother fought him; his sisters stood by with bared teeth. And his father and mother watched.

By morning, a beautiful sunny late-winter morning—bright as new jewelry to human eyes, and certainly pleasant for a wolf—Shooksh walked along a frozen creek, alone.

In four days, he was starving.

On the fifth day, he smelled meat—only the slightest bit spoiled—and coming out of a stand of spruce, he stared down a hillside of snowberry bushes. The meat was there. Moose.

Shooksh was already trotting down the slope when, below and to the side, a dark brown boulder grew fur, rose up, and became a bear.

The grizzly stood on its hind legs and searched short-sighted over the brush to see the wolf it had already smelled, had already heard come trotting down the hill toward meat that wasn't his. The bear swayed from side to side, then it dropped to all fours and began to grind and clack its teeth together, making a sound like breaking branches.

Shooksh ran back up the hill, his legs trembling from fear and hunger. He looked back to be certain the bear was not coming up through the berry bushes after him—and even when he saw it wasn't, he kept running.

The next morning, he ate the fine green needles from a small white spruce. They made him sick.

When he felt a little better, he chewed alder bark and willow bark, and then lay denned in dwarf willow mouthing his left foreleg as puppies do, biting it gently, whining, until his foreleg was wet with saliva.

Then he slept, and dreamed of chasing.

When Shooksh woke, he walked in the evening and smelled something warm in tangled willow brush along a thawing creek. He shoved his shoulders into the willows, then pushed his nose into what was warm, and found a nest of baby snowshoe hares.

He did to these babies what he'd done to himself, and gently mouthed the tiny bodies that squeaked and squirmed. He whined and licked at them, and made to bite but never did.

After a while, he went away.

The next morning, he saw animals that weren't there, and he ate snow. By afternoon, his stomach hurt so much he had to lie down. He lay on brown spruce needles damp from melting snow, lay curled to keep his stomach from hurting. He slept and dreamed of eating meat from a moose the pack had pulled down not too long ago—not too long ago to be remembered. He dreamed many bites of the moose, and whimpered and drooled in his sleep, and dreamed he heard foxes barking.

He woke to that barking, smelled almost-wolves, and got up slowly to see if these almost-wolves had made a kill and might let him share. It was hard for him to walk without bumping into things.

For some time, Shooksh lay downwind in snow-dusted grass, watching a big den made of dead trees. Then he saw the dweller come out walking like a bird on two legs, to greet the almost-wolves. He saw the bird walker bringing strange food to the almost-wolves—who hadn't killed anything for it, and perhaps had earned it by barking.

Shooksh tried to bark once or twice himself, though it sounded strange. He hoped that the bird walker would come out to him with food—though not too close.

He barked several times, and the almost-wolves barked back.

Then the bird walker went inside its den of dead trees and came out with a stick and pointed it, and barked as well, a hard bark that took Shooksh's breath away—and never gave it back. . . .

Sara closed her notebook, slid it down into a side pocket of her pack, then got up to say goodnight to the dogs. Dutchy turned away when she tried to hug him.

"Well, fuck you, too," Sara said. Her voice sounded odd to her. She thought she might have been pitching her voice differently to accommodate the dogs' hearing, and would sound odd now, speaking to people.

"Hello," she said to the nearest tree—a fragile spruce, hardly foliaged at all. "Hello. Hi. This is Sara Maher. I called you about the position you advertised, in sales?" She held out her gloved hand as if the tree might shake it. It sounded awkward to have said 'position you advertised in sales.' It didn't sound the way she remembered people talking.

"—Hi. My name's Sara Maher. I called you about the position in the paper. . . ."

That sounded worse. 'The position in the paper. . . .'

Sara walked over to a new tree. Sturdier tree. "Hi. I'm Sara Maher. I called about the position you advertised. Delivery driver . . .?" It sounded ridiculous. The trees were the problem, foolish to talk to— though not bad to be. She saw herself staying in the mountains, but staying as a tree. Imagined standing here just above summer's snow line—standing still enough, long enough in all weather, freezing and thawing—using what sunlight came blazing down through aching blue to slowly turn her toes and feet to clusters of roots that in time broke her boots, snaked gradually down through yards of snow to finally find stone, its trace of soil, and root her there in line among the trees, safe from everything but avalanche and weather. Passed—if ever passed by humans—unnoticed and unknown, a small spruce to whose branches scraps of cloth still clung, to blow in uncoiling ribbons on the mountain wind. . . .

Sara looked up at the mountain. With her head held all the way back, she could see the haze of blowing snow that plumed its summit. "Hi," she said to the mountain. "I called about your notice in the paper—secretary?" That seemed better. She wondered if she'd developed an old person's voice, alone the past year. It sounded odd, a sort of pinched voice. She spoke to the mountain again, talking to it as if it were a big man—a nice man but busy, a superintendent or school principal.

"My certificate has lapsed, but I taught for three years up in Inuviak—that's in Alaska—and four years teaching third grade in Montana before that. Butte." The last part of the sentence Sara tried to make her voice sound younger, not so . . . direct.

Then she thought she'd overdone the youth thing. A little too breathy, too teenage. Talking to the mountain, was the problem.

"Alan," she said, and turned to look at an empty place in the snow, where he might stand. "—I'm sick of moose. Either go up and hunt us some mutton or kiss your wife good-bye." Said that, not because she meant it, but because she knew he wanted to go hunting, was getting restless sitting in the cabin webbing snowshoes and waiting for trapping snow.

"Want to come with me, sweetie?" Which company he didn't want.

"No, I don't. You go and get us some mutton, and I'll work with the pups on the red-sled."

"You got a deal," is what Alan would have said to that, and would have been up and provisioned and packed and rifled and out of the

cabin—then returned for a kiss, his mouth tasting of lunch's sourdough and honey, his rough red beard smelling of pipe tobacco—then gone again, for three or four days. She would have three or four days without him—the first and second days passed in the pleasures of solitude, the third and fourth in increasing anxiety. . . . Alan crawling with a broken leg high on the mountain, firing gunshots into a distance too grand for their sound to carry. Or Alan slipped through a snow ledge that had seemed so solid, now falling, falling right now through a thousand feet of air. . . . Falling to meet his shadow on the mountain's knee.

Two days of this—the last day particularly. Then, in a moment she wasn't thinking about him, his call as he came snowshoe-shuffling down the slope through birches to home, bent beneath his slung rifle and the pack-board weighted with a hundred pounds of fresh mutton, wrapped in its own fleecy, red-stained hide. . . .

"—I'll work the pups on the red-sled." It seemed to Sara her voice had sounded all right in that conversation with the air. Not too strange. . . . The dogs, each chained to its spruce, were staring at her. Dutchy, perhaps puzzled by her different voices, had been listening carefully, his big head cocked to the right.

Sara walked over to him. "I'll forgive you, if you'll forgive me," she said, and as if she'd given him a command, Dutchy lay down and rested his heavy muzzle on the toe of her left boot-pac. It was surprising, so sudden a surrender—Dutchy usually sulked for days, only gradually relenting—so sudden and complete a surrender that Sara was embarrassed for him, worried he wasn't strong as he seemed . . . not strong enough for the work and to take care of her, if he surrendered so swiftly.

She crouched in the snow beside her lead, stroked him, spoke to him, and wished she and the team might travel beyond this three-day journey down the mountain to the west—past today's mountain running—past tomorrow's ancient gold works at Backache Creek, and down snow slopes and spruce forest. Past the third day's lowland breaks and brush, the meadows and frozen creeks stretching to the river. She wished they could keep traveling beyond that country, beyond the river and Fort Billy Mitchell and on across more mountains, to wind in and out of hills and high ranges—over smaller silver rivers frozen still and bright as broken mirrors—and move on, running fast and slow, hunting their food as they went, until she and her dogs (their passage unseen by anyone, unknown) had traveled a thousand wending miles to rest at last by the Chukchi Sea.

*   *   *

On the third day—having come down the day before from blue-white mountain light to air almost amber through the hills . . . then descending this morning into low country, storm gray—having come down in three days from viewing landscape, into the landscape, they reached the river in late afternoon.

Sara, Vanilla panting alongside, was running behind the sled through a foot of soft snow—the team hauling hard, their shadows sprawling beside them—when Dutchy led through bare-branch alders down a sharp slope then up another so steep that Sara (shouting "Hike! *Hike*, god-damnit!") had to bend, shoving, her shoulder under the sled's drive-bow taking some of the load's six hundred pounds on her back as the dogs strained, scrambling, to haul the sled up and over. She thought the sled was going to hurt her, break something inside her with its weight before the dogs took hold.

"Hike," she said, the third time—couldn't say it loud, grunted it—and the team heard, or found footing, and dragged the sled's weight slowly up and off her, then over to hiss down a gentler slope running to the river.

Frozen five feet deep, the river lay nearly half a mile wide from this shallow bank to the steeper bank across. The ice, almost everywhere white and smooth, was ridged in places by series of low snowdrifts, and dotted with an occasional upstanding rubble of black tree trunks or paler driftwood imprisoned. A small hump of island, its snow furred with evergreens and bare alders, rose from the river halfway over. Behind the far bank—where, high along the bluff a faint dark stipple of tiny cabins and sheds showed—slow, low hills rose white with black spruce sprinkled over, to grow to larger and larger hills as they marched away, so the mountains they swiftly became seemed near as the nearest rises, seemed to stand directly behind the distant small sheds and cabins of Fort Billy Mitchell.

Sara *whoa*'d the team, found them glad to stop after such hard hauling, lifted her snow-hook from the sled's near-right stanchion, and stomped it in. Vanilla, panting, belly heavy, trotted up limping slightly off her left fore, and lay down in the snow with a sigh.

Sara went over to lift the tender paw, found a small ice cut in the pad's rough black center, and went to the drive-bow to dig into the possibles-sack for Cut-Heal.

Vanilla lay on her side, watching intently as Sara smeared the ointment on . . . then pulled a poly bootie over the paw and tied it off.

"Leave it alone," she said, and Vanilla looked away, pretending not to hear. An intelligent dog.

Sara went back to the sled and knelt to check her mend—two left-side stanchions had broken when the sled, running fast downhill, had tipped and slid into a tree the morning before.

Her knee had been hurt, bruised dark blue. She'd whittled birch braces, wired them to—then rigged a gee-pole to manage the sled better through such rough going. And after, had ridden the runners or hopped along through the last of that day, until the knee would bend. The splinted stanchions were still holding.

She stood and walked down to the riverbank through deep snow to look out across to the village. It was warmer in this low country. She hadn't needed the tent last night, only the tarp hung as a lean-to off spruces.

"Hi," she said. "How's everybody been?" That sounded all right.

"Good trip down," she said. "—Frank Solokoff around?" It seemed to her she sounded fine.

Sara went back to the drive-bow and dug among her possibles for her purse. The big purse's brown leather was stiff with cold, its snap difficult from not being opened for so long. Taking off her gloves, she opened the purse, and found her small makeup kit (pale blue with dark blue flowers). Then she hunted through her purse for the mirror and found it at the bottom, with a nail file and two old ballpoint pens.

She walked away from the dogs for some privacy—was annoyed when Vanilla rose with a grunt to follow her—sat on a small frozen log (flooded down last year, or the year before) and looked at herself in the little mirror. She was startled at first to be stared at so closely by a stranger—an animal, dark-eyed, long-nosed, and surprised, its skin brown as her purse's leather. Weather-burned . . . squint wrinkles at its eyes. Tough eating.

Sara rested the mirror on her left knee, and dug into her makeup kit for mascara, powder, lipstick. She noticed her chapped, dirt-dark hands were spotted with blood—blood the snowshoe hare had spit when she'd broken its neck. Vanilla, lumbering along, had started the hare that morning as they were running through willow breaks and over small frozen creeks reflecting sunlight like burnished steel. The snowshoe, a purer white than the snow it fled on, had run from one thicket toward another, then unaccountably jinked in the wrong direction—perhaps confused by so many dogs—and run into the team. Smiley had snapped it up out of noisy confusion, then let it fall as Sara ran up, shouting, to untangle the harness.

The hare's back had been broken. She'd cradled the animal against her breast, taken hold of its neat head, and turned that sharply to a snap like a breaking stick's. Then, the hare had spit blood on her hands. . . .

Sara bent over her mirror, and used the mascara brush to darken her right eye's upper lashes. Her breath fogged the glass. The mascara didn't apply well in the cold; she had to brush it along her lashes several times. Bending so near, with only that eye looking and looked at, it was hard to see any improvement. Seen so close, the eye seemed like a reptile's, all emotion gone from it. The iris—brown, striated dark green—might have been a plain blossom's petals, with round black at its center.

The other eye appeared more gentle as she made it up, seemed to look at her, recognize her, its lashes accepting the mascara.

Sara powdered her face lightly, thought it helped, and spent some time putting on lipstick, carefully drawing her lips slightly fuller than their natural shape. Her lower lip, split to the right of center in the cold and dryness, had bled. The lipstick soothed that place as Sara put it on, but the color, Coral Rose, seemed more orange than red. She wished she'd gotten another shade in Fairbanks. She'd gotten the wrong shade and been stuck with it for three years. Two—three lipsticks, all Coral Rose. So stupid it was hard to believe, and the result of listening to Alan saying it looked really good. He would have said that if she'd picked anything. —A little less condescension, a little more honesty would have been helpful.

Finished, she held the mirror up to see her whole face—saw the black-and-white wolverine of her parka's ruff, then an edge of sky above her head—light uneven gray, tinted slightly sulfur where the setting sun still shone.

"Not pretty," Sara said, looking at herself, and turned her head a little to one side, then the other. She thought she looked like her mother, but much thinner, with a dirty face and bigger nose. She'd certainly looked better a year ago. Had less gray in her hair, too.

Vanilla sidled up, sniffed at the blood on Sara's hands where she held the mirror, then licked them.

Sara sighed and put her makeup away in the purse, then stood and walked back up the drift to tuck her purse into the possibles-sack. She called the team up from their snow beds, hauled out the hook, and hung it on the sled's right-side stanchion—then hike-*hike'*d them out at a run, the sled jolting, then gathering way, hissing after them. Sara paced beside it, Vanilla toiling just behind.

Team pulling nicely (Lobo doing very well), they mushed down-slope, broke through brush at the river's frozen edge (Sara ducking branches as she ran beside the sled, gripping the left rail with her gloved right hand as they went over)—then rode out onto the river, the runners whispering through drifted snow, then sliding with a stony sound over the river's ice. On the ice, Sara slipped slightly and swung in, reaching to hold onto the sled's drive-bar—feeling, as she ran along, the almost steady surge as the team leaned to its har-ness—almost steady, but not quite. She could feel through her fin-gers the faint tremors as different dogs slacked, then leaned into their harness again.

They ran very well—Sara thinking someone from the village might be watching across the river, watching to see how fast a fine freighter team could travel after three days mushing down the mountains.

They tracked out onto the plain of ice, frosted white under the sky's darkening gray—Vanilla lagging, panting, farther behind. . . . When, after a while, they were almost halfway over—just passing the wooded island rising from ice to their right—wind came gusting down the river in clouds of snow driven whirling up into the air to fall a second time. The sled was blown skidding, and Sara had to run faster, run up left alongside the load, and lean into it to keep it tracking straight.

The wind blew buffeting away down the river valley, left snow settling, and Sara, looking back, saw Vanilla trotting far behind them and called, ''Ho, ho, ho,'' to Dutchy to slow him slightly, ease the team off running quite so hard.

Then the sled slid easily along, rumbling here and there over black ice caverned below by some underflow, so the river boomed softly as they went by. And sometimes as they passed, stressed ice cracked like rifle shots.

Sara slowed the dogs still more, nearing the village, ashamed she'd wearied the team to show it off . . . and let them settle into a steady trot, a pace in which, their harness jingling, the huskies rested almost as well as standing still.

As if she'd sensed game, Sara looked up while she trotted along and saw two humans standing on the village bluff looking down, watching her outfit travel. Men in parkas. They looked the size of mountain sheep, just out of rifle range.

A little while later, she *haw'*d the team to the left, past two long logs frozen in and a fish-wheel raft hauled near the bank . . . then past the village dock (black pilings and timber standing out on the ice) and on to the river beach. This snow beach, rising out of dark, fractured ice, was littered with flat-bottom river skiffs (two half-built) stored upturned on sawhorses—as well as drying racks for summer's salmon, and cannibalized outboard engines lying in the snow beside the nets of monofilament, heaps of cloudy green.

The team swung on upslope over drifts of dirty snow scattered with rusted tin cans and bright shards of broken glass—Everclear's transparent, Jack Daniel's dark, beer's brown—and an occasional blue oil-drum rusted through or lying on its side half full of drifted snow.

Past these and along the bluff (the two men no longer standing there, watching), Sara stepped onto the sled's runners, called "Gee . . .!" to Dutchy, and rode right . . . and up into the village. Its thirty-odd sheds and houses, its clotheslines and skeletal racks for drying household salmon struck her as a city, and smelled richly of cooking food and woodsmoke, engine oil and gasoline, dog manure heaped frozen and freezing in backyards, and faintly of sewage lying beneath the snow and ground surface in cesspools, dispersion fields, and pits.

Slight sounds seemed racket to Sara—the village generator's mild thumping, some faint indoor murmurs of televisions and radios, and suggestions only of conversation, argument, or laughter within the places she passed—all half-buried by months of snow, roofs draped thick with it. Even the scattered barking of tethered dogs behind the houses (alert to her team's traveling by) seemed loud noises to her, and obscured the sounds the runners made. She heard children, and saw a trotting pack of them—small, plump with parkas or heavy sweaters—playing a distance away at the clearing's edge, where the first rows of forest spruce stood ranked.

Sara was glad they weren't near, that most of the people were indoors. She wondered if the two men who'd been watching from the bluff had reappeared behind her and were watching again.

She drove the team across one narrow deep-rutted lane, its snow stepped into frozen mud, and wished she could keep straight on, run straight through the village and on into the forest. Run on away. . . .

After passing a shack—the clothesline beside it hung with shirts frozen stiff as metal—she rode a sharp right turn onto a steeper path, and into an uproar of strange dogs barking, snarling threats from behind their houses. She slid past two small government-built ply-wood cabins, their yards choked with snow-drifted old machinery, fuel drums, and walls of cut firewood—the second cabin decorated with wide moose antlers nailed over its narrow door. Just past these, Sara *whoa*'d the team to a jostling, inconclusive stop in front of a third house standing across the road, a good-sized cabin built of peeled black weather-scored logs.

The cabin had a washing machine, a red Suzuki three-wheeler, and a snow-machine (ruined) resting in its small square front yard, roughly fenced. Also a glass reflecting-globe on a cedar post, reflecting sky, yard, and its neighbors in bright smeared curves—gray, white, black, and plywood brown.

No noise was coming from this house.

Sara, suddenly tired—as she hadn't permitted herself to be, mushing—stumbled as she stomped her snow-hook in, lifted a coil of light cable off the sled's left back stanchion, and walked up to restless Dutchy to snap one end to his harness, the other around the far corner fence post.

Sara started up the path to the cabin's front door, changed her mind, and came back to sit on the sled load. Vanilla, grunting, climbed up to sit beside her. The children were shouting a rifle shot away. Sara wished she could take a square mile of spruce forest and icy air, sky gray with the failing light of winterset—take that aloneness with her wherever she went, to walk away into. . . .

The team rested in the road, their ears alert, listening to the village dogs bark.

After a while, Sara stood up and walked to the cabin's front door— the path's trampled snow frozen to a jumble by thawing, then freezing again—stepped up onto the stoop and knocked on the door. She listened, thought she heard voices, then knocked again, harder, standing with her eyes lowered so she wouldn't suddenly see the face (so close) of whoever answered the door. She'd be able to look up gradually, get used to it.

Nobody answered the door after all, and she forced herself to knock again, harder.

"Who the hell are you?" Followed by what sounded like the same question, but in Athabascan.

Sara started, turned around to look across the narrow road, and saw a very fat old man, a Native, sit down on his front doorstep under the palmate moose rack, and stare at her. The old man was wearing a blue baseball cap, mukluks, bib overalls, and at least two flannel shirts—the top shirt red-and-black plaid.

It startled Sara to see another person out in the open, near enough to see clearly. Dark eyes and brows at the same slant, fat cheeks, small nose, his face looked like an old brown owl's. She'd never seen him before. He was an unhappy old man, and sick. There was something wrong with him, and he would dress out to a hundred and thirty, hundred and forty pounds of meat, fatty, pale, and fibrous. She smiled at him in a friendly way, then saw he wasn't pleased. It was wonderful and sad how much she could see in his face. Alan had always tried to get into poker games the first day or two out of the bush—it was so easy to read people's faces.

The old man said that same thing again, in Athabascan—Koyukon—and Sara cleared her throat and called "Sara Maher," loud enough, she thought, for him to hear her across the road. It seemed to her her voice sounded all right—maybe a little hoarse.

The old man, frowning, asked his question again.

"My name's Sara—*Sara Maher.*"

He said something to that, but Sara couldn't hear it because a woman called from just inside the log cabin, "You out there! You shut up an' get the hell outta here!" Mary Toby's voice (a girl's voice, seamless) singing from the side of the house, probably through her kitchen window. "—I'm cuttin' somebody!"

Sara turned and sat down on the house's split-spruce front stoop to be quiet and wait. She was cold now, from running so long then sitting still, and tugged her parka hood up.

The old man across the road sat on his front doorstep, his cabin's plywood facing rotted along the foundation edge, and stared over at Sara and her team. His breath was smoking in the cold. Then he called something more in Koyukon, and Sara called back, as softly as she could, "I don't speak Koyukon. I'm white!" Her voice sounded pretty good. She thought she was already getting used to talking to people.

"You are, like shit," the old man called back in English. He reached in the left-side pocket of his overalls, took out a pack of cigarettes, shook one free, then lit it with a yellow plastic lighter and said something more in Koyukon.

When Sara said nothing, the old man sat puffing on his cigarette for a while, the tip glowing bright in rhythm with his breathing—then called to her in English, "Why are you sittin' out in the cold?"

"Why are *you* sitting out in the cold?" Sara said, loud enough for him to hear. Her voice sounded fine to her.

The old man said nothing for a while, sat smoking, staring back down the road where the river stretched from below the village bluff, a reach of ice frozen out to its small dark island, and beyond into dusk. "I guess you are white, after all," he said, raising his voice for the distance. His breath clouded in the cold, mingling with cigarette smoke. "—You sure as shit don't look it." Then he stood, opened his front door, stepped inside and shut the door behind him.

After almost a minute the door opened again, part way, and the old man leaned out. "You ain't got dogs there," he called to her, nodding at the team. "—You got elephants." Then he withdrew into his house and shut the door.

As his door closed, the one behind Sara clacked and swung open. "What the *hell* do you think you're doin'—whoever the hell you are—yellin' out here? Didn' you hear me say I was cuttin'?"

"Sorry," Sara said, put back her parka hood, stood up and turned to the doorway.

Mary Toby, sixty or seventy years old, was short and fat in boots and a blue dress buttoned up the front. Her face, wrinkled as a catcher's mitt under gray, bowl-cut hair, was a mitt's soft brown. Her small eyes, almost concealed beneath epicanthic folds, were bright and black, so dark it was difficult to differentiate their pupils. She held a cigarette in her plump right hand.

"Well, great goodness to godness Agnes," a puff of frosted breath with the girlish voice, "—look what the cat dragged in." Mary Toby'd never kept a cat; the village dogs would have killed it. None of Fort Billy's women had ever been able to keep a cat.

"Hi," Sara said, "—sorry I disturbed you." She wished she could stand back a little farther.

"Well, you sure as shit disturbed me. You hear me say I'm cuttin' somebody in here, and you go on an' hit my door and start yellin'." She raised the cigarette, took a drag.

"Sorry."

"An' what's wrong with your voice? You sound like a damn frog— out here yellin' at that old jackass, Bruce Sam. Don't you know a drunk when you see one? That old fool come up from Nulato with his kids."

Sara didn't say anything. It was troubling for her to be standing so close to Mary Toby. She felt she could see all the words Mary Toby was about to speak running down her face, rushing to her mouth to be spoken. She could see too much happening in Mary Toby's face.

"You're goin' to have to put those dogs out back, chain those dogs up; we got enough trouble without strange dogs fightin' around here. —What happened to your face?"

". . . Makeup."

Mary Toby stood staring at her. "Well . . . well, you still got that Dutchy dog?"

"Yes."

"Well, you be sure an' chain that son of a bitch up—we got too many dogs fightin' around here as it is. I had enough of dogs when Ralph was alive—always goin' out mushin', playin' like he was George Attla. You want to come in? I suppose that's what you want to do."

"If it wouldn't be too much trouble."

"That's a laugh," Mary Toby said, turned and went inside. Sara followed her quick waddle past a thick cluster of hanging parkas, past a short candle smoking in a small red glass beneath an icon of the Archangel Michael with a sword . . . and into warmer and warmer air rich with smells of woodsmoke, wet cloth, moose soup, kerosene, sweat, and smoked salmon. It was too warm.

Mary Toby led into her small living room—dark, crowded with Native men, women, and children watching television. The sound was turned off, colored light wavering in quiet broken only by the dull ruffling of fire from a big woodstove in the room's far front corner. The fire seethed behind the stove's small square window.

"Hello, Mrs. Maher." A child's voice.

Sara looked at dim faces tattooed by shifting light, and saw three children sitting on the floor in front of seven or eight adults. She bent to avoid interfering too much with the silent TV picture, went nearly on all fours over to the children. She was afraid the adults would move suddenly, would startle her, being so close—then saw a little girl's face she thought she recognized.

"Carla . . . ?" Keeping her voice down as if there were program sounds to interrupt.

"Hello, Mrs. Maher."

"Hello, sweetheart. —You know, I almost didn't recognize you. You've gotten so *big*."

Carla Demientieff, four years old, sat small in jeans and gray sweatshirt, her round face shadowed in the TV's light by a shaggy fall of hair, black and glossy.

Sara went to her knees to gather Carla up and hug her. Hugging Carla felt like hugging one of the dogs—but a soft dog, a puppy not even in training. Carla smelled strange, sweeter than a dog. Like a monkey house in a zoo, but sweeter.

"Did you bring the puppy back?"

"Yes, but Lobo isn't a puppy anymore. He's almost grown, and he's getting to be a pretty good hauler, too."

"What are you doin' down there?" Mary Toby said, "Come on."

"Can I go see him?" Carla leaned back in Sara's arms, and Sara let her go.

"Yes, sweetheart—but don't go out to visit the dogs alone, O.K.? You wait and I'll take you out to see them."

"O.K."

Sara, still staying low, backed away from in front of the TV—noticing, as she went, several of the Koyukons watching her, black eyes shining in the screen's troubled light. She recognized Edna Paul and her husband, Richard. Handsome Charlie Batten. . . . And there were strangers there.

"Will you come *on?* —I'm in the middle of cuttin'!"

"O.K."

Someone—a man, Sara thought—was weeping in the back of the house.

"You take that shotgun off your back," Mary Toby said, leading down a narrow hall. "—I don't have people walkin' around in my house with guns."

Sara said, "All right," lifted the harness strap, swung the sheathed Remington off her shoulder, and carried it balanced in her right hand as she followed along the hall and into a back room, the kitchen—Mary's bedroom to the right, off that. Mary Toby's kitchen was new the past two years. This had been the back porch before, her cooking done in the living room.

". . . Mary Toby wants to cook white, like on TV." Pauline Demientieff confiding to Sara last summer, while Sara'd been resting after a morning spent talking to the State Police, the Corporation and Fish-and-Game people. She'd been trying to get to sleep on Mary Toby's kitchen table. "—Cookin' white, an' livin' white in this big house," Pauline had said, leaning against the kitchen counter with a can of Budweiser in her left hand. Pauline, married four times and Carla's mother, was black-eyed, dark and slender, her oval straight-nosed face still beautiful at almost forty. She was being bold during Mary Toby's absence at the outhouse. "—You see those real old Donna Reed shows? Reruns on the TV? That's what Mary Toby likes, 'cept even Donna didn' have this shit on her walls. . . ."

Sara, following Mary in, saw the small kitchen—having commenced plain peeled log and plywood—was now even more richly decorated in lower-forty-eight country style, more tole paintings and dried wildflower wreaths nailed up, and (new) a small wagon-wheel chandelier with four light bulbs hanging only inches below the sheet plywood ceiling. The same heat stove, however, a battered little twenty-gallon drum, lay on its side, muttering in the corner.

A big man in white socks, jeans, and a blue-and-white sweater— little blue figures of caribou marching across the white—was lying on his right side on the long kitchen table, facing away. The man's Bean boots were set neatly side by side on the floor. He was crying, soft, childish sobs, broad shoulders shaking slightly. The back of his neck was pale Indian brown, his hair long, anthracite.

Two Native women stood on the other side of the table, both with their hair in braids, both in boots, dark wool pants, and unzipped Sears parkas the same shade of khaki. The older woman—wearing glasses, her hair iron gray—was holding the man's hand. The other, much younger, a short, fat girl with wide cheekbones, was patting his shaking shoulder.

"He's been drinkin' or he wouldn' be cryin'," the older woman said, stroking the man's hand. The fat girl had nothing to say. She patted the man's trembling shoulder in time with his sobs, and looked at Sara without any expression.

"Sara, you put that gun away in here," Mary Toby said, opened a narrow broom closet on the other side of the refrigerator, then walked back to her propane stove, took a teakettle off the left front burner, and went to the drain-sink to pour a stream of steaming water over a paring knife—holding its handle with two fingers in order to rotate and turn the narrow blade to be scalded. The small knife's steel had been worn almost away with honing, leaving only a gleaming slim suggestion of a blade, only sharpness.

Sara went to the broom closet, checked the sheathed shotgun's safety, and stood the 12-gauge up amid brooms, sponge mops, and a jumble of old sneakers, Ajax cans, and spray bottles of household disinfectant.

"What the hell Cary gave you that gun for, I'll never know." Mary Toby shook the small knife free of water droplets, and set the teakettle back on the stove.

"He sold it to me. I bought it."

"What for, I'll never know—walkin' around with that thing on your back. . . . Now, Ronnie," she said to the weeping man, "I'm goin' to be finished in just a minute. So you stop all that cryin'."

Ronnie drew in a long, shaking breath, swallowed, and lay silent. The two women stood away as Mary Toby stepped between them, took hold of the man's left earlobe, tugged it sharply back, and slid the knife's so slender blade slowly down into the ear's opening. Ronnie murmured . . . and Mary Toby's fat brown hand paused, shifted—then suddenly jerked as she stabbed slightly down. There was the softest snap inside the ear, and Ronnie yelped and kicked as the snowshoe hare had kicked when Sara broke its neck. "Oh, God!" he said. "Oh, *shit!*"

The knife was out and held to one side, and Mary Toby's mouth had replaced it at Ronnie's ear. She sucked hard at the ear, her lips fat, enveloping, as if she were kissing it, desperate with passion— and Ronnie kicked so that both Native women reached to hold him. His left arm was flung out toward Sara, and she stepped forward without thinking, took hold of a thick, sweatered wrist, a thicker forearm, and gripped them hard, held on as bulky Ronnie bucked and thrashed, tried to rise off the table as if he were some reluctant sacrifice, a captive of women, their knives, their greedy mouths.

Mary Toby stopped sucking with a smacking sound, stood up and went to spit in her sink, worked the pump-handle to wash that away, then picked up the teakettle and rinsed her gleaming blade with hot water.

"I got some stuff out of there," she said. "You'd come in early with that ear, I could have just cut a little behind there an' got some bad blood out. I wouldn' have to go inside an' pop it like I did."

"*Jesus.*" Ronnie jerked his arm out of Sara's grip, pushed the two Native women away, and sat up. He put his left hand up to his ear, and sat gently pressing his palm to it, comforting. His face was contorted as a sorrowful child's. "—That's the worst thing in the world, what you did. . . ."

"You come to me earlier, it wouldn' hurt so much. It's your own damn fault, takin' a bunch of pills. Pills don't do a thing for a red eardrum inside. You got to pop that."

"Oh, man," Ronnie said, and rocked back and forth, his head canted to the left, broad hand at the ear. Now that he was sitting up and she could see his face, dark and heavy-jawed, Sara recognized him—Ronald Parry. He was a pipe fitter for Alyeska on the Slope. Sitting up, he looked older than he had lying down. In his thirties, anyway.

He took his hand away from his ear, looked at the palm, then showed it to them. There were dots of blood at the center. "Bleed-in'," he said.

"That's fine," Mary Toby said. "—Now, you get off my kitchen table an' go home an' put a hot damp cloth on that ear. You got any more of them pills?"

"Four."

"Take 'em. Do you some good, now that stuff's runnin' out." She dried her little knife on a paper towel and put it away in a drawer to the right of the sink. "—Go on, get off there; I got to fix some dinner."

"Thank you, Mary," the older woman said.

"Don't thank me," Mary Toby said. "—You know Sara Maher? Woman went up in them mountains? Well, there she is. . . . You goin' to get off my table, or not?" she said to Ron Parry.

"O.K." He stood up, hand still at his ear. "Thanks."

"Don't thank me." Mary Toby took a stack of green plastic dinner dishes from her kitchen counter, put them on the table.

"I know you," the older woman, the one with glasses, said to Sara. "—I'm Nancy Hodges. This is my daughter, Christine."

The fat girl looked at Sara, but didn't say anything.

"Hi," Sara said. "I'm sorry Ron is sick."

"He's not sick no more," Mary Toby said, and put out a stack of green plastic bowls, "—if he puts a hot cloth on that ear."

"I'm goin' on home," Ronald Parry said, and walked out of the kitchen and up the hall in his stocking feet.

"Drunk," Mary Toby said. "Lucky I didn' do his other ear, too."

"Well, thanks anyway." Mrs. Hodges bent to pick up Ronald's boots.

"Don't thank me—you goin' to stay for dinner, or not?"

"No, we'll go see Ron's O.K."

"Good-bye, then, 'cause I got work to do."

The women left, walked back up the hall into the noise of studio laughter. The TV's sound had been turned up.

"I suppose you want to stay here," Mary said, put a handful of soup spoons on the table, then turned back to a lower drawer for knives and forks.

"If it's all right." Sara's voice sounded fine to her, now. Or she was getting used to it. "—Just for the night. Then maybe I can get a lift downriver."

"I got kids stayin' in my livin' room. You can sleep in here. —An' goin' down that river, there's always some fool goin' down that river." Mary Toby took two boxes of raspberry Pop-Tarts down from a cabinet, put them on the counter beside the sink. "But before supper, you go put them dogs out back. An' lock your stuff up in that shed out there, if you want to keep it. We got a lot of people come to town." The light bulbs in her wagon-wheel chandelier flickered, dimmed almost out, then surged back to full illumination. "—That damn generator . . . it's goin' to hurt my refrigerator."

"I saw some people I didn't know in the living room."

Mary Toby stepped to her stove, used two yellow pot holders to lift an eight-quart aluminum pot off the right front burner, brought it to the table, and set it down on the scarred wood. "—Those are some. We got people in town this week from every damn place." She took the lid off the big pot, looked inside. "Got a *heeya* goin'. Stick Dance the whole damn week." She sniffed the rising steam. ". . . Lots of fools come in town for that, suppose' to be sayin' good-bye to dead people, potlatchin'. An' that's a laugh—expectin' people to feed 'em, is what that is." She put the lid back on. "An' it's suppose' to be in the spring; isn' suppose' to be this early. They don't know what the hell they're doin'. . . ."

"Why are they having it early?"

"So the men workin' on the Slope can come down now, an' they couldn' then. That's what they call a reason. They don't know what they're doin'. . . . Father Yermy says they're crazy, an' he's right."

"I need to get down to Chancy."

"There's always some fool goin' down that river." Mary Toby went to her sink, reached above it where a small oak rack with a calico bow tied beneath was tacked to the wall, and took down a speckled blue tin ladle.

"Can I buy something for the dinner, Mary? Some honey—something sweet?"

"If I wanted to be servin' somethin' sweet beside Pop-Tarts, I'd buy it—that damn *K'oyitl'otsina* store don't have nothin' I want, anyway. You want to be doin' somethin', you just go out there an' bring in some wood. They got the damn oil heater up at the center, but they won't pipe none of it to us. Hell, no; that costs too much money! —An' chain them dogs in the back. You put your stuff in the shed, an' I'll give you the key an' you can lock it. You already got more stuff out there in my own shed than I do. You bring a wolverine skin down here?"

"Two."

"Well, you put them two hides way away at the end of the shed. I got kids sleepin' in my livin' room." Mary Toby came to the table, lifted the lid off the pot, dipped her blue tin ladle and gingerly tasted the contents. "I tasted worse. On your way out, you tell that bunch to come eat, if they want. An' if they don't want, they can turn off my TV an' go home an' watch their own TVs. Ear's done—show's over."

"O.K."

"What's the matter with your finger?"

". . . Nothing."

"Well, go on an' tell 'em. This Moose isn' much good cold. —Think they're goin' to be gettin' head soup, an' what they're gettin' is ass soup, an' that bunch won't know the difference."

4

After dinner, in early evening light the shade of caribou tallow's dark cream yellow—one of the first shades of late winter's long evening—Sara and small Carla stood in Mary Toby's wide backyard amid the team, their chain-stakes and weather-stained old plywood doghouses. Sara stood stooped, holding Lobo's harness and scratching behind his ears—watching his ears for signs of impatience, temper—while Carla, only a little taller than the wolf-dog, patted his heavy head, spoke to him softly in Koyukon. Lobo, usually shy, seemed content enough, perhaps remembering Carla's odor from so many months before, from his puppyhood. The child's language sounded in soft clicks, humming vowels, and *sssk, sssk, sssk.* . . .

Dutchy sat chained beside his house at the lot's back uphill corner. He was watching them, watching to see what favors, what attentions Lobo was receiving.

Sara had settled the dogs, fed them from one of the four big sacks of Trail-O cached in Mary Toby's shed—a log shack standing alongside three fat steel propane tanks—before going in to stand silent against the kitchen wall with several Native women, eating her dinner: moose stew with potatoes, cabbage, and pilot bread. Miller's cold-draft beer and a raspberry Pop-Tart. . . . The dogs hadn't jumped on the Trail-O—a change from the rice-and-gut mulligan they were used to—but they'd drunk a lot of water.

Sara knew five of the Native women eating dinner—Pauline Demientieff, Tanya Jackson, Stevie Sam, and two sisters (older women) Carrie and Margaret Batten. These women had nodded to Sara as they began to eat, the Batten sisters sitting at the table with the men. The women had nodded to Sara, but said nothing.

Most of the men had behaved as if she weren't there. Ron Parry had stayed at Mary Toby's after all, though the Hodges women had gone on to some other house, and sat eating with the others, occasionally reaching up to touch his left ear. The men, bulky in boots or mukluks, sweaters and windbreakers, despite the house's heat, had talked and joked their way through dinner in mixed Koyukon and English, dunking pieces of pilot bread into their stew, and drinking as many beers as Mary Toby let them have. One tall boy Sara hadn't seen before, visiting Fort Billy Mitchell from some village down the river, sat across the table and had looked up at Sara from time to time. Thin, with black hair to his shoulders, the boy had a darkly handsome high-cheekboned face and a damaged left eye that spoiled those good looks. The eye was blue-white, and had no pupil. . . .

Small Carla, her red parka bright in pallid twilight, leaned against Lobo's gray shoulder and stroked his fur-ruffed neck, already thick with muscle.

"He was scared when he was little—but he isn' scared no more," she said.

"He's scared of some things," Sara said, "and he was slow learning to haul. But he's learning, now."

Lobo stood beside them, looking a little away, a wolf trait—looking a little away, as if the present and present company were not as important as what might be seen or scented off at an angle. What may have been there once . . . what might be there again.

"He's big."

"Yes, he is, honey. And he's going to get bigger."

"Look, look at Dutchy over there. Dutchy don't like him."

"No, Dutchy doesn't like him."

"Some people don't like you," Carla said, still stroking Lobo, so Sara thought for a moment she meant the wolf-dog. "—My daddy says you're a bad-luck white person."

Sara said nothing.

"Are you?" Carla turned to look up at her.

"I don't know," Sara said. "—I don't think I am."

"He says you call bears like a *nahani*." Carla sighed, and stepped back from hugging Lobo. "—An' you're not pretty, either."

"No—that's for sure."

Carla put her arms up, and Sara stooped to lift her, stood for a moment enjoying the child's pliant weight beneath the parka's softness.

"Well," Carla said, "I like you, anyway."

"I like you, too," Sara said, and carried Carla out of the yard, her boot-pacs crunching over trampled ice and snow.

"Good-bye." Sara felt rhythmic movement at her right shoulder as Carla waved to Lobo. "Good-bye. . . ."

Sara set Carla down by the cabin's front door. "Remember, honey, don't go out to see the dogs without a grownup person with you."

"I won't," Carla said, went up the front steps, opened the door, and went inside. She left the door open, and Sara reached into a billow of warm, stew-smelling air, into a noise of conversation, and swung it shut. Then she went back out into the dog yard, walked across to Dutchy, and bent to stroke him.

"Don't worry so much," she said to him—Dutchy sitting, looking up at her, black-centered blue eyes very intent, ears forward, listening to tones beneath tones as she spoke to him.

"I'm going away, and I probably won't be back. Mr. Solokoff will take care of you. —There are plenty of mushers who'll want you, Dutchy. Such a good dog . . . *such* a good lead. There are people in Fairbanks who've heard about you. Wouldn't you like to run the Quest? Wouldn't you? Well, maybe you will. . . ."

She was talking too much, and Dutchy began to pant and look left and right for whatever trouble or chore she might be indicating.

Sara bent and kissed him. "Good dog," she said. "I'll see you before I go." Then she walked away in the twilight, patted Fatso as she went by, and left the yard. She passed the side of Mary Toby's house and went out the front yard to the path . . . turned right, and walked uphill past two more cabins, then went left along a ragged line of spruce to the edge of the village.

Frank Solokoff's house was two government plywood houses joined together. There were a tarped three-wheeler and two snow-machines in his front yard. Ski-doos. One dismantled, its battered aluminum and steel frosted inches deep by snow, its tread-belt gone, skis gone—the other, in running order, had been modified for trapping, windshield built higher with riveted Plexiglas, outfit boxes bolted to its body.

A dog was barking behind Solokoff's house—wolves answering from high in the hills, yelping like foxes.

Sara knocked, and Solokoff's oldest son—a big man in his forties, his black hair cropped crew-cut short—came to the door, and stood in striped cotton coveralls and heavy white-rubber bunny boots, looking down at her.

"Charlie," Sara said, "is your dad in?" She could feel the house's heat billowing out the door.

"We just come back from huntin'," Charlie Solokoff said, "—saw you mushin' in," and turning, called into the house. "Pop! Mrs. Maher's out here. . . ."

"*All right. Well . . . tell her to come in!*"

"Come on inside," Charlie Solokoff said, held the door open while Sara edged past him, then shut it. "Pop's in there. . . ." a nod to the right.

Sara looked into the living room, saw several men and women sitting around two card tables, and walked to the right along a big Sears maple dining table to the kitchen door. She looked in and saw Frank Solokoff gutting a skinned beaver on the cutting board beside his sink. It was a big beaver, and the flat black scaly tail lay severed beside the carcass. A small pan of water was heating on the propane stove. The kitchen was very narrow, an aisle of plywood-panel walls and rough pantry shelving—the stove, refrigerator, well pump and drain-sink all packed into the room's far end.

Solokoff, wearing black horn-rim glasses, peered into the animal's sliced-open chest, tugged out lungs, then the heart, cut them free and put them on a large chipped white platter at the left side of the sink. The kitchen smelled of blood. Frank Solokoff was small for an Athabascan, very small to have fathered such large sons. He was old, besides—more than sixty—very dark, shrunken, standing lean and weathered in moose-hide mukluks, stained old jeans, and a blue-and-gray-checked flannel shirt.

"Well, here you are, come down off that mountain. Come down early. You didn' have to come down off that mountain this soon." The pan of water on the stove beside him began to gently boil.

"Pretty well trapped out, Frank—four packs. If I'd cleared more line I could have done a lot better. But it was time I came down."

"Um-hmm. Saw you comin' there, across the river. You was runnin' them dogs like Alan—showin' off them dogs." Solokoff put down his knife, a Chicago Cutlery five-inch slicer, stepped to her and hugged her, holding his bloody hands away from her parka. The hug felt startlingly good, and Sara stood still in Solokoff's arms, tensed in enjoyment. The old man smelled of tobacco and blood, faintly of beaver castor.

He hugged her only that once, then let her go.

Frank Solokoff and two of his four sons had lived in their double house alone the three years since Frank's wife, Selma, and their little girl, Merrie, had fallen through the river's ice on a snow-machine.

"You O.K., Sara?"

"I'm all right."

"Been up there alone almost nine months. Long time."

"Yes."

"You shouldn' ever have gone back up there. Didn' I tell you that?

—I told you that, an' those Fish-an'-Game people told you that. Didn' Don Terry say stay down on the river?"

Sara nodded, but said nothing. In the office at the community center, last summer, Don Terry had remarked that Alan shouldn't have built below a bear trail—no matter how old, how unused the trail had seemed. Said further, the same bear might well come through there again the next year, early or late, depending if she had a new cub. Terry'd asked Sara many questions about the grizzlies: about the big cub—how well grown? how ready to go on its own?— and he'd wanted to know about the sow, her coat's condition. He'd been very concerned with the animals' health, how well they'd wintered over. Sara hadn't answered those questions. She'd imagined Don Terry screaming beneath the bear.

"So, you're O.K.?"

"I'm fine, Frank. —Charlie said you were hunting."

"That's right. This isn' no trapped beaver; I shot him off the bank of the creek up there."

Sara stepped to the counter to look. "What was he doing out so early? Not much left—what did you shoot him with?"

"Got hungry, came out for some fresh bark. And there's plenty meat left on this animal." Frank Solokoff reached into the beaver's body cavity, took out kidneys, each rich red, filling his hand. "Best stuff, right here."

"What were you after?"

"After what we could get."

". . . I read the letter, Frank. And whoever brought it carved up my table when I wasn't home."

"Jerry and Powell Talbot went up there with that letter. Huntin' sheep."

"Well, one of them carved a bear on my table."

Frank put the kidneys on the plate with the heart and lungs. "Jack probably done that."

"Jack Donell?"

"Jack Joseph, Bill Joseph's kid—he was with 'em. He's Mary Toby's sister's grandson, knew Alan from when he was livin' over at Fort Yukon. Guess he felt bad about what happened— and Mary Toby's been sayin' you were bad luck."

"Mary Toby's letting me stay at her place."

"Mary Toby isn' scared of bad luck. She's bad luck herself." Solokoff looked into the beaver carcass again, as if it might hold a surprise, some organ he'd never seen before . . . never heard of.

"You're having a Stick Dance."

"That's right; ends up tomorrow night. Nulato has one, so we got to have one. Some people wanted us to do it—get a chance to say good-bye to people died . . . you know, they come back an' say good-bye. You know Joan Bruce is gone?"

"Joanie? Why, what happened?"

"That girl shot herself. Seventeen years old."

"Oh, Frank. . . . Why? Why would she *do* that?"

"You tell me. Young people dyin' like flies around here. All down the river. If somethin' don't kill 'em—they do it themselves. Got people worried sick. That Joanie took Sidney's shotgun down to the beach and killed herself."

"Poor Sidney. . . ."

"Good as dead, himself. He's not good for nothin' anymore." Solokoff turned the beaver carcass over on its back, began cutting the ribs and rib meat away.

"I'm sorry, Frank." Sara watched as Solokoff worked, the knife blade dancing in and out, running a cut, withdrawing, slicing again . . . the beaver divided and portioned out. "By the way, about that notice or whatever from the Porcupine Corporation people."

"I'll tell you what that amounts to. —What's the matter with your finger?"

"This one?" Sara held up her left hand. The little finger of that hand was bent slightly inward at the second joint, that joint swollen. "I broke it harnessing the dogs a while ago. They jumped and broke it, so I put Furacin on it and a splint. You think it looks bad?"

"Bone stickin' out?" Solokoff leaned to examine the finger, interested.

"No—you could see it in there, but it wasn't sticking out. Not protruding."

"Looks like you busted the joint, there."

"I can use it." Sara demonstrated, wriggling the finger. "It just looks a little strange."

Solokoff turned back to the beaver carcass. "Well, what that letter you got amounts to is, you're down out of there. Off that mountain. Unless you want to go to Fairbanks, pay some lawyer a couple thousand bucks an' appeal. Corporation says lease is up—it's up."

"I understood that lease ran two more years—"

"Not no more." Solokoff cut into the joint of the beaver's right hind leg.

"—And it was renewable."

"Not no more."

"Frank, did you do this? You ask them not to renew our lease? My lease?"

"Anybody ask my opinion, I told 'em. Anybody ask me if you belong up there all alone, three days up in them mountains you can't even get a Ski-doo up there—I told 'em."

"You asked them not to renew that lease."

"Don't you give me that bush look. Corporation doesn' give a damn what I say." Solokoff cut into the joint of the beaver's left hind leg. The blade tip grated on bone, then the joint came free.

"The hell they don't. You run the village, Frank. You were an officer of that corporation."

The kitchen's ceiling bulb flickered and dimmed.

Solokoff glanced up, watched as the bulb brightened again. " 'Officer of the corporation.' That's a laugh. They don't give a damn what I say; you white people run that corporation more than us Natives do."

"Bullshit."

"—Anyway, this is all *Dena* country up here, why do you want to stay? You're white. Alan was white. Why do you want to stay in Koyukon country? You people take our country and go up there and play Indian, is all you people do."

"Who do you think you're talking to, Frank?" Sara said, and noticed her voice sounded suddenly hoarse, as if she were talking to the dogs, was angry with them. "First place, this isn't Koyukon country—it's Kutchin country, and your people took it away from them. What are your people doing this far up the river, anyway? This is Kutchin country, so don't you lecture me about whose country this is. And as far as playing Indian—that isn't what we do. If we played Indian, we'd sit down on this river and take government money and complain and get drunk and catch salmon when they come swimming by. That's what we'd do if we were playing Indian."

Frank Solokoff didn't seem to be listening. He carefully cut the front legs off the beaver. Left one first.

"—I don't need to be told about Indians," Sara said, surprised she was so angry. "I grew up in Montana and went to school with real Indians when I was a little girl. Cheyennes—who were horseback Indians, fighting Indians, not just fish-eaters sitting by a river on their butts."

Solokoff bent to a cabinet beneath the sink, brought up a handful of plastic bags, and put them on the counter. "Could be you got some Indian blood yourself, that mean tongue you got," he said, and cut off the beaver's head.

"I don't like people to talk as if Alan was a fool. —Your people don't even like it up in those mountains, Frank. You go up and hunt there twice a year and that's it. Caribou, or sheep."

"Now, you listen to me," Solokoff said, took a long flat stone from a drawer beneath the sink, and began to sharpen his knife, easy rhythmic strokes back and forth. "Every man's a fool one way or another, one time or another, and Alan Maher—who was real smart for a white man—still got caught workin' down below a berry patch without his rifle. An' a bear track runnin' right through up there . . . *an'* in the spring, cubbin' time."

"We never saw a bear on that old trail."

" 'Cause you didn' see 'em, don't mean they wasn' passin' through. —An' doin' that was his fault, not your fault. Not your fault for stayin' out of it, neither. Nobody blames you for not takin' a run for that rifle. You're a woman; you're not a man. An' people down here give you a lot of credit for not lyin' about it, for not sayin' you wasn' anywhere near there when that happened—even though anybody lookin' in your face could tell you saw it. Mary Toby knew right away, for one. She said she saw that bear in your eyes like in a mirror. We give you credit for not lyin' about that."

He shook out a plastic bag, picked up the beaver's tail, slid it down inside, then twisted the bag shut, fastened it with a green wire tie.

"You don't—"

"People here don't think you're a coward—they think you're bad luck. They think you called that bear last year by havin' your periods or whatever—an' excuse me for mentionin' it—havin' those out there in the woods where a woman doesn' have any business."

"Oh, please, *please* don't give me that crap, Frank."

"I'm not sayin' they're right, an' I'm not sayin' they're wrong. So you go on an' insult people all you want; they know where that anger comes from—comes from bein' ashamed, comes from bein' so scared you just run down out of them mountains couple months early. . . . An' whichever way, they don't want you up on our mountain anymore—whether you're playin' Cheyenne or Sioux or goddamn Aztec. You understand me? An' that's that. That mountain is in our country an' the goddamn courts say so. *White* courts. So you stay off it. You want to play Daniel fuckin' Boone, you find somebody else's mountains. You go there an' I don't know whose land it is, an' we don't give a shit."

Solokoff put the beaver's head in a plastic bag, fastened the bag
with a yellow wire tie. The beaver's small dark dead eyes peered
through the cloudy plastic as if desperate for a last look at the kitchen,
before the refrigerator's lightless cold.

"I didn't mean to hurt your feelings, Frank."

"Oh, yes, you did." Solokoff opened the refrigerator and put the
beaver's head away. "—An' let me tell you a little somethin': we
never got the horse up here. What we got was winters them lower
tribes wouldn' believe. We didn' have no buffalo or corn gardens an'
two-crop seasons an' so forth. What we got was those winters—an'
we handled 'em. I'm proud of the *Dena*; we took a lot of crap from the
Russians and from you people, and we kept our dignity and kept our
faces straight."

" 'Kept your faces straight'?"

Solokoff smiled. "That's exactly right. An' it wasn' easy, either."
He chuckled, trimming slices off the beaver's side. "Best eatin' there
is," he said. "—Tell you somethin' else. White men may run this
country, but white women run them. An' you're a real good example
of just what I'm sayin'."

"So, you asked them to cancel that lease."

"Damn right. Lease is up this spring, unless you're dumb enough
to waste money gettin' a lawyer, appealin' an' all that. Alan dead up
there is enough. I'm not goin' up there next time, find *your* foot in a
berry patch. An' you can't run that trapline anyway, not worth a
damn. What did you say you brought down—just four packs? Needs
a man to clear those lines every year, bush 'em out. What is it, a
hundred, hundred-an'-eighty-mile line?"

"I wish you hadn't asked them to do that. . . ."

"You don't even want to go back up there. —You really want to go
back up there? Well, do you? You intendin' to go back?"

". . . No. I don't think so."

"Well, then what the hell's your *problem*, woman?"

"My problem is I would like to have the choice, Frank. All right?
. . . Anyway, I'm going out of the country, now. I'm on my way
Outside."

"Well, thank God. An' you're glad to go, right?"

"I'm going."

"An' do us a favor an' don't come back." He reached out and
patted Sara's left hand with his own bloody right. "I'll miss you. An'
I been missin' Alan; we liked him. The young people, kids all liked
Alan this part of the river—here an' Chancy an' Fort Yukon. He'd go

dancin' with 'em, fool around. Crazy white people are the only white people we can stand, tell you the truth. Rest of 'em are too damn cold, always plannin' somethin' . . . schemin'. You people got winter inside you all year long—could be why you're white."

Sara was outside in failing light, trudging through drifted snow down the tree line to the path, when she remembered her dogs. She turned around and walked back up to the Solokoffs' house, went to the front door and knocked.

Charlie answered the door again, and didn't seem surprised to see her. "Pop's still in the kitchen," he said, stood aside while she came in, then closed the door behind her.

". . . What now?" Frank Solokoff said. "Don't you know it's bad luck to say good-bye to somebody twice?" He was rinsing the cutting board with hot water poured from the small pan. "I thought I saw the last of you." Parts of the beaver were still lying on the white platter; the rest of it, back and bones, was in a plastic bag. Solokoff dried the cutting board with a blue-and-white-striped dish towel, then opened the refrigerator's freezer door and tucked the plastic bag in among cartons of frozen milk, frozen butter, other plastic bags of salmon and meat.

"My dogs. . . ."

Solokoff sighed. "What do you want me to do?"

"Frank, could you hold the team for me—put them up for sale in the spring, after break-up? I'd ask Mary Toby, but she'd sell them to anybody. Somebody could mistreat them."

"Honey, not many people want dogs down here, now. Cost too damn much to keep, unless you're racin' 'em."

"Well, that's what I was thinking. I was thinking someone might want them for the Quest. Dutchy's the best gee-haw freighter lead I've ever seen."

"He's a fighter."

"Dutchy has spirit, that's all."

"He's goin' to fight somebody's dog an' cripple 'im."

"He's a great lead—he just doesn't like other dogs coming near his food."

"Yeah, sure. . . . An' speakin' about dogs, how's that half-wolf pup doin'?"

"Lobo."

"Right. How's he doin'? You keepin' in mind that's a Kottke-bred pup, there?"

"We—I take good care of him. Hard to train. . . ."

"Sure he's hard to train. You got a wolf there with some husky in him. Damn right he's hard to train; but you get him goin' right, you got a real piece of machinery."

"Well, he's sweet, but he's spacy."

"What about that Boots dog? How's he runnin'?"

"Boots is dead, Frank. Something happened to his kidneys, and I nursed him for weeks and kept him on low protein. It didn't work; he was an old dog. His legs got swollen and he was moaning and he couldn't pee. I had to shoot him."

"Damn. Shot that Boots. . . . I saw you were runnin' an eight team, one comin' along behind. Should have figured you lost one. Don't know how come you an' Alan didn' have more dogs up there, anyway. You didn' have enough for the work."

"We had all we could feed."

". . . Shot that Boots. That was a damn good dog."

"You mean he liked you, Frank—that's why you think Boots was such a good hauler, because he was always happy to see you. Boots was sweet, but he wasn't much of a teamster; wouldn't keep his mind on his business. —Why don't you run my team, Frank? Why don't you keep them?"

"I'm not racin' any more dogs. I'm an old guy. You want old guys runnin' your dogs, you go down to Huslia, don't come to me."

"Maybe Charlie—"

"Honey, don't make me laugh. My boys don't know about dogs. They don't know the eatin' end from the crappin' end. All they know is snow-machines—an' all they know about snow-machines is call the Ski-doo people in Fairbanks an' order a new one."

"That's not true. Ed's good with machines."

"Ed can put a new tread on. That's it. He can change the plugs. That's it."

". . . Well, will you take care of the dogs, Frank? I have a one hundred pound bag of Iams and four hundreds of Purina stored over in Mary Toby's shed from last summer. You can use that feed—and when the river opens in May, if you really decide you don't want the dogs, and you find somebody nice to take them, you could sell him the harness and sled, whole outfit. My two-man tent's over there, and the ax and cooler. —I'd write and let you know where to send the money. And if you want, you can have the stuff up at the cabin to keep if I don't come back. Another sled up there, and tools and the traps—just keep those for your trouble."

"If you don't come *back?* You just forget about that comin' back stuff. You want to come back up in this country, you go over to the coast or somethin'. Not back here. —You still runnin' all basket sleds?"

"Keeps the load dryer than toboggans. You could take the cabin and outfit up there, Frank; keep the money for any expenses taking care of the dogs till spring. Vet bills."

"Is that a hint? I'm supposed to have a vet fly into Chancy, fly all the way up here, take a look at 'em they get kennel cough?" He put the plastic bag of lungs and kidneys into the freezer. "I love it. You women are all alike. Come in here an' call me a shitty fish-eater Indian to my face—which most people wouldn' think of doin', I can tell you that—then turn right around an' come back an' want me to baby those dogs. The lead of which team would just as soon take my leg off as look at me. . . ."

"I'm sorry, Frank, for saying that. I apologize; I shouldn't have said that to you. Vanilla's about to pup. You could have the whole litter. Feels like four."

"Great . . . great." He put a careful drop of Dove dishwashing detergent on the white platter, then used the last of the water in the pan to rinse suds and beaver blood off the china.

"So, you'd rather not do it?"

"Damn right I'd rather not do it." Drying the platter very thoroughly with the striped dish towel.

"Well, all right. . . ."

"But I will do it, just so you get out of here."

Sara was so pleased she stepped forward to touch Solokoff, perhaps hug him, enjoy another hug, but he glanced at her in an odd way, so she didn't, but only held out her hand to shake.

Outside the house, walking away, Sara picked up a handful of snow and rubbed the beaver blood off her hand. It didn't seem she should have blood on her hands in town. She wondered if Frank had thought her makeup looked strange. Now, she wished she hadn't put on any makeup across the river.

As she walked down toward Mary Toby's house, the snow—freezing drier as the temperature fell toward early night—squealed softly under her boot-pacs. Sara heard amplified drumming begin to thump through the village from the community center, the drumming seeming to slowly coil around the generator's softer, rapid, and perfectly regular beat. When the path turned steeply downhill, she saw groups of men and groups of women moving separately along the bluff above the river, walking through darkening evening toward the sound. The men were talking, joking as they strolled, their hands thrust into parka or windbreaker pockets. The women, in boot-pacs or fur-fringed mukluks, knit hats, parkas, blue jeans or wool skirts, walked quietly along.

Sara stood for a while outside Mary's house, feeling she'd talked enough for the time being, had enough to do with people. She thought no one would notice her in this near-darkness—no one would bother to look up the path to see her, would bother to look out their windows. She stood resting for a while, taking the deepest breaths she could, as if the air's coldness and freezing weight could be taken inside with her, stay with her there as comfort. . . .

Mary Toby, wearing a blue apron with a small white duck embroidered on its large left-side pocket, was in her living room sweeping, smoking while she worked, when Sara came through the front door into warmth and odors of cooking and the menthol smell of the cigarette. There were no adults in the living room, now—only Carla and a little boy a year or so younger, sitting watching television. They were watching the news out of Fairbanks, the weather report. Snow.

"I hope you stomped your feet on that stoop."

"I did."

"I sure hope so. I got enough to do, cleanin' up after these people—raised in a damn barn."

"I did; I'm not tracking anything in."

"You'd be the first one didn't. —Well, what's the matter with that finger?"

"Broke it—broke the joint a few months ago. I splinted it, and it's fine."

"Call that fine? Sticks out like you was havin' tea at the Munsters. I could bust that again for you—set it right."

"No, thanks, Mary. It's fine, doesn't hurt at all."

"You got some mail—Frank Solokoff left it here a couple months ago. Top drawer in my dresser in the back, there."

"O.K."

"Top drawer. You don't need to be goin' all through my dresser back there."

"Mary, I don't want to go through your dresser. All right if I take a bath?"

"You pump the water, you heat it—you can take a bath. Just don't use up all my propane. I got an empty tank out there, an' a half-empty an' one full one supposed to last me till the barge. So don't waste that propane." She stepped to the TV, and tapped her cigarette ash into a small round white-china Anchorage Sheraton ashtray resting on a lace doily on top of the set.

"I'll just heat one bucket."

"You can heat two buckets—two buckets is O.K." Mary Toby, yellow plastic dustpan in her left hand, stooped with a grunt to gather up her sweepings. When Sara came and knelt to hold the pan for her, Mary jerked it away.

"What are you doin'? I don't need help sweepin'. Why don't you just go an' take your bath? I need help doin' somethin', I'll tell you."

Sara walked down the hall and through the kitchen to the back bedroom, looked in the top drawer of Mary's small dresser—Sears oak veneer—and found a bundle of letters in a red rubber band. There were various small sizes of cardboard boxes in the drawer, all with costume jewelry in them. Sara'd never seen Mary Toby wearing any of this bright stuff—big brooches of pot metal and thin brass, pins colored nearly gold, beaded bracelets and fragile rings with stones like rubies, like emeralds, pearls, diamonds. . . .

She supposed that Mary stood here before the dresser mirror sometimes, and tried her finery on. Stood and looked at herself for a while—a fat, elderly Koyukon lady—then took her pretties off and put them away.

There were eighteen letters, all dated last year, come after she'd gone back to the mountains. Fifteen were from Alaskans Sara didn't know. She opened one, read how sorry that woman was to have heard of her tragedy, the risk of frontier living—and put it down on the oak-veneer dresser. She sorted out all the letters from people she didn't know, and put them on the dresser unopened. There was an advertisement letter from Eukanuba—they had a new concentrated dog food for racers—a letter from Bud LeBeck, and two letters from Anne. Bud wrote a clear, looping hand; had probably been taught at Catholic schools.

SARA—*I heard the news June 8, and it shits. I'm going to miss our boy. You need anything, anything I can send up, have Batten or Frank Solokoff write me a note.*

Business is real good, considering the States is now a lousy market. Europeans are buying everything anybody can trap—especially marten and fox. Their red fox is crummy, so they're glad to get ours. Lynx is good, too. Wolf, not so good. Coyote is taking that over—a measly fur, but what are you going to do.

*If you decide to stay up and run the line, go for fox. Bill Sellecka
and Andy say hello and crappy news about Alan.*

Love,
BUD

Sara read that letter twice, then put it on the dresser. She opened
one of Anne's letters, dated June 29, saw the smooth rounded rise
and fall of her sister's handwriting. Black ink on one small blue page.

DEAR SARA,

*It's dreadful news, and Connor and I never even met Alan. I'm
terribly, terribly sorry. I wish you at least had let us know by phone
or radio or whatever—as it was, a friend of ours read it in the paper!
Please come home. After this, after years of being up there, I imagine
the wilderness has lost its charm.*

We send you our love; Kevin too. I'm so sorry.

ANNE

PS Mom doesn't know.

Sara put that letter down on the dresser top, then opened the
other, dated July 26. Two blue pages.

SARA,

*Since we didn't hear from you last month, and of course we
haven't heard from you for months before that, I contacted a Rev.
Paley, an Episcopalian minister up there you may or may not know,
but who did know about you.*

*Rev. Paley was able to tell us you went right back up where you'd
had your cabin, and apparently were going to continue fur trapping
or whatever.*

*I won't comment on all this, dear. I'm just not going to comment
except to say that it stinks. I would think, after what happened,
you'd be extremely tired of the Sheena Queen-of-the-Jungle bit.*

*Well, that's unforgivable, so forgive me. Really, though, you are
not the only one with troubles, and you will find, believe you me,
that running up to the North Pole for five years is no help at all. You
already have found that out.*

*It will not be surprising news that Connor and I have stopped
dancing around, and just went and did it. Divorce was a great relief.
And I think it was a great relief to Kevin, too. He'd been acting like
a nine-year-old all through it. Now, at least, he's a normal pain-
in-the-ass thirteen. And by the way, Connor is not at all interested*

*in having Kevin with him for more than one night a week, max. His
own son. A really wonderful man. And even so, I go in and smell
Kevin's sheets the night he's gone, as if he might leave me, too.*

*I know it's much too much to ask you to write. And I am very
very sorry about Alan, although we never met. But I really think it's
time for you to come home. You haven't seen Kevin since he was a
little kid, and even Connor—if he can tear himself away from the
very young prostitute he's supposed to be in love with—wants to see
you.*

*God knows I can sympathize about losing a man. There doesn't
seem to be that much to them, and then they're gone and suddenly
you're up the creek. It's as if we need their farts to stay alive.*

Love,
ANNE

*PS Mother's house is sold. No choice about it. She's worse, and can't
get out of her wheelchair anymore. I have her in The Arbor, which
is better than most, and costs $2,500 dollars a month.*

Sara folded the blue pages, put them with the other letters, and
stacked them all together. She went out to the kitchen, opened the
barrel-stove door, and put them into the fire. Then she pumped two
buckets of water to heat for her bath.

"Mind if I come in? Jesus, woman, you're skinny as shit." Pauline
Demientieff—her pale-brown oval face still lovely after so many hus-
bands, so many harsh evenings at the Tick-Tock Lounge in Fairbanks—peered around the edge of Mary Toby's bedroom door.
Pauline was wearing a pretty parka swinging open, a Native caribou
parka trimmed in blue beadwork, its ruff thick wolverine.

Sara, standing in Mary's big laundry tub washing herself with a
cloth soapy with Camay, had been at ease, glad the house was almost empty. She'd been listening to Mary Toby in the living room—
apparently, from her voice's high pitch and gentle repetitions, talking
with the children.

"I know I lost weight. . . ." The gray washtub barely fit between
the small dresser and a single bed decorated with a yellow-and-green
rag quilt. Mary Toby had sewn the quilt to represent a fish wheel
turning in the river's summer current, the great salmon it caught
pieced in various shades—leaf-green, gold, pale lime, rich butterscotch. The Camay soap, which Sara had first thought wonderfully
scented, was smelling more and more chemical.

" 'Lost *weight'*?" Pauline stepped in, closed the bedroom door behind her. "Honey, you lost everything. You look like you're twelve years old and been sick, except you got muscles." She sat down in one of Mary Toby's two metal folding chairs.

Sara felt that Pauline, so casually beautiful, was staring at her breasts—seeing how small, how inadequate they were. She soaped them again, covering with the cloth . . . then, afraid that would just draw attention, soaped her stomach instead. Too much pubic hair. . . .

Stooping to soak the cloth, she quickly rinsed her body, half-turned away, supposing now Pauline was observing the scrawny butt so inferior to her own . . . something wrong wherever she looked.

"What the hell happened to your knee?"

"Nothing. Bumped it on a tree."

"Shit. Want to be private? Want me to go?"

"No, no, don't be silly." Sara stepped out of the tub, picked a towel off the back of the other folding chair, and began to dry herself. Mary Toby's bath towels, off-white, had rows of little yellow chicks running across their top and bottom hems.

"You O.K. from bein' up there all alone? Gone a long time up there."

"I'm fine."

"I wouldn' do it, man. I wouldn' be up there alone after what happened. . . . Hear that? Those people are goin' crazy over at the Center—you hear that drummin'?"

Sara hadn't noticed the drumming for some time, those distant heavy rhythmic thuds becoming part of listening to anything after a while, then part of listening to everything—then indistinguishable from silence.

"Been doin' that for five days—an' you know why all those people come over an' eat at Mary Toby's?" The last said more quietly.

"No, I don't. Hospitality isn't her thing."

"You come stay with her."

"I like her."

Pauline smiled. When she smiled, she revealed stained teeth, as if a jealous forest spirit had cursed her with those at least, to a little spoil her loveliness. "She don't like *you*. She don't like nobody except kids."

"I think she does like me . . . in her way." Sara finished drying herself, still held the towel against her. She hadn't dried her feet, and decided not to rather than put her leg up on the chair and expose her groin to Pauline. Pauline had been drinking enough already to make some remark about Sara's having too much pubic hair.

"Well, that's why they come over—'cause they know she don't like it. People up here for the Stick Dance come over all the time so she'll have to feed 'em . . . start sweepin' an' everything minute they're gone. They think it's funny."

"It is funny." Sara wrapped the towel around her, tucked its corner under her right arm.

Pauline nodded, gleeful. "—An' what's so great is, she don't get it. Meaner she is, more they like comin' over, makin' her cook that bad soup."

Sara stood looking into the dresser mirror, brushing her short brown hair back with her hands. Mary's black plastic brush-set lay on the dresser top, but Sara didn't think she should use that. There was a comb in her purse; it didn't seem worth the trouble to go out to the kitchen for it, dig through the pack. . . . There was more gray in her hair than there had been. Looking in a regular mirror, she could see it.

"You been cuttin' your own hair."

"I don't think it's very good."

"You didn' get it good in back. You got some stickin' out back there, looks like a duck's ass." Pauline shifted in her chair, restless. Her parka was beautiful, the beadwork done as leaping little blue salmon migrating up the zipper trim.

"I suppose I should go to somebody, have it cut. . . ."

Pauline put her hands up to her own hair, gently touching, stroking that combed richness, black as raven feathers, falling down her back. "Mine needs cuttin', too, I guess. You know, get it cut so I don't have to be all day washin' it."

Pauline saw Sara's clean socks, bra, and panties folded on the bed with jeans and a faded green sweatshirt, all creased from the pack. She picked up the panties and handed them to Sara. "Cotton, right?"

"Yes. And falling apart." Sara put the towel down, stepped into the panties.

"I don't know why all you white chicks like those cotton panties."

"Healthier, get more ventilation. More air." Sara went to the bed, set the socks aside, and put on her bra.

"I don't need no air down there. Guys like a little smell, know what they're gettin'. —I'm embarrassin' you, right?"

"No." Sara pulled the sweatshirt on over her head.

"Well . . . you got nice legs. Real long."

"All I've got." Sara shook out the jeans, stepped into them and buttoned them up, wishing Pauline would stop looking at her, making remarks.

"No, you're real interestin' lookin'."

"Like a cow moose, right—long legs and everything?"

Pauline laughed and shook her head. "No way that bad," she said. "You want to go over? See the dancin'?"

Sara sat down on the bed to put her socks on. "Pauline, I don't think so. It isn't any of my business. I think people would rather I didn't go over there."

"Hell, they don't care. Not if you just sit up in the stands, watch. Why should they care? Some of those young guys up there so stoned they don't know what's goin' on. Could be watchin' TV, far as they're concerned."

"I don't think so. . . ." Sara bent to pull on her boot-pacs.

"You want a drink?" Pauline took a pint Jack Daniel's bottle from her right parka pocket.

"No, thanks."

"Bullshit. I'll get us some glasses." She stepped out of the bedroom; Sara could hear her sorting through one of the kitchen cabinets. Heard glass clinking. Through the bedroom wall, through a Norman Rockwell print of a family's Thanksgiving (thumbtacked neatly at its corners to the plywood), Sara could hear rapid little spanking sounds, Mary Toby playing pattycake with the children. Her voice, so youthfully light and sweetly pitched, sounded almost like a third child's joined in the game.

"Here we go." Pauline came in, black eyes lit with mischief. She held a small, flowered Kraft-cheese glass in each hand, the glasses (treasures of Mary Toby's girlhood) almost half full of whiskey. "—She hates people takin' a drink in here," handing the one in her right hand to Sara, the glass decorated with vines of little yellow blossoms. "Her an' that priest are always goin' on about it."

"Father Yermy?"

"You ever meet him?" Pauline sat down in a folding chair. "Episcopalians don't like him comin' up, but he comes up anyway."

"No. Almost, when we were down two years ago. Mary Toby's always talking about him."

"He comes up durin' the winter, now. About every six weeks except in January—does services an' stuff." Pauline sipped at her whiskey. "He's cute for a white guy. Got a beard an' everything. I don't have to tell you; Alan was real cute with his beard. Priest's not a bad guy, an' he sings a lot, you know; he sings in the services. Got a nice voice. Sings in the original Greek."

"Alan said he was nice." Sara tasted the Jack Daniel's, was surprised at its sweetness. It tasted sweet as store sugar to her, its harshness hardly mattering.

"Oh, Alan met him down here long time ago—an' they was foolin' around right away. You know, just foolin' around. Alan makin' fun of all that religious stuff."

"Yes. . . ."

"Still hurts you a lot, right?"

"I'm just waiting for it not to be so bad."

"You need to get out of this country. Then it'll start to fade, you know."

"I don't know how that ever fades. I'm afraid it won't ever."

"How did you stay up in them mountains all alone, thinkin' about that? Alan gettin' killed. I can't understand how you did that."

"It's beautiful up there."

"Not to me. You should hear the stories I heard about them mountains, when I was a kid. —I saw a guy killed in Fairbanks. Did you know that? You hear about that?—but it wasn' so bad. An Eskimo guy. He just got shot an' went outside an' fell right over in the snow an' that was that. They kept servin' people right at the bar, like there was nothin' to it. Cops came—they just kept servin' right at that bar. I didn' even know the guy an' I went back in the bathroom an' cried. That's all there was to it."

Sara sipped at her drink and wished Pauline would get up and go—wished they both could get up and go somewhere, and not be talking so much.

"Not like Alan," Pauline said. "Lot of people here cried when they heard what happened. Man, some people were real upset—guys were goin' out an' kill a bear just for the hell of it." Pauline finished her drink. "I'd rather be drinkin' beer; this stuff isn' good for you. Especially you're havin' a kid. I learned that with Leonard. It's just irresponsible to be drinkin' this stuff if you're havin' a kid."

"Carla spoke Koyukon out there to the dogs. That's nice, that you're teaching her that."

"Not me—her grandmother's the one talkin' that to her."

"Well, it's nice that she knows it."

"Tell you what, let's get out of here—go up an' see the dancin'. Last night they're goin' to be dancin'. Then they're takin' the stick down, you know, just before mornin'."

"I think I better stay away."

"Bullshit," Pauline said, and stood up. "We're goin' to have another drink, an' we'll go."

The drumming wasn't only one rhythm, or two or three. It seemed to Sara the drumbeats filled all the time there was, with no pause between. The icy air outside the community center shook with them, so the falling snow—a slight fall amounting to nothing much—trembled in twilight shading to night.

"Come on." Pauline pulled open the right side of the outer double doors, led in, and opened the inside door to thunderous noise, light, and heated air. They'd drunk some more Jack Daniel's from the bottle, walking over; Sara could faintly smell the whiskey on her breath blowing around her face like a scarf. The light seemed very bright.

The basketball court, half the community center—the locker room, bathroom, schoolrooms and small office the remainder—was packed with people. In the middle of the court, a tall spruce pole was fixed from the floor up to the ceiling, fastened high amid the steel members. The pole was draped so densely with pelts it was thick as a living tree—a spruce tree with gray, bronze, and dappled foliage of furs. Wolf, marten, lynx . . . wolf again. Sara saw several lynx pelts, red fox and wolverine, but mainly wolf skins threaded through with many smaller pelts of marten, bitter-sweet chocolate brown.

At the base of this—so active, so crowded that Sara avoided looking too closely—what seemed two hundred women danced packed around the pole, dancing there in an extended file several women deep that swung to reach the edge of the right-side grandstand. The women, arms over one another's shoulders, danced together in a sturdy, roiling, many-ranked line, like a slow surging river—parka brown, sweater red, blue, green, and white. They did a slow-footed then quick-footed dance, steps stomping forward and back that advanced the line very slowly, so it heaved and turned and turned back and heaved again, moving slowly no matter how fast any one woman danced.

Sara couldn't tell what rhythm the women were dancing to; they seemed to dance to none of the rhythms being drummed. They were dancing to their dancing's rhythm—and seemed different people, dancing, than they'd been eating dinner or watching TV.

The lights high on the court's ceiling blinded Sara when she glanced up at them, disturbed by seeing so many people. It didn't seem possible to be in a place with so many people. She looked down again and thought they seemed like a dancing herd of animals, fast-footed animals moving slowly. Very much like caribou, clicking, clicking, trotting along, always moving and moving unless you shot one—the rifle's weighty cracking sound echoing away as the animal, far upslope, fell over as if ordered to, kicking. Then the others would trot faster, filing by. . . . It relieved Sara to think of these dancers as a herd, moving together. The music was all drums—recorded drumming, some of it, she thought—chattering, thumping, roaring over the big speakers at the court's corners. The sounds, complete as silence, took up all her listening.

Men were gathered across the court, only a few dancing. Most of them were standing talking to one another. Four old men were sitting in the first row in the left-side grandstand, clapping, nodding to the drumming. Sara couldn't tell what drumming they were clapping to. The drummers sat farther down that row—seven or eight men drumming. The drums were big Native hide drums except for one, white and gold, a band bass drum. Sara thought she could hear its muffled deep dry thudding amidst the hide drums' humming, ringing thunder. The drum sounds rolled and rolled out; the polished yellow wood flooring shook and buzzed beneath Sara's feet as Pauline led her off to the right along the forecourt wall.

There was barely room to sidle along between the wall and the dancers. It was too hot; dancers bumped into them as they went, shuffled past them singing, packed together, boots and furred mukluks stepping those small steps—now quick, now slow, but moving so slowly all together. Heaving along. Now Sara could hear the women singing high-pitched *HAAAY*-ya . . . *HAAAY*-ya while they danced. Some were singing something else, shouting out more complicated phrases in Koyukon, but Sara couldn't hear them clearly—only saw their mouths moving, thought she heard those slight complications through the drumming. The drumming pressed its hands against her ears.

Pauline was looking back, calling something through the noise, tugging her toward the right-side grandstand. Sara saw the Hodges women, Nancy and Christine, dancing side by side deep in the file as the ranks dipped, stepped up and back, then shuffled forward one two three, and stepped back and forward, dipped and danced forward again so the wide court seemed to slip free of its foundation and slide behind them step by step, spurned away from under their feet. The gym floor now shook more from their dancing than from the drums.

The lights were so bright Sara's eyes teared—the dancers were swinging close to the wall again, crowded in, dancing step step step, so Pauline held Sara's right hand hard, tugged her along as if she were a child, took her to the grandstand and past other people sitting. They climbed up four or five rows of seats before Pauline sat down, Sara sitting at her right side. Sara felt that people were staring at her for being white, and unlucky.

"Look over there—" Pauline pointing down at the near corner of the gym, where a small middle-aged Koyukon woman wearing glasses stood singing alone in jeans and a heavy blue sweater that reached below her waist. Sara saw the woman was praying, shouting out some prayer or incantation over the slamming vibration of the drums, the dancers' shrill voices, the thud and shuffle of their feet.

"She's tryin' to call Joanie back," Pauline said, and Sara saw it was Erline Bruce, Joanie's mother. "You hear Joanie killed herself?"

"Yes."

"Went on down to the river an' shot herself right there. You tell me why a kid would do that—'cause I sure as shit don't know why."

Joanie Bruce's mother looked smaller and older than Sara remembered her. Two summers ago, she'd seen Erline at a fish camp twenty miles downstream—Erline running the fish camp, cleaning the big salmon, *flash, flash* with a bright-bladed knife, laughing with the other women at the tables, splitting the huge hook-jawed humpies, gutting them, whacking the heads and tails away, sliding the trash down the table where the dog barrel boiled . . . then unfolding the fish, butterflying brick-red filets wide. Joanie Bruce had been fifteen that summer—wearing black-rubber boots and her brother's cut-down cotton coveralls as she helped her mother—trotting to the smoke sheds, ducking into coiling haze-blue alder smoke to hang the red salmon up in shingled rows along the pole rafters.

Joanie, a big girl, had been cheerful then—joking, making fun. She'd upset her grandmother, threatening to fall in love with a black bear. In the heat of afternoon, all flying things—yellow-jackets, black flies, and jays—had been clouding, darting over the salmon racks, the cutting tables, stealing tiny oily red bites while the women worked. . . . Alan had stayed out on the river with the men, helping empty fish-wheel traps. Sometimes Sara, slicing with the women, had heard the men's voices from far down the river. Shouting . . . laughing. The women working at the tables had looked up when they heard the men's voices, looked up from their work and made amused faces at each other, as if they listened to children playing. . . .

Sara sat buffeted by drums, watching Erline Bruce in the corner of the court shouting her prayers in Koyukon—all unheard amid great noise—watched Mrs. Bruce's clenched hands pump up and down in time with her shouting, as if she were calling her daughter to her for punishment for such thoughtlessness in shooting herself on the riverbank, careless of how those who loved her would partly die as well, for nothing but a pulled trigger.

"I see Sidney didn' come tonight," Pauline said, voice raised above the drumming, speaking into Sara's ear. "Erline lost the both of 'em."

The lights in the gymnasium—high on the structural steel, and screened from unlucky or deliberately lofted basketballs—seemed to Sara to become brighter, harsher, heated as if the shouting, drumming, and dancing were increasing their currents of electricity. The grandstand boards trembled beneath her.

The women, jammed together, danced their slow circle around the pole in a haze of light through which the wolf pelts and lynx and fox pelts, through which the marten pelts swayed like spruce boughs on a morning wind. Sara looked across the court and saw the men less serious—saw two men, drunk, shove each other until separated, then saw a blue baseball cap like Alan's, that might have been Alan's cap . . . saw his red hair, or at least a man's red hair, perhaps a man with Russian blood in him. Saw this man—Alan's stocky size—standing at ease in his blue baseball cap, checked shirt, overalls and boot-pacs, the small round outline of a snoose can showing in his right back pocket. He was talking to a Koyukon Sara didn't know.

'That isn't him,' Sara said to herself, and leaned forward to look more carefully. The man who was Alan's size was busy talking, didn't even turn her way. He could be anybody. Sara felt her heart beating; it was shaking her. She was afraid her heartbeat would begin to argue with the drums.

"Look," she said into a rattle of drumsticks on the rims, the wooden drum-sides. "Look."

"What?"

"Look. . . ."

Pauline looked where Sara was pointing. "They're just fightin'."

"No," Sara said, and staring across the room, now saw nothing of the man who could have been Alan—had seemed the same as Alan would have, back turned. Then stared harder, determined to find that one—and saw so many men, all alike in being men, all close to being Alan, but not quite. "Not him . . ." Sara said out loud, so Pauline turned and looked at her.

"What?"

"Nothing." It seemed unfair that of so many men, none were Alan.

"See them?" Pauline was pointing at seven men sitting across the gym, sitting together on the top row of the left grandstand.

"Yes. . . ." Sara tasted the whiskey lingering in her mouth.

"They're suppose' to bring the messages from the dead people—you know, say good-bye for the dead people to all their friends an' family an' everything tomorrow mornin'."

The seven men—two of them young men, boys—were sitting in a row, joking, watching the dancers.

The gymnasium's air, smelling of sweat-damp wool and cotton, glowed dull gold above the dancers' seething, stepping up and back. The air, thicker than it had been when Sara first came in, was hard to breathe. The dancers seemed to be using all the good air up, so Sara had to breathe harder to get her share.

"I think I'll go out for a while."

Pauline didn't hear her, was talking to a woman sitting on her other side.

Sara felt her face, her shoulders, her breasts oiled with sweat. Up in the cabin, she would have gone to open the vent board over the door. And if it stayed hot as this, would have had to open the door and let all the thick, slow, steaming air slide out—let the other, emptier air, quick and icy, rush in to refresh her, let her breathe.

"I'm going to go outside." Sara's stomach ached, but when she burped—whiskey and moose soup—felt better.

"Look at that," Pauline said, almost shouting over the noise. "See those red boots that girl's wearin'?"

"Where?"

"She's wearin' glasses, dancin' in the front—between them two old ladies."

"I see her." Sara saw the girl in red boots dancing wonderfully well—rising slowly off the floor, drifting slowly back down again—dancing halftime to all the others. She moved in a halo of heat, her glasses flashing reflection as though a fire burned one step before her.

Sara heard a humming in her ears growing louder than the drums, and felt her hands tingling. As she watched, the dancers began to dance at more and more of a slant—as if they were dancing up a slope of yellow gym floor, as if the building were tilting up on its side so they had to climb as they danced. But when she moved her head, the floor and building swung slowly down and across and up the other way, so she expected the women dancing to begin to stumble, to be unable to keep their feet. . . . It was so odd she supposed it wasn't happening, was only dizziness from the whiskey and heat. She closed her eyes and felt better, not so sick. And even better when she covered her ears, but still not well enough. She lay down on her right side along the grandstand bench; the board vibrated beneath her and was so narrow she was afraid she'd fall off it, fall and get tangled in the structure below . . . and all the angles down there would make her more nauseated.

"Sara?"

"I feel . . ." Sara intended to say 'sick' but was afraid saying it would make her sicker.

"You O.K.?"

"Yes," Sara said, gagged and suddenly vomited a mouthful, lying on her side, and spat it out between the grandstand boards. Moose soup and whiskey.

"Oh, shit—" Pauline, stronger than she looked, took Sara by the shoulders and sat her up.

"I better go outside. . . ." But when Sara looked out at the dancers, they seemed to swing all together slowly back and forth, the floor swinging away with them—up and up to the right . . . pausing like a carnival ride . . . then swinging swiftly down, down—then up to the left. She couldn't bear watching. *"Outside,"* she said.

"Fuckin'—a." Pauline took Sara's right arm and pulled her to her feet. "Come on—come on!"

Sara stood and stepped down the grandstand boards with Pauline coming down behind her—stepped down and reached the gym floor, which seemed so hard it was difficult to walk on, not springy as the grandstand boards had been.

Her sickness and the man who could have been Alan came together and made each worse, so Sara couldn't stop for the dancers but put her head down and went into them, into those ranks, tried to push through them to look at that man again, and get to the door. She didn't know which she needed more. She shoved into the ranks of women—Pauline following, pulling at her—so she was lifted off her feet and carried along for a moment and dropped, then was able to wrestle through, elbow her way through, and thought of shouting as Erline Bruce had been shouting.

And did call out, "Not here!" to the man who might have been Alan—though she couldn't see him now, in the crowd—as if calling was better than nothing. She shouted, unable to hear herself above the noise of drumming, but certain she was doing it. *"Not here . . .!"* A woman caught her arm but wasn't strong enough to hold her, and Sara fought free of the dancers, broke through them and came out on the other side. Then she stopped and stood with her eyes closed, afraid she was going to vomit on the floor.

A man was saying something to her, and she opened her eyes and saw an angry face standing by the drums, and she pushed past him and went to where the other men were drumming. She thought there might be a door there, to get out before everyone saw how sick she was. And just then, she saw the man almost Alan's size—and he turned slowly from the men he was talking with and seemed to keep turning, seemed to spin slowly around and around . . . and grew darker and older each time, so by the last turn he was a Native, so unlike Alan there could be no mistaking him.

A man in a red sweater took her left arm and pulled at it, and when Sara yanked her arm away, reached for her again, took her arm and held it hard.

"Out!" The drums hammered the same thing he was yelling. *"—You get the fuck out of here!"*

Sara ducked her head to bite his hand and the man let her go. She walked along the line of drummers and stumbled, feeling the drumbeats pulsing through her as she passed each instrument, as if the drums were huge squat dogs—Outside dogs, deep-chested as mastiffs, bellowing as she went by. She heard Pauline behind her, and two boys were standing in her way, and when she turned, looking for the door, Frank Solokoff was there saying, "Come on now . . . come on now."

An angry man in a dark green windbreaker came up to them, and Frank waved him away. "You come on and get out of here, now," Frank said to Sara. That's what she thought he said, though she only heard it slightly over the drumming, the stomp, stomp, stomp of the dancing. "—You don't belong in here at all."

"I know it," Sara said, and when Frank bent to hear her better, said, "I had too much to drink." Frank nodded as if that was no surprise and took her arm and handed her to Pauline like an awkward package. "You take her on out of here," he said to Pauline. "—I thought you had more sense." Pauline, breathless, looked annoyed.

"I'm sorry," Sara said, "I feel better, now." But Pauline still looked angry, and wouldn't let go of her arm—kept pulling and pulling her through all the noise, the drumming thumping against Sara's back, pushing her along toward the double doors. The floor was shaking under her feet, she felt it through the soles of her boots.

Women were watching her as she went through the dancing. Sara saw Carrie Warren and Stevie Sam—then suddenly bent over and vomited, with nothing she could do about it. Things wanted to come out of her, and they came out of her and spattered on the shining yellow wood floor. That was just for a moment, just for a moment or two, and then she could stand up straight and let Pauline haul her away. Sara had gotten some of it on her jeans and her boots. She was so embarrassed she would rather have been dead. Dead up in the mountains. She hoped she was dreaming and this wasn't happening for everyone to see. Pauline tugged at her and she heard a woman shouting, and was past the dancers and at the doors. Pauline pulled her through the inside doors and coolness, then through the outside doors and out into emptiness, darkness and cold—twilight become night, at last—and Sara felt better and tried to forget the heat and light and smells and drumming. That was all past.

The nighttime snow, frosted whiter than snow by a rising moon, was frozen dry, and blew and ran and eddied around their boots like sand. The aurora shifted slowly above them in deep leaf-green curves softer than the moonlight, and so sheer the stars shone through.

"Thank God," Sara said—for the cold—then doubled over and tried to vomit again, but there was nothing there. She felt better, even so, and soon stood up. The cold was her friend.

Someone came out of the gym's double doors, stood for a moment, then went back inside.

"I'm shit sure not givin' you no whiskey, anymore." Pauline stood furious on sifting snow, her breath clouding in glassy moonlight around her, the ruff of her beautiful parka standing around her head, a black-and-silver halo.

"I just got sick," Sara said, and bent to scoop up a mouthful of snow . . . then more to scrub at the front of her pants, the toe of her right boot. She was feeling much better now, much more natural. "—And he wasn't there. Now I feel better," and meant she was crying. "See?" she said, and knelt in front of Pauline, then fell on her face in the snow and wept.

"Oh, my God. Come on, now," Pauline said, bent down and took Sara under the arms and hauled her up to her knees. "Stand up, come on. —I sure as shit am not givin' you no more drinks. That's for sure." She held Sara around the waist and helped her up onto her feet. "There, come on now, honey—you don't want anybody seein'

you fallin' all over. Come on . . . you're not the first one got drunk
an' vomited in that gymnasium."

"I like you, Pauline," Sara said, and wiped her eyes with her right
parka sleeve, her nose with her left. "I'm going to do you the biggest
favor. I won't ever tell you what I saw happen to Alan. That's the
biggest favor. . . ."

"I know . . . I know, sweetheart," Pauline said.

"But then I liked being up there alone. . . ."

"Sure. That's O.K."

The outer double doors to the gym opened again, and two men
came out, one in padded dark-tan coveralls. Then another man came
out; an older man, big, who wore dark glasses as if against the
moonlight. The three of them stood staring at Pauline and Sara.
"Hey, you fuckin' bitch," the one wearing the dark glasses called to
them, his breath smoking like a demon's. "*Gussuk* bitch!"

"You shut your mouth," Pauline said.

Sara reached into her right parka pocket, took the Clipit out,
opened the blade with her thumb, and held the knife behind her.

"—I know you," Pauline said, "an' you aren't even from here.
You're Fred Beetus from Ruby. Well, this isn' Ruby, so you just shut
your mouth."

While the three men were thinking about that, the doors opened
again and Frank Solokoff and his son Charlie came out of the gym.

"You men, go on back inside," Solokoff said.

When one of the men went but the other two didn't, Charlie
Solokoff walked over to them. "You heard what my pop said, didn'
you? Go on back inside." Then the other two went.

Frank Solokoff came over, his mukluks squeaking on the snow,
and looked at Sara. "You know better than that," he said. "You don't
belong in there, an' especially not drinkin'."

"I just got sick in the heat," Sara said. "—Too many people. I
didn't mean any disrespect, Frank."

"What have you got in your hand back there?"

"Nothing."

"Pauline," Solokoff said, "—you take her back to Mary Toby's,"
and turned and walked away through bright powder snow that
stirred with his steps like silver. His large son, turning into his father's tracks like a moonlight shadow, followed him to the gym and
on inside so the double doors swung shut behind them.

Sara closed her knife and put it away. Her mouth, her tongue
seemed thick with the acid taste of whiskey and moose meat. She

bent down for more snow, took a mouthful, and wiped at two small spots of vomit frozen down her left pants-leg.

"Shit," Pauline said. "Goin' to stick somebody with that knife? Woman, I can't take you *anywhere*." They both began to giggle clouds of frost, then linked arms and walked away down the hill past the TV down-link's gray steel box, its wide steel-webbed dish—Sara feeling better as the cold closed around them, the night opened wider . . . so that above, the northern lights seemed to chime, and green as willow, swung half a slow circle past the polar star.

5

Carla, wide awake, small and light taffy brown in a white Snoopy T-shirt, lay beside the sleeping little boy on an unfolded couch-bed in Mary Toby's living room. She waited for Sara to find her place in her blue notebook.

"Flying Squirrel," Sara said. "—That's the title."

"What's a title?"

"That's what it's about, Carla," Mary Toby impatient, sitting in her rocker in the corner. Mary was wearing a white terry-cloth robe and sheepskin slippers against the cabin floor's still pond of cold. She was rocking, her slipper toes just touching the floor's planks, lifting as she rocked slowly back and away . . . then returned to touch the floor again, only with her toes. "Go on," Mary Toby said. "—If you're goin' to read us a story, then read it." And, more softly, "Comin' in a house drunk in the middle of the night . . . supposed to be a mother," the first referring to the two of them, the last to Pauline, who, bored, had gone back to the Stick Dance.

"A Flying Squirrel," Sara read.

"Title. . . ." Carla.

"Shhh," said Mary Toby.

"A FLYING SQUIRREL. . . .

Three years ago, down in the West Alaska Range, a parky squirrel was born who seemed to be like all other parky squirrels. She was very small when she was born in spring under a big white spruce, deep under the tree in a nest among its tangled roots. Parky squirrels aren't very smart—and never call each other by name—but we'll name her Tusna. Tusna was born tiny, fat, and blind, and had two brothers and three sisters. *And for weeks, in this little warm nest, Tusna and the other babies drank from their mother, wrestled, and squeaked.*

By summer, the squirrel kits were much bigger. Their mother allowed them outside the nest, and they played in soft pine needles beneath the trees. It was here that Tusna began to seem strange. Parky squirrels are ground squirrels; they're not much for climbing trees. But Tusna, even when she was so young, climbed a tree almost every day. She didn't climb very well, and she didn't climb very high, but she climbed.

As she grew older, she climbed higher in the trees—she even climbed big rocks, as high as she could get. She would have climbed higher if she hadn't been so fat. She was fat, even for a summer squirrel.

It sometimes surprised the other ground squirrels to see Tusna up in a tree, or high on a rock like a mountain marmot—but squirrels don't think very much, so they never wondered why a ground squirrel seemed so dissatisfied being a ground squirrel. It seemed she would rather have been a red tree squirrel, or even a flying squirrel, so she could run off the high branches up there and glide and glide."

" 'Glide an' glide . . .' " Carla said.

"None of the squirrels were smart enough to see that Tusna didn't want to be a squirrel at all. She didn't want to climb. She didn't want to glide. She wanted to fly."

"Mmmm. . . ." Carla wiggled her hands above the edge of the quilt, as if they were small wings.

"It's hard to say why she began to want to do something so strange for a parky squirrel. Perhaps, when Tusna first came waddling out of the dark nest into the sunlight, a fat furry little baby, the first thing she saw was a jay—bright-feathered, quick, and noisy—fluttering near her, then suddenly flying away up into the air. Perhaps that was the reason that even as she grew older, even after the next winter's long sleep, Tusna still climbed as high as she could and sat looking out through the spruce branches. She stared at birds every time they flew by, stared at them until they flew high, and higher, and out of sight. And sometimes, excited, she would give a little hop, as if she, too, should be able to fly.

Perhaps it was her strange behavior that kept Tusna from mating with a male squirrel. Male squirrels don't like anything strange. Anyway, she didn't mate, and she didn't have babies.''

"No babies," Carla said.

"She nested all alone under a small black spruce, and when she wasn't eating seeds or chewing pine cones, she climbed and she watched birds. She watched ravens and jays, sparrows and blackbirds; she watched them all. And sometimes, when a bird would light near her, peck at this and that, then suddenly fly away, Tusna would give her little hop as if she were about to fly, too."

Carla hopped under the covers, and wiggled her hands.

"Discontented," Mary Toby said, rocking forward. "Plenty fools right in Billy Mitchell just as dumb," touched slippered toes to the floor, and rocked slowly back.

"And that's how her second summer went. It was a good summer for parky squirrels—lots of seeds and pinecones. A long, warm summer.

Then, one hot day in August, a day so long that the sun would throw shadows until midnight, Tusna was in the smallest clearing in the grove. She was sitting up, peeling a thin strip of spruce root, when a goshawk came whistling down out of the sunshine and struck her hard. It was such a surprise, and so hard a hit, that Tusna didn't feel any pain, only a blow that made her dizzy and rolled her on the ground."

"Oh, no. . . ." Carla put her hands up to her mouth.

"The goshawk—a big hawk with bronze and silver-colored feathers, a beautiful hawk—"

"What's bronze?"

"Bronze is a shining dark brown color. . . .

The hawk hopped after Tusna and gripped her in his talons. Then the bird flapped his wide wings and heaved the squirrel up off the ground. And that wasn't easy, because Tusna was so fat.

But even though she was hurt, Tusna wasn't frightened and didn't mind the hawk's sharp odor or its hard grip. She just hung still in the bird's claws and watched with small bright black eyes as the ground fell away beneath her, then the spruce trees, then the tops of the spruce trees, until all the country lay stretched out below her, the wide spruce forest covering the land all the way to the mountains.

Held firmly, her short brown fur ruffled by the wind from the big hawk's wings, Tusna traveled along through the sunny summer air, blinking, looking down at everything.

She was flying at last, and found it wonderful even though she felt sleepy. Tusna was happier now than she'd ever been. And a little while later, carried high over a small river that ran gleaming through the forest, she closed her eyes, went to sleep, and died sailing through the air. . . ."

Carla lay staring up at Sara, astonished. "She died?"

"Yes."

"Good story," Mary Toby said.

"Well . . . she got to fly, anyway," Carla said, and sighed. "But I don't like it that she died."

"Good story," Mary Toby said again, stopped rocking and stood up. "Time for bed."

Sara dreamed it was still deep winter, without sunlight, only the soft pinks and blues of noon fading back to moonlight's black, silver, and several grays.

She was snowshoeing through taiga, comforted by miles of ringing silence broken only by her shuffling passage, and lit with the aurora's pale draperies a hundred miles above the mountains. She stood still in a wide snowfield, eased her pack, and looked up to watch the northern lights filter lower, then slowly bloom from mauve to rose. Sara's face stung with cold as if she'd been slapped. She breathed deeply in, and felt the frigid air run down her throat heavy as ice water.

Standing still, she heard only the faint crackle as she breathed out, her breath freezing before her face—that, and the slight thump, thump, thump of her heart . . . some barely felt disturbance through her throat, where blood pulsed up . . . and the faintest static of molecules roiling against her ear drums.

Nothing else sounded, nothing else shook the moonlit air. If any breeze blew to loose a handful of soft snow from a spruce, it did so five or ten or fifty miles away.

She stood still a little longer, reluctant to introduce a sound—then had just shifted to travel again (already making the noises of cloth and pack straps moving) when she heard wolves begin to call as if they'd lain for hours silent, waiting to hear what might dare to make a sound, then made their own.

They were behind her, at least two miles, more likely three or four. She thought it doubtful they'd be hunting her—thought that until they called again. Closer by only a quarter of a mile perhaps, but coming on.

She dreamed she reached up over her right shoulder for the shotgun, touched its checkered pistol grip, then felt that soften as if the cold were heat, soften still more, and run through her fingers like syrup.

The wolves sang again, and Sara, as if the long, sweet howling had suddenly permitted a vision, saw three wolves trotting through dark spruce miles away. Only three—but strange wolves. The leader, particularly, seemed strange—big, dark-furred and high-shouldered, running with an uneven bobbing gait, more like an Outside dog's than a wolf's way.

As Sara watched through the echo of their singing, she saw this leader stop half in a spruce's shadow, shrug, and slowly stand up onto its hind legs, hunching its shoulders then easing them, until Sara saw it was a man. Or almost a man, since its feet remained paws, its hind legs the legs of a wolf, trembling now with the weight of the standing man's body resting on them in perfect moon-white snow.

Sara saw by this moonlight the lead wolf had half become the older Koyukon man, chest now bared, who'd cursed her outside the dance. And the other two men now appeared half-naked out of their wolf shapes, wolf fur, wolf bones and teeth, apparently changed for conversation impossible for wolves.

The leader bent to the snow and drew on it with a human finger, his right hind pad stepping half a step forward for balance. The other two came staggering to look—their moon shadows the oddest shadows—and spoke with him in Athabascan.

Sara saw her snowshoe tracks, their run reaching away before and beyond them. Now, talking done, the leader threw back his head, caught moonlight in his face, and let that slowly melt it to a muzzle . . . slowly out of shadows make his pelt complete, as the other two did, shivering until they were furred.

Then, weak with hunger, drooling, the smallest snapping at snow, the three yelped, scurried and sprang away into their kind's quick trot. They were starving for her meat and guts and bones. . . .

That was all she saw, but having seen it (and now, being back to herself) Sara found the vaulted emptiness, the line of forest far across the snowfields, the mountains miles beyond—frosted, immense, still and silent—found all this no longer beautiful since there was no help in it, and began to run, waddling, shuffling swiftly as she could, snowshoeing over snow at least packed fairly well by some hammering cold wind the night before.

Her heart rattled in her chest like metal as she ran. She heard the werewolves howl behind. They had her almost in sight, she was sure. Almost in sight—as if when they did, when they could see her small struggling shape so far ahead, just that seeing, that viewing, would slow her and make her stumble out of fear so terrible she'd prefer to run more slowly, to struggle less and so hasten her end.

She sweated as she thrashed along, sweat warmth under her clothes, sweat freezing to sleet down her forehead. And sweating, she gave them another rich scent to follow, a banner to wave them on and in upon her—an encouragement to wolf-running already nearly perfect. Her snowshoes, webbing clotted with snow, weighed heavier every shuffling step.

Her right knee hurt; she must have twisted it hauling the snowshoe up, swinging it forward, planting it to pick up the left one, swing that forward. . . .

She could hear herself breathing; she sounded already injured. Frightened by how tired she was, making small grunts of effort, she whimpered, pleading as she ran, all rhythm lost in heaving the snowshoes along, kicking snow, nearly tripping once as she let the toe of the left one droop. She saw the forest less than half a mile away, saw trees just big enough to climb. —But then, those three (now paws and tongues and teeth) could alter just enough for hands, and climb after her, smiling up through small soft dumps of snow the spruce shed, shaking.

She heard (above her busy thumping sliding noises, her gasps and little cries) heard high above these—as if an owl made them in the air—other sounds, swift paws pattering, cantering, changing gait to gallop . . . all muffled slightly, whispering slightly in the snow. It was happy running she heard. Now, they hunted by sight.

Then Sara shared what caribou knew, and moose, and her eyes were wide, her mouth open, and she staggered and whooped for air. She hoped when they caught her, it would be as wolves. She hoped to be killed and eaten by them as wolves—have innocent canine muzzles sniffing, rooting in between her thighs, biting into her belly for the guts—as wolves, not as men, so she could keep her privacy.

Still running, but lumbering, laboring along, worn out with waiting, Sara stumbled through the snow and called for Alan just once, as if calling only that one time had the best chance of being heard, being answered. An almost casual call, to prevent his being completely dead.

A moment later, when she looked up, struggling, and saw still how far ahead the forest lay, she heard Alan say softly, *"Don't be scared. —Don't be scared. I'm just visiting. . . ."*

She thought she was waking, then thought not. She opened her eyes to Mary Toby's dark kitchen, heard the small woodstove's metal ticking in the cold, felt the kitchen table firm beneath her, the comfort of the sleeping bag. Sara closed her eyes again and was certain she was awake, that the three running as wolves must have seen her waver in their sight, become more and more moonlight, then vanish away and depart the dream, leaving them only the cold and their hunger, unless they could catch her moon shadow before it fled, and as dream creatures, find that food enough. . . .

Her heart was still pounding from the chase, and she relaxed, not minding her foot being held through the soft bag's thickness. Then she was awake.

"Carla . . . ?"

Still the gentle holding.

"—What is it, sugar? You have to go potty?" And certainly awake, Sara opened her eyes again, raised up in the sleeping bag, and saw Alan standing shadowed in moonlight at the foot of Mary Toby's kitchen table.

"Don't be scared," he said; his gold-rimmed glasses glinted as he moved his head. "I'm just visiting. Tell you everything's O.K." He sounded hoarse, recovering from a cold. . . .

Sara sat up in the sleeping bag and saw him smiling at her.

"Just came to say good-bye," he said. The moonlight bleached the red from his short curling beard, left only darkest gray. He was wearing his Oshkosh overalls and a checked flannel shirt she'd never seen. His Bean down vest.

"Oh, you were so hurt," Sara said, and was surprised she said it; she felt her heart lying motionless in her chest.

"Don't worry about it," Alan said. "Event was natural new planet." And Sara felt, as if she'd forgotten it for a moment, how he held her foot through the sleeping bag. She looked down and saw he was doing that, his hand barely visible against the dark fabric where he gripped her—and she twisted and convulsed away and shouted something loud as she could, to wake up or be thrown far away just by the sound.

"I don't blame you," Alan said, and Sara wished she could die to get away, and made that shout again, felt wet warmth run in her underwear where she was peeing, kicked out and kicked free of the sleeping bag and writhed and fell off Mary Toby's table onto the frigid floor, knew she was awake, and scrambled back screaming past the barrel stove and refrigerator toward the closet.

"Don't," he called to her, "—*don't be afraid.*" And Carla cried out of sleep from the living room.

Sara reached up to open the closet door, in to get the shotgun—snapped off its safety and turned as the bulbs in the kitchen's wagon-wheel light flashed on and Mary Toby, small and fat in a yellow flannel nightgown, came out of her back bedroom with an aluminum softball bat and hit a strange Alan in the head with it—not with her full strength, but firmly. Then hit him again, the bat ringing softly with the blow, and knocked him up against the drain sink and down on his knees.

Sara crouched to stare under the kitchen table, the shotgun staring with her, and saw a tall thin Indian boy sitting against the spruce-wood cabinets in overalls and a brown down vest. A small bundle of red wool yarn was tied at his mouth and chin. The gold-rimmed glasses had fallen off, and his blind left eye shone white.

"Jack . . . oh, Jack Joseph," Mary Toby said, and put the bat down on the table hard enough so it sang the same dull song it had hitting the boy in the head.

"Sara," the one-eyed boy said, "—why would you want to shoot me?"

"What happened to your knee?" Mary Toby trying to change the subject.

"Never mind my knee; I bumped it. —Listen, I don't care what he thought. I don't care what he wanted to do." Sara, in deep night's humming stillness, stood in Mary Toby's back bedroom in the wash-tub—a second bath so soon by soft lemon light from Mary's bedside lamp—splashed to rinse the urine from her legs, and stepped and stomped on her underwear and the sleeping-bag liner. "Just keep him the fuck away from me."

"Well, I sure don't believe any of it." Mary Toby, still too upset to talk tough, sat on the side of her rumpled bed, watching Sara bathe. "It's just pagan superstition. Father Yermy tries an' tries. . . . Episcopalians let 'em do it, that's what happens. Those white fools come up here—last word out of their mouths is Jesus. Never hear that word out of *their* mouths."

"It's a Native thing; that's fine. Just keep it away from me." The barrel stove, freshly loaded, thumped and grumbled in the kitchen.

"Got drunk over there," a meaningful look, "—an' not the only one, either. Just got drunk over there with those people an' saw Alan climbin' down that pole. Said he told him he was angry Jack carved on your table, an' told him to come say good-bye for him. . . . Just ignorant superstition."

"He said that? You must have hit him harder than you thought."

Mary Toby, at this mention, began to rock a little back and forth, sitting on the bed. "I thought I killed him. Thought I killed that boy, eighteen years old an' my own sister's grandson. I didn' know who he was or what he was doin' in there or nothin'."

"That asshole's fine. He's all right."

"I know he was all right. Just a big bump." She put a soft brown hand to her right eye. "He's stayin' with Eddie Sams—an' they're not even *supposed* to be comin' sayin' good-bye for dead people until tomorrow. That's how much those fools know. Can't do nothin' right. . . ."

"And that saying 'Sara, why would you want to shoot me?' as if I ever met him in my life! He's lucky I didn't shoot him. —And about new planet stuff. How would he *know* to say that?" Sara stepped out of the tub.

"Gettin' water on my floor." Mary Toby, calmer now and sitting still, handed Sara a towel, this with red chicks running at its border, left to right. "Alan knew Wanda an' Ruth an' them in Fort Yukon. Didn' he tell you about them?"

"Told me about Ruth."

"Jack an' Wanda was always followin' Alan around, goin' fishin'— that's how come Jack said that stuff. . . ."

Sara began to dry her breasts and arms. "Since we're talking, Mary, Frank told me what you've been saying to everybody. —I'm bad luck. Isn't that what you've been telling people? People like that boy, Jack? And then he went and carved a bear on my table."

"Well, you are bad luck. Look what happened to Alan! An' usin' up all my propane. . . ." She sat pouting, plump light-brown legs descending from her yellow nightgown to fat little feet.

"You want me to leave this house?"

"You better put some weight on you, you talk about leavin' peo-

ple's houses middle of the night. You're so skinny, you look sick.
—An' you didn' eat much dinner, neither."

"That's because you're a terrible cook," Sara said, and saw a startled look of hurt on the old woman's face.

"I am *not*."

Worried Mary Toby might do something sad and surprising, perhaps begin to cry, Sara said, "No. I didn't mean that, Mary. You're
really a good cook." Drying her belly, then her back.

"I am a good cook." Looked close to tears.

"I just wasn't hungry. The moose was all right."

"I don't cook my best for those people; that's all. But if I want to
cook good, I can cook damn good."

"That's true; you can." Sara bent to dry her legs.

"You go up in that graveyard an' ask my husband if I can't cook."

"I know you can. Remember when Alan and I came down the year
before, and you made the cake?"

"I remember that. Raisin cake. Raisin and cloudberry."

"It was very good." Sara draped the towel over the back of a
folding chair, and dug through her pack for clean underpants.

"So don't say I can't cook. You're not eatin' anything—you're not
used to good food, is your problem. You're so skinny your bones are
stickin' out of your skin. Good thing you never had no kids; you sure
don't have enough tit to feed a kid with."

"I always thought if we had a baby, and I couldn't nurse," Sara
stepped into the panties, "—I'd put it on one of the bitches." She
pulled her T-shirt on over her head.

"Well, that's the most heathen thing I ever heard," Mary Toby
said, "—and I've heard a lot."

Sara bent and reached down into the water to find her underpants, wring them out into the tub, and drape them over the back of
the chair beside the towel. Then stooped again for the sleeping-bag
liner. "Help me wring this out."

"Gettin' water all over my floor . . ."

Later, the house dark again, Mary Toby was back in bed and softly
snoring. She'd left her bedroom door open, perhaps for early warning of any other visitor bringing greetings from the dead. "I don't
want to hear nothin' from my husband. Far as I'm concerned, Ralph
Toby is gone an' good riddance. Man was only good for gettin' our
moose an' foolin' with dogs an' fish-wheels. Period."

"Good night, Mary," Sara'd said.

Mary had muttered, "*Bad cook . . .* ," getting into bed, turning off the small bedside lamp so her complaint trailed off into darkness.

Sara, barefoot in her underwear, had climbed from the frozen floor onto the kitchen table, wriggled down into the linerless sleeping bag, smelled a trace of Alan's odor in the fabric . . . that less and less. Now, mostly remembered.

She lay in the cooling kitchen (the barrel stove ticking, conversing with its failing fire) and wondered what had frightened her so about Alan's coming back—why he'd been so unwelcome. And if, when the lights had come on—and she'd been ready with the shotgun from the corner—what if the lights *had* shown Alan, come magically back to her? Maybe come crawling down the fur-draped pole, or swimming down through thick gray, brown, and spotted pelts—soft waterfall from a world above—come swimming down to the dancers, called by the drums.

What if Alan had come down himself, instead of only in a Native boy's imagination after too much whiskey? And she'd seen her husband sitting against Mary Toby's kitchen cabinets, rubbing his hurt head and smiling at her. And he'd said, "Why would you want to shoot me, Sara?" What would she have said, then? —That after all, she'd liked being alone on the mountain? That she'd loved him, but he'd taught her all he knew, and she was tired of his repetitions? None of that seemed reason enough to point the shotgun at Alan, or Alan's ghost, unless to be rid of his witness—or it was death she was pointing the shotgun at.

She wished Dutchy had been in the kitchen with her. Then, there would have been no confusion. Dutchy would have known who was who, and acted on it. As it was, except for the noise and sorrow and blaming, except for all the trouble it would have caused, she wished she'd killed the boy. Then, Alan would be entirely dead.

He'd come to her before, but only in a dream one evening, during a gentle blizzard blowing, when she'd taken the rum bottle down from the second-highest canned-goods shelf, and drunk enough to make her dream, awake.

Then, Alan had come to her, but only after the lamp was out. He'd come to her, and sat on the bunk's edge and talked in the dark about other things—not the bear. Other things they'd done together before they ever came up to the mountains. . . . Alan had sat and talked. She never answered. He sat in the dark and talked for a while. Then he stopped talking and they listened to the wind and snow come humming, hissing down the mountain, until she went to sleep. . . .

Sara lay in darkness on Mary Toby's table and thought it would be a pleasure being among white people again, safe beyond their narrow range of vision, where a person could simply step aside and be forgotten and comfortably alone. Free of animals' sniffing and observation—never being out of sight of at least one of them—a vole or squirrel, a balancing hawk a mile high, or some wolf resting on a ridge or standing under a spruce on the mountainside, looking down, watching while Sara hung her clothes out on the line. Free of the Natives, too—all that looking at people so closely, keeping them in mind, making judgments about them only because that used to be so important, so vital. Now, in these little villages, they still studied each other, made internal notes. . . .

It would be a pleasure to leave this rich, ancient civilization where everything and everyone depended on one another, leave it for a modern wilderness where no one was responsible, and she could be free in a desert of crowds.

She began to sleep, saw Alan again—the Native boy as Alan, with raveled clumps of red knitting yarn for mustache and beard, with gold-rimmed glasses. . . . From what granny had Jack Joseph borrowed those glasses? And had Mary Toby broken them? They'd certainly slipped half off, been dangling when the boy was knocked down against the cabinets. Mary Toby with her softball bat. Fat little brown lady, courageous, coming out of her warm bed at Sara's screams, ready to battle—what?—in her flannel nightgown.

Anything? . . . A bear?

"You don't have to come," Mary Toby said, dressed for outdoors in a long brown wool skirt, heavy Sorel boot-pacs, and an old-fashioned blue wool parka decorated with huge horn buttons. She'd stuffed a thick fold of yellowed newspaper into its left side pocket.

"I'd like to." Sara just in from cleaning the dog yard, feeding the team, carrying water out to them. There'd been no sounds through the falling snow but the generator's faint thudding; no heavy, rushing pulse of drumbeats ringing through the village. "Mary, those were really good pancakes."

"O.K. for an old woman can't cook," Mary Toby said, snapped her dish towel, folded it, and draped it neatly over a turned-oak rack on the inside of the cabinet door under her sink.

"They were real good." Carla—cushioned in her small red parka, fur-trimmed mukluks—come in behind Sara, pleased with having helped feed the team, having another opportunity to talk to Lobo, gently pinch his cold nose after he'd eaten. "Where's Jeffy?"

"His mama came an' got him," Mary Toby said. "Well, if you're comin', then come on," and sallied out of the kitchen and down the hall with a breakfast (pancakes, syrup, a caribou-sausage patty) piled on a paper plate and covered with a crumpled square of thoroughly-used foil.

Carla, running ahead to open the door, was startled to find some-one standing just outside in a bitter breeze and small swirl of snow only beginning to brighten with morning.

Christine Hodges, short and toughly fat in her khaki parka—and looking, Sara supposed, much as Mary Toby must have when she was a young girl (and probably equally sullen)—stood and stared at them as if it were they who'd come to her house, and uninvited.

"What is it, Christine?" Mary Toby shouldered past the girl and on down the front steps. "—Carla, shut that door. All the damn heat is goin' out!"

"I'll get it." Sara, last one out, shut the door behind her and came on down the steps past Christine, who fell into line behind, stump-ing along as they all followed Mary Toby out of the yard and up the path to the right. Mary Toby, paper plate held out before her, went at a quick march, plowing through or over small snowdrifts as if she ran on a cleated tread rather than short fat legs. She called back through the blowing snow without turning her head, "What *is* it, Christine?"

Christine, huffing along behind Sara, called, "Jack Joseph wanted me to come over an' say he's sorry!" Then, to Sara, "Said to say he was sorry, Mrs. Maher, but he was drinkin'."

Carla was stumbling alongside, the snow here too deep for her, and Sara stepped over and picked her up. "That better?" and Carla nodded that it was. Sara pulled up the small parka's hood, so Carla's face was framed in it as she gazed past Sara's right shoulder, a passenger.

"How's his head?" Mary Toby called back while passing a last cabin on the right, then angling up a steeper slope, climbing through deeper snow toward a small grove of white spruce.

Christine raised her voice. "His head's O.K."

"All right," Sara said. "You just tell him to stay away from me. You understand? You tell him that?"

"I'll tell him." Christine stopped walking, stood still in blowing snow as they walked away from her, then called after Sara, "—Don't you want to go down the river? He's goin'. We're both goin' down on the Bravo. I'm goin' to Nugget, an' he's goin' past there right down to Chancy."

"*Thanks,*" Sara called back. "*—But no thanks.*"

Ahead, Mary Toby, the snow dusting her parka hood from dark blue to blue white, walked up into the stand of spruce and out of sight.

Carla set down to kick through snow among wooden crosses, Sara found Mary Toby already at Ralph Toby's grave, digging small holes in the snow and frozen ground beneath it with a sharp broken branch still tufted with green needles. Working without gloves.

"Ground is hard as a rock," she said, grunting with effort, pushing, twisting the stick down.

"Can I do that?" Sara said. "—Let me do that."

"I don't need help diggin' a hole in the ground," and finished with one, Mary Toby stepped to the side and dug another down through deep snow. Then went on to dig seven more holes in a rectangular pattern around the grave, twisting her spruce branch like a drill for each—and after the last, stood erect, puffing, and threw her branch away.

"More trouble'n he's worth," she said, bent down and picked up the paper plate, uncovering it carefully so as not to tear the foil.

"Here." Sara took the foil, folded it, and put it in her left parka pocket. Carla was shaking a low spruce branch, trying to duck the soft shower of snow sifting down. Then she turned away and kept slowly turning, making herself dizzy, her red parka a small beacon through snow falling faster now . . . as if the winds carrying downrange brought to the cemetery veils of mourning.

Mary Toby stood silent by Ralph Toby's marker, apparently praying, her clenched bare hands frosted with snow, her round brown face and blue parka darker against so white a field. Then, done praying, she crossed herself in the Eastern style, dug into her parka's breast pocket for an almost empty pack of Salems and an orange plastic lighter, tapped out a cigarette, and lit it despite the wind. "Well, Ralph," she said, "I miss you sometimes, but not much." Then she bent with a grunt, went to all fours, and crawled along the grave's edges, putting her face to each of the small holes dug down into the snow, blowing vigorous puffs of cigarette smoke into them. She dropped the lit cigarette butt into the last one. Then she knelt, catching her breath. "He'd like some whiskey, but he isn' goin' to get it," she said. "Carla—find us some wood." And Carla scurried away between the trees, as if she knew just where to go for twigs and small branches beneath shallow drifts, and so cold they needed only a sharp shaking to be dry enough to burn.

Mary Toby sat down in the snow and wiped snowmelt from her face with her parka sleeve. "What are you goin' to do?"

"I'm not going downriver with that nut. That's what I'm not going to do."

"*Carla . . . hurry up, honey.*"

"—Unless you'd like me to get out of your house." Sara turned her head, looking for Carla—for anything else approaching through falling snow. She was uneasy, standing in forest without the shotgun on her back.

"That boy," Mary Toby said, apparently comfortable sitting in her snowbank. "—If Naomi knew what was goin' on with her daughter's boy, she'd be spinnin' in her grave. . . ." Mary Toby's only child, a boy named Barry, had died on the North Slope during development—frozen to death when a snow-machine's engine had quit and left him to try walking thirty-nine miles at fifty-two degrees below zero and a hard wind blowing. Barry Toby had walked thirty-two miles before, on the evening of the second day, lying down to sleep. "That Christine is not a bad girl; she's real smart. But she sure is bad for Jack, 'cause they're two of a kind. A boy needs a friend is just the opposite he is."

"I suppose it wasn't that serious. He was drinking. . . ."

"Don't tell me about drinkin'," Mary Toby sitting resting in the snow amid snowfall as if it were her natural bed and place of ease. "I know all about drinkin'. All them drugs is better than drinkin'. You people just as well cut our throats as bring that booze up here."

"I would never have done that."

"I don't mean you, an' I don't mean Alan. —*Carla! Come on, honey; we got to get goin'!*"

"*I got it. . . .*" and Carla came burdened with brown branches through the spruce trees, struggling in drifts, her gripping arms and mittens caked with snow.

Sara took the wood from her. "Mary, where do you want your fire?"

"I'll make it."

"*I'll* make it. Where do you want it?"

"Here, foot of the grave—not that it makes any difference. Ralph wouldn' be doin' this for me; I'll tell you that."

"Here?"

"I can make it."

"Is this place all right?"

"That's all right."

Sara scooped a small depression in the snow and laid two green-needled branches there for a base. She took the wad of newspaper

Mary Toby held out, shook fallen snow off it, and crumpled it over the branches . . . then laid the rest of the slender branches on, criss-cross, took a blue-tip from her parka pocket, thumbed it alight, and set the paper burning.

When the branches caught, Mary Toby leaned down and set the paper plate of food on the fire. "More'n he'd do for me. . . ."

Christine Hodges, trudging up the path through clearing air, met them coming down—Mary Toby leading, Sara carrying Carla.

"Jack Joseph says he's real sorry," she said to Sara. "He's too sorry to come an' say so. An' he's not drinkin'."

"You may as well go on down with 'em," Mary Toby said. "Isn' nobody else goin' down that river while they can fool around here, get 'em a few more days free eats."

"Why is Jack going early, Christine?"

Christine seemed surprised to be asked. "He's got business, Mrs. Maher."

"I just bet," Mary Toby said, and walked past. "I bet he has business," she said, and went on down the path.

"When are you going, Christine?"

"Are you goin'?" Carla put an arm around Sara's neck.

"Probably, sweetheart. I can't stay forever. —When are you go-ing, Christine?"

"Anytime—Jack says anytime you want."

"Like in an hour?"

"Sure. Anytime. We got that big Bravo, an' we tow a sled so all your stuff'll fit just fine."

"And you're going to Chancy? —no long stops?"

"Just droppin' me at Nugget, an' he's goin' right on down to Chancy. That's where he's headin'."

"You goin' now, Sara?" Carla said.

"Pretty soon, sweetheart. —All right, Christine, if you want to come by Mary Toby's, I'll be ready."

"O.K." Christine turned and walked away down the path, boots squeaking in the snow. Now in slight sunlight, she had a pale shadow.

"You takin' Lobo?"

"No," Sara said, following Christine's deep bootprints down. "Lo-bo's staying here, at Mr. Solokoff's house."

"That's good."

"Carla—"

"Yes?"

"Lobo's friendly—but sometimes he gets nervous, you under-stand?"

Carla nodded, her face shaded by her parka's red hood.

"So, you always ask a grownup to go out with you when you want to pet him. Understand? Every time."

"I will."

"Promise me?"

"I promise," Carla said, and as if Sara had asked for a kiss instead of a promise, kissed her cheek.

At Mary Toby's house, Carla wriggled to be put down, and ran inside.

Sara went around back to the dog yard—to Lobo at the first stake, bent to hug him, murmuring into a furry left ear the same singsong baby talk she had when the half-wolf, a thin, leggy, unhappy puppy, had woken her in the cabin's icy dark . . . yelping, mourning his mother, so Sara'd had to ease out from under her caribou skins, walk barefoot over frost-streaked flooring, pick the sufferer up out of the big kindling box, and take him back to bed to murmur to and com-fort.

She went to Dipsy's stake next, stroked him and said good-bye. Dipsy, Samoyed-white, sweet and stupid, always such a willing hauler, closed his eyes like a cat as she scratched his ears. Doodle, his brother, staked alongside—as big, as strong, but clever and less steady—was restless under her hands, willing to be left alone. Kick-apoo and Cherry, the swings, nervously alert, thought she might have more food concealed, and nosed and shoved at her in their turn, then accepted stroking as second-best. "Good-bye," Sara said to them, wasting a good-bye—then walked up the lot and went to her knees to hug Vanilla and gently stroke her gravid belly—the bitch's response, as often, to nuzzle and lick at Sara's throat, as if to indicate how love's attention had so completely replaced biting and ripping there.

Staked in the last line at the back of the yard, Fatso and Smiley—wheelers, and alert to words and warnings—enjoyed her good-byes as praises, the tender tone the same to them, Fatso licking her right hand as if it held food, and if not this time, then certainly held the promise of it.

Dutchy, chained in the yard's north corner, stood concerned, watching her slow approach—delayed by so many pauses, so much attention to inferior dogs. As Sara came to him, she saw he was panting, his long tongue lolling bright as blood, his pale-blue eyes unfocused, so their round black pupils—usually direct as rifle muzzles—now were softer, almost smeared into the blue.

She knelt beside him, heard his faint suggestion of a whine, put her arms around him and hugged until he grunted as he had when a puppy—fat and temperamental, his fur blotched black-and-white—and she'd held him high over her head so he gazed down at her, on guard . . . then was inevitably brought down to hug, his warmth, softness and odors enjoyed, hugged until a grunt escaped him. Difficult to do now, compressing such muscle and adamant ribs.

Sara stood, said, "Good-bye—and behave yourself," turned and walked out of the yard.

"I hope you know what you're doin'." Mary Toby wrapping a large chunk of squaw-candy in a piece of brown butcher's paper.

"Now, what do you mean by that?" Sara just back inside from visiting the outhouse, then bringing her pelts, duffle, and guns from the shed to Mary Toby's front steps. "You just said I should go downriver *with* them. Is there a problem, or what?"

"No. Did you stomp your feet?"

"Yes, I did. —Then, what is it? Don't tell me you're going to miss me."

"No, I'm not goin' to miss you." Mary Toby reached up into an oak-laminate cabinet over the stove, took down a Ball jar of cranberry jam, and set it beside the smoked salmon.

"Well, they'll be here in a minute—if they're coming."

"I'm not goin' to miss you," Mary Toby said. "I always liked Alan better'n you, anyway. But I'm goin' to miss seein' you." She bent with a grunt, opened the narrow cabinet under the sink, took out a jar of *kamamik,* and set it beside the salmon and cranberry jam. "—I don't suppose I'm goin' to get these jars back."

"I'll ask Christine to bring them back."

"That'll be the day that girl brings back my jars. —An' you don't need to be givin' them two all this food, neither. It's for you." Mary Toby opened her counter drawer, took out an old soup spoon, and put it beside the food. "You give him a chance, Jack'll eat all of it. Way that boy eats, you wouldn' think he'd be so skinny. . . ."

Sara heard a snow-machine outside, come snoring up the path. "Time to go. Mary, thanks for letting me stay—and thanks for hitting Jack on the head."

"Better'n gettin' him shot. Where's your furs?"

"I hauled them out front. . . . I won't be seeing you again."

"So you say," Mary Toby said, and Sara went to the broom closet, took her shotgun out, sheathed it and slung it across her back.

"That damn thing," Mary Toby said—and when Sara came and hugged her, said, "Don't do that; I don't like it," but stayed still.

"You take care of yourself," Sara said, and let Mary Toby go. "You know, you have the most beautiful kitchen in Billy Mitchell. I love what you've done with it."

"Well," Mary Toby said, "—it isn' bad."

"It's beautiful."

"Well . . . not bad." Mary Toby followed Sara up the hall to the living room and front door. Carla and three grownups—a couple and single older man Sara didn't know—were watching TV. 'Sesame Street.'

Carla got up and came to the door, and Sara bent to kiss her, then went outside into nearly full daylight, now—pale sunshine, soft shadows—and saw a big black-and-silver Bravo parked on the path. Jack Joseph, slender in jeans and a torn blue down parka, sat at the handlebars wearing large-lens dark glasses and a marten-fur cap. The right side of his face was bruised dark along the cheekbone below the concealment of his glasses.

Christine, squat in padded khaki, sat just behind him on the jump. She had her parka hood up.

The Bravo was towing a manufactured sled, very long and narrow, with plastic runners and aluminum struts. There were two five-gallon gas cans, a backpack, tent roll, and possibles-sack bungeed up front.

"Them four bales?" Jack Joseph dismounted and walked up to the steps to hoist one big bundle of pelts as Sara lifted another, and carried beside her to the sled. They stowed the two bales just behind the gas cans, cross-corded them on, then walked back to the house together, and Jack took the last two bundles of fur while Sara picked up her pack, duffle, and cased rifle. They went to the sled, fastened Sara's goods and rifle mid-sled, and stowed the two fur-bundles at the back for Sara to sit against, away from the snow and ice the Bravo's belt would rooster-tail.

Mary Toby, Carla beside her, stood watching from her doorway, smoking a cigarette. "Write me a postcard, daughter," she said.

6

Jack Joseph sat, settled himself, and pushed the Bravo's starter so the engine cleared its throat—then, snarling like a large chain saw, the machine jerked and hauled forward over the snow, kicking a swift glittering snow cloud up behind its broad tread.

Sara looked back to wave to Carla and Mary Toby, was jolted on her perch at the sled's end, and put her gloved hands up to her ears to guard them from the noise as the Bravo ran swiftly up the path's slope for several yards, then turned as if it had changed its mind, passed a smoke shed on the left, turned again, and swiftly—its sled bucking over rises—ran down the village street past several cabins toward the river.

The engine noise seemed very fierce to Sara—too harsh and continuous—not like a rifle shot's magical crack, that only divided silence for an instant, then echoed.

She took care balancing, swaying with the sled's motion as they reached the shore, dropped down the bank very fast, struck the frozen river beach—jerked suddenly right and right again . . . then drove out onto the river's ice, the engine's harsh racket fading slightly at this easier, smoother, faster running.

The wind stuttered into Sara's face in swift gusty breaths, each taking some feeling away, and she opened her mouth wide as if she were singing, felt her teeth begin to ache from the cold, and breathed in such heavy, definite air, that it seemed to fill her like food.

If it weren't for the noise, the idling-boat stink of oil and gas, it would have been wonderful—such speed, that seemed to leave a white world behind, always introducing another world of white.

No bear could catch the Bravo.

Behind them as they racketed along, Fort Billy Mitchell was quickly reduced to only traces of settlement along the northern bank, lit by a cautious late-morning sun. Then the village vanished, erased by distance. Now, only the river and its borders were present.

Sara sat cross-legged on the sled's jumpy deck, her gloved fingers curved down around the platform's edge to hold herself in place. Now they were traveling only as fast as a fast team might, Jack Joseph apparently watching for crevasses cracked through the river ice by the ice's weight or by currents upwelling as the river still flowed, massive and silent, below.

They swung slowly around a minor bend, the river narrowing here to less than half a mile across of ice—white, but scaled with imperfections that refracted light yellow, soft gold. Sara saw the Kellner cliffs rise on the right, layered like a chocolate-and-angelfood cake sliced four hundred feet up from the snowed-over ice and drift-wood along the river's edge.

Golden eagles—a mated pair flown north early—were drifting along the cliff's layered ramparts, tilting, kiting in the updrafts high above a narrow blue-green streak of overflow along the wall's pleated foot, as if in anticipation of the merganser and teal certain to paddle there soon, if not quite yet.

Sara leaned right as Jack Joseph swung the machine left, out into the river's center . . . to race, engine revving, alongside an island decorated with fallen spruce that hemmed its banks—sweepers top-pled out onto the ice, their foliage still rich green and fresh as if determined to live, revive in spring, and stand upright again.

There were seven islands in this stretch—one huge, its landscape varied, thickly forested above a comforter of snow, and edged with bleached angled bones of driftwood along a pebbled beach that took the snow-machine a while to pass.

Sara was troubled by the engine noise. It made her ears ache, and separated itself into too many voices—some even lower, harsher than the engine sound, others choiring so high they became almost quiet except they hurt her ears, especially as she turned her head to watch the country come to meet them along the riversides, pause even, then parade on past.

This way of traveling disturbed her, after two years of going on foot, and the team—it hardly seemed like traveling at all, it was so effortless. A sort of cheating way to go, insulting to something . . . only sitting, bearing noise as if the noise were what shoved the country past and back behind them. It seemed odd that this sort of traveling should result in arriving.

Six or seven miles farther down—where a flight of ptarmigan (for-ty or fifty birds, wings flashing silver-white) flew over them and into forest lying left along the river—the river's ice had buckled, shattered and refrozen early in the winter. Now it lay a shambles, deeply cracked, chunks and slabs rising six to twenty feet above the rough plain of white. It was slow going for the snow-machine, the Bravo grating along at a dog team's trot. Jack Joseph, torn blue parka leaking a small puff of white down at his right elbow, leaned into the handlebars, steering slow curves around each slab and splinter, bucking the machine over ridges and down ice steps to smoother ice, so the trailing sled jolted, skidded sideways.

"I'm going to run awhile." Sara thought they hadn't heard her, and called again, *"I'm going to run awhile,"* and Christine half turned to look at her through the fringe of her parka's coyote ruff.

Sara uncrossed her legs, knees stiff from sitting so, and when the snow-machine ran smoothly for a moment, stepped off the sled, caught her balance, and began to run as if she ran beside her dogs. Felt as though the machine was a team of dogs, noisy barkers and stupid, but pleasant to run with. Sara trotted along, uneven ice crunching under her boot-pacs—then angled away farther to the left, farther from the engine's sound, so at least her left ear was somewhat comforted with silence from the frozen river's southern bank, now almost a mile away.

She settled into running the way she worked or settled into sleep, allowing herself any effort needed, not allowing any effort to disturb her . . . pleased with the touch, cling, and rub of her clothing, satisfied with the sheathed shotgun's weight riding her back like a baby. And comfortable with her breath frosting, clouding before her as she ran through it, stepping swiftly over small obstacles—low ice ridges windblown to waves before they'd finally set, frozen many months before—and running up and over larger barriers, old tilted ice-pan shelves and slabs, always keeping the snow-machine's racket roughly even to her right.

They traveled, she and the machine, from a slightly sunny midday . . . into gradually, over one or two hours, a dimmer light under the first of mackerel clouds becoming darker and darker, rippling forty or fifty miles along the sky above them. These ranked, corrugated clouds lay a deep and deeper gray above the lower mountain range to the river's south, though barely clearing tooth-white mountains rising beyond the river's northern bank. Beneath these clouds the air grew colder, heavier, and harder to breathe deep—and once in the lungs, reluctant to be breathed out until it was warmed. Winds began every now and then to rise off the ice, always blowing north in quick small gusts and squalls, so Sara put up her parka hood and leaned to the left, into the wind as it blew, to keep her course. The wind lifted ice crystals with it that sparkled, spun, ruffled around her, and whirled away.

She could feel the delicate field of warmth layering the outside of her parka and wool trousers—from her body's heat in running—torn and blown away by these small winds, felt suddenly colder and didn't mind. . . . She thought of a story, a story about a young female polar bear who, as she grew older, couldn't stand the arctic cold. Always sought heat—sought heat's comfort in a landscape without it. A strange, beautifully-white young bear wandering for warmth in forever winter, then swimming at last toward the pale barely risen sun—until, in a blue-green endlessly deep polynya far out to sea, an orca found her.

A while later, the small storm winds blown out, the mackerel clouds blown mostly over, the machine trundled off the last of the rough ice (Sara still trotting in echelon), and they stopped to pee.

Pleasantly weary, Sara kicked through shallow drifts across a small island spit, and saw wolverine tracks—a large male's—across a patch beneath four alders. The tracks were softly wind-worn, hours old; the wolverine had been scavenging the river's islands. The animal's right hind turned inward a little each stride, the leg injured some- how, or its hip.

Through scattered spruce and down the sandspit's other side, Sara found privacy enough to pee. . . . Then fastened her trousers and belt, and walked on down that limited northern beach to a stretch where broken willow showed the path a moose had plowed. Bull moose; the branches splintered high by wide antlers. —The largest rack she'd seen, she saw with Alan almost three years before in an autumn meadow, when two female moose had circled and presented to a small, burly bull, hugely decorated. After the bull staled, the females had gone to their knees to root and rub on the wet ground in a daze of sharp odor and longing.

Sara heard one light crisp rifle shot—then another—and trudged back up through drifts to the spit's other side. Jack Joseph, carrying a .22 (semi-auto, Remington or Marlin), walked up along the peb- bled southern bank with two ptarmigan hanging from his hand— white bundles upside down, their small broad wings unfolded, gently fanning in the last of the storm's breezes. The sun, emerged, shone over the hills on the river's right, and threw Jack Joseph's walking shadow out onto the ice.

"Dinner." He held the birds higher. Sara saw he'd shot each bird through the head. The .22 was a Marlin.

"You have any trouble with that action?"

"Not shootin'." The bruise lay sooty alongside his right eye, the eye concealed behind his dark glasses. "—Gets stiff, sometimes. I just use graphite, or stomp the sucker open."

They walked along the pebbled beach together, Sara on his left. There was no sign of Christine. "How are you feeling?" Sara said. "—You're lucky Mary didn't hit you harder."

Jack Joseph turned his head to the left to answer her—turned it far enough to favor his sighted right eye. "That's right. Lucky you didn' kill my ass with that shotgun, too." The boy, though speaking quietly, had a man's rough voice sounding as if it came from an older throat, a broader chest.

Sara stepped back and behind him—past his narrow blue-parka'd back, the heavy fall of long black hair bound in a loose ponytail—then up to his sighted side and walked along, her left arm brushing a dead bird's wing. "Where's your girlfriend?"

"Chris isn' my girlfriend. She's my near cousin, my mom's sister's kid; can't be my girlfriend. She's just my friend."

"You scared me in the kitchen—that's why the gun, Jack."

"Yeah? Bullshit," Jack Joseph said, and lifted the dead birds to greet Christine as she came trundling out of the trees along the island's narrow spine, her khaki parka unzipped, the bunched leather fingers of her gloves sticking out of the parka's right pocket.

"What do you mean by that?" Sara said.

Jack Joseph stopped walking, turned to face her. "Hey—I mean you were real ready to blow poor fuckin' Alan right back into the fuckin' grave, man. That's what I *mean*."

"O.K. You just stop right there. Look, I don't know you, and you don't know me. I think we better not talk about this anymore."

Sara walked away down the beach, feeling her heartbeat in her throat. She noticed how many colors of white to gray showed in the pebbles, noticed bird tracks—ravens'—printed across a drift of snow along the shingle. Hard to see what had brought them here.

She heard Jack Joseph and Christine talking on the beach behind her, and walked faster back to the snow-machine and sled, bent to check the crossed bungee cords holding the four pelt-bundles on. One hook was fastened to the edge of the sled's deck, and Sara took a strain on that, unhooked it, stretched it a fraction more, and hooked it around the top of a stanchion, holding harder.

She heard the others' bootsteps in gravel, saw their pale shadows from the corner of her eye, but didn't turn around . . . checked the cords on her pack, duffle, and rifle case.

"Let's eat somethin' while we're stopped—O.K.?" Christine bent over their small pack behind the seat, unfastened a flap, and pulled out a clear plastic sack holding long dark narrow strips of smoked salmon, a box of Fig Newtons, four large Snickers bars, and a square dark-blue package of pilot bread. Jack Joseph unlatched the Bravo's seat, lifted it to the side, and took two cans of Miller's, then another, from a small red-plastic cooler—closed the cooler, put the seat back down, then swung his leg over and sat down on it, facing backward. Christine did the same, and leaning back against Jack Joseph, rummaged through the plastic sack, took out a strip of salmon and passed it over her shoulder to him, then passed him the box of Fig Newtons.

Sara opened her pack, took out the jar of *kamamik*, the spoon and wrapped piece of salmon, then sat on a bundle of furs, unscrewed the jar-top, handed the *kamamik* and spoon to Christine and accepted a can of beer. The beer, still slightly warm from the cooler, was chilling fast in the light wind off the river's ice, would be frozen in a few minutes.

Sara unwrapped her package of salmon, took out the Clipit, cut herself two thick slices dark as liver, ate one—richly salty—then opened her beer and took a swallow. Small crystals of ice were already gathered in it.

Christine was eating the *kamamik* with great attention. "That's good oil," she said, ate another spoonful, then passed the jar over to Jack Joseph. Jack Joseph, dark glasses reflecting a curved sled and Sara, took a spoonful, then passed it back. He sat sipping beer, looking out at the river over the pale center-part in Christine's glossy black hair, looking across the frozen river as if Sara weren't sitting in the view.

Sara took the cranberry jam out of her pack, unscrewed the lid, and passed the jar over. Then accepted two Fig Newtons.

The sun set in late afternoon; white ice turned gray and grays grew darker—so dark at last the mountains couldn't be seen along the river on either side, and the Bravo's small headlight made only the shortest path of warm orange, running over the ice.

Beside the Bravo's light, after some time faint starlight shone so the softest pinks glowed over the river, and faint blue, and silver. The starlight was just bright enough to make out wooded islands by as they ran along. Sara rode carried on the engine's noise, the passage wind freezing her face through her parka's ruff, the machine and sled vibrating, jolting occasionally over some unevenness.

They rode for a long while down the river, Jack Joseph driving fairly fast . . . and Sara felt the darkness expand farther and farther away from her until all the country was distance. Then she didn't mind the Bravo's noise as much.

When the moon rose, almost full, it spilled its light along the river in a flood of silver, washed the starshine out, and filled the river bank to bank so it seemed to thaw and flow again. The mountains ranked in brighter light on both sides as they traveled, and against a near spruce slope, Sara saw a snowy owl flying upriver, low along the bank—big as an eagle, silent, and white as chalk.

Long after that, and deep into winter night, when the moon had swung a little way toward setting, Sara felt the sled shift as Jack Joseph turned the machine and slowed it, driving to the river's right bank through shallow mists of ice crystals, so the fog divided, stirred as they drove through it, then flowed together behind them. It was getting colder.

Jack Joseph—driving now very slowly through shadowed moonlight, past driftwood . . . ice hummocks—found a slope he liked, gunned the engine, drove high up the bank, and turned the machine off.

Happier with the silence than the stopping, Sara climbed stiffly off the sled, unfastened her pack, then helped Christine tug the tent roll and their small pack free, helped carry those to a level past a row of bare-branch cottonwoods leaning hard to the river, helped shake the tent out, then went for firewood.

Back in the trees, searching by moonlight for fallen branches under the snow, Sara felt herself ease in being alone, only troubled by the others still being near. They wouldn't have disturbed her if they were farther away, just a mile or two. But they were close—and Jack Joseph's nonsense the night before made it worse. The boy apparently eccentric, and probably drunk at the time. A ridiculous end to being in the country.

She gathered her fallen wood, knocked the snow off it, and broke two green branches for a fire base. Then she stood for a while under a tall white spruce, listening to the slightest wind moving in the trees around her, hissing softly through the evergreens, making a hollower sound through leafless alder, cottonwood, and willow. She closed her eyes and imagined herself in the kitchen, scrambling across the floor for the shotgun—saw Mary Toby sallying out with the softball bat, saw Jack Joseph knocked silly, the gold-rimmed glasses and knitting-yarn beard awry. Sara began to giggle in the darkness under the white spruce, tried to stop and couldn't. It was the sort of incident she and Alan would have laughed about for weeks—except he would have taken the Native thing more seriously, shamanism and so forth. Would have taken that seriously . . . made some pontifical comment.

Now Dutchy would be wondering where she was, why she hadn't come to say goodnight to him.

Sara was pleased with the fire—she'd built it the way Alan had liked them built, the kindling and dry wood arranged in a neat shallow crescent, protected from melting snow by green branches.

She sat on Jack Joseph's blind left side, Christine on his right, and they passed roast ptarmigan—the flesh tasting a little of pine sap from the seeds the birds had eaten—back and forth, tearing off small legs and wings, other pieces. Christine had cleaned and plucked the birds, spitted them on whittled branches leaning into the fire.

They had the birds to eat, the *kamamik*, Mary Toby's cranberry jam, beer, pilot bread, the last of the Fig Newtons, and a thin joint Christine had rolled with quick, stubby fingers by firelight.

Jack Joseph passed a wing to Sara—his hand grimy, brown, fairly slender—took a toke and passed her the joint as well. It was the first pot Sara'd had in almost a year, a little harsh, but sweet.

"Mrs. Maher, you still mad?" It was the first thing Jack Joseph had said to her since the afternoon.

"I'm not mad. I was angry last night, Jack, but I stopped being mad after Mary Toby hit you with that bat."

"Oh sure—an' that shotgun wasn't about anything, right? 'Cause I already got hit, an' you had that shotgun on me."

"Come on, Jacky," Christine said from his other side.

"Why don't you just butt out," Jack Joseph said to her.

"You've got a hell of a nerve, kid," Sara said, "—even complaining about it. Just because I was scared when a ghost woke me up in the middle of the night? Where do you come off, dressing up like my husband, pretending to *be* my husband? I mean I've kept my mouth shut not to hurt your feelings, because of this Stick Dance . . . your beliefs. But you got in *my* face—I didn't get in yours. You were way out of line."

"Yeah? Well, there's lots of things you don't know, white lady." Thin dark face flushed darker in firelight under those dark glasses. Sara wished he'd take the glasses off.

"Oh, right—I don't appreciate your ancient customs of carving nasty hurtful things on my table, and then daring, *daring* to come in the middle of the fucking night and pretend to be my husband! Don't give me that Native customs crap!" Sara found herself exhilarated by disagreement, happy to continue it, grow even more angry.

"I don't expect," Jack Joseph said, and Sara found herself, at ease in the eye of the argument, touched by the boy's fragile dignity. "—I don't expect a white woman who thinks she's hot shit," Sara watched Jack Joseph take a breath and lose his temper; she wondered if he'd call her ugly, say something about the way she looked. "—an' knows everything an' we're just a bunch of Natives an' kids an' what the fuck do we know? Meaning that you have no idea what really goes down. We watch you people all the time you're watching us. You think we don't know what goes with all your white bullshit? You don't have the least idea what's real in this country."

"And what does that have to do with Alan, Jack Joseph?"

"I knew him."

"So? You played softball or something with him down at Kaltag, or what?"

"I knew him."

"You knew him. . . ."

"That's right."

"And that means you can borrow somebody's glasses and put on a fake beard and come and scare a woman in the middle of the night? And I don't even *know* you."

"Come on, Mrs. Maher," Christine said. "Come on."

"—No, really, I'd like to know about all these great customs. You come and say good-bye for a dead man—you come and you've got his spirit in you or whatever. Were you drinking, Jack?"

"Oh, fuck you," Jack Joseph said, and stood up. "Yeah, I had somethin' to drink, but Alan came an' said hello to me at the dance—an' it was him an' I knew him, drinkin' or not."

"What? What the hell is that nonsense?" Sara stood up, and Jack Joseph walked away with a can of beer in his hand.

"—Don't walk away from me," Sara said. "You tell me what you mean by saying that."

Jack Joseph turned to look back into the firelight, the bruise showing smeared blue-black at his cheekbone. "I mean that maybe there's some shit about people an' bears an' everything else you don't know about, Mrs. White Schoolteacher."

"Jack," Christine said.

"Oh, great." Sara's face burned, and she felt herself balancing on her temper as if it were a toboggan on a slope—and let it carry her away, didn't care how ugly she looked. "And what do you know, Jack Joseph, except how to carve on my table when I'm not home? I wish to Christ *you'd* been there, Mr. Big-mouth, when that grizzly came. I just wish you'd been there! . . . And what are you doing now? Taking that sled down to Chancy for what? Wouldn't be alcohol—right? Whiskey? Wouldn't be running some whiskey, would you, Jack? Help your people out? Give me a break from all that Native Wisdom crap, and grow up!"

"I didn' say anything about that. About that bear."

"The hell you didn't. Don't tell me what you said."

Jack Joseph turned and walked away, gone into the dark at once.

"*Son of a bitch*," Sara said, reluctant to let such refreshing anger go. The pleasure of dealing with a man again, all that clumsy roughness and surprise.

"He isn' the way he seems," Christine said, and ate a piece of ptarmigan.

"Could have fooled me," Sara said, and sat down. "So, you're not his girlfriend?"

"No. My boyfriend's at TCC in Seward."

"Well, you're lucky."

"Jack Joseph is nice. He isn' like that. He's been drinkin' a lot last few days, that's all." Christine dragged the joint to a glowing roach, and passed it over.

Sara lay crowded too close to Christine, listening to her breathe with a fat girl's faint wheezing. Christine had watched Sara check the shotgun and set it down along the canvas tent's side wall . . . then had said goodnight, withdrawn deeper into her sleeping bag—taking by necessity more than her share of tent—and, with the flashlight off, whispered a prayer: "*From all ill dreams defend our sight, from fears and terrors of the night. Withhold from us our deadly foe, that spot of sin we may not know. . . .*" then had farted softly and gone to sleep.

Sara, regretting her mountain tent, had offered to sleep out, had wanted to. But Jack Joseph—returned to hunker at the fire after tossing a weighted cord over an alder branch, and hauling the food and packs up out of animals' reach—had taken off his dark glasses and exposed his white left eye as he turned to her. "Guy sleeps out," he said. "Women have the tent."

Sara thought she might wait for a while, then move outside after Jack Joseph was asleep. In the morning she could explain she was used to sleeping alone, so Christine wouldn't be offended. It was annoying to have to worry about offending people. In the past many months, there'd been only the team and Dutchy's occasional sulking to deal with. Now she had these two late adolescents, hung up between cultures and very angry. —Needing, in Jack Joseph's case, a kick in the ass. Showing off his Nativeness by scaring the shit out of a white woman—and a teacher (an ex-teacher). That was the big thing with Jack Joseph (who probably had attended about one class a week, if that). How anybody could teach junior high, high school . . . it was just amazing the crap people would take.

If Alan had been at that dance, ghost or whatever, he would have talked to her, not some one-eyed Indian boy who looked as if he needed three good meals a day . . . would be handsome except for that eye. —Sara decided to get up soon, take her ground cloth and sleeping bag outside, to the other side of the fire. Then thought that if a bear was out this early (and one might be, in late winter)—if a bear was out and came into camp, it might kill Jack Joseph. Or he'd run away, which would be a really good lesson for him. If it came into the tent, ripped the tent and came in, then it would probably take Christine, because Sara would just shrink herself smaller. . . .

Then Christine would be killed and Sara would have a chance, a clear shot with the Remington as the bear dragged the girl away. And it would be the same bear, with the light-brown fur reversed in that sort of cowlick along its neck and shoulder. And she would have just one clear shot—too bad Christine was already dead—and the sabot slug would take the animal just exactly on the shoulder and knock it down. It would kick and piss on itself, and she'd put the second high in the chest and that would be that. So much for brute strength. Then, when Jack Joseph came back—and she would be taking care of Christine, who was only hurt after all . . . terrified, but only hurt—then Jack Joseph would come back ashamed, and she would look up and say, "Where were *you* . . . ?"

In the morning, Sara woke as Christine woke, said "Good morning," as Christine's round brown face surfaced through a flock of red ducks flying in fabric across the exposed yellow lining of her sleeping bag. The tent's dark-green sloping sides were frosted with their frozen breath. Sara sat up and reached to unzip the tent's door flap, saw fog, frigid and still, and smelled gasoline. She wriggled out of her sleeping bag to pull her trousers on, her boots and parka . . . then crawled outside, with Christine stirring behind her.

"Good morning." Jack Joseph, apparently done fueling the Bravo, stood smiling in his blue quilted parka, his dark glasses off. Beside him, a small fresh fire snapped under a teapot hung from a horizontal green branch supported by two others, upright and forked. The fog, waist-high, roiled and recoiled from the fire's heat.

"Mrs. Maher, I guess I was an asshole," Jack Joseph said, yesterday's angers apparently to be set aside so simply.

"That's right," Sara said, "—you were. But I was, too."

"I was out of line. An' what we do an' what you do is different, an' that's that."

"Yes, I think 'that's that.' "

"Uh-oh; you're still pissed off, right?"

"No. No, I'm really not. We just had a bad experience, that's all."

"All right. O.K. —An' I shouldn't have cut your table." Jack Joseph, now a cheerful boy, stooped with a folded black leather glove to lift the teakettle off the fire. "We got sweetener, if you want some."

Midmorning, most fog gone, the sun just rising, they saw two distant snow-machines heading upriver, glinting in golden light across the ice, and Jack Joseph drove the Bravo left and faster, bumping across snow ridges to intercept them a quarter mile down.

Eskimos were driving the machines, big bright-red Yamahas, and slowed them as the Bravo came near. One of the men, stocky and smiling, with a thin mustache, had his wife sitting up behind him with her baby—tucked into her long parka hood—riding her back.

Sara didn't know the people—saw by his casual wave that Jack Joseph didn't know them, either—but the Eskimos drew up and stopped their machines to talk. Their soft voices, punctuated by the ticking of cooling metal, were barely audible to Sara, her ears ringing from the Bravo's noise.

A short conversation, in any case: the ice fine, farther down—had they heard that a plane had crashed at Chancy? Pilot came in three nights before, late and low on gas, radioed for headlights along the strip, got them, then went ahead and put the Super Cub down on a steep slope far to the side, as if the lights hadn't been there at all. A pilot just up from Pennsylvania (both Eskimo men shaking their heads at that, amused). The pilot from Pennsylvania had been flown out the next day with no feeling below his belly button, and crying for his wife all the time.

"Had no business up here," Jack Joseph said, and the Eskimo men agreed—'Cryin' for his wife all the time.' Then said polite good-byes, pressed the Yamahas' starters, and roared away—the woman, arms akimbo, adjusting her baby on her back as they went.

"Eskimo people are O.K.," Jack Joseph said, "—but they're comin' higher an' higher on the river. Huntin' caribou." Then he started the Bravo and accelerated fast, swinging back toward the right side of the river so Sara, sitting at the back of the sled, had to hold hard, hanging on.

The river here was growing wider, fed in summer by several lesser streams, none small, whose mouths were now concealed by distance and the ice fog still drifting low along the river's banks.

The sky, late-winter sun half risen, was milky blue fading to almost white along the mountain ridges to the north. South, the mountains were slowly subsiding as the Bravo ground along . . . slowly becoming smaller mountains, tending toward hills. As they grew lower, the rises retreated from the river, leaving forest behind like gray-green fur covering the miles-wide plain where, millennia before, the river had occasionally run through other beds, had spread to flood and level the land.

A clear day, still and cold. Sara rode the vibrating sled with Jack Joseph's and Christine's exhaled breaths wisping with her own past her hooded head. The Bravo's harsher breath smoking past as well.

Two ravens came to pace them for a while, black against the light blue sky as they flew high . . . blacker against the ice when they dipped, flapping closer to observe, heads tilting left and right to give each eye a chance. The ravens slowed together, glided, sharply swerved away toward the river's right bank.

For a time after that, Sara saw nothing alive along the river. She felt her hands grow stiff with cold in her gloves, her butt wooden on the sled's frigid aluminum, knees also icy (her trousers' wool drawn tight against them as she sat, legs crossed). Jack Joseph was driving too fast for her to run alongside.

A while later, Sara noticed—half a mile away in a clump of leafless cottonwood above the right bank—a tiny piece of brown other than log-brown, or dirt-brown, or the brown of some slumped mud. It was moose-brown, she thought . . . then was certain as she noticed distant branches that were antlers among the cottonwoods. By then, the Bravo had gone past—but suddenly slowed so she was pushed forward against the pack and rifle case in front of her. Jack Joseph slowed the machine again and took a swift rounding curve to the right, so Sara swayed left. Completing a full turn, he drove the machine bucketing back the way they'd come, jouncing over uneven ice closer to shore, running along the bank toward that inlet where the moose was grazing.

He drew the machine up to a bank-edge spangled with broken diamonds of ice, then shut down the engine and swung off the Bravo's seat—easy, limber with youth. He pulled a Remington 7400 (the carbine in .30–06) from the sheath behind the snow-machine's windshield, and stepped over the broken ice to shore. He climbed the steep bank, click-clacked a round into the Remington's receiver, and walked into the woods—Sara stepping just behind him, ducking to avoid a small bare cottonwood branch swishing back at her from his passage.

She worked the Winchester's bolt, nodded left as Jack Joseph turned to look at her. Then she walked away left, stepping carefully over frozen windfall and driftwood trash brought downriver last summer, walking around larger logs and branches come down summers before. She heard Jack Joseph walking away to the right, a little fast and noisily, it seemed to her.

Her share—at least four hundred pounds of meat—though winter moose meat, lean and stringy, would divide to a gift quarter for Bud LeBeck, a quarter to help pay for a flight to Fairbanks.

She walked into the woods relieved of the snow-machine's noise and motion, relieved of company, at least for these few yards. Unobserved, except of course by the moose—which would have heard them come, would now be hearing them walk their separate ways . . . and if the slight slow breeze shifted northeast instead of west, would scent them.

Jack Joseph had had a scope sight on the carbine, so Sara watched to her right as well as before her, in case he should take the scope's narrower field as gospel, not notice her to his left if he drew down on the animal as it moved. Alan had hated scopes. "—If you need to use a telescope to find an animal and kill it, you have no damn business doing either. A rifle with iron sights, a folding leaf, is more than advantage enough. Besides, scopes cloud, and they break if you just fall into some rocks. . . ."

Sara walked straight back through the cottonwood grove, up a mild rise into alders, and through them to their edge and an empty channel the river must have sent a stream through some time before.

The stream bed was thirty to thirty-five feet across, seven or eight feet deep—four or five feet of that depth, snow.

She stayed under pale tree shadows and didn't cross. From here, she could see to the right along the channel as it curved slowly away into black spruce—see for a good rifle shot's distance. If the moose didn't run out onto the ice upriver when Jack Joseph drove it, it would have to come this way. Sara thumbed the Winchester's safety off and stood almost between two slender alders only a few feet taller than she, the old Model 70, a patient weapon, resting lightly in her hands.

. . . After a while, she saw movement out of the trees far to the right, looked that way, bringing the rifle up, and found the moose in rocking-chair gallop down into and across the empty stream bed— and up onto the other bank as she laid the sights, took up the trigger and knew she would hit him (but far back, through the ham and into his belly)—and held her fire as he was gone.

Without Jack Joseph, and Christine waiting at the machine, she would have shot the animal, then walked after until she tracked it down to finish—or would have held her fire, and gone after it up along the river (swinging out left or right to stay downwind). Following through a moonlit night to next morning . . . when the moose, forgetting, would have stopped to browse again. Easier in the fall, when the rutting bulls smelled like spoiled vegetables, could sometimes be located by that. Now, these other people with her and someplace she had to be, there was no time to stalk.

Sara worked the bolt to eject the round, caught it as it flew, pushed it back down into the magazine well, and slid the bolt shut over it. Then clicked the Winchester's safety on.

She heard something the direction the moose had gone, and saw Jack Joseph coming along down the stream bed's near edge, walking her way with the Remington slung on his back, frowning beneath dark glasses. A disappointed boy. . . . He needed a new down parka; the blue one was coming apart. Alan's would have fit him.

When Jack Joseph got near enough, he looked along the gully bank, saw her, and climbed up through a patch of frozen willow.

"Fucked up," he said, breath fogging. "Rushed him out of there, an' he ran."

"I saw him."

"My fault for pushin' him." Jack Joseph walked to her. "An' my fault, too, for showin' up the way I did the other night, when you wouldn' understand it. An' also . . . I do feel bad because of when I was drinkin' up in the mountains there, an' cut that shit about the bear on your table. Showin' off to those other guys, like a kid." He held out a gloved hand.

Sara said, "All right, Jack," and took his hand (not much larger, not much stronger than her own), and shook it formally.

"—An' the thing is, I was tryin' to make up for that when I came over. You know, take the message to you, make you feel better. . . ."

"O.K. But what was that about seeing Alan at the dance?"

"Hey—that's a different subject." Jack Joseph let go of her hand and walked away through the alders toward the river, pushing leafless branches aside as he went. His jeans weren't in any better shape than his parka. It seemed there was little money in bootlegging up to Billy Mitchell.

When they got back to the river, Christine was sitting where she'd been left, heaped on the Bravo's seat in her khaki parka. She was staring across to the river's south bank, or the weather coming in over it—a series of long irregular black clouds that seemed to wrestle with each other, jostling then easing apart, sailing high. The sunlight was still bright enough to lay the clouds' long shadows on the hills beneath, so they and their shadows drifted shifting along, high and low in replica.

Christine turned to watch Sara and Jack Joseph push through frozen brush, then out onto the ice. "Didn' hear no shootin'."

"He spooked," Sara said.

"An' I was the spooker." Jack Joseph sheathed his rifle, swung into the saddle, and started the Bravo's engine.

"Tell me somethin'," Christine said to Sara, raising her voice over the motor's noise. Christine's head was turned back over her shoulder, turned around as far as an owl's to watch Sara case the Winchester, then settle onto the back of the sled. "—How come you carry that shotgun on your back all the time? You go huntin' with a rifle, an' you take the shotgun too."

"I don't need it when I have the rifle, but the shotgun's a habit, I guess," Sara said. "I'm still afraid of bears, winter or not."

"I can understand that," Christine said. "That's understandable." As the snow-machine started with a jerk, then accelerated out over rough ice onto the river's main channel, she held her place, kept her head sharply turned back to Sara, and raised her voice to shout over the engine noise, "Jack can't hunt for shit."

Jack Joseph called "Thanks, buddy!" then turned the machine to the right in a long, long curve to head downstream. It was growing colder, and sun dogs glowed pale lemon beside the sun.

*   *   *

Near dark in afternoon, almost eighty miles from trying for the moose—and one stop more, on a narrow island, to eat, pee, and gas the Bravo again—Nugget's few lights shone from the left bank of the river (low bank among the trees). Jack Joseph swung the machine that way, so they buzzed across almost a mile of uneven ice gleaming silver to copper in the sun's last light. Nugget, once boiling with gold seekers, now held nine homes—small cabins and plywood shacks—and flooded often.

Jack Joseph drove slowly coming in, the Bravo grumbling, wended past two fish wheels frozen into the ice, then several flat-bottomed skiffs drawn higher, half drifted over with snow. He stopped the snow-machine on a shelf just under a low bank overhung with frozen brush, and Christine climbed off the Bravo's jump-seat, bent over the sled to open the pack she and Jack Joseph shared, and took out in turn a heavy blue sweater, gray boot-socks, pink panties and bra . . . a red baseball cap, a small plastic freezer-bag of pot, and a paperback book. "About comin' to terms with stuff," she said, seeing Sara notice the book.

Sara got up off the sled, stood on black ice and stretched, hearing her shoulder joints crack softly, and supposed she and Jack Joseph would be walking back to the village with Christine to visit, have something to eat before they went on. But Jack Joseph stayed where he was, firmly on the Bravo's seat, gloved hands on the bars and dark glasses in place despite the fading light. Ready to go.

"You want to come on back for a while, Mrs. Maher?" Christine stomped slowly in place, thin edge-ice popping softly under her boots. Left foot, right foot . . . left foot, right foot, like a walking machine warming up. "My daddy doesn' like Jacky. Does he, Jacky?"

"I don't give a damn what he likes."

"Doesn' like you. . . ." Christine glanced at Sara, amused, and Sara saw her as the student she must have been in high school—a girl apparently as thick, slow, sturdy as her body, but actually quick and clever, so what seemed dull speech, proved sharp.

"Well, I don't think I'll come up," Sara said. "It's early to quit traveling—not far, now. If that's all right with Jack Joseph."

"I'm not stayin' here. —Chris, I'll pick you up in a couple days. Goin' back up to Billy."

"Makin' a delivery," Christine said to Sara, brown round face expressionless. "Big business." She suddenly smiled, showing teeth small, white, and even as a child's—then trudged over to Jack Joseph and hugged him one-armed, her right burdened with her goods.

"O.K.," Jack Joseph said. "Go on."

"An' take off them glasses," Christine said. "It's gettin' dark an' you need to see. Mrs. Maher knows you only got one eye."

"Just go on," Jack Joseph said.

"Take 'em off."

"Just go on."

"Good-bye, Mrs. Maher," Christine said, turned and tramped off the ice to drifted snow, then up the shallow bank where only two houses showed in dusk back among the cottonwoods. Both were small plywood shacks, mean, stained and spoiled by flood. Soft light at their windows, kerosene's wavering pale orange.

Sara considered going to sit up behind the boy, then thought not and settled back onto the sled. "I heard the government put those houses back up on the hill—higher, off the flood plain."

Jack Joseph turned on the Bravo's seat, said, "Yeah?" as if that had been Sara's plan and proposal. "I guess they just don't like bein' way up on that hill, havin' to go down a fuckin' mile to the river to get water. Just a bunch of weird Natives. . . ."

"Jack," Sara said, "—take off the dark glasses. Christine's right; I've seen your eye. And I want you to be able to see what we're hitting out on that ice."

Jack Joseph took his dark glasses off, folded the temples carefully, and slid the glasses into the left pocket of his blue parka. He turned to look at Sara directly, the right eye dark brown, and still bruised by Mary Toby's bat. The left eye, set neatly in the boy's narrow face, looked in this light not injured, but only a different sort of eye, snow white, for different viewing.

"O.K.?" Jack Joseph said, then turned front to start the Bravo's engine, listen to it idle.

Sara thought she looked like a fool sitting back on the sled—and insulting the boy, doing it. She got up, stepped to the Bravo, swung her right leg over and settled in the saddle behind him, put her arms around a waist surprisingly solid for so slender.

"O.K.," she said, and felt the machine come alive beneath her as Jack Joseph drove it away.

7

Sara felt relieved by Christine's absence, that much less company. And the Bravo's noise seemed less severe sitting up on the engine than riding behind it, the evening wind less edged behind the boy.

She caught, in conflicting currents as they rode, various hints of Jack Joseph's odor, as she had with a different driver so many years ago, night-riding from Butte to Bozeman. The prairie, stretching across each horizon left of the highway and right, had smelled of wheat, refinery smoke, hints of sage blossoming by the summer's moon as she'd ridden behind Kirby Dodd, the Harley's dampened vibrations trembling up her spine. Kirby had smelled of sweaty denim, cattle, and Old Spice. He'd been a cowboy biker, unsettled and intelligent. A beef highjacker, too—a high school bad boy, never grown up.

Sara'd always expected to see Kirby in Alaska. He was made for the country—stumpy, big bellied, sandy-haired and almost squat, a ready fistfighter, pothead, and rebel—whose gray eyes (slightly walled) had expressed alert curiosity in every circumstance, as if whatever or whoever, and right then, were the most important mysteries—mysteries, Sara found, that left him less tough and more worried as he thought of them.

Kirby Dodd was the second man—boy—Sara'd had sex with. That in her junior year of high school when, talkative and troubled, Kirby'd worried her into bed in his mother's mobile home. Class bad boy and class dog—they'd made a self-pitying pair for three or four months, fucking and complaining . . . then began to joke more and more, screw less, and slowly become good friends. Friendship finished when she went to college—Kirby working first on the Lariat, then on Four Forks as ranch hand and jeep mechanic. Then jail . . . then truck mechanic in Butte, for Kennicott Copper. . . .

She'd seen him only once, years after—looking shorter than she'd remembered, his belly bigger—saw him climbing down from the driver's side of an old blue Ford pickup in front of the 7-Eleven on Belford Street. There'd been, as Sara drove past, an impression of others still seated in the vehicle. Blond hair, thin faces—a woman, and perhaps a little girl—and Sara had gone by.

"Oh, that boy," Sara's mother had said years and years later, in civilized Seattle. "That was a success story waiting to happen, that Kirby Whoever." Smile. "Had Evan worried with that motorcycle, but I said there wasn't enough serious to him to be dangerous. And I was right. . . ."

The Bravo—headlight a pool of orange fleeing before—struck booming black ice just before the moon rose, and bucked, slid, then roared along down almost the center of the frozen river . . . running, after a while, through soft blue light glowing from a moon risen silver as salmon scales.

For this moonlit traveling, Sara forgave the snow-machine its noise, and rode holding Jack Joseph through a pleasant wilderness of vibration, near darkness, and cold. The moon appeared to ride just over the peaks of mountains due north, sixty or seventy miles away, to hang and slowly roll in brighter and brighter light against a sky blue-black and dense with stars.

No stars showed south. The night sky there was ribbed with dark cloud streamers blowing west, the direction the hidden river still flowed beneath the ice and the Bravo's spurning tread.

Sara, through a dream of sound and motion, saw the country clearly as she ever had—clearer than by day—and wished she might call a great owl to her, then half stand to swing astride the bird, sit into soft plumage, sense clenching muscle, beating pinions—and rise up from the Bravo's shaking to smoothly silently fly away into air so dark and definite, so like an arctic ocean for distance. Jack Joseph might turn his head just then, his blind eye, to see a snowy owl sail away, kite away in moonlight through the Bravo's kicked-up cloud. An owl so big and ember-eyed, with such a soft rounded white spread of wings it might take its passenger to safety, fly with her so far she'd be forgotten, flown too far to be remembered even by Mary Toby . . . as if she'd never been.

The western storm blew across the river's turning course a good while later, drove clouds underneath the moonlight, obscured it, and introduced hard winds that spanked humming across the ice out of darkness into darkness, and swung the sled skidding to the side behind the snow-machine.

The storm arrived and they arrived on bad ice almost together, so that under shadowed moonlight the Bravo—running fast—passed in deep drumming then gunshots, as black ice, hollowed to caverns by the river flowing underneath, echoed and cracked beneath them, disturbed, wakened even by the Bravo's faint vibration, its minor weight.

Jack Joseph slowed and steered to the right, past the dark wreckage of several big trees floated down and frozen in. . . . This new track down the river was good for several miles. Then, while Sara leaned forward against Jack's back, almost asleep, the ice—as if a great river beast, following them, had swum along in darkness beneath it—began to groan, make sudden sharp splitting noises through the sound of the Bravo's engine.

Jack Joseph called, *"Better camp up, tonight,"* over his shoulder, and steered farther right as storm clouds sailed beneath the moon again, so the plain of ice turned from white to silver, then gray, then darker.

When the light went, the wind sighed as if drawing a long, long breath. Drew another. Then suddenly shouted as the storm came booming and seemed to miss them at first, streaming over—then, as if seeking, turned and came again from the dark. It hit the Bravo, shoved it sliding several yards to the right so the engine roared as if the machine were surprised. Jack Joseph hauled on the left handlebar to stay on course. The wind shifted, turned, and came again, howling behind a surf of ice crystals. Sara felt the needles of ice, then the snow-machine heave as the trailing sled was lifted, blown sideways and turned over. She felt the leverage, then the Bravo tilt.

Sara left the machine as if she were dreaming, sailed, hit, and skidded along ice surprisingly rough. She tried to stop herself sliding, frightened there might be overflow and she'd skid into it, freeze suspended in night-black water before there was even time to drown.

She spun on her back, hissing along, and tried to brake herself with her right boot heel—sprained that ankle but turned onto her belly and was able to get her gloved fingers into the ice. She dragged and scraped, ripping her gloves then tearing the fingernails off the first and second fingers of her left hand . . . and slowly slid to a stop in darkness and the sounds of wind.

She got to her feet fast as she could, afraid the snow-machine or something would come out of the darkness and hit her . . . then reached over her right shoulder and found the shotgun still in its sheath on her back.

She saw the Bravo's headlight to the left, slight as a match flame.

Her right ankle hurt to stand on, and hurt more when she walked.

She heard Jack Joseph calling *"Mrs. Maher . . ."* but mislocated the sound, and was startled when he came trotting out of a blowing haze of ice and snow on her right.

"You O.K.?"

"Fine. How's the machine?"

"I don' know." Jack Joseph had lost his fur cap. "—You're O.K.?"

"Fine."

Sara limping along, they walked through buffeting wind—gradually slackening, less furious—guiding through darkness on the Bravo's headlight glowing dim on battery, then vanishing, then glowing again through blown drifts of snow, ice crystals.

Jack Joseph took Sara's arm. "What's the matter?"

"Just sprained an ankle," Sara said, raising her voice over the wind, and lifted her arm out of his grip.

The snow-machine lay on its side. The small steel hitch-knob had been twisted out of true and broken off, and the sled was gone, slid away across the ice.

"Great. . . ." Jack Joseph knelt to check the Bravo's skis and drive tread by what diminishing yolky light the headlamp threw, angled into the air. His cap gone, the boy's long black hair tangled whipping on the wind.

"My goods are on that sled. I'm going to find it!"

"Wait . . . wait. Give me a hand."

Lifting together, Jack Joseph on the right handlebar, Sara at the left, they levered the Bravo up on their second try. It thumped and squeaked upright, and Jack Joseph swung onto the seat to try the engine. The motor whinnied . . . then coughed and caught as if there'd been no difficulty, the headlight's beam suddenly bright across the ice.

"All *right!*" Jack Joseph half turned to her, his blind eye visible— pale in darkness.

Sara trotted downwind, limping off her right foot, the snow-machine chuckling, trundling behind—and after minutes of searching, saw through blowing ice the gleam of aluminum. The sled was on its back against a driftwood log stuck half upright through the ice. The packs, rifle case, and two fur bundles were still bungeed on.

"I lost some furs out here!" Sara saw Jack Joseph's silhouette frosted with ice behind the Bravo's windshield as milder winds sighed past them, and he drove up and stopped at the sled. Wishing for moonlight, she jogged unevenly on, keeping most of her weight on her left foot. She searched by the snow-machine's headlight, then leaving that behind, looked by the night's own faint illumination—light reflected from streamers of sailing snow, starlight intermittent, the pale underglow of ice.

She saw the pelts almost a pistol shot away, both bundles still skidding along a little in stronger gusts as she hobbled up. The cording had held; all the skins were there.

". . . Gettin' off this fuckin' river," Jack Joseph said when she got back to him, dragging the bundles along. Blinking snow out of his good eye, he was bent over the Bravo's hitch-bar, winding wire from a short coil to fasten the sled's bow to it. "This hitch wasn' supposed to be able to break. . . ."

Sara fastened the fur bundles back with the load, checked all the bungees . . . then stood idle, favoring her sore ankle, enjoying the storm's echoes. A river storm, sudden, windy, but warmer than weather in the mountains. Just below zero, maybe ten below. Nothing without the wind. . . .

It took them a while to find an inlet off the river's right bank. This finally found—after two false turns into only shallow bays with high banks and no shelter—Jack Joseph drove deep into it, then up and over a shelving pebble beach into willow seedlings too frail to bar the way.

In the narrow clearing the machine had won, Jack Joseph pulled up, turned off the engine, and they unpacked to camp in freezing darkness, no moonlight visible. It took some time—the tent's material flapping, billowing, snapping out of their hands—to set that up, stake it out, get their sleeping bags, packs, and food inside, and fasten the entrance closed.

Sheltered—packs shoved to the back, sleeping bags unrolled to cushion the ground cloth—Sara lifted the sheathed shotgun off her back, and while Jack Joseph sat watching by the flashlight's dull glow, worked the action, checked the safety, and laid the gun along the tent's side. Then they knelt facing each other over the food, sorting out Snickers bars, jam, rounds of pilot bread, the last can of beer, and pieces of smoked salmon as if they were playing checkers—then drinking or eating the pieces.

"What's the matter with your fingers? You're bleedin'."

"Lost a couple of nails." Sara raised her voice a little over the storm's noise, the tent's rattling canvas. "They'll be O.K." She ate the last of the salmon, and passed the *kamamik* over for Jack Joseph to finish.

. . . Then, food gone except for pilot bread for breakfast (and no cranberry jam left to have on it), Sara screwed the lids on the jars, and handed them and the spoon over to Jack Joseph. "When you and Christine go back up, I'd appreciate it if you'd return these to Mary Toby."

"O.K."

Sara sat back and tugged off her left boot—was more careful with the right. She worked the boot off, then her sock, and checked the ankle to make sure a bone wasn't broken.

Jack Joseph looked down at her bare ankle, stared as if he was startled at its injury—already mildly blue, and swelling. "Can I?" he said, reached out to hold her ankle, hold her foot with his other hand, and move it gently side to side. "It's not busted."

"Just a sprain," Sara said, but Jack Joseph held her as if he could heal the hurt by holding, and said, "Shit, we should have come off the river sooner."

"Not your fault," Sara said, wishing he'd let go.

"Sara, I'm sorry," Jack Joseph said—seeming too close to her in the tent—and the first time he'd called her by her name. "I'm sorry. . . ." And as if that were excuse enough, leaned down and kissed her ankle where it was most swollen, most sore.

"You can just stop that shit right now," Sara said, and tried to pull her foot away. But Jack Joseph held it so she was afraid it would hurt if she pulled harder, and he bent and kissed it again.

"Hey—just let *go*."

Then he said "Please," let go of her foot and reached up to put his arms around her, hold her instead, as if that were a substitute. She saw by the flashlight's mild beam that Jack Joseph looked ready to cry—as if he'd hurt her badly, not just sprained her ankle, and not responsible even for that. It was so unreal, it seemed not to involve her at all. She saw his narrow face, saw a tear pale in his pale eye, and let him hold her.

"That's enough, now," Sara said after a while, enjoying the hugging so much she felt she owed him for it. They were leaving the flashlight on, running the batteries down. ". . . That's enough."

Jack Joseph stopped holding her, said "Please," and while she was wondering 'please' what? gently pushed her down. "Please," he said again, leaned down and kissed her throat, kissed under her right ear as she turned her head. That was too personal, and she turned back so he'd kiss her mouth instead. "O.K.?" he said—then kissed her so roughly she was surprised and opened her mouth and let him do what he wanted. She thought of saying, "Get the fuck *off* me!'' and kneeing him away—picking up the shotgun if she had to. Then that seemed so much trouble she thought of saying, "Do what you want,'' but he was so busy with her mouth that she couldn't. He was kissing her as if she had something in her mouth he wanted, and after a while she opened her mouth wider so he would find it and then leave her alone. At least, no one could see them. No one would be standing outside in the storm, no one to open the tent's entrance and see her looking so stupid with her bare foot sticking out and this boy lying on top of her, heavier than a dog, and kissing her.

It was so cold in the tent, she was shaking. His face, too close, was hazed with fog as he breathed. He seemed to want her tongue, and she let him have it, let him suck on that and do what he wanted. That might satisfy him—he was so young, not really a man—then they could go to sleep.

He did that for a while, smelling of sweat and woodsmoke, his breath of sweet youth and salmon, and she had enough close company, was ready to tell him to stop if it hadn't been so awkward. It was less embarrassing to let him keep on than tell him to stop, push him away . . . talk to him.

"Sara,'' Jack Joseph said, and it seemed too intimate a thing, his saying her name. "—I'm sorry.'' Then he put his hands under her sweater and pulled her long-johns shirt up out of her pants, slid his hands up onto her. His hands were so cold she wanted to warm them, and her breasts were the warmest things when her bra was pushed up. He felt her there as though he owned her, and had every right. She felt him touching, squeezing her nipples. She thought if he was too rough he would give her cancer. He pushed the long-johns shirt up higher, bent and sucked on her left breast, sucking the nipple. Now he could see her breasts, how small they were, how odd, and Sara wished the flashlight would go out. Her breasts were cold where he left spit on them.

She supposed he would want to look between her legs now, pull her pants down and look at her there—this whole thing was so stupid, a mistake, and had gone so far. She raised her hips so he'd be able to if he wanted, and unbuckled her belt . . . unbuttoned her trousers so if he wanted to, he could pull them down, then her long underwear and look at her. She didn't care if the flashlight was on. He could see anything he wanted. He could see how much hair she had there . . . if he wanted to look at that, he could.

Jack Joseph said "Jesus,'' sat up, reached down to unzip the front of his jeans. He unzipped them and reached in there—to push his underwear aside, she supposed—and took his cock out, slender, long and stiff. Let her look at it, curved up out of his trousers, red and angry as a small third person in the tent, making it crowded. Sara hunched up, propped on her elbows, uncomfortable as he knelt over her—leaned forward and kissed it. She wanted to, and she didn't see why she shouldn't, when that made her feel less lonely. She held her cheek against it . . . then arranged and wet it with her tongue as if she had no hands, enjoying the heat and smoothness, a slightly salty taste. She took it in her mouth, got her mouth too full and was breathing noisily through her nose—she supposed he was listening—and licked and sucked as if she were starving. Then she pulled her head back and let it go, so it pulsed, stretching up before her, wet, sore-looking.

Sara didn't know what he expected her to do; it was too embarrassing to look up at him. She was afraid he'd say something to her, so she bent forward again and kissed his cock as if she loved him. Then sat up farther, put her hands on his legs to hold herself up—gripping, through thick denim, thin thighs harder than hers with muscle—then bowed her head, took it again and sucked, listening to the noises she made, how she swallowed, almost gagging, breathing through her nose as if she had a cold.

Jack Joseph said something in Koyukon. He sounded frightened, and he bent slowly over her, obscuring the light. Though it seemed he wouldn't be able to leave her, he did, knelt back and drew his cock out of her mouth so it stood glistening, smelling of her saliva. It seemed to her, though, he must have loved her for a while when she was doing that. He was only a boy; how could he not love her then, for just a minute? She wondered if there were many things he would want her to do, so there'd be no end of them. She wondered if there were enough things to do to fill up all her time.

She wished he would do something—she didn't want the responsibility—and was very relieved when Jack Joseph, wrestling in the tent's cold confines, tugged off his sweater, boots, and socks, then his jeans and underwear . . . and moved, it seemed to her, much more freely naked. Very thin, dark, every rib showing. His cock nodding stiff and swollen—his lean body's most important part.

Then he came to her, very serious, businesslike, pulled her pants and underwear down and took them off, so she was cold—then squatted, looking at her by the flashlight's adequate light, gently pushed her legs apart so he could see more.

Sara, glad she'd shaved her legs, held them apart for him, even though she felt she was ugly there. He wanted to so much, it seemed the thing to do—hold her legs, knees bent, far apart so he could see. If he didn't like it, too bad.

Jack Joseph looked at her, his breath frosting, clouding slightly—then put cold hands on her, put his thumbs there and pulled her vulva painfully apart, as if he were beginning to turn her inside out. Then he put his finger in—pushed it slowly deep into her and then another one roughly enough to hurt, so she made a sound like humming. She could feel his fingers in there, moving. Hear the wet sounds they made, even over the noise of the wind. She could smell herself.

Sara's sweater, shirt, and undershirt were gathered at her armpits—her bra, too—and she sat up and wrestled them off over her head, had to get the bra off separately. Then, naked, she was worried she'd have to say something, but Jack Joseph suddenly took her left leg, lifted it and turned her over so she was on her belly. She felt his hands again, pulling her open as she lay on her belly, her legs spread out. He took her hips and pulled her up onto her hands and knees as if he'd done this many times—it hurt her sprained ankle a little, hurt her damaged fingertips—but Sara for some reason stayed that way, put her face down into her sleeping bag's softness and arched her back so her rear end was up, showing everything. Anything he wanted. She was glad he couldn't see her face. She was trembling with the cold; it was too cold in the tent for this for not being in the sleeping bags. They could have zipped the sleeping bags together. . . .

She felt something behind her, at her vulva . . . and realized he was smelling her, had his face there. Then he knelt up and took hold of her like a man, his hands painful, gripping her buttocks, and she felt something nudging, pressing. Missing and then finding . . . pushing against her. Uncomfortable, shoving—then suddenly in, bigger than his finger had been, and slowly pushed inside her.

It felt so good Sara said, "Oh . . . *oh.*" That sounded stupid, and she was sorry she'd done it; she hadn't sounded like herself. He pulled it almost out, then pushed it in again, deeper . . . and that felt so painfully good, made such a stupid noise—liquid, sort of liquid farting—that she wasn't ashamed then to call out something that wasn't a word.

He was sticking it so deeply into her that she ached, and hollowed her back to take more. He was doing it too slowly. It was humiliating; Sara wished he would do it faster, so she could make noises without being heard—so he wouldn't be fucking her so completely she had no privacy.

She supposed he was looking down, watching what he was doing to her. And when she thought that, she came . . . but only a little, just the start of coming, one knot slipping undone. She imagined she was erasing Alan, doing this—fucking him away with this boy. . . .

She could smell herself, like grade school glue—and he was going at her and going at her. If he didn't stop he'd find out too much.

"You're doing . . . something," Sara said out loud, her face turned from the sleeping bag so he would hear her. "Stop—you're *doing* something!" And meant he was hurting her, was going to hurt her—and it felt so serious she cried out, and he shoved it into her again and again, smacking and smacking against her. She shook and hunched back so her ass was higher and anything could be done, and she felt it move inside her and something else, and all knots came untied and she twisted on it, clenching to keep it, and shouted "Alan . . . oh, *Alan!*"

Then, after a while, calming and tired, crouched resting with the boy on her back, his cock, soft as cloth, now slipping free of her—his liquid . . . her liquid cool on her soaked vulva, damp down her thighs—Sara almost slept so deep was her repose, so free of thinking. His weight was bearing her down. It was strange to have another animal so close, who was not a dog.

She half-sat, turning, so he lifted off her; then she reached up through cold air and drew him down, hugged him—and though Jack Joseph had fucked her like a man, now he tried to turn his face away, a boy not caring for this sort of hugging. But she held him anyway, held his neck crooked in her left arm so he couldn't avoid tenderness. She had her revenge then for the fucking—how he'd made use of her, made her use herself—and kissed his mouth gently, against his wishes. Forced tenderness upon him, kissed his mouth . . . then, murmuring, his blind eye, whether he wanted it or not.

Sweat-slick, smelling of woodsmoke and the starchy odor of his coming, the boy settled naked into her arms, surrendered, his long black hair undone. "Sara," he said to her. "Sara. . . ."

The late morning was clear as glass, the air transparent, ringing, sunrise flashing off the river ice. There was no wind.

Sara had wakened to the canvas tent's translucent filtered light—had recalled, and been relieved Jack Joseph was already up and out. She lay reviewing the night before, and found it first humiliating—

being screwed by an angry Native boy who undoubtedly thought even an ugly white woman represented at least a minor trophy. So humiliating she wished Jack Joseph would fall through the ice somehow before reaching Chancy, and be gone with all his knowing. . . .

First that, then found it funny—saw herself groaning, butt in the air, happy to have the attention, closeness, even from a one-eyed boy so thin . . . obviously hadn't ever eaten properly. . . .

Sara smelled brewing tea, and it seemed to her the longer she stayed in the tent the harder leaving the tent would be, so she sat up—found she was sore from the sex, her vagina irritated—pushed the sleeping bag away, and searched for her socks. She found the socks near her shotgun, then untangled her bra, shirt and sweater, and put them on. She found her trousers and long underwear beside her pack, and finished getting dressed.

She crawled out into shallow snow and perfect weather—ten, fifteen above—stood, and saw Jack Joseph below, on the pebble beach. He was gassing the Bravo, his blue parka leaking its puff of down from the right elbow. He'd built a neat fire on green fir branches two or three yards from the tent. The small dented teakettle was hanging by its wire bale over low, occasional flames. Sara called "Good morning" and bent to the kettle, looking for a cup. Her ankle felt better.

"Good morning. . . ." Jack Joseph walked up the bank and squatted by the fire. Apparently shy, he had nothing more to say, his shyness relieving Sara's. He tugged the aluminum cups out of his pack, and handed her one. Then took the last rounds of pilot bread out of the plastic food sack, and handed her more than half.

"Pretty day," Sara said. She used her bandanna to hold the kettle's hot bale, filled her cup . . . and squatted, keeping a little distance from Jack Joseph, who said nothing more, didn't look at her. They ate pilot bread, drank the tea in silence, until for Sara the silence became more difficult than talking.

"Jack Joseph—it's just something that happened." That said, Sara glanced at him and saw him making a boy's quick grimace of embarrassment, mouth drawn down, eyes rolling up. It was so childish, she was charmed.

"—Really, you know? It was a natural thing. I'm not upset." Jack Joseph looked down into his tea as if he hadn't heard her, and she felt a disastrous urge to laugh, he looked so young. "Jack, it just *happened*—you know? Shit happens."

"Yeah." Jack Joseph sipped some tea.

Sara supposed she should just shut up, let it go for a while. She finished a last bite of pilot bread, wished for *kamamik,* then poured herself more tea. She missed feeding dogs in the morning. . . .

They struck the tent, packed up, and broke camp without talking . . . then loaded the sled and set out, riding on wind-polished ice smooth as fine paper—going so easy, it seemed to Sara even the Bravo's noise was muted. Here, the river took a grand slow swing south between low brushy banks only half a mile apart. The hills to the left, the mountains on the right stood farther away than they had, fencing this lower country along its horizons.

Sara twisted to look back over her right shoulder as they rode, and was just able to see her mountain—its peak snowy, shrunk by distance to seclusion among other summits of its savage range more than two hundred miles northeast. The air shimmered in sunshine, ran like cold ribbons past her as she sat the Bravo's humming seat.

Far behind them, in that range of mountains, glaciers dammed forested valleys she had not yet seen—tree-fall ravines, snow slopes falling to granite steeps split by small gray-water mountain rivers. Rivers foaming, rushing down . . . ice lacing their courses descending through stone, then tundra, then willow. Somewhere in that spacious country, under a great spruce stump, or deep, deep into the side of a frozen hill, the bear lay sleeping, dreaming of salmon or grayling swum up to spawn . . . dreaming of berries. Dreams to become less satisfactory in time—their sounds unconvincing to her, their odors fragile—dissolving, fading away as she begins to rouse to spring.

Then, high in the mountains, the crocus's green blades and small yellow buds would come sliding up through snow where it lay shallowest. Those yellow buds, and the windflowers' white. When the little flowers found the sun—in a month or two, so high—the bear would wake.

Somewhere along the ridge above the cabin, they'd buried what was left of Alan. They'd started to tell her where—Frank Solokoff had tried to tell her—but she'd put her hand up and turned away, not wanting to know. What was left of Alan was buried among black spruce, high above where the blueberries grew in summer. . . .

The Bravo rumbled past two fish wheels on the right, frozen in, and a little while later passed the fish camp set along the same bank, its smoke shack and ramshackle tables draped with snow among cottonwoods.

Sara'd been careful this morning how she put her arms around Jack Joseph as they rode, avoiding the slightest hugging . . . clasping, so the boy wouldn't get some notion of romance. As it was, she supposed he wouldn't be too quick after all to brag of having screwed a woman so much older, not pretty—and probably desperate for attention, let alone fucking, after almost a year by herself.

She supposed he'd tell Christine Hodges, or more likely wouldn't have to. That clever fat girl would smell triumph on Jack Joseph. Or shame . . . satisfaction, something out of the ordinary.

Christine would say, "How was the trip?" and stand watching him, her black eyes deep as petroleum. "How was the trip?"

"O.K."

"O.K.? You didn' argue with her?"

"No."

"No? Well, what happened?"

"Nothin'."

"Nothin'? Then how come you're not talkin'?"

"I'm talkin'."

"So, what happened?"

"I told you. We just rode down."

"You didn' stop with that storm? Drove through that storm at night?"

"What . . . what the fuck do you care, Christine? We stopped, went on in the mornin'. What's your problem?"

"Not *my* problem," Christine would say. "—What happened?" And would, of course, get it out of him. Then would be able to imagine anything about Sara, and it might be true. . . .

Her fingers—the first and second fingers of her left hand—ached where she'd lost the nails the night before. Sara took off her left-hand mitten (the gloves too badly torn to wear) and held her hand out into the windstream until the cold had numbed her fingers to no longer hurting. She rode along that way for a while, until her fingers grew pale, then put her mitten on and slid that hand back around Jack Joseph's narrow waist to meet the other.

It would have been very easy to discourage him—not to use a boy just because she'd felt so lonely. It was the worst thing for a teacher to do, even a teacher who hadn't taught in so long. Even though the boy was eighteen. So simple to have said, "Jack Joseph—I am *not* interested." If she'd just said that, and let him know she meant it. If she'd just said that, and reached down and taken his hand off her sore ankle, that would have been it. Maybe a little awkwardness, but not as awkward as this—a Koyukon boy and a white woman thirty-seven years old who looked as though she ought to be riding a broom, not a Bravo. She knew what she looked like. . . .

And as she felt ashamed, and so reminded of what else she'd failed in, and being afraid, the forest and all the country on both sides of the river began to appear more and more like country in a picture—something only to look at. Now, it would seem strange to have Jack Joseph stop and let her off to walk away through the trees. Walk away back toward the mountains. That would seem the oddest thing, now—while only the day before, it felt proper to go in among the trees, hunting.

The country was withdrawing from her. Sara didn't turn to look again. She rode in the engine's racket with her eyes squinted in the wind, peering over Jack Joseph's blue-padded left shoulder. Watching the river's ice rushing toward them powder-white, lead gray, then powder-white again as a cloud passed over—these shades seen through the hazed complication of scratches on the Bravo's windshield.

A few miles after, the snow-machine swung left, then nearer that bank, then left again just off a point of forested land the river had allowed (or had formed, as an oxbow)—and an orange-and-white Piper came over the trees, low, its engine louder than the Bravo's . . . then tilted to the right and flew off upstream, rudder working, the small plane skidding a little in the current of heavy air that ran above the river.

Past the point, Chancy lay scattered along the bank, its several docks (black-tarred pilings, joists and planking) stilting out onto the river's ice. The processing plant's heat had melted the snow off its corrugated metal roof, so the galvanized steel reflected a smeared sun shifting slowly to the left as the Bravo traveled by.

"Ruinin' the river," Jack Joseph said, voice raised above the engine noise as they passed. "Over-catchin' an' then wastin' salmon just for the roe."

It was the first thing he'd said since the morning.

Chancy's waterfront was trampled clear of snow at two landings near the plant, and the Bravo motored on beyond the company dock, then another, bumping over ice shelved in folded soft greens and browns and ivory white—disturbed, melted, refrozen and rejoined many times. Jack Joseph turned into the bank where grimy snow lay piled among beached boats—left the river ice and geared down so the Bravo growled up the ramp onto a level where three net sheds stood, waddled past those on mud and snow mixed, then up a narrow path (the towed sled bumping behind) to the flat where Chancy's houses lay. The store, community center, school and clinic were up on the hill behind the town—Booze Hill, it had been, now officially Lookout.

Sara observed from her perch behind Jack Joseph—a place she

now wished she could keep, rather than dismount to deal with Chancy, its forty or fifty houses, its processing plant, post office and airfield. Rather than deal with Bud LeBeck. Sara wished Jack Joseph were older, didn't look so odd—skinny, one-eyed, and Indian. She wished he were a man who loved her, who'd insist she go back up the river with him—would just let her have a bath at Bud's, a breakfast at the store, then would take her back upriver in the morning. A man even better with an ax than Alan . . . and not always lecturing, making pronouncements. A man who'd killed several grizzlies. Who always had his rifle with him in the spring.

Jack Joseph stopped the Bravo a few yards along, let the engine idle, and looked back over his right shoulder to see Sara with his good eye.

"I got some business. Where you want to go?"

"LeBeck's." On the wind, in the pauses when it blew more gently, Chancy smelled slightly of rotten fish and sewage. Rich odors—not unpleasant carried for a few local yards on wind flavored only by a thousand miles of spruce and frozen river.

"LeBeck's. You got it. . . ." Gunned the engine, made a skidding U-turn left, and ran back down the path they'd traveled—passed the ramp and rode up along a row of cabins, their snow-machines and three-wheelers parked among old oil-drums . . . washtubs and rusting drive chains hanging from nails along their walls, decorative moose antlers nailed above doors.

Chancy looked bigger, seemed to have more houses than when Sara'd been down with Alan two years before. The oil people coming in. . . .

She saw two white men walking down the path, their parkas swinging open in the sunshine—burly, bearded, in their twenties. They were strangers and looked peculiar to her, their faces misshapen, long, their jaws heavier than Natives', skin pale as underdone biscuits beneath their windburn. Their odd eyes noticed her for an instant as the Bravo grumbled up—dismissed her swiftly, as plain, while the Bravo passed. A different dismissal than Native men's, who hardly seemed to notice she wasn't pretty, and dismissed her for other reasons. Sara thought it must be the most extraordinary thing to be beautiful—to see approval and desire in almost every man's face. Possibly a burden, too.

Bud LeBeck's house was a two-story cabin built high on the edge of the bank; the processing plant and river his view from a roofed back porch.

Jack Joseph ran the Bravo along LeBeck's dog fence to its low gate, stopped the snow-machine and left its engine running—so as not to have to talk to her, Sara thought. He dismounted as she did, and walked back to the sled to help her unhook bungee cords from the load. Then she hoisted one big fur bundle (favoring her sore ankle), he two of the others, and they lugged them into the yard and up the steps to the front door.

Jack Joseph left the two fur bundles, went down the steps and out the gate to bring in the fourth and her duffle—then walked back out and swung onto the Bravo's seat, ready to go.

Sara followed him down, picked her pack and rifle case up off the sled, then went to the snow-machine and held her hand out to him.

"Thank you for the trip. You're a good driver."

"That's O.K." He shook her hand gently, as if to leave no impression on it, and seemed so much to want to get away he reminded her of Lobo, half-wolf and young, shrinking away when she came too close and stayed too long.

Out of mischief, she supposed—or angry at him—Sara leaned to Jack Joseph and kissed his cheek (saw close the boy's blue-white eye, pupil-less and perfect, reflecting only light). Jack Joseph bore that well, didn't shy . . . then said "Take it easy," turned the Bravo's throttle, and drove away—the sled, nearly empty, jittering behind. He turned right almost at once and rode the snow-machine over boot-printed snow up along a scattering of shacks and cabins, then turned right again a shotgun shot away, and disappeared behind jeans and several plaid flannel shirts frozen stiff along a clothesline.

"You bootleggin', lady?"

Sara turned and saw Bud LeBeck, lanky in blue coveralls, standing by his front door—a baby, pink-blanketed, tucked in the crook of his right arm like a package. He looked odd as the other white men had, skin so strangely colored. His mottled paleness more striking than his bony height, six foot six, though he always stooped.

"No, not bootlegging," Sara said, and walked up the path.

"Saw you come with that kid, an' he damn sure does business," LeBeck said, and opened the door for her. "I'll bring in the pelts. Day's long gone you can leave shit out in this town. Assholes we got now'll steal it, not give it another thought—goin' up to those new oil fields. Fuckin' up the whole goddamn country." In a narrow hallway hot with oil heat and smelling of cured hides, he held the baby out to Sara. "Take her on in. —What do you think? First chick; we're callin' her Cynthia. Two boys, now this one."

"Is Terry O.K.?" Sara put her pack and rifle case down to hold the baby. It smelled of talcum powder and pee, smelled to Sara almost the way Carla had smelled in Billy Mitchell—sweet young monkey. Sara supposed she'd spent too much time with dogs. The baby had a face like a soft white knot. From that, cold round blue eyes observed Sara as nothing special.

"Terry. . . . That nasty bitch is fine. She's in Fairbanks, spendin' my money; I'd say she's fine." He bent outside the doorway to pick up two fur bundles, handling the weight more easily than Jack Joseph had, and nodded her on down the hall ahead of him. "Just lay her on the bed in the front bedroom, an' I'll get the other two in. Only brought down four packs? Not much fur. . . ."

Sara walked through white people's odors in a white person's house, her sprained ankle aching. The house smelled sweeter than Native places had—different from the mountain cabin as well. This smelled of pot smoke, hot chocolate, hides, and store sugar. The big ground-floor room was crowded with stacks of skins, fur hanging thick as smokehouse salmon from the low ceiling around a wide brown plywood table—LeBeck's trading table. She had to push curtaining pelts aside—caribou, black bear . . . another black bear, wolf, two more caribou—to get into the front bedroom, also Bud's office. A neatly kept desk with a Macintosh computer stood against the wall beneath the window . . . and a double bed, draped with a yellow-and-brown patchwork quilt, against the wall.

Sara put the baby gently down in the center of the bed so she'd be less likely to roll to the edge and fall. The baby stared at her all the time, not smiling, looking into her eyes, and didn't seem sorry to be left alone.

Bud brought the last of the fur bundles into the room, and Sara's duffle—had the backpack and rifle case hung over his shoulder as well. He put the hides down on his trading table, set the backpack, duffle, and rifle case under the table on the floor.

"Now, come here," he said, "an' give me a damn hug."

He was a strange man to hug—so tall there was chest muscle against the left side of Sara's face, his unshaven chin looming when she looked up.

LeBeck was very strong—she could feel the long muscles of his arms around her in casual compression. He smelled of coffee and tanning mixture. Pot smoke, too.

"You do O.K. up there alone all this time? Get my letter?"

Sara didn't like hearing his voice through his body, so she leaned away and he let her go. "Yes. Thanks, Bud."

"Always go round with that shotgun on you?"

"I guess not." Sara lifted the strap off her shoulder, swung the shotgun sheath off her back and set it down beside the rifle case.

"Maureen an' Bill Sellecka sure would like to see you. Bill's in, now—got the nicest two black-bear pelts you ever saw. Big ones, an' not a bad flaw on 'em. Some oil-company asshole'll buy 'em, claim he took 'em one shot each."

"I'd rather not see anybody, Bud."

"Shit—Maureen's crazy about you; you know they want to see you."

"I'd rather not. Maureen'll understand."

"Hell she will. . . . You do know Alan owed six hundred from last year. The traps an' chain an' shit I shipped to Fort Billy, an' vitamin syrup, wormer, Iams, an' ten nylon harnesses. What do those dogs do, eat that harness?"

"Yes, I knew we still owed that."

"O.K. Well, I just wanted to mention that so you wouldn't think I was waitin' to see if *you* were goin' to mention it."

"That's all right."

"Business is business, an' that's that. —But the goddamndest news I ever heard," LeBeck stepped to the table, drew a Randall Hunter off his hip and cut the cords binding the pelt bundle. "I mean the *goddamndest*, was Alan Maher killed by a fuckin' bear. . . ." Le-Beck had the bundle open, was slowly sorting through martens. Stooped once to blow on dark brown fur, watched it comb richly away from the breath. "Nice martens. This fox is a little measly."

"No, it isn't. The pelts would look a lot better outside."

"What the hell's the matter with in here?"

"Light's better out there, Bud. Fur looks like shit on that brown table."

"Oh, great," examining a wolverine hide, "—now you're tellin' me my business like I was goin' to jew you."

"Let's go through them out in the daylight, Bud. O.K.? That's the way you did it when Alan and I came down, and that's the way I'd like it now."

LeBeck shook out the wolverine pelt, set it aside, and looked at the last red fox Sara'd taken. "Shit, you got hides in here only salt tanned!"

"I had to leave early."

"Don't doubt it—was me, an' been through what you been through, I'd *damn* sure want to get off that mountain before the fuckin' bears wake up."

"It isn't that. Not only that. . . ."

"Well anyway, I don't suppose you want me to pay you finished prices for raw skins?"

"No. But most of them are finished—and I'd like us to take them outside."

"It isn't goin' to make a bit of difference. You think you can get a better price in Fairbanks? Go pay airfreight an' try with Curry or that Italian. I don't give a shit."

"I want us looking in fair light, Bud. There's good fur there."

"Oh, sure. Just four bundles, an' some salted. Honey, you are not goin' to make much of a livin' trappin'. That's a man's job, keepin' long lines clear up in them high mountains—which are damn thin trappin' anyway. Got to keep them lines clear, cut 'em to go with the flow on that furbearer traffic. Four bundles isn't goin' to make you shit. —Now here's a good wolf; this is a good wolf. Europeans'll buy this fucker."

"I'm leaving the country, Bud. I won't be trapping anymore."

LeBeck put the wolf pelt down, a soft heap of cloudy gray. "Leavin' the country? After what—five years? Why the hell are you goin' Outside? Just live somewhere else up here!"

"I wouldn't want to live anywhere else if I was here. And I wouldn't trap anymore, anyway."

"Oh, come on, 'I got to get away' an' all that shit. Get *serious*. Everybody up here knows what happened. You think they blame you? —Nice marten. You got some good martens. Wish there was a fuckin' market for 'em. . . . It's all horseshit. 'Leavin' the country.' You had a rifle *with* you, that would be another matter. Not one swingin' dick in this town—an' we get some good people in here, some real trappers still come in—not one of those boys would have climbed down an' run for a rifle, given that situation."

"Bullshit. And what if it was their wife?"

"Probably glad to see her go. Now, you listen to me, because you're a friend of mine an' Alan was a friend of mine, despite the element of you sellin' an' me buyin'. It is a fiduciary relationship, but it's also a friendship. Now, you can eat that guilty vomit many times as you want, barf it out an' eat it up an' barf it out again. I'm just givin' you a friend's advice, which is you did what most would do, an' you couldn't do more at the time an' fuck it. An' that's what Alan'd say, too, an' I knew that dude damn well."

"I'd be leaving anyway, Bud. The Koyukons want me off that Porcupine land, canceled my lease. And the only thing I could do is back up way deeper in the mountains."

"So—fight 'em in court, or back on up. What is that back there, Federal land? They'll run you, too, if they find you. We ordinary white people don't own shit up here. It isn't even like fuckin' America."

"Unlikely to find me, there—and if they did, I'd just back up farther."

"Then what's this 'leavin' ' shit?—unless you're just gettin' out for spring, figure the fuckin' grizz'll come back down that bear track an' kill your ass, you goin' out to take a dump. Which she might. Sure as shit would be on my mind. . . ."

"Bud, I'm just leaving—and if I wasn't, I still wouldn't trap anymore."

"Oh, sure. An' you'd do what? Process fish eggs?"

"I'd build some sluice boxes up on Backache Creek, and placer. There're already old gold workings up there."

"Oh, come on; I *know* that setup—which is on Federal land, by the way, so it's a Bureau thing. —What happened to your fingers?"

"Lost a couple of nails."

"You got a crooked little finger there, too. You bust it?"

"It's fine."

"An' what the hell do you know about minin', anyway?"

"I helped Karen Ismay placer her claim one summer."

"Oh, give me a *break*. Look, I was minin' four years before I found the fur business—you know that?"

"Yes. . . ."

"—An' I can tell you there isn't shit for good color up there in that creek. It's too high—high as your homestead, just other side of the mountain. Right?"

"Yes."

"An' you couldn't use scrap iron 'cause you can't afford one, couldn't get it in, an' you couldn't fix a 'dozer anyway if it threw a tread or broke down. Water's too damn fast for suction dredgin'. You'd be buildin' sluices an' shake boxes an' shovelin' your ass off all alone, an' if you showed enough for four thousand a year I'd be fuckin' amazed. Maybe four thousand five, if you busted your butt."

"I could make do on that."

"Do dirt poor."

"I could get somebody to help me. I could get a man up to help me."

"Some bush rat, an' then you'd make seven or eight thousand bustin' both your asses, siftin' the little you get out of that heavy hematite. —But you're leavin' the country, anyway." LeBeck flipped a marten pelt over, thumbed the underside.

"That's right. And Bud, I won't be taking my guns. Would you sell them for me?"

"What do you have? You got Alan's Model 70?"

"I have that, in the case. And the shotgun, and a Redhawk, stainless, and a Single-Six .22."

"Well, I might want to buy that Model 70 off you. Other stuff—O.K., I'll hold 'em for you. You write me in a couple months, you really want the guns sold off. Till then, I'll hold 'em."

"If you would, keep my duffle, too. There's just ammunition in it, mainly, and binoculars and stuff. I can send for that. —I won't be coming back, Bud."

"Sure . . . sure. You know, just because you did shit this year doesn't mean you couldn't do better, trappin' up there—even back in there so high. If you got some dude to partner you, trappin', bush out them lines, you could cover more'n a hundred, hundred an' fifty miles, pull maybe fourteen packs if the hare don't crash. Prices swing way up again, could clear you fifteen thousand dollars." He bent to sniff at a fox pelt.

"I just don't like it."

"Oh, I don't believe this shit! You feel sorry for them animals? —'Cause you ought to know no animal's feelin' sorry for an animal. You ought to know them other animals an' nature kills the poor fuckers a lot harder than you do."

"I just don't like it."

"Didn't mind it when Alan was doin' the work."

"No."

"But you don't want to do it yourself." LeBeck stepped away from the table. "—Gotta check the kid." He walked into the bedroom, stayed a minute or two, murmuring, then came back out.

"That's exactly right," Sara said to him. "I don't want to do it myself. It's unfair."

"Isn't huntin' with a rifle unfair?" He stood at his trading table, leafed over a marten's hide and stroked it.

"At least that's quick unfairness."

"You're tellin' me the same fuckin' nonsense those wimps do down in the forty-eight, shootin' their mouths off about fur as if some people didn't make their livin' with it. Assholes never did their own killin' for anything. Buyin' all their shit already killed *for* 'em." LeBeck rolled the marten fur in his hands, testing the cure. Then put it down and stooped to lift another bundle up onto the table, used his belt knife to slice its cord, then slowly dealt out the hides. "—An' then they go in some fuckin' restaurant an' do recreational eatin', chunks cut off little lambs an' calves. An' little chickens been through hell, had their beaks cut off for Christ's sake! Doin' that—an' the meat's so fat it's *bad* for 'em. They don't care."

LeBeck turned a wolverine hide over, looking for the bullet-mend, and found it behind the ear. "Nice fix-up. You do good sewin', anyway." He combed the pelt with his fingers, then put it down. "Havin' millions of little animals killed for 'em so they can go pay some wop fifty dollars, sit on their ass an' recreationally eat an' swallow all that grease those little animals suffered an' died for. Disgustin'. . . . But, hey, don't let a woman keep warm in a pelt some dude busted his nuts runnin' line in the boonies to get. Don't let *that* happen." He checked a small marten, bent to sniff at the fur, then set it aside and looked at the hide of the lynx Sara had strangled.

"Vegetarians," Sara said.

"Oh, right, don't tell me about those people. They may not eat recreationally—but have you ever been in a health-food store? Seen those sad chicks, those faggy guys come in with 'em. You ever see one person in a health-food store looks healthy? They look like shit. Skin all broken out; they're a mess. —This lynx is a little measly."

"It is not. Bud, I'd like to deal the skins out on your porch in the daylight."

"God damn it. . . ." LeBeck gathered furs into his arms. "Then open the fuckin' back door. As if it was goin' to make a damn difference in the world. . . ."

"Thank you."

"Great to be trusted," LeBeck said, carried the pelts out onto his back porch, and dumped them on the spruce flooring in the sunlight so they lay the softest heap, capturing many shades.

Chancy's airfield was a wide level west of town—two gravel runways plowed to light snow cover lay alongside a log shack and small maintenance hangar. There were two rusted pickups and three snow-machines parked at the shack when LeBeck stopped his four-wheeler on the beaten path from town. Five planes, ski-rigged, were parked off the near runway—two green-and-white Huskys, a Cessna 180, and a big Otter with its engine pulled. Farther back, three dark-blue oil company helicopters rested side by side, their long rotor blades drooping. And there was a tangle of scorched wreckage, black bent ladders of aluminum—apparently the Pennsylvania pilot's unlucky ship—cleared off and dumped.

"That's Halsey's Cessna. —He's O.K. He can fly." LeBeck shifted his baby daughter, bundled in her blanket in a blue cloth sling.

"Thanks for the lift, Bud." Sara climbed off the seat, took her backpack (rolled sleeping-bag bungeed to it) from the ATV's rack.

"Glad to. An' those furs weren't bad. I don't suppose you think I cheated you on those furs. Shit, for just four bundles, an' some skins only salted—an' subtractin' that six hundred owed—eighteen hundred isn't bad."

"It's all right."

"Well . . . you think I took advantage of you?"

"I think those lynx were worth more than two hundred apiece. I do think they were worth more."

"Well, you're just dead wrong. They're good skins; I'm not sayin' they're not. But they're worth just what I gave you. You're thinkin' of last year's prices; you got no idea the way the market is these days—fuckin' prices swingin' up an' down, an' I got to at least stay even. Wasn't for the Japanese an' Europeans buyin', I'd be broke."

"All right, Bud." Sara shouldered her backpack, missing the shotgun's weight. "Thanks for the sandwiches and shower." She walked away through the snow to the shack. There was a loud radio playing in there—or TV.

LeBeck started his four-wheeler, called after her, "Take it easy. Take care of yourself. . . ."

The people in the shack looked up while Sara stood in the doorway, stamped snow off her boot-pacs, then came inside. The door, on a strong coil spring, slammed shut behind her, the heat from a small fuel-drum stove washing back where the cold had drafted in. Sara set her pack down against the near wall, its plywood covered with push-pinned maps.

The shack's floor was thumping with old-fashioned rock and roll—some group before Sara's time.

There were three Native men—one old, the other two much younger, perhaps his sons—sitting in folding chairs at the stove, drinking bottled beer and using small yellow-plastic forks to eat sardines out of cans. A short fat white man, middle-aged, clean-shaven with neatly parted iron-gray hair, was talking to an elderly woman seated behind the desk. The woman was in her seventies, with a 'dough's weathered face, her hair permanented into frost-blue curls.

The radio was on the counter beside her. Sara supposed she was a little deaf.

"Mister Halsey?"

The fat white man turned to look at Sara, then raised his voice over the music. "I'm Halsey." He was wearing big-lensed aviator's dark glasses and a bright red parka.

"Mister Halsey, I'm looking for a ride to Fairbanks."

"I'm going pretty soon."

"O.K. What's the fare?"

"One hundred and fifty dollars."

"I'd rather walk," Sara said, and to the elderly woman, "Any other pilots in?"

The woman opened a blue-covered loose-leaf notebook, consulted several pages, then closed it. "Man called Robinson's supposed to fly that green Husky out. He was waiting for a part. Now he's got it, I suppose he'll put it in and go in a day or two."

"I'll wait," Sara said, went back and sat down on the floor, leaning against her pack.

The fat man said something to the woman behind the desk, then turned to Sara. He looked amused. "And suppose Chuck Robinson asks two hundred?"

"Then I'll walk," Sara said.

"One hundred fifty's my price."

"I heard you." Sara found a place along the wall with no wet from tracked-in snow, and stretched out on the floor, her head propped on her pack. She felt the planks beneath her vibrating slightly with the music's deeper strumming, and closed her eyes so she wouldn't have to see these strangers. It would be only three or four days walk to the highway. She could hitch into Fairbanks from there. She'd have to go back and get the shotgun from Bud, some birdshot shells for snowshoe hare. . . .

The shack smelled of woodsmoke and sardines, more faintly of high-octane gas from the hangar next door. The two white people were talking through the music, their voices louder than the Natives'. Talking about another pilot; he'd flown into the east face of Voonerak in a storm. Sara, drifting, her eyes closed, wondered if he'd had a moment, a last instant when the sheets of buffeting snow before him were transformed to granite, to wake him from flying as from a dream. . . .

She slid into sleep, and the Bravo was flying, sailing high over the river's ice while people talked around her. In the dream, Bud LeBeck came walking to them in the air, and Jack Joseph stopped the Bravo to listen. Bud said, "O.K.," reached out, shook her, and she woke.

"It's just a fuckin' gift, is what it is," LeBeck said, standing bent over her, annoyed—his baby hammocked, muttering in her blue sling. He was holding out some money. "I don't really owe you this."

Sara reached up, took it, and counted it. Five twenties, ten tens. "Thanks, Bud." She dug the eight hundred he'd given her in cash out of her left parka pocket, added the two hundred to the roll, and replaced the red rubber band.

"Subtractin' last year's six hundred, makes two thousand even, O.K.? Cash an' check. I just didn't want you leavin' thinkin' you got screwed by somebody was a friend."

"I appreciate it."

The three Native men, the fat pilot, and the woman behind the desk were all watching.

"Well," LeBeck said, straightening up, "—so long."

Sara got to her feet, held out her hand to shake, but he stepped in and kissed her quickly on the cheek. "Can't tell you how fuckin' sorry I am."

"I know."

"You got your ride O.K.?"

"Everything's fine, Bud."

"Well, you take care. . . ."

"I will."

LeBeck went out, the door slammed behind him, and the fat pilot said, "Guess now you got the money for your fare."

Sara didn't answer him, lay down on the floor again, and closed her eyes. Now it would be too awkward to go see Bud again, get her shotgun and say a third good-bye. If she had to walk, she'd buy sardines and three or four cans of beans at the store. It would be hard traveling, some stretches, without snowshoes. And unpleasant, not having the shotgun with her.

After a while she turned toward the wall for privacy, and thought that Alan would never know what she'd done with Jack Joseph. Ridiculous. On her hands and knees in a tent with a boy, the flashlight showing how scrawny, how sad she was. It was almost worth Alan's being dead that he could never know about it.

"I'm sorry," Sara said to the wall, but only moving her lips, not making any sound. "It's the second thing I'm sorry about, but I'm sure it was because of the first thing." She whispered that last to the wall, but very softly . . . certainly couldn't be heard over the music and talking. Then went to sleep.

"Hey!"

Sara woke and looked up. The fat pilot was standing over her, his red parka zipped.

"—You make up your mind if you're going? Isn't anybody else flying out this afternoon."

"I'm not going for a hundred fifty."

"You tell him, honey," the elderly woman said from behind her counter.

"Up to you," the fat man said. He called "So long . . ." to the elderly woman, walked to the door and went out. Sara saw it was darker outside. Afternoon.

"You can stay here tonight, if you want," the blue-haired woman said. "Anybody says anything, tell 'em Charlotte said it was O.K."

"All right. Thanks."

"Plenty of wood. You got something to eat?"

"Yes."

The shack's door swung open and the fat man stuck his head back inside, looked at Sara. "You ready to go?"

"No."

"I give up. One hundred."

"O.K." Sara stood and picked up her pack.

"What a guy," Charlotte said.

Carrying her pack, Sara followed the fat man out into sunset weather, cooling, shadowy, and pleasant. She could see the distant night swinging in from the south, swinging closed like a dark door made of half the sky. There were faint stars above the setting sun. The river ice had turned to Irish gold.

The fat man, Halsey, trudged a path through snow to the Cessna, the plane striped cream and crimson, and bush-rigged—wheel-pants off, bungee-cord gear above its skis, doors split. There were riveted half-covers on the engine bug-eyes. A pair of bear-paw snowshoes and an ax were padlocked into a strap-steel rack on the side of the fuselage.

"You're going to have to carry that pack down in front of you," Halsey said. "—I have cargo in the back." He stomped a quick track into the snow to the front of the plane, looked the engine over . . . then walked around and out of sight, to reappear at the tail, checking, stretching up to move the rudder a little. He came around to the passenger-side door, reached up and opened it. "In you go. You look smart enough not to touch anything." Then ducked under the Cessna to its other side, stepping over its long skis lying half buried in snow.

Sara stood on the right ski, shoved her pack up in front of the passenger seat, then fitted her boot toe into the step-notch, climbed up and settled in, the pack wedged fatly between her legs. She swung the door slamming shut. Frigid woven plastic touched the back of her neck, so she reached over her shoulder to tug her parka hood up slightly. It was colder in the plane than it had been outside.

The left-side door swung open, and the fat man hauled himself up, settled with a grunt into the pilot's seat—closed his door, and reached under his butt to tug his parka-hem free. "Now, listen," he said, "I don't know what you have in that pack—" he turned in his seat to reach behind, touch a duffle bag wedged in front of a netted load of cardboard boxes. "But in here is a .308 and cartridges, pemmican bars, a good aid-kit, matches, and a sleeping bag." He leaned forward and touched a raised red-plastic square under the dash. "See this? Paying attention?"

"Yes," Sara said.

"I don't give a damn how much a sourdough anybody thinks they are. All my passengers get told about that duffle bag and this locator. We have trouble, land a little rough—and I'm not in a position to be helpful?—then you check this tell-tale. If it's blinking at you, then you just stay put by the plane; somebody'll be along sooner or later. If it isn't blinking, then you set up a camp, next morning you're on your own . . . stay with the aircraft, or try and walk out. Your choice. You understand that?"

"Yes."

"I don't give a damn how bushy anybody thinks they are. Far as I'm concerned, every passenger gets this little lecture. O.K.?"

"Fine."

"Now, I'd like that hundred bucks. Pilot's like a whore, wants to be paid up front. Day gas comes cheap, that'll be the day that won't be necessary."

Sara reached into her parka pocket, took out the roll of bills and slipped off the rubber band. She peeled off the ten tens, and handed them over.

"All right," the pilot said. "Now we're in business." He tucked the money into his shirt pocket, held out a plump right hand. "Jim Halsey."

Sara shook his hand, strong, but padded soft.

"You're not much of a talker," Halsey said. "—But that's all right. Less chance of an argument." He pulled a small clipboard down from his sunshade, ran a methodical checklist, lips moving as he read, and reached to flip switches, tap gauges as he went along.

"You were an airline pilot?" Sara was pleased at how easily she was talking to people, when she felt like it.

"That's right. —Delta. And military before that. I don't have much patience with the 'any-landing-you-walk-away-from' philosophy of bush piloting. I've been flying up here three years and I have had no accidents—none. Zero. Zip." He reached back for his safety harness, settled the straps over his shoulders, buckled up, and waited for Sara to do the same. "You got that tight?"

"Yes."

Halsey gripped the yoke, eased it forward and back—Sara saw his short, booted legs pumping on the rudder pedals. Then he leaned forward, pushed the starter, and listened with attention as the engine ground, the prop suddenly shifted, turned a half-circle . . . then turned and turned again as the engine spat, tripped, thundered and kept on—so much louder than the Bravo's—shaking the small ship. Sara put her hands over her ears, and saw Halsey glance at her before he looked out through the plane's windshield, gunned the engine, and drove the Cessna suddenly swinging out to the right, taxiing over the snow past the small hangar and out onto the level field and runway. Then he swung the ship again to the right, and got his line, the runway's dimming length leading into night.

Halsey reached down to his right to advance the throttle slightly. He sat listening to the engine for a few moments, watched his dials . . . then applied more power and allowed the Cessna to start with a slow, then faster, then gathering rush—let it go as Sara let her dog team go, allowed them to do what they did best—and the ship seemed to pay no more attention to what anyone wanted, as her dogs at running starts paid no attention, as she with Jack Joseph had paid no attention. The plane ran roaring along the snow, eager, shuddering, and soon shrugged gently, then shrugged again and lifted up into the air. Swayed in the wind, sailed on the wind it made for itself, rose over spruce trees sweeping in, then took a slow, slow curve up and out over the river, trembling to its engine. Steadied, then rose again, turning, turning as it climbed . . . and a thousand feet high, flew southwest into darkness, away from the country.

8

Sara'd remembered the odd serpentine outdoor lights, their steel supports painted rust pink, above the entrance to Fairbanks's airport. She'd forgotten the interior, its carpeting and long counters. It was as if she'd never been in the building, never known it full of people, and so noisy.

Halsey had said nothing more to her on the flight, hadn't mentioned her sitting for so long with her hands over her ears—that, and turning to look back. Looking back several times, as long as sunset still ran along the river, still showed the mountains so far behind them.

They'd landed in Fairbanks in lights on the far west runway—left snow-over-gravel for ski-planes—the fat man very alert, his earphones on, talking to the tower, listening, then talking to them again before he banked the plane left . . . banked more steeply . . . leveled off and flew the Cessna skimming just above the snow for a while, in no hurry. Then, flaring only slightly, settled it down to the slightest jolt, some shaking.

He'd taxied past dim ranks of parked small aircraft to a row of hangars as another prop plane, twin-engined, navigation lights winking in the dark, roared strenuously away behind them, taking off. Halsey'd spoken to the tower again, then turned off the runway onto an access ramp, traveled along it for a little way, then turned again to slide slowly into a parking bay and stop the engine. Silence had washed in over the engine's ticking while it cooled, soft creaking as the Cessna's metal settled into gravity. Then Sara'd seen a white van, parked behind the nearest shed, blink its lights.

"O.K.," Halsey'd said, unbuckling. "Out you get. Cut around to the terminal parking lot." He'd gestured, "—That way. Stay behind the fence, *off* the field."

Sara'd said "Good flight," opened her door, swung down, found the step notch and stepped to the ski, hurting her sore right ankle a little—then reached up to haul her pack out. She walked away through a warm night's soft snow—around the Cessna's tail, then along the dark front of a boarded-up one-story building. She could see the lights in the parking lot ahead . . . a wilderness of lights at the terminal, over to the left. Behind her, the soft mutter of the van's engine. —Come out to get the pot. Warmed in flight, the Cessna's small cabin had smelled green as summer with the crop from some boony weed farm, stored until the last months of winter raised the price. . . .

"Seattle coach one way is five hundred and thirty dollars. And I can get you on a plane leaving in a couple of hours. Anchorage, Vancouver, Seattle. Next departure would be . . . five o'clock in the morning. So you're lucky to get this one."

"That's expensive."

"Well, when you don't reserve a ticket, buy in advance, it does get more expensive."

The girl behind the counter was white, had a pleasant plump face and dark-blond hair cut shorter than Sara's. She was wearing a green uniform suit and a pale-pink blouse. She'd seemed surprised when Sara first came to the counter—had stared for an instant. Sara wasn't sure why; she'd showered at Bud LeBeck's. She was certainly clean. Her jeans and shirt weren't as clean as they should be, but not really dirty.

"They have gone up a lot. . . ." The girl stood poised over the ticket paperwork, waiting for Sara to make up her mind. "Plane'll be boarding in about an hour and a half."

"That's the cheapest?"

"Cheapest we've got, now." The girl smiled, being patient. There was no one in line behind Sara.

"Well, O.K. . . ." Sara took the money out of her parka pocket, pulled off the rubber band, and put the ticket money down in careful twenties, tens . . . then six fifties, one by one. 'Like an old lady in a grocery store,' she thought, but couldn't make herself count faster. She saw the girl looking at her fingertips, swollen and scabbed where the nails were gone.

"All right." The girl—she wore a small black-plastic badge with *Chris* engraved in white—seemed relieved to have the money, swiftly recounted it, and gave Sara her change. Sara supposed the green uniform had a short skirt. Some other women in the terminal were wearing short skirts.

"O.K." Chris made small notes on Sara's ticket. "Checking that backpack?"

"Yes."

"Boarding in about," she glanced up at a row of clocks, "one hour, twenty-five minutes. Gate Five. And I guess I should mention, some people come through with things. . . . You know, guns and ammunition and knives and stuff can't go aboard with you. Right?"

"I have a knife," Sara said.

"Well . . . tell you what, let's put it in the pack, O.K.?" She sounded as if she thought there was something wrong with Sara.

Sara searched her parka—found a small coil of light wire, a Chap Stick, a Guide Line compass and a sharpening stone in the left breast pocket . . . her match safe, bandanna, a cluster of safety pins and a candle stump in the right, and put them on the counter. Then took a twelve-gauge sabot shell from her lower left pocket, along with a Tampax, a small flattened roll of toilet paper, and a curved fur-needle stuck in a leather patch wound with dental floss for sewing.

"Oh, wow." Chris looked around to see if anyone had noticed. "Honey—the bullet's going to have to go. I don't know what we're going to do with the bullet."

"It's a shell," Sara said. "You keep it. Give it to somebody you know who hunts."

"No, no. You take it back and go and put it in the wastebasket in the rest room or something. I never saw it—right?"

"That's an expensive shell."

"You can't take it on the plane."

"All right." Sara emptied her lower right pocket, took out the Clipit, the roll of bills, a little round tin of powdered graphite, and a short piece of medium-tooth file. She had wire-cutter pliers in a hand-sewn belt sheath, and she took those out, too, and put everything on the counter. ". . . Lot of stuff," she said.

Chris nodded, agreeing it was a lot of stuff. "You know what? I think we ought to put everything that's metal in your pack, and just check it through. O.K.? We can just put everything in your pack except the bullet, and you keep this and your money and your handkerchief, O.K.?" Handed the Tampax, the roll of bills, and bandanna back, and watched while Sara stooped to set the pack upright on the rolled sleeping-bag bungeed to its bottom—then unzipped its long side pocket, tugged out her big brown-leather purse, and put the Tampax and her money away in that. She also took out a sandwich in a clear plastic bag, and put that in her purse as well. Then she took the wire, file, and knife—everything but the shotgun shell—and tucked them into the pack's various spaces, unzipping, unsnapping . . . then zipping and snapping shut.

"All done?"

"Yes."

"O.K. Put it up here on the scale." Chris wrote on a tag, tied it to the pack's left shoulder strap, tore the tag in two, and gave half to Sara. "And you're going to throw that bullet away, right?"

"It's a shell. —I will."

"O.K. Now, Flight 221, and Gate Five, and they're going to be boarding in about an hour and a half. Here's your ticket and pass—just give them to the stewardess."

"I've flown before," Sara said, putting those in her purse. "I may look odd, but I'm not an idiot."

"I don't think you look odd," Chris said.

"Well . . . good-bye."

"Good-bye, and have a real good flight."

Sara stood at the counter for a moment—Chris smiling at her—then nodded, turned and walked away, looking for the rest room.

She found it down the concourse and around a corner to the left, went in and saw a woman's leather boots under the near stall door. There was no one else there, so Sara started to put the shell in the wastebasket—then, worried someone might burn the trash and get hurt when the shell went off, put it down under a sink instead, against the wall. Anybody cleaning the floor would find it and see what it was.

She walked out into the terminal, then back around to the ticket counters so she could see the clocks. An hour and twenty more minutes. Two white women walked by, and one looked at her. She supposed her hair looked funny, badly cut. Pauline Demientieff had said it looked like a duck's ass. Sara saw there were no seats where she could watch the clocks, and decided she'd better buy a watch.

There was a small newsstand down the concourse. All the papers in the rack mentioned things she knew nothing about. . . . There was a small revolving stand with black plastic watches in it, digitals. A Native woman was behind the counter—a Chilkat, she looked like, her black hair braided.

"I'd like an inexpensive watch, please," Sara said.

The Chilkat woman—sturdy and small, wearing a white pullover sweater—stopped the display's revolving, and took two women's watches out of the back.

"How do you like it up here?" Sara said.

The woman shook her head. "Too damn cold. Too dry—hurts my nose. Which one you like?"

"Whichever's less."

"This one." The woman picked out the one with the smallest square face. "Want me to set it?"

"Please."

"I can set these things in my sleep." The woman pushed at the watch's side with quick blunt brown fingers.

"How much?"

"Eleven dollars an' thirty-seven cents. Get the same thing at Safeway for seven bucks."

"O.K." Sara opened her purse—was frightened for a moment she'd lost the roll of money, then found it in another compartment. She paid, took the change, and put the money away in the same side compartment. The purse was bigger than she needed; looked ridiculous.

"Here you go. . . ."

Sara put the watch on, saw she had more than an hour left, thanked the woman and walked back down the concourse. She sat in a blue plastic chair in the middle of a row of chairs, and watched the people going by. Almost all white. Two women wearing short skirts, high leather boots. Boots not good for anything serious.

She was struck by the absence of any animals except people. Every time some went by, she could smell them—a lot of perfume, and a slight monkey smell under that. They were talking and talking. . . . The men smelled like the women, and she saw several wearing earrings. Some of the people looked happy, some didn't. Two of them walking past—both men—had looked frightened. Sara supposed they were scared of flying.

There were too many white people to look at, it became disturbing, so Sara got up and walked to the rest room, went in, saw a very thin woman making up her face at the second sink—saw the shotgun shell still lying under the first sink. She went into a stall, hung her parka on the door hook, put her purse on the floor, and sat down on the toilet to wait in privacy. The toilet seat felt funny—its black plastic curved to fit a fatter butt. Sara closed her eyes, then put her hands over her ears so she couldn't hear anything, either.

In Seattle, she felt much better, but a little hungry. They'd been given a snack on the plane, cheese melted over tortilla chips. The chips were all right, but the cheese had smelled strange, so instead she'd eaten the sandwich LeBeck had made for her. Egg salad on store bread.

Except for being too warm—she had to carry her parka over her arm—the Seattle airport was all right. And after traveling with the odors and crowding in the plane (she'd sat on the aisle with her eyes closed, listening to Peter Nero over the earphones), the Seattle airport didn't seem to smell too bad. There was some cleaning chemical, the odors of paper and something else . . . and fading scents of crowds of people. The terminal was almost empty this late at night. She was getting used to people, anyway; didn't think everybody was looking at her.

The plane ride had felt odd at first, so different from flying bush—smoother, rushing through the dark. It was like skiing a steep slope all the way to Anchorage, then on down to Vancouver, then Seattle—down to each of those pretty patterns of lights, as if they were all downslope on one great mountain. At first flying so fast had seemed strange, then familiar. The people and their smells had bothered her more than flying.

Sara walked to a bank of phones. Her sprained ankle felt much better, hardly hurt at all. All the sitting had rested it. She used change out of the bottom of her purse, coins left over from buying the watch, and called information for Anne's number. The operator still had it listed under Connor Rittman.

"Hello?"

"Anne?"

"Who is this—and do you know what time it is?"

"It's Sara."

". . . Oh, my *God*. Are you in Fairbanks—or is this some call from the wilderness?"

"I'm in Seattle."

"Jesus Christ!"

"At the airport."

"I don't believe it. Sheena has come out of the jungle. An on-my-way phone call would have been nice."

"Well, I'm here."

"I'm glad, Sara. I'll be very happy to see big sister at long last. I mean it. —So, welcome back to the Emerald City, and I'll be right down to get you. Baggage claim?"

"O.K."

"Wait for me at baggage claim, and I'll be there in, oh, forty-five minutes . . . a little more; I've got to get dressed."

"O.K." Sara thought Anne might say something else, listened for a moment, then hung up.

She walked down the corridor to the right, and into a two-story space with a platform in the middle. There was a half-scale model of a Haida war canoe on display there, its polished planks decorated with glyphs of seal, walrus, and killer whale—the creatures taken apart, rearranged into folded and refolded black-painted designs with only eyes, fins, or teeth recognizable. The empty canoe seemed to be waiting for warriors and water.

There was a row of closed stores beyond that, and a cafeteria down on the right. The cafeteria was open, had melons and fruit displayed on cracked ice in a glass case. Had odd-looking brown carafes of coffee on a short counter. Sara stood for a little while, looking at the melon-slices and fruit, and a thin black girl wearing a white paper hat came behind the case and asked her if she wanted coffee.

"I'd like a piece of melon."

"If you come around the counter, I'll get it for you. You want honeydew or cantaloupe?"

"Could I have both?"

"Sure; you want somethin' to drink?"

"No."

The girl got a slice of each kind of melon from the case, put them on small plastic plates, and brought them to the counter. "That's two dollars, eighty." She took three dollars from Sara, stepped over to the cash register and made change. "There's silver an' napkins over on the servin' counter."

Sara took a cream-colored plastic fork and knife from metal bins, a paper napkin from a stack of napkins, then went to a small black-topped table with chairs at either side. She put her purse down on the table, her parka over the back of one chair, and sat down in the other. A man and woman, both middle-aged, both dressed in sweat-pants and shirts, were sitting at a table to her left. The man had a long sad face, reminded her a little of her father. His sweatpants and shirt were blue; the woman's were beige, with dark brown stripes down the sides of the pant legs. The woman was a little too heavy, Sara thought. Almost fat. A lot of the people she'd seen were fat—perhaps looked fatter and softer, being white.

Sara tried to eat the slice of honeydew melon with the plastic fork, but the fork was too fragile. Then she tried to cut the melon with the knife, and that worked but seemed a lot of trouble, so she picked the melon slice up and ate it to the rind. She'd intended to just take a bite, maybe two, then put it back down on the plate—but it tasted so startlingly good, so sweet and strange, that she ate it all in a hurry.

Then she picked up the slice of cantaloupe, and tried to take just one bite, but the taste of the honeydew was still in her mouth, and her first bite of the cantaloupe mingled with that so wonderfully tears came to her eyes, and she ate all that melon, too, without being able to put it down.

Sara finished, dabbed at her eyes with the napkin, then wiped her mouth. The woman sitting over to the left was watching her . . . probably thought she was crazy. That kept her from going back to the counter, asking the black girl for more melon. And an apple.

She stood, picked up her purse and parka, and when she walked past the couple's table, paused and said, "I'm not crazy. It's just been a long time since I ate melon." But the woman looked at her as if she were really crazy to have said that.

Sara went back through the passage, then to the right, following "Baggage Claim" arrows, and down two flights of an escalator. The escalator seemed stranger than anything else.

At the bottom of the second flight, she saw the bright steel baggage carousels, a blinking sign over the second one: Flight 221. She walked through an entrance in a low chrome-metal barrier, dug into her purse and found her baggage-claim ticket. There was luggage already coming around the carousel on sections of sheet steel that expanded and contracted, sliding into and under each other as they carried the luggage along. She'd forgotten how that worked. Other people stood waiting—two women very well dressed. Slacks . . . pretty sweaters and puffy nylon jackets. Eleven suitcases were traveling along, all colors, and a big khaki duffle bag. Her backpack wasn't there. After a long pause when there was nothing new on the carousel, a small blue suitcase came sliding onto it. Then, as if it had been waiting for Sara to arrive, to begin to worry, her pack suddenly came spilling down the chute. It toppled, its dark-green nylon torn and stained, then rocked almost upright, carried along.

When the pack got to her, Sara lifted it off the carousel, slung its left strap over her shoulder, then went back to the claim-area entrance and showed her receipt stub to a nice-looking old man in a gray uniform.

She looked for Anne, wondering if she'd spent too much time upstairs eating in the cafeteria. Anne could have come and gone. . . . There were a few people waiting in rows of plastic chairs. Sara saw a woman far down to the right, walking toward her, but it wasn't Anne; five years wasn't long enough to change her that much.

Sara took the pack off her shoulder, and went to sit at the end of the front row of chairs. Her heart was beating as if she'd been working hard, running behind the team.

She waited a longer time than she thought she'd be waiting—long enough to wish herself out of there, wish she'd stayed in Fairbanks, gotten a job. She could have rented a room and been left alone to think, at least for a few days. Or she could have gone to Montana . . . seen about a job with an outfitter, a guide, with nobody knowing anything about her.

She'd just thought about that when she saw Anne walking down to Baggage Claim.

Sara recognized her as she came, as if Annie were walking through years toward her, walking through time. Younger, almost a child . . . then swiftly a girl . . . a young woman . . . then older as she saw Sara, smiled and waved, a woman in her mid-thirties, her long light-brown hair—always two shades lighter than Sara's—coiled up into a French knot. Sara saw her sister had taken a little extra time to make up, dress well in a dark-gray wool skirt, a light-gray silk blouse, a silk scarf dark pumpkin under a beautiful trenchcoat—the coat, pearl-gray and worn open, almost a cloak. Anne had dressed as if she'd been afraid Sara had turned beautiful in her five years gone.

Anne walked faster, smiling, struck perhaps by the difference between them, how they looked—how crucial a little less nose, a slightly less bony face had been to make her pretty, leave Sara plain.

"Oh, God," Anne said, swept up to Sara in her coat's flowing fabric, put her arms out and embraced her, holding hard. Anne smelled of cigarette smoke, perfume—a rich odor of flowers. Gardenia. She let Sara go, stepped back. "What do you weigh? You don't weigh anything! And you're sunburned *brown*."

"Windburned," Sara said. "—Just weather. Just my face. . . ." She remembered Anne's eyes, so light a brown, almost their mother's hazel.

"Well, you look wonderful, really—in a kind of witchy elemental way."

"Anne, I look like shit."

"Well, a little bit like shit—but interesting." She leaned forward, held Sara lightly at the shoulders, and kissed her on the cheek.

"You look beautiful," Sara said, and thought of kissing Anne back, then thought they'd kissed enough. "How's Kevin?"

"Kevin's fine. Very smart, and a little spoiled. Child of divorce and so forth. —How was the flight? Did they feed you?" Anne's voice was exactly as Sara remembered it, various as an actress's. A full-bodied voice, richly individual even over the telephone.

"Yes, I had something to eat. It was fine."

"Where're your bags?" Anne looked at the pack. "Don't tell me. This is your bags."

"That's my bags."

Anne bent to pick the pack up, but Sara lifted it. "I'll take it. It's not heavy."

"O.K. . . ." Sara saw her sister make a small stirring motion with her hands, as if a bird were considering flight, easing its wings—and was surprised to remember that as notice Annie was uncertain, pausing to launch herself into slightly different social motion. "O.K. Greetings over. Well—let's go to the car!"

Sara felt she'd disappointed her sister, and—still missing the shotgun's weight—hoisted the pack onto her back and said, "I love you, Annie." But that was apparently the wrong thing to say, because her sister looked a little startled, said, "Me too," and turned to lead the way.

Sara, following—watching Anne stride along in slate-gray high heels—supposed she should just have said, 'It's wonderful to see you. You look lovely.'

That wouldn't have surprised her sister. It would have pleased her, made her happier to see Sara. Wouldn't have been a lie, either.

Anne led back to the escalators, up two flights, then turned left to go through a high bridge passage, out double doors, and into the parking garage—Sara remembering coming that way years before. The garage, smelling of wet concrete, was a forest of square concrete pillars under a low-beamed concrete roof. Sara recalled it, the top of several levels. Here was almost outside air, better than the terminal's but damp and too warm—forty above, maybe warmer.

Anne turned right, away from a large C-3 in faded yellow paint down a pillar . . . walked before Sara along a street-wide aisle, and stopped at the tailgate of a maroon station wagon, snapped open her purse for her keys.

"Mercedes, of course," she said, found her keys and opened the tailgate. "A remnant of past glories."

"It's a beautiful car," Sara said, swung her pack off her shoulder, and put it in; put her purse in, too. The gray carpeting in the car's interior looked soft enough to sleep on.

Anne pulled the tailgate down as Sara stepped back. "Not so

beautiful after you've spent three hundred dollars for a new taillight. Believe me, this overpriced object gets less and less beautiful the broker you are."

The road from the airport was wet with fallen rain, and reflected from shining black every color of light along it—gleamed brightest where the Mercedes' headlights struck it just ahead. The car's interior, heated too warm, smelled sweetly of tanned leather. Sara stroked the upholstery with her fingertips—a chemical cure, and pieced cowhides stretched before and after, machine-scraped and roller-dyed. The seats were comfortable, though so soft, and everything—the dash, controls, and glove compartment—looked nicely rounded in dim light. It was a fine car, but it seemed to Sara that Anne was driving it too fast.

"Sara, the first thing I have to say—need to say—is apologize for sending you what I'm afraid was a very asinine letter. Did you get my letters?"

"Got two. . . . Fast car."

"—That's all I sent, thank God. And sis, I have to apologize for the second one. I think it was the second one; I was not terribly together at the time. I was in such deep shit I didn't care about you losing Alan or anything else. And I wasn't . . . I didn't react properly to that ghastly tragedy. Problem being, it has a dreadful humorous thing about it, too. 'Eaten by a bear.' It has this grimly humorous ring. —I haven't been able to tell some of my friends what happened. I told Jennifer that your husband had been killed by a grizzly up in Alaska, and she understood that. God-awful. But if I'd said he was eaten by a bear, she would have laughed. Well, Jennifer'd laugh at anything, if it wasn't her precious Chinese ass in a sling. Do you understand?"

"I understand. I know it sounds funny down here."

"Not funny. A little odd, like something out of a fairy tale. One of the original versions."

"I know."

"But I didn't tell you, and I should have told you in that damn letter that it nearly killed me to think of you finding a nice man who loved you, and then seeing that terrible thing happen. Because the Reverend Whoozis said you were right there and saw it. You were up in a tree or something."

"I was up in the cache."

"—Up somewhere. I looked at pictures of grizzly bears at Waldens, on the Nature rack? And I imagined it, and it gave me the shakes. Anyway, I'm very sorry, sweetheart." Anne took her right hand off the wheel, reached over and stroked Sara's cheek, then put her hand back on the wheel. "It was such an awful thing. Are you down here to stay?—I hope to God."

"For two or three weeks, anyway."

"Shit. *Weeks?* And you've been gone for five years. Five! —Well, that'll be a big help. That's just great."

"I thought I'd go out to Montana—"

"Oh fabulous, recreate our wonderful childhood on the Bow Tie. Eight thousand acres leased—two hundred owned. Sara, the ranch is long gone; some other guy is ruining his back on that land just like Daddy did. The ranch was great—for kids. But what the hell are you going to do out there now? You don't have any money, do you? Well, I know you don't have any money. . . . So what are you going to do out there? Wait on tables in some café in Pronghorn, and hope Mister Miracle is going to come bowlegging in the door? Order steak, eggs, and you? Take you out to some hundred-thousand-acre paradise where there's an Indian woman to do the shit work?"

"No. I thought I'd get a job with an elk hunter, a hunting guide. Cook and wrangle until I earned enough money to set up my own outfit."

"Jesus H. Christ." Anne steered left into another lane, passed a small black car going slower.

"I'm a very good hunter. Two years, I was the one who got our meat. Both years, I got young bulls down along the river. We butchered there, and cached the meat to freeze—then when the snow was right, we'd take the dogs down and sled the meat up the mountain. Eleven, twelve hundred pounds, two three-day trips."

"Sweetheart, very impressive. I'm sure you're a wonderful hunter."

"A lot of women hunt. They might like going out with another woman, instead of a man."

"Sis, if you think women would rather go hunting with you than some good-looking leathery 'I can handle anything' guy with great bones and probably a huge dick, you have been up in those north woods way too long."

"Well . . . then I'll hire a handsome cowboy to come along. He can wrangle."

"And cook?"

"That's right."

"Good luck."

". . . I think I could do it." A swift spatter of rain struck the windshield, then the wipers thrashed it away. No more fell.

"Sara—why the hell do I have to be the big sister when you're the big sister? Sweetheart, I'm sure you can do it; you can do just about anything you want to do. I'm really not quite such a jackass I don't have some idea what it takes to live the way you lived up there for all those years. —What I'm asking is, does doing that make sense?"

"It does for me."

"That's great, for you. Leaves me in the shit, but it's great for you. I was the one who watched Dad go—now I'm elected for this one, too."

"Anne, if you need me, I'll stay."

"What I need is money." After saying that, Anne drove awhile in silence. Sara, glancing over, saw in the glow of a passing car's headlights a trace of pale down along her sister's upper lip before the dark returned, then saw Annie's face soft as a child's, heard her voice—when, insistent, she'd come walking along the back porch to follow when Sara went out to feed the chickens. Sturdy, small in small blue-jean overalls, determined to trail after. That was the first time Sara'd felt a sudden love for this creature—as if her bones, recognizing sister bones at last, had halted her, forced her to wait for Annie . . . suggested she bend and hug her, take her hand and lead her out into the yard and past the pony pen to feed Hannah and Citrine and all the others, so long gone, little feathered chicken ghosts. . . .

Sara, sitting beside her sister, found that Anne—through the car's odors of plastic and tanned leather—smelled slightly like a monkey, scented floral.

She found the button to lower her window, brought the glass down slightly, and sat breathing in warm damp rushing air smelling of rain, engine oil, and gasoline . . . while other cars sped beside them, surged away or fell back, all shining under backward-racing lights along the concrete vaulting. Warm, wet air, many degrees above freezing.

Then the car slowed a little, shouldered to the left, and fled down a dark curving ramp, its tires sizzling on wet pavement, its headlight beams barely staying ahead.

"We moved out to the Island, you know." Anne's profile was outlined in light as she drove off the ramp and slid into another stream of traffic moving swiftly as the first. "—If you can believe that. It's wonderful what a really creepy CPA can make, working for other creeps."

"Traffic." A big white pickup truck was running up close along-side them on the right.

"Yes, indeed. You're looking at twenty-four-hour-a-day traffic right here in Emerald City, thanks to I-5 and a horde of Califor-nians."

The white pickup had dark tinted windows. Sara couldn't see the driver.

"—I am at long last on Mercer Island, and I have a big beautiful brick-and-cedar house on a pond, and it's a white elephant that's eating me alive. I owe for half the goddamned payments! And I am *not* a creepy CPA like the swine I was married to—who undervalued his holdings for the divorce and community property, and now, *now* has suddenly started earning a fucking fortune. Which I think and Charles Guttfreund thinks (he's my lawyer—was my lawyer in that mess), which we think was very carefully planned by Connor and his buddies. 'I helped you screw your wife—you help me screw my wife.' The cash held for him by his crooked friends in return for CD interest. Isn't that nice? And try and prove it in court. Good luck."

"Annie, doesn't he owe child support?" The white pickup was moving ahead, passing them.

"Oh, yes. I get child support—from a trust fund established for Kevin."

There was a dog standing in the bed of the pickup, an old golden retriever balancing with the truck's swift motion.

"—Specified amounts at specified intervals, and all disbursements to be fucking accounted for. And why? Because I had to go for counseling, some treatment two years ago—and three days in the hospital."

The old dog was wet from rain the truck had run through. He was too old to be riding out in the pickup bed.

"—Connor told me to go for counseling because I was so unhappy I wanted to fucking die. I told him I would just as soon kill myself as go on the way things were. So . . . 'Go get some counseling, *honey.*' Gave me the doctor's name, gave me everything. . . .'"

Sara put her window down all the way, looked out through blow-ing wet wind, and smiled at the old dog. Braced against motion, he looked back at her as the truck pulled ahead . . . then out of sight into a lane to the right.

"—And guess what his lawyer told the judge at the support hear-ing. 'Suicidal tendencies, markedly unstable, two years of counsel-ing. . . .'"

Sara put her window up almost all the way.

" '—Some control, your honor, a modicum of control over the funds would seem to be indicated, for the child's welfare.' Do you believe that? Do you believe it?" Anne turned to look at Sara, eyes off the road, waiting for an answer. Sara saw, by passing sulfur light, a tear bright as jewelry on her sister's cheek.

"Yes," Sara said, "—I believe it," so Anne would turn back to her driving. There were skyscrapers off to the left, rising into the night. They reminded Sara of mountains, but much too small, and lit with occasional lights. Without the dignity of darkness.

"—My last complaint, then I'll shut up about the whole thing. My very last complaint is he waited . . . he waited until he knew Mother was going to be a complete invalid. A complete—wait till you see her. You're going to be shocked, so just start bracing yourself. This isn't like that little fall she had when you came in from Butte to see her, and she'd bruised her hip. This isn't like that at all, so brace yourself. Tomorrow's Sunday; we'll go over in the morning. I don't let Kevin go, anymore."

"You wrote me it was benign! I got that letter at Fort Billy beginning of last year."

"*Benign.* Listen, you are damned lucky you were up in the Arctic or wherever the last five years. Five *years.* . . . You were very smart to get the hell out, because that left me holding the shitty end of the stick with Mom. The tumor didn't grow at all for months, and I thought, 'Well, thank God, not as bad as they'd told us.' Then it started growing again and they operated once, an exploratory, nine months ago—and they put a bead in her head and that was it. 'Additional surgery is contraindicated,' etcetera. 'It would kill her,' etcetera. —What the hell do they think that so-called benign tumor is doing? It's just doing it slower, that's all. And at very great expense. A radioactive bead stuck in her head and bombardment with neutrons or neutrinos and everything else in the kitchen sink. . . . Well, Connor must have smelled something coming down when she first started to have really bad headaches, have more trouble talking. Then, when she'd really had it, when the bills came in for Long Term, he just bailed out."

"You should have let me know before it got so bad."

"Mom didn't want me to write to you about it. She didn't want anybody to know. She was angry *I* knew. —It was a weakness, a serious illness. Couldn't have that; didn't want anybody to know *that.* Besides which, I've got to tell you, writing to you, trying to get in touch with you—why you didn't even have a radio up there I will never understand—trying to get in touch with you was weeks of effort, and frankly, I just said fuck it."

It seemed to Sara that Anne stepped on the gas for emphasis; the car went faster.

"—Anyway, Connor waited for the really bad news. He waited for that. Mom's house sold—she couldn't stay there alone, anyway—and most of her money gone to those bloodsucking doctors. I do not understand what Medicare is supposed to *do*. So, Mom winds up stuck in a wheelchair in that Pine-Sol hell for three thousand a month. By then, Sir Galahad had taken off." Anne reached down to punch in the dashboard lighter, used the same hand to search blindly into her purse beside her as she drove . . . found cigarettes, shook one out of the pack, tucked the pack back in, and was ready when the lighter knob clicked out, its coil-tip scarlet as she lifted it to light her cigarette. "And don't talk to me about smoking," she said. "I get remarks from every earnest jackass everywhere. The women are the worst."

"It all doesn't sound like Connor. I always thought he was crazy about you, Annie."

"He was, he was! I hung the fucking moon for Connor. I was his sophisticated M.A., his class broad, his *lady*. He ate me up in bed; that man would screw me and cry with pleasure. —You believe that?"

"Yes."

"Well, you can believe it—it's true. And he *liked* me; he wrote a poem to my goddamned boobs. And in that same poem he said he loved my spirit even more! And we're talking about an accountant. If that isn't love, then what the fuck is love?" She reached down, pulled the dash ashtray out and tapped the ash off her cigarette. "So, if you think that helps—knowing he was crazy about me, and that can change so fast. It doesn't help."

"Not all men are like that."

"Oh hey, sis, that's so helpful. So . . . that's so original. Now, let me tell you something—and I'm not going to go on and on with this—I have said zip about it to Kevin. As far as Kevin is concerned, Connor is King of The Accountants and a great guy who, unfortunately, got stuck with me—a bitch—and has now found a sweet, sweet girl. Young. A fabulous cunt. (To the vision of which, I'm sure, Kevin jerks off like crazy.) And this leaves me being the Wicked Witch of the West and a total pain in the ass who's always working in the store or making very healthy breakfasts with bran muffins and wheat germ on his cereal and all that vile-tasting shit on Saturdays when Kevin just wants to have pancakes and sausage and get out and be with his friends. I have become a goddamned caricature." Anne braked the Mercedes, said, "Go on, cut right in, asshole! . . . And twice a month, sometimes *three times* a month, the great man pulls up in his BMW convertible with, you guessed it, young, *young* Miss Cunt by his side, dressed in breezy flowing Laura Ashley crap—to take Kevin to a basketball game and a big dinner with lots of pork chops and ice cream and whatever he wants (so he'll weigh a ton and die of a heart attack when he's thirty-five). After which, they deposit him in front of the white elephant, and go zooming off. . . . The good father. The wonderful father."

"I'm sorry."

"You should be—you don't know how lucky you are. At least your husband loved you. Alan loved you; he didn't want to leave you. He was killed; he didn't just slowly change into some huge nasty adolescent with a lot of money, and then walk out on you. I am thirty-five years old. Is that a fucking crime? Only thirty-*five*. That's young! It isn't as though I were forty; Jesus, that would be unforgivable. Thank Christ I wasn't forty; he would have had me committed."

"You look very young, Annie," Sara said. "You're young enough to meet a terrific man, have a life of your own. You have no problem with looks."

"Sure, the family beauty, right?" She leaned to tap more ash away. "Listen, you're an interesting-looking woman. —Don't laugh; you are. And as far as terrific men go, if you knew what was out there . . ." She steered down another exit ramp, lit aquarium-green, and drove onto a wide street that swiftly narrowed, declined, and dipped near the lake shore into a tunnel lined with yellow lights sliding by as they traveled.

"So, there hasn't been anybody since Connor?"

"Nobody I could bear to even listen to, let alone have climb on top of me, naked. And you? Nobody since Alan died? None of those big, bearded Alaskan guys, can build a cabin with a jackknife and so forth?"

". . . No big, bearded Alaskan guy."

"Oh, speaking of sex, two women approached my salesgirl, Marie—we're talking about two *straight* women, one of them supposedly a stock analyst—approached Marie and asked if she'd be interested in masturbating with them."

"I don't believe that," Sara said.

"A damn vibrator group! Believe it, big sister. Does that give you some idea of the supply of eligible males? Of decent *men?* Marie doesn't know, but she thinks they rent a video of Mickey Rourke or somebody and have some Chablis and talk about their problems and just buzz off together in the living room."

"I don't believe it."

The station wagon surged up out of the tunnel, ran along a highway that first curved swiftly right, then straightened to become the floating bridge. Lake Washington shone softly black on both sides of them. Lights on the island ahead were reflected in shifting uneven lines, pale yellow, pale green across the water, broken where the lake moved against the shore. The moon—riding high—was smaller, less radiant than it had shone in northern mountains. Sara could see its track wavering across the water.

Anne, silent, leaned forward to stub her cigarette out in the ashtray, then settled to her driving, intent as they crossed the long bridge and took the exit off it, right, onto West Mercer Way. She drove down that narrow winding road much more slowly, still in silence. Sara, grateful for less speed, for quiet, sat watching the long dreamy side-slipping parade of hedges, road signs, plum trees and house corners into and out of the headlight beams. The plum trees were already, at the end of February, foaming softly pink in early blossom. . . . After a while, Anne turned left. Sara saw "SE 72nd Street" on the corner sign.

Anne drove two blocks, then along a high fence, and turned right and up into a shadowy neighborhood of houses looking almost alike, and standing very close together—big two-story houses, clapboard and brick, their entrances deep-shadowed. Some houses had three-car garages and rows of dormer windows on their second floors, and all of them looked new, were built on small lots neatly landscaped with shrubbery and small trees showing dull yellow-green under the streetlights. As they drove along a slow-curving road, Sara saw moonlight shining on water behind a house.

"Are they on a creek?"

"No. Ponds. I think they dammed a stream into ponds—miniature spillways and everything. That part's all right, if I didn't have to help pay for it." Anne took her left hand off the wheel, gestured to the left. "Kevin's school is right over there. —This place is called The Lakes. Ponds, is what they mean."

"It's really nice." Sara could smell grass . . . and the trees. This smelled better than any place had since she'd traveled to Chancy.

"You mean it looks expensive—and you're right. It's too damn expensive. But Connor said we were moving up . . . and we moved up."

Anne pulled over to the left, turned up into a wide driveway, and stopped. The house was big—angled across and to the right of the drive. It seemed to Sara to show more pale clapboard than some of the others. The brickwork at the entrance looked very fine, even in shadow. There was a small amber coach lantern lit over the front door.

Anne turned off the car's engine and headlights, and sat looking at the house with Sara as if she hadn't seen it in a while. "What you have here," she said, "—is a five-hundred-thousand-dollar house, with almost three-hundred-thousand still to pay on the note. And the problem is that I've got to come up with half that monthly payment, or lose it. And another problem is, the market shits right now—so I can't sell it without taking a loss I can't afford to take. I am spending every dime of my so-called half of our community property. I'm spending *more* than every dime. I have this fucking house— that Kevin loves, that is the only evidence at all that I have achieved anything on this earth . . . and I have the store."

Anne reached up to her sunshade, took down a small brown-plastic garage opener, and pressed its top three times. The nearest of three garage doors slowly rose, revealed a lit white-painted space— empty except for three long shelves of cardboard cartons along its right side—then slid up and back, out of the way.

Anne started the car and drove up onto spotted cement, stopped, turned the engine off, and pressed the brown-plastic remote control to lower the garage door behind them. "Home sweet home," she said, picked up her purse, and they both got out.

Sara, tired of riding on machines and in machines, felt better standing on her feet. The other two garage bays were empty except for a row of gardening tools on the far wall. The wide space smelled of cement. When Anne opened the back of the station wagon, Sara reached in, pulled her pack and purse to her, and slung the pack's right strap over her shoulder. "Anne—you sure it won't be inconvenient to have me here?"

"You must be kidding." Anne closed the tailgate, walked across the garage to steps and a door. "We have four bedrooms in this house. Four bedrooms, three and a half baths, and so on and so forth. Of course it isn't inconvenient—you're my damn *family.*"

She went up the steps, unlocked the door, and led Sara down a blue-carpeted hall with a big laundry room off it to the left. The house was very warm. Anne turned the lights on in a kitchen.

The kitchen was very large, with cream-painted walls and a blue-tiled floor. A U of counters and white cabinets curved around a central serving island and cook-top; tall white-upholstered bar stools with backs and padded arms were ranked around the island. The kitchen's counters were surfaced with what looked like light-gray marble, and were interrupted by a big stainless-steel refrigerator with two doors, and a stainless double sink beneath a wide window with white café curtains across it. It looked like a kitchen in a magazine, a kitchen no one had ever cooked in.

"Annie—this is a hell of a kitchen. . . ."

"This is nothing." Anne took her fine trench coat off, draped it over one of the upholstered stools. "—Wait till you see the rest of the elephant. Debt city, but fabulous. Come on upstairs . . . get you settled."

Sara followed, noticing her sister's fine ankles in the gray high heels, her legs' delicate curves in dark stockings. It struck her how decorated the women were down here—Anne, and some of the women at the airport—everything arched and strained, slippery and smooth, as if anywhere a man might look or touch, that look or touch would slide up or down to the woman's sex and be stuck there. Watching Anne walk, thinking of the other women down here, Sara was surprised Jack Joseph had wanted to do what he did with her—windburned and so plain, thin, and smelling of dogs. She thought Jack Joseph must have been desperate. . . .

They walked through a formal dining room, walls painted ivory—the ceiling at least twelve feet high, a chandelier hanging from it made of slender concentric curves of bright brass circling wide above the table, each holding a descending row of little candle bulbs above small crystal lusters. The dining-room table, its wood a deep reddish brown, apparently mahogany, was a long oval, centered with a crystal bowl. The chairs and a tall dish cabinet behind the table were made of the same richly polished wood.

Anne's heels clicked on into the entrance hall, its walls the same ivory, but two stories high, and floored with marble—white, streaked with chocolate. The staircase curved up to a landing, then up again to the second floor. There was a room across the hall, dark through open sliding double doors, and above the front door, a large rose window (leaded glass) was lit by the amber coach light shining through from outside.

"Cool?" Anne said, stopped and turned slowly on her heel, smiling at Sara. "Well, maybe not cool—but classy?"

"Classy."

"Back hall goes to half-bath, den, Florida room, and back door. In there," she nodded to the open double doors, "—living room, and TV room behind that."

"It's beautiful, Annie."

"You think I was kidding about this house? We're talking about a major show-off piece. Even if I can't afford the son of a bitch, and it's breaking me and I'm going to have to sell it as soon as some idiot makes an offer, I still like to show it off. It's such a *long* way from the South Side. —All gas, thank God; I couldn't afford electric heat." She started up the stairs. "Don't worry about waking Kevin; he's a major sleeper, and his room's down at the end of the hall, anyway."

There was a window arch looking out from the landing. Sara could see a pond's curving black margin just behind the house, across a narrow lawn.

The second-floor hall was carpeted in light beige, the walls painted a lighter color than downstairs, barely off-white. "—Master suite over here on the left; guest room (your room) there on the right, and the spare room and Kevin's down the hall. You have your own bath." She opened the guest-room door, and Sara followed her in, waited just inside the doorway while Anne turned on a bedside lamp.

The guest room was slightly larger inside than the mountain cabin. There was a wide window past two big beds side by side on the right. The beds, an ivory lamp table between them, had white tufted coverlets and low curving white headboards. The bedroom's walls were papered with a small print of trellised roses, and the carpet was pale green.

"What do you think?"

"It's like the house. It's very nice." There was a small watercolor seascape on the wall above each bed.

"Too damn much, is what you mean."

"No; it's beautiful." A lowboy dresser and a vanity with six drawers and a mirror stood against the far wall, with a white bentwood rocking chair between them. There were cut-glass bottles on the vanity.

Anne walked back through a doorway, turned on the bathroom light, and came out. "And the closet's over there by the dresser. . . . Sis, put the pack down. Don't look so damn ready to run. You're staying here, O.K.?"

"O.K." Sara put the backpack down on the rocking chair. Put her brown leather purse on the dresser. The room smelled of wool, and a chemical—two different chemicals.

"Why don't you settle in, pee or whatever, and come down to the kitchen. I know it's late; I know it's the middle of the night, but maybe we could have some decaf or something, just visit. . . ."

"O.K."

Anne smiled at Sara, went out the door, closed it behind her— then opened it again, put her head in. "Have I shut up since you arrived?"

"Not for long."

"Right. That's what I thought," Anne said. "I was nervous." She pulled her head back, shut the door again, and called through it, "*See you downstairs.*"

Sara stood in the room, wishing she could stay there, not go back down. She didn't feel like peeing, but it would be odd to just leave the room right after Anne had gone, follow her down the stairs. It seemed there should be a pause, just a few minutes before they saw each other again.

She walked over past the beds, opened the window—it swung out to the right when she turned an angled handle—and looked outside onto a wide shelf of roof, sloping slightly down to gutters. Beyond, at the foot of the lot, the pond shone darkly by moonlight.

The view through the window didn't look like real out-of-doors. It looked as though someone had built it—as if it were more house, without a roof.

Sara stood and looked out, then checked her watch. It read 3:13 A.M. She'd lost an hour coming down; had spent a lot of time on the plane pushing buttons, getting it reset. She sat on the bed beside the window, and waited. When the watch read 3:18 A.M. she thought it was all right to go downstairs.

"Instant decaf O.K.? Or I've got real coffee, or you can have tea— we've got Constant Comment and Zinger. Irish Breakfast, too."

"Instant's fine." Sara, sitting at the island on one of the tall white-upholstered stools, swiveled a little, left to right, then back again.

Anne took a small lead-colored pot from a cabinet beneath the counter, filled it with water at the sink, then brought it over to the island and set it on a front burner. She turned the burner on and up to high. "You must think I'm the jackass of the world."

"No, I don't."

"Oh, yes you do—you have to. I meet you at the airport, and I'm too damn self-involved to let you know how wonderful . . . what a relief it is to see you. I'm probably the only younger sister on earth who really, really loved her older sister. And I still do—and I was so glad to see you, and then I gave you that ridiculous social hug, and I wanted to cry and I couldn't even do that."

"We were both a little nervous."

"And you just lost your husband—a terrific guy, probably—and I spent the entire drive home, complaining."

"I didn't mind. . . . I love you, Annie. I've loved you since you were five."

"Not before that?"

"Before that, I wished you'd fall in the well."

Anne went to a section of counter beside the curtained window, reached up and tapped a white cabinet door. The door swung open and she took down two white mugs decorated with designs in black. "You're sure instant's all right? I've got real coffee. I could make real coffee."

"No. That'll be fine." Sara touched the smooth countertop surface. Seen this close, the gray was subtly accented by swirling irregular darker-gray patterns drifting through. "—Is this marble?"

"No—it's almost-marble, and almost as expensive." Anne reached up to a different cabinet, tapped it open, and took down a white sugar bowl and a large green-labeled jar of instant coffee. She brought those over, set them on the counter by Sara, then went to the refrigerator and opened its left-side door. "You want a sandwich? Piece of pie?"

"No. Nothing, thanks."

"Fabulous apple pie."

"No, thanks."

"There are some people—friends of mine, you don't know them—who'd really like to meet you. And I don't mean setting you up with a guy; I'm just talking about a dinner get-together."

"I'd rather not. . . ."

"Sara, you cannot shy your way through life."

"Maybe later."

"Maybe never. —O.K." Anne took out a half-gallon carton of milk and closed the refrigerator door. "You probably could use a drink, but Connor cleaned out the den bar, and I'll tell you . . . I bought just one bottle of Smirnoff, and I finished that in about three days and a little voice told me not to get any more booze, to just forget about it."

"I don't want anything. —Annie, I don't mean to be such a stiff. I'm just not used to people."

"Well, you have been a stiff." Anne put the milk down on the island counter, then sat on the stool beside Sara's, took the lid off the jar of coffee, and put a spoonful in each mug. "You've been a stiff, and I've done nothing but whine, so we're even. Poor sis, flies down here out of that frozen wilderness for long-postponed get-together, and is greeted by rage and fulmination."

"You had some rage and fulmination coming. You're the one who's been dealing with a divorce . . . Mom's illness." The bar stool's seat was very comfortable, but the pale padded arms seemed to close Sara in. She leaned forward and rested her arms on the countertop. Its surface was cool, but not as cool as marble would have been.

"Well . . ." Anne reached over to turn off the burner, then lifted the pot and poured hot water into the mugs. "—a sympathetic ear is what I've been waiting for. And of course, what really scares me is I could have just driven him away. Maybe it was me. Maybe I changed, or I was always a complaining stuck-up bitch and he just had enough. Have some sugar; this stuff needs sugar. Anyway, I wish I knew if that was true or not—milk? I do know everybody's tired of hearing me go on and on about it."

"No milk."

"I mean, half the women in Seattle are raising their kids alone, and everybody's tired of hearing about it. Now you come down, and I've got a fresh listener."

"I'm glad to listen, Annie. I know you're in trouble." Sara saw the black designs on the mugs were wading herons, their slender necks perfect S's, their legs prancing, angled and elegant. Around each lower leg, a delicate indication of water, concentric circles of fine black lines.

"I'm in trouble—and I *am* trouble. You know, except for arithmetic, Connor's really very lazy. I was amazed he put out all this effort just to get rid of me."

"Maybe he fell in love, Annie. Even accountants do that." The coffee didn't taste as good as Mary Toby's. A different instant.

"Well, you don't know how lazy he is. And fall in love with that? We are talking about the young whore of the world. She's an assistant hygienist, for Christ's sake! A smiling, vacuous pussy—looks as if any man stuck his finger in her navel, she'd fall on her back instantly, skirt up and legs apart so fast her shoes would fly off."

"Must be something more than that. . . . I'll have some milk."

"Here. Coffee's terrible, right? —I'm probably the 'something more.' Connor wasn't simpatico, but he was always sort of sweet, so I have a sinister feeling I was the 'something more.' And I've just now been demonstrating exactly what I'm talking about by babbling on about my shit when I haven't seen you for five goddamned years, and you just lost your husband up there miles away from anything. I would have gone crazy and still be wandering around in the woods."

"And you haven't met anyone you like?"

"Hell, no." Anne sipped her coffee. "Not wonderful coffee. —No, I just crotch-watch and daydream. Who'd want a spoiled and furious bitch with a thirteen-year-old boy? Would you, if you were a man? Would anybody?"

"I think you're beautiful. I think a lot of men would want you."

"Want the bod, maybe, for a few more years. Want the package? Never. . . . And there hasn't been anybody for you, nobody you even think about?"

"Nothing serious."

" 'Nothing serious.' Are we talking . . . like one dance, one conversation, one smile or something?"

"Something like that. That's about it."

"What's so funny?"

"Nothing."

"And no future?"

"No future."

Anne sipped her coffee, then put her mug down and poured in a little more milk. "If it wasn't the middle of the night, I'd wake Kevin. He's looking forward to seeing you—stories of the Alaskan bush and wolves and everything by a sourdough trapper and so forth—"

"By a real weird old aunt."

"Bullshit. Although of course, he's very very cool. Middle-school cool. —What in God's name happened to your hands?"

"Nothing. I broke a finger a few months ago."

"*Nothing?* Your nails are gone!"

"I lost a couple of nails sliding on the ice."

"Sliding for fun?"

"No, it was an accident."

"I guess they'll grow back. . . ."

"They'll grow back. —I remember Kevin playing cool when he was eight."

"Same kid. Other people think he's rude, and sometimes I suppose he is. I guess I spoil him."

"I'm sure he's O.K., Annie. You've always been a very good mother. I don't know anything about raising kids, anyway. I know *about* kids, from teaching. And I know about dogs."

"Well, I think the main difference is, kids potty-train. You and Alan didn't want to try?"

"Oh, we were talking about it. You know, just talking. I think we would have had a child."

"And now you wish you had?"

"I don't know."

"And you still miss him."

"I miss him," Sara said. "But more some times than other times. I don't mind being alone."

"Would you tell me something? Just curious. What was he like? I'm just curious; I mean you married the guy. What was he—was he handsome . . . what?"

"He was a nice-looking man. You'd notice Alan, even with other people around. He was short, stocky, very strong. He wore coveralls a lot—I always thought he looked like a handsome mechanic who just comes out to work on your car, and you realize he's very nice. He had red hair, short red beard—I trimmed it short. He had white skin, very white skin. And he was quiet for a lot of the time. Had a soft voice. He never raised his voice—almost never. Blue eyes, very bright blue eyes, always looking at everything. Very energetic—"

"And in bed, I hope. —You're not drinking that coffee."

"It's fine, really. I'm drinking it. —In bed . . . energetic. Alan was a very directed person, the way he dealt with things. He was interested in wilderness living; he thought that was the only decent way to live. Very directed that way."

"And he loved you."

"He loved me, and he trusted me. . . ."

"Would he have loved you no matter what? Would he have come down here and lived with you, if you had to come down? If you had a baby and it was sick or something?"

"He would have come down, but he wouldn't have stayed for long."

"You mean like 'for two or three weeks.'"

"Annie, I didn't mean I didn't want to see you—"

"You just don't want to see us for too long."

"No. It's everything else, all the people and everything."

"And Alan liked you—*liked* you? You were best friends?"

"Yes, we were. There were things I didn't like. He always knew the best way to do things. Got a little pompous, sometimes."

"That's all of them; believe me. It's just a male thing."

"I know. But, except for that, we were best friends."

"And you loved him."

"I did love him. I respected him."

"Well," Anne took a sip of her coffee, made a face. "—then you lost a lot. It's harder to respect them, than love them."

They sat side by side in silence for a while, Sara still surprised at all the things she could smell—Anne's perfume (fading gardenia, now) along with the odor of her skin, and cigarette smoke. The coffee, and kitchen odors; the kitchen smelled of ammonia. Sara hoped she'd be able to smell less as time went by. ". . . Tell me about Mom."

"Just what I said. They say it's a very slow-growing tumor. It's benign—won't metastasize—and it began above the brain stem, and it's growing out, and it's slowly crushing the rest of her brain—and it will definitely do that. Will kill her. They put a radiation pellet in there about nine months ago, and she wasn't that bad then. Just headaches, and she'd get dizzy. Said she didn't want you coming down, said it wasn't that big a deal, because they thought the radiation might stop it from growing. But it hasn't, and the last few months it did grow and it's just destroying her, is what's happening."

"Oh, Annie . . ."

"And of course, the hospital didn't want her to stay—can't have a dying woman hanging around a *hospital*. No, no, a 'long-term facility.' They just transferred her right out, and if the nursing home doesn't monitor the medication perfectly day-to-day—tough titty. And this tumor can grow very slowly. Doctor Cherkin says maybe even another year. The thing can grow faster, or much slower. The problem is, the more they try to slow it down, the longer it will take to kill her. Toward the end, it may push her eyes right out of her head." Anne drank some coffee. "Can you imagine something like that? Can you imagine that?" Anne's eyes, light butterscotch, were wide with fright as a child's.

"The doctors are absolutely sure?"

"There are basically two doctors, now. And she's been to four—five, really. And they're sure."

"And Mama knows all about it?"

"You'll see. Now, I don't know what she knows. She can't talk very well, anymore—at least not until she warms up. If she's interested, after a while she can manage to speak all right. Then, next thing you know, when she gets tired, it's all baby talk again. They have no idea why that happens. So I don't know what she knows. And she was so *tough*; that's the terrifying thing. She looks ancient— she had us late, but she isn't old enough to look the way she looks."

"You should have let me know exactly what was going on. I would have come right down, Annie."

"There wasn't that much going on until a few months ago—and it wouldn't have made a bit of difference. She didn't want you coming down, anyway. She didn't want me going to see her, and I don't think she likes it now."

"And it costs a lot of money—did you say three thousand?" Sara drank more of her coffee. It was too weak; the milk just made it weaker.

"Three thousand dollars a month is what The Arbor costs. Everything the store makes, and a regular chunk out of my so-called community property settlement."

"I thought it was twenty-five hundred a month."

"That was six months ago, big sister. You're behind the times. And Medicare would have paid for a lot, but not in The Arbor—too expensive. They had two other places, both dreadful, they would have helped pay for."

"Anne, I don't have any money—I mean I have some, but that's just to live on until I get a job. Otherwise, you could have it."

"Sara, relax—I know you'd help if you could. Anyway, money wasn't your thing. Money was *my* thing. That's what makes all this so grimly appropriate."

"But the store's doing O.K.?"

"It's doing O.K." Anne finished her coffee. "That was terrible coffee. —Listen, if you want to go out to Montana, guide fat ladies up in the mountains . . . sis, you go and do it. What the hell do I know."

"It was just something I was thinking about."

Anne sat looking at Sara as if there hadn't been good enough light to see her by, before. She looked and didn't say anything, then put out her hand, took Sara's, and they sat at the handsome kitchen island holding hands.

Sara was uncomfortable at first, but then it became pleasant. They held hands for a while, and didn't talk.

Then Anne said, "I've kept you up long enough." She let go of Sara's hand, and got down from her stool. "It's bedtime."

"O.K." Sara was glad to get down from her stool; its pale soft arms had closed her in.

Anne took the mugs, put them in the double sink, then opened the left side of the refrigerator to put the milk away. "Goodnight, sis. I'm glad you came down. . . . Tomorrow's Sunday, no reason to get up early. We can go see Mom about eleven. Maybe come back and have lunch at Tangerine. . . ."

"O.K. 'Night, Annie." It didn't seem enough to have only said goodnight, so Sara went over and kissed Anne on the cheek, then walked out of the kitchen, through the dining room (strong smell of furniture polish), and across the entry hall to climb the stairs. . . .

Sara closed the door to her room, glad to be alone, then took off her clothes, started to hang her jeans and sweater in the closet, then folded them instead, and put them up on the shelf.

She took off her long-johns and put them in the big middle pocket of her pack, then walked naked to the bathroom, went in and turned on the light. She sat on the toilet—its padded ivory-colored seat soft as a cushion—peed, and wiped herself with soft pink paper, blossoms printed on it. She stood, flushed the toilet, stepped into the shower stall and closed the glass door behind her. The stall was light beige, and so big there was room for a seat built out from the fiberglass, and little shelves and sunken dishes, all the same smooth material. A small bar of soap, coral-colored and shaped like a seashell, lay in a niche just below the faucet. The faucet was one slender gold lever; the shower head, above, was also shining gold.

Sara moved the faucet lever just a little, to get used to it, and nothing happened. 'H' for hot was engraved on the right side of the boss. 'C' on the left. She remembered faucets like it, but not exactly how they'd worked. She tried to keep the lever right in the middle, and gently pulled it up and toward her. She heard a humming in some pipe, and thought water would come out, but none did, so she pulled the lever up a little more—and suddenly the water came spraying down at her in a rush and much too cold, so she pushed the lever to the side and very hot water came flooding down.

Sara jumped, moved the lever again and the water got hotter, so she had to push the stall door open and get out in a cloud of steam, laughing. Then she looked across the bathroom and saw herself in the mirror above the sink. She looked like a drenched scarecrow, hair cut raggedly short, wet, plastered to her head. And she so thin, plain face burned dark by weather, looking as though the mountain winds had blown all of her away except her bones, and just enough skin to cover them. The reflection's eyes, hooded brown, looked out at her as if she were a rude stranger, staring.

Sara hadn't thought she looked that bad—worn, but not like that. Turning from the mirror—anxious to get into the stall and away from her reflection—she reached into the haze of steam and hot spray, and pushed and pulled the faucet lever until she saw how it worked. Tugged the lever inward a little, then slightly to the left, toward 'C' . . . and was able to step in and stand under water only very warm, water that was a pleasure.

Sara stood under the spray for a while, trying to think of something beside how she'd looked in the mirror. She thought of Vanilla's possible pups, of what she would have named them. Whipper . . . Snapper . . . Flower and Folly were the only names she could think of. Sara held her arms cradled to her chest, pretended she was holding one of the puppies (Folly) in the shower. Holding her, soaked and soft, wriggling under the spray. She bent her head, pretended to kiss the imagined puppy. . . . Then she stopped pretending and soaped herself, the coral-colored soap smelling better than Anne's perfume had. She soaped herself taking no extra time, no more enjoyment from the shower, then put the reduced shell of soap back into its niche.

Sara turned under the spray to rinse the soap off, then pushed the faucet lever in to stop the water. She stepped out of the stall, took a big pale-green towel off a rack . . . and drying herself, thought of glancing into the mirror—perhaps to find she looked all right after all (only too thin and tired)—but decided not. She dried her hair, hung up the towel, and went out to her pack to get her toothbrush. She brushed her teeth at the sink—looking down, away from the mirror—rinsed her mouth, then turned off the bathroom light and walked back into the bedroom, the carpet feeling like oddly warm snow to walk on, barefoot.

She turned down the coverlet and fat white comforter on the bed nearest the window, then climbed naked in between the sheets, reached out to the left to switch off the bedside lamp, and lay on her back in coolness, smoothness, softness, and ease.

The pillow was so plump it puffed up on either side of Sara's face, so she couldn't see anything but the ceiling, barely lit by light reflected from some streetlamp across the pond. She lay still, and felt herself sinking deeper and deeper into softness. The sheet was too warm over her, and she kicked it off.

She lay that way for a while, then turned on her side. That felt better at first, then began to feel as strange as before—as though she were sinking into the bed, and would sink until it closed over her. It was worse with her eyes shut. Sara pushed the pillow away, and that was better, less smothering, but still not comfortable.

She got up and took the comforter off the foot of the bed, spread it on the floor, and lay down on that.

That felt much better, but the room's odors still bothered her—detergent from the bed linens, and something else rising from the carpet. And it was too warm. Sara lay there as long as she could, eyes closed, trying to get to sleep. Trying not to think about her mother, or Annie, or having come down here. Trying not to think of Jack Joseph, or getting drunk at the Stick Dance, or about anything after the team had crossed the river to Fort Billy Mitchell. She should never have crossed there; she should have taken the team across the river miles upstream, and just kept going. Now she'd have Dutchy beside her in the mountain tent. . . . She imagined how her mother would look tomorrow—frail now, instead of strong and stocky. Sitting in a sunny room, smiling but unable to speak, her clever, sardonic eyes still bright hazel and almost able to conceal her pleasure at seeing Sara after so long a time.

The carpet smelled too strongly of whatever it was . . . cleaner. Sara got up in the dark, went to the rocking chair, bent and unhooked the sleeping bag's bungees, took it from beneath her pack, and went to the window. She saw how the screen clipped to the window frame, unfastened it, lifted it down and stood it against the wall. Then she leaned out and unrolled the bag onto the roof, spread it open. She climbed out the window and felt the cedar shakes, still damp from rain, rough beneath her hands and knees.

She stretched out on the sleeping bag, naked in much cooler air, her head upslope, and lay looking up at several stars faded by moonlight. What constellation they might have made was interrupted by breezing dappled clouds, distant and pale as Dall sheep, drifting over the night. Sara reached out with her right hand to touch shingles where her shotgun would have been, then tugged a fold of the sleeping bag across, up to her waist.

She smelled water and damp cut grass, heard two finches sleepily quarreling off to the right—ten, twenty yards. A dog barking farther away than that.

9

"The Alaska aunt," Kevin said, sat at the island counter and stared at her. When Sara held out her hand, he shook it softly, then let go. In yellow sweatshirt, gray jeans and denim jacket, Kevin seemed to Sara big for a thirteen-year-old—pale and pudgy, blue eyes so wide apart they looked odd. "Mom told me about your husband. Sorry." He glanced down at his breakfast, a sausage patty and a blueberry-bran muffin.

"You remember me, Kevin?" Sara sat at a place set beside him.

"Oh, sure." His reddish-blond hair was cut short in front; at the back it had been left long, fell to the jacket collar. "Well, is it weird up there, or great, or what?"

"It's weird *and* great," Sara said.

"Everybody goes around with guns?"

"In the bush they do." She drank some of her orange juice.

"But your husband didn't have one?"

"*Kevin.*" Anne, from the sink. She was wearing a light-blue wool dress and a necklace of two strands of bone beads. Slender and pretty, she seemed to Sara to complement the kitchen's mild blues, grays, and whites.

"That's all right. Good question," Sara said. "—No, he didn't, not when he needed it. We made a mistake."

"Heavy. . . . Where do you get your food?" Kevin forked a tiny bit off his sausage patty, tasted that, and put the fork firmly down.

"Hunt it, or grow it in the garden; summers, we have a big garden. And we trap—trapped for fur and sold that, and cure some of the skins to wear."

"Man. . . . Sounds a lot easier just to buy stuff. Earn some bread, and buy it."

"You're right. That would be a lot easier," Sara said, and finished her orange juice.

"But you like living that way, right? That's your thing."

"Yes."

"What a conception." Kevin tasted his own juice (looking at Sara over the glass's rim), then drank it down, reminding Sara suddenly how Connor Rittman looked, seeing the father in the son.

"Kevin," Anne dried her hands on the dish towel, "—would you just try that patty? More than one bite, please? It's a regular sausage patty, just without all the fat."

"I don't want it, Mom. O.K.? Is that O.K.? I do not like it, and I do not want it."

Anne glanced at Sara, made a 'See?' face as Kevin slid off his stool, went around to the refrigerator and opened the left-side door, reached in to shift things around, looking. "—Truth, Mom? Painful truth? It tastes like shit, but precisely. Davey and me'll get something later; all right?"

"No, it's not all right—because for lunch you'll eat two cheese-burgers and one of those disgusting McDonald's pies, and that stuff is bad for you, Kev. So please—just try this."

"I tried it before, and it's gross and I don't like it." He swung the refrigerator door closed. "There is nothing . . . to eat . . . in this house," he said, and started out of the kitchen.

"Kevin—"

"Mom, don't panic. We will not—I repeat—we will not eat at McDonald's."

"I mean it."

"Davey won't do McDonald's, anyway." As he walked out of the kitchen, "So we'll eat at Burger King."

"*Kevin*—" Anne stood by the stove, listening. They heard the front door close. "Goddamn him."

"Smart boy."

"Smart ass, you mean. . . . I think he likes you."

"You think he *likes* me?"

"Oh, sure. Probably thinks you're an interesting aunt, as aunts go. —Do you want fried or scrambled?"

"Can I have scrambled with milk? Soft scrambled?"

"That's how I do them. How many eggs?"

"Four.—Is that too many?"

"No. No, that's all right." Anne went to the refrigerator, opened it, took out a carton of eggs and put them on the counter. "You want sausage?"

"It doesn't have any fat?"

"Well, not much. It's a special lean kind of sausage. It's really not bad. Really. . . . You don't want any."

"I don't think so."

"All right. It is not the most delicious stuff." She bent to a low cabinet, took out a large lead-colored frying pan. "In about a minute, Kevin will be sitting down to a late breakfast right over at Davey Rolvaag's house down the street, and Katherine Rolvaag (who has the spine of an earthworm) will be stuffing both those kids—and it's damn near lunchtime—will be stuffing both those kids with her very dry overcooked waffles and lots of syrup."

"Annie, while I'm here, I want to pay for my food."

"You don't have to pay for your food." Anne opened the refrigerator again, brought out a loaf of whole-wheat bread, milk, and a small plastic tub of margarine . . . left the bread on the long counter, and brought the milk and margarine to the stove.

"I want to."

"Well, you're not going to."

"Yes," Sara said. "Yes, I am."

"I can afford the fucking eggs," Anne said, and put a dab of margarine in the frying pan.

"Well, I am, Annie."

Anne put the frying pan down hard, made the left front burner's metal ring. "Don't insult me. I mean it."

"Don't you insult me," Sara said, "—by not letting me help even a little. You're not the big sister here, no matter what you think."

"Well," Anne said, and put another, smaller smear of margarine in the pan, "—are we having our first fight in five years?"

"A little fight," Sara said. "Not much of a fight, Annie."

"All right—then give me some money for the goddamned food if you want to. I don't really need it. Food money is not the problem here."

"I'll give you five dollars a day while I'm here."

"Right, while you're here—'two or three weeks.' And since you want to do this, five dollars a day won't cover it. You've been out of touch."

"How much?"

"Six will cover it."

"All right."

Anne mixed the milk and eggs in the pan, and started cooking them on low. She walked back to the long counter, plugged in a white-metal toaster, and put two slices of whole wheat in. "Well, I'm a slow learner, but I do learn. I'm getting so I don't give a damn what Kevin eats. —I don't suppose you still have your driver's license."

"Yes, I do. I renewed it by mail; I renewed it two years ago."

"Good, because you'd get very tired of waiting for the buses around here. You can drive me to the store in the mornings, and then use the car for anything you want to do."

"I'd rather not drive your car, Annie."

"Oh, don't be silly; just do it. What, you think the Mercedes is too fabulous for you to use? Sis, we're just talking about an overpriced vanity item. So drive the goddamn thing . . . but for God's sake, be careful." Anne used a cream-colored plastic spatula to stir the eggs, turn them in the pan. She paused a while, stirred them, stirred them again, then shoveled them onto a plate and went back to the long counter for the toast. She sliced two pieces diagonally, stacked them on a smaller plate, and handed that and the eggs over to Sara. Then salt and pepper shakers—one a fat white china rooster, the other (the pepper) a hen.

"Coffee?"

"I'd rather have milk."

Anne went to get a glass—a tall faceted tumbler—and poured milk for Sara, handed it to her, then stood leaning against the island counter, watching her eat.

The eggs tasted so good, Sara felt tears come to her eyes. . . . The eggs and toast were wonderful, but not as sweet as the milk.

"Want more milk?"

"If you have it."

"We have a lot of milk. Give me the glass," and poured it full.

"Aren't you going to eat?"

"Breakfast is not my meal, sis. I'm a lunch person. Christ, you eat as if you've been starving."

"Just haven't had eggs. No real milk—only powdered." Sara tried to eat more slowly, take more time between bites.

"I don't dare ask, but I have to ask—do you have anything beside jeans and sweatshirts to wear?"

"Why? Do I have to dress up?"

"Well, not *up*—but you might want a dress or slacks or something if we go out to dinner some evening. Meet friends, whatever. What do you think?"

"I really don't want to meet anybody."

"Right. Of course. Of course you don't want to *meet* anybody. But if we should happen to . . . you know, bump into another human being, you might want something beside jeans and a sweatshirt, that's all. We could check Nordstrom's out—wouldn't be a big deal."

Sara finished the last of the eggs. She wished she'd put a little more pepper on them while she had them.

"Want some more?"

"No, thanks."

"Sis, do you want some more goddamn eggs?"

"No, really. I'm fine. They were very good."

"More milk? We have a ton of milk."

"No; I'm full. . . . Maybe a little more milk."

Anne took the glass and filled it. "And what do you think about shopping—just for a few things, you know, give you some choices?"

"Is Penney's still at the mall?"

It seemed to Sara, after she said that, that her sister looked at her with real affection, smiling. "Penney's," Anne said. "Now, why didn't I think of that? I could have guessed. Sweetheart, if you want, you and I will go shop the shit out of Penney's."

The Arbor had two small trees in its front yard. In a neighborhood zoned light industrial, where even minor companies had left a number of firs or alders to grace their lots, The Arbor had cleared all trees out except for two young plums—each lonely on its side of the central walk—and otherwise left only lawn in a wide sweep across the front of a long one-story building sided in gray board-and-batten.

They drove half around a long semicircular drive to a row of diagonal parking places, and pulled in beside a white delivery truck with *Gai's* printed on its door in dark blue letters.

Anne got out the driver's side, pushed the door lock and closed the door, then walked around the front of the car.

"Sara—you are coming in?"

"Yes, I'm coming in."

"Well, then come on."

Sara got out, made sure her door was locked, and hurried to catch up with Anne at a set of shallow brick steps. There was rich enough sunshine to paint their shadows alongside as they stepped up, then walked together. Sara saw her shadow folding in and out of Anne's . . . part of Anne's if she stayed close.

The Arbor's double doors looked like a bank's—thick sheets of glass, chromed steel handles. The reception area was carpeted umber, with a couch and two armchairs in figured brown fabric set around a long coffee table on the left, fronting a fireplace, and two more formal armchairs on either side of a low lamp table to the right. The room was too hot; Sara could hear warm air thrumming up out of floor vents.

"Hi." A very big man in a gray tweed sports coat, white shirt and dark gray tie, was sitting at a desk in an office through open double doors off the room's right. He got up and walked into the reception room. "Hi, Mrs. Rittman. This your sister?"

"Yes, it is. She just got in last night—hasn't seen Mom yet."

"And it's Sara, isn't it?" He reached out to shake hands. The backs of his were furred with light-brown hair.

"Yes," Sara said. "—Sara Maher." There was such a strong sweet smell of roses in the room that she looked for flowers, but saw only a large rose-colored candle, a scented candle burning in a cut-glass dish on the fireplace's narrow white mantel.

"Sis, this is Tom Couvelier. He manages The Arbor."

"I try," Couvelier said. "—Well, I'll log you in, and that's all there is to it. You can come see your mom any time you want, during visiting hours." He walked back into the office, took a white pamphlet from a small stack on the desk, and came back to hand it to Sara. His eyes were a very light blue—almost as pale as Dutchy's. "Hours and staff, little details of our operation here. Phone numbers . . . it's all in there."

"Thank you."

Sara wished the man would delay them a little, tell them how old the building was, how many people lived here. Just spend some time talking about things.

"Sis . . ."

"O.K." Sara followed Anne through double doors at the back of the room. These were edged with rubber strips, and hissed on black-and-white squares of composite tile as they swung open into a smell of urine so sharp Sara looked down, thinking some must be puddled right there. But the tile was clean.

This was a long hall of doorways, ceiling and upper walls painted white, and a light-brown veneered wood lining the walls from waist height to the floor. Slender-leaved palms in big green plastic pots were set each side of the hall, a plant past every room door.

A woman so old her hair was gone but for fluff here and there, sat in a wheelchair against the left-side wall. She wore a pink-flowered robe, and sat with her head fallen to the right so it lay along her shoulder. Her eyes and mouth were open—eyes milky gray with fluid, toothless mouth a dark pouched opening. . . . There were women, and perhaps two or three men, in wheelchairs beside the palm plants—pale, pale as the walls' white paint, shriveled and folded in upon themselves, rich green palm fronds fanning up behind them. A dozen or so were spaced along on either side, all in robes or hospital gowns, light blankets draped over their laps, and all crumpled down into their chairs as if they were made of paper, heads lolling. One sat unblanketed, her bare legs bone-white sticks wormed with light-blue veins, her feet fat mushrooms dotted with small bruises. These people's heads looked too big for them, their hair only wisps over gleaming scalps, noses bony as bird beaks, mouths either gaped too wide or shrunk into small purses.

Sara walked beside Anne down an aisle of age. She hadn't seen people this old in several years. No animals this old, no humans quite as old as this, even in the villages. It shocked her. It seemed she could still see the faces of the young people lost, trapped and rotting behind these faces. Two women looked at them as they went by; the second of these grunted when they passed her, produced a soft burr of flatulence.

Another corridor opened to the right; Anne gestured that way. "A lot better in East Wing. Down there they can walk around, and you can talk to them and so forth. Still human, down there. . . ."

Sara saw elderly people in bathrobes down that hall, walking. The plants lining their corridor weren't palms—they had small leaves, and knotty, treelike stems.

At the next doorway they passed, on the left, a tiny woman with a yellow-plastic bib tied down her front made a gargling sound. Sara stopped to make sure she was all right.

Anne looked back. "What's the matter?"

"Is she O.K.?"

"She does that all the time. Come on."

The woman didn't notice them when they walked away past other withered people left and right. Only one woman—bony, with busy spider hands crawling in creamed food on a white plastic tray—seemed to see them coming. "Hello," this woman said, and nodded to them. "Hello. Hello. . . ." But as Anne and Sara walked nearer, the woman seemed less certain. And when they passed her by, she didn't notice them at all—instead craned a wattled neck to look back down the corridor where they'd been. Stared that way as if expecting them to reappear.

"Oh, damn it." A nurse, elderly herself, but looking decades younger than her patients, walked out of a room on the right and went to the bony woman, lifted her hands out of the food, and cleaned them with a paper towel unfolded from her uniform pocket. "Carrie! Why has Catherine still got her lunch?"

"I don' know. I picked 'em all up." Carrie, palely plump, with short, curling ginger hair, stood in the doorway the nurse had come from. She wore a light-blue uniform smock, and was a grown woman with heavy hips, but she talked like a child. Her eyes were slanted, and Sara saw she had Down's syndrome.

"Well, you didn't pick up this one," the nurse said, looked up and saw Anne and Sara. "Mrs. Rittman . . ."

"Mrs. Solmssen's the head nurse," Anne said.

"—And only RN," said Mrs. Solmssen.

"How's Mom doing today? No more turning the wheelchair over?"

"No. Hasn't done that for a while."

"Sis, Mom turned over in her wheelchair. Rocking side to side hard enough to do that, if you can believe it. We had her restrained in bed for a week."

"Could have fractured her skull." The nurse held out her hand. "Mrs. Maher?"

"Yes," Sara said. The nurse's grip was surprisingly strong.

"I've seen that before, but not often—take a wheelchair right over on its side. She was having some headaches that were just over-whelming for her. Leveling off, now; I don't think there's quite so much discomfort."

"Agony," Anne said.

"Well, I don't think Helen's having that degree of discomfort right now; we don't see as much crying." The nurse tucked the dirty paper towel into a plastic sack hanging off the back of the bony woman's wheelchair. "—I sure would ask the doctor to continue medication at current level, though." She looked at Sara again, examined her. Sara saw her notice the two swollen fingers where the nails were gone. "Mrs. Maher, you haven't seen your mother, have you? Since she's been sick?"

"No."

"Well, you'll find her changed, aged a good deal. Why don't you go on in and see her? Over there, room twenty-four. My experience is it's better just to go right in. Half the time it's not as bad as you're worried it's going to be."

Sara couldn't think of a reason to ask Anne to come with her, so she went down the corridor to twenty-two, then to the room past that, same side, and walked in.

But it was the wrong room; there was a little old man in it—one of the few men she'd seen in here. Wasted away, except for an old man's breasts and fat little belly evident in a white hospital gown, he sat heaped in his wheelchair alongside a rubber-sheeted bed. There were only tufts of iron-gray hair on a downy scalp, and a few small hairs curling from the chin.

Sara said, "Hi," smiled—and as she turned to go, saw her mother's eyes in the ruined face.

Sara stood where she'd been, half turned, and it seemed to her she floated slightly off the floor . . . then found herself looking past that person and out the window across the small room. Out the window past a second, curtained bed. They'd left trees there, behind the building—evergreens. The light in the room, when she looked back, pulsed in time with her heart.

"Mom?" she said, and was able to imagine she was mistaken until she looked into the hazel eyes again. Helen Whaley made a slow rubbery face, wry, conscious—then shrugged and said a word Sara couldn't understand; it was a vowel, a drawn-out short *A* wreathed in hisses.

"She knows you," Anne said from the doorway. "She's saying 'Sara.' It's really weird; she has to sort of warm up—don't you, Mom?—and then she can talk better and better. And of course they don't know why. Pressure on speech centers and so forth. . . ."

Now Sara saw her mother more clearly, saw this was certainly she—stocky, bald, and collapsed. There was the slightest smell, dark and musty, of remnant shit, the brighter odors of urine and pine-scented cleanser. Sara wondered if there was anyone in the curtained bed beside the window. She thought that might be where the smells came from.

Anne went past her, bent and kissed Helen as if she were demonstrating something to Sara, showing what she'd had to do for so many months, as their mother became a monster.

Sara walked over to kiss her mother, too, found it easiest to look into her eyes—the same clear hazel, not faded, not yet beginning to bulge as the tumor, growing larger, slowly forced them from their sockets.

Her mother's cheek was soft as cotton wool, and smelled of talcum powder. After the kiss, drawing back, Sara saw Helen peering at her, as if making certain it was her daughter who'd come and stared and looked away, then bent to kiss her. Hazel eyes, pupils faintly splintered with tiny wedges of gold—the same shade they'd been when Helen Whaley was young, her torso, arms, and legs almost too deeply curved, tanned and strong.

Now her ankles were fat, mottled, and spoiled. Her arms skin-draped bone.

Anne dragged two small straight-back chairs, their seats upholstered in light-blue plastic, from against the wall. "Sit down, sis. . . . Mom? Mom, are you having headaches?" She took Helen's left hand and sat holding it, stroking its spotted back. "You having headaches?"

Mrs. Whaley considered the question, nodded slightly, but not as if to say yes. They seemed to be nods of consideration as she thought about it. Then she let her head fall back a little, opened her mouth to get sufficient air, and answered with a humming noise that became "Yooouuu . . ." and when Sara was certain she meant "You," turned with less hooting and a hiss into "Yessss."

"Oh, shit," Anne said. " 'Less discomfort,' my ass."

"We can have the doctor give her a stronger sedative."

"You kidding?—depress her *breathing?* No, no, no, Cherkin's not going to do that. You try him, see what he says."

"Then let's get another doctor!" Sara saw Helen watching them as they talked. The handsome eyes seemed only slightly interested, as if her daughters were the ones in trouble.

"Sis, Cherkin *is* another doctor. You should have heard Bob Owens, that super internist, that asshole, on the dangers of Demerol. Hey—habit-forming, addictive—gotta watch those doses. . . ."

"Why don't we bring something? We could get prescriptions and then bring stuff to her."

Anne smiled. "What about that, Mom? Great minds . . ." Mrs. Whaley was watching Sara as if she were still not quite sure of her, not certain she was Sara. "Sis, I already tried that one. I brought Darvocet and gave her two and she vomited all night long."

"I don't think she really recognizes me. —Do you, Mom? Do you know me? . . . I think she just thinks I'm a visitor."

"Sara, she's not an idiot, just her thought processes get interrupted. She knows damn well who you are. Mom, you know who Sara is?"

Their mother grinned suddenly, toothless gums revealed, and nodded once, looking amused at Sara's stupidity.

"She's lost her teeth."

"Mom's been wearing false teeth for years, sis. Where the hell have you been? —Well, we know where you've been. Absent."

"I would have come right down if I'd known it was like this. I don't think you wanted me to know—you didn't call me about Daddy, either."

"Oh, please. Now I'm the ghoul who likes to keep Dad and Mom all to herself when they're dying, just to shut Big Sister out. Big Sister can't be expected to keep up. She's having *adventures*. She's way the hell out of town. . . ."

Helen Whaley sneezed, and her nose began to run. Anne got half off her chair, reached to the bedside table and tugged a Kleenex out of its box, then very gently wiped her mother's nose and upper lip. "Want to blow?"

Their mother shook her head. She didn't want to blow.

"I used to brush her hair, but after the radiation it just started coming out in the brush. I tried to snip off that little goatee, too, but she wouldn't let me do it. Embarrassed her—if you have to take it off, then you're admitting it's *there*."

"I'm sorry, Annie."

"You're sorry. I'm sorry. . . ." Anne balled the tissue, dropped it into a bronze plastic wastebasket against the wall.

Helen seemed bored with them, with their talking. She turned her head toward the window, looked out at the backyard view, and revealed two long scars, ridged and light pink, crisscrossing the back of her scalp beneath a sparse gray fluff of hair. Her hospital gown, freshly ironed, was white enough to gather light. Sara remembered white was the color of Chinese mourning.

Whoever was in the curtained bed by the window moved slightly, sheets rustling. Sara looked an inquiry at Anne.

"Don't ask me," Anne speaking softly. "Some poor woman. Very gross. She never says anything while I'm here, and Mrs. Solmssen says she never says anything at all, period. Occasionally you'll get a whiff," Anne sniffed to demonstrate, "Bed sores, even though they do their best to keep her turned."

Helen had closed her eyes—and as if this provided Sara her only chance to get away, she said, "I think she's asleep." It became urgent to get away, even if only to the corridor. She and Annie could talk in the corridor.

"She's not asleep," Anne said, and their mother, eyes still closed, began to say something. Hissing . . . droning as if she were about to sing.

"What did she say?"

"Said she's not asleep," Anne said. "Talk to her, for Christ's sake. She'd like you to talk to her."

"Anne, just leave me alone."

"Jesus." Anne got up. "—I'll be glad to," and walked out of the room.

Sara felt better right away, much better without Annie in there angry at her. Sisters competing for the last of Mom's attention. . . . She moved her chair closer, reached out to hold her mother's hand. It felt unfamiliar, too small and bony. The freckles on the back of the hand had spread into splotches.

Helen turned, opened her eyes to look at Sara, and said a word that sounded like 'New.' Sara thought she might mean 'What's new?' Her mother used to say that.

"Well, I've been married. You remember I was up in Alaska?"

It seemed to annoy her mother to be asked that; she frowned and nodded once very definitely.

"Well, I was—I'm married."

Another nod. Her mother put out the tip of her tongue—swollen, coated cream-white—and tasted her upper lip, licked slowly from the right corner of her mouth to the left, as if she were wondering whether that tissue would be good to eat. She watched Sara while she did it, then, when she was finished, closed her mouth and turned her head to look out the window. The row of evergreens across the back lawn was stirring slightly in a breeze. Small green waves.

"Mom, I would have come down sooner," Sara said. "I didn't know how serious it was. I thought since it was benign, it wasn't so serious."

Helen shrugged, and still staring out the window, said "Husband," quite clearly.

"Oh, his name's Alan. He . . . he's very nice. Likes working outdoors. Living rough. You'd like him; he's a very gentle man, really. Stocky, redheaded guy—much shorter than Daddy. He has a beard."

Her mother turned her head to look at Sara again—and this time with such an unpleasant look, alert, full of amused contempt, that Sara felt goose bumps run down her arms as if, in her agony and terror, her mother had gone mad.

" 'Ed,' " Helen said, concentrating. " 'Ed." Apparently displeased with that, she paused and took a deep breath. "Dooo . . ." Looked furiously impatient and said, "Dead."

Sara felt angry enough with Anne to hit her in the face. "I'm sorry. Annie wrote me that you didn't know."

Her mother grinned a toothless grin, then said, "Oh, sure," almost clearly.

"He was killed by a bear," Sara said. Then, not certain her mother had understood, said it again. "Killed by a bear."

Helen nodded—she knew all that—rolled her eyes up in exasperation.

"It was my fault," Sara said, then decided not to say anything more about it. Her mother wouldn't care, anyway—or if she did, would be upset. "Would you like some water, or a Coke?"

Helen shook her head.

Sara sat holding her mother's hand, hoping to become more comfortable that way, to feel she was really sitting there, and Helen come to this. That simply the passage of time—unimportant minutes, days, and weeks—had gathered their slow momentum and smashed her mother as if she'd been hit by a truck. Simply a passage of time, and a single cell recalling an ancient independence.

Her mother hadn't changed, before—as her father had. Evan Whaley had diminished for a long time, once he was off the ranch and on the road, an unconvincing businessman. On the ranch, he'd been one person—afterward, another. But Helen had never changed, she'd been the same self working on Bow Tie—shifting the horses, worming calves—as afterward. She'd done the ranch chores as if they'd been office work, and seemed to take no pleasure from them. No pleasure in much, except irony.

"I think you'd like Alaska, Mom. Not many people there."

"Then . . . I like. . . ." her mother said, speaking much better now. And withdrew her hand.

It seemed to Sara she hadn't made clear how she felt, her sorrow at seeing her mother—so coldly strong—brought down to this wreckage. She felt if her mother knew, then she would love Sara better, be glad to see her though Annie had always been the favorite sister—not afraid to argue with their mother, even when Helen was swiftly, lightly cruel to her. Cruel with a hunting bird's cold courage, which could not be shaken.

"All that to one side," Annie would say, and jump right back in, apparently unwounded—while Sara and her father (if he was home) sat waiting for what Helen might say next. Once, after Annie had stood arguing in the kitchen of the Seattle house at dinnertime— arguing with her mother about dating a boy in high school named

Jesse Zelm—Helen had said, "Anne, you're very young. Your mouth is bigger than both your breasts put together." But Annie had seemed to pay no attention, had ridden right over that, and kept saying, "Except for prejudice because Jesse's dad drinks, what's your problem, Mom? We are not screwing, if that's your big worry!"

But upstairs that night, Annie had cried. And in the next year her breasts had grown and become beautiful, as if she'd insisted on it.

"Do you want anything, Mom? Want some juice?"

"New . . . head," Helen Whaley said with some difficulty, pausing to draw a quick breath, mid-phrase. But still well enough so her familiar voice sounded, and Sara could see that person quite clearly—could see her mother as she had been, perhaps now standing by the window watching her dying self, watching Sara, almost amused by its having come to this. Not surprised at all. Not surprised either, to see her plain daughter, still unsatisfactory, come down from the wilderness late.

"Mom, I'm so sorry. Oh, I'm so sorry. I wish this hadn't happened to you." It seemed such a stupid thing to say—and it wasn't what Sara meant. She meant that her mother had been beautiful and strong, and now was broken. "You were so brave—I didn't think you were afraid of anything. Really . . . you always scared me, and I was afraid of you but I loved you so much. I just wish I'd been pretty for you. And I'm so *sorry*."

Sara heard somebody behind her, and turned and saw Anne standing in the doorway, listening. "Hey—you get out of here." But Annie just stood there. "Get *out* of here!" Sara was shouting, and she didn't care.

Anne started to say something, then didn't, and left.

"—*And stay the fuck out!*" It was . . . just so stupid to be shouting like that; Sara couldn't believe she was doing it. She shut her mouth. There wouldn't be any more shouting while her mouth was shut. She looked back at her mother and saw that Helen was laughing, dappled gums exposed, shaking her head—laughing in little grunts, so Sara couldn't help smiling.

"I know, I know. I just got . . . absolutely hysterical." She remembered Annie ducking back out of the doorway. "I was really ready to kill her, and I don't even know why. . . ."

Someone was at the door again, and Sara turned to apologize to Annie, but it was the retarded woman, Carrie, peering around the door frame, looking apprehensive.

"Carrie," Sara said, "—you need to come in?"

"I don' *need* to."

"Come in." Sara stood and smiled at her. "I'm sorry I shouted. I was . . . just upset." And Carrie sidled in, carrying a red-plastic sponge mop in a white-plastic bucket. Eyes lowered, she went to Helen's wheelchair, shoved it rolling back a foot or two, swiftly swabbed up a small puddle Sara hadn't seen, then put her sponge mop back in the bucket and went out, eyes still lowered, sturdy legs stumping. She was wearing white sneakers.

"I'm sorry," Sara said to her mother, and reached out to hold her hand—although after she said it, she wasn't sure what she was sorry for. For shouting, she supposed.

Her mother withdrew her hand and put it in her lap. She said something that started with "Yooo. . . ." and ended in ". . . airs-mesh." She wasn't speaking well, anymore.

"What? I didn't understand. . . ."

"She says your hair's a mess," Anne, back at the door. "Have you calmed down?"

"I've calmed down."

"I don't know about you," Anne said, came in and sat in the other small chair. "—But I find it a little humiliating that we still act like seven-year-olds around Mom."

"I know."

"You actually woke up some of those mummies out there. They thought it was feeding time."

"That's what she said, my hair is a mess?"

Helen hissed a *yessss.*

"Mom, you want something to drink?"

"No, I asked her that," Sara said.

"Well, one of the things she doesn't do is drink enough water." Anne and Sara both looked at their mother to see how Helen might respond to that, and saw her nodding slowly, but apparently only to something remembered.

"Doesn't drink enough water, and that's terrible for her kidneys—and she'll eat anything, and that's not good for her."

"What do they give her?"

"Oh, they give her the usual not too dreadful institutional stuff—but Carrie keeps bringing Mom extras. At least I suspect it's Carrie. I found *three* trays in here one afternoon."

"Well, they need to stop her from doing it."

"You tell them. I've already told them."

Sara was watching her mother as they talked—saw her seem to

sail along while sitting still, sailing through their discussion, their offers and concern as if she were already a memory about whom they might talk and talk, but do nothing.

Early afternoon had turned uneven gray when they went down The Arbor's steps. They threw only momentary shadows on the walk. It seemed the day should be cold at that shade of gray, but it wasn't.

"I'm sorry I upset you, Sara. That stupid argument. I don't think we really had an argument. You just started yelling at me." Anne was walking briskly alongside; they both were walking fast—getting away.

"I'm sorry, too."

"And she was worse than usual, today; lot of difficulty talking. Well, welcome to the real world. I've about decided that everything outside The Arbor is just bullshit to keep us from thinking about The Arbor."

"That isn't the real world. In the real world, some animal would have taken them, long ago."

"Oh . . . right. Very Darwinian. —And in any case, I have the very definite suspicion Mom would not have gone to quite this much trouble for either of us, if we had something growing in our heads, getting ready to pop our eyes out."

As she stood by the Mercedes' passenger-side door, waiting for Annie to unlock it from inside, Sara whispered the good-bye she'd said to her mother: *"I'll be back, and I'll visit as often as you want me. I love you."* The original had also been whispered as she kissed Helen's powdered cheek—whispered for some privacy from Anne, who'd already stood and said, "See you Wednesday, Mom."

Helen Whaley had looked up at Sara then, reexamined her, and said, "Airsmesh. . . ."

The door unlocked, Sara climbed in, settled into the car seat. It was a little too soft to be comfortable. "I suppose I ought to get my hair cut."

"No 'suppose' about it." Anne backed out of the parking place, turned down the drive, and took a left. Sara saw a fat tabby cat, front paws folded, lying deep in shadow under an evergreen hedge across the road. The cat, surveying the street, noticed her watching and stared back with apple-green eyes.

"You hungry?" Anne searched in her purse one-handed, found a pack of cigarettes, Winstons, and fingered one out.

"Yes."

"I'm always starved when I get out of there." She leaned forward to push in the dash lighter. "Seafood? Want some seafood? We can go over to the Market."

"And vegetables."

"My treat. —Is that O.K.? I treat? We'll call it a recovery lunch. Death's-door lunch; next time, you buy. And afterward, we'll go to Penney's. . . ."

The restaurant was called Sea Shells, and they'd walked through the Market to get to it. Sea Shells was new since Sara's time—fancier than the shrimp-and-crab stalls along Pike Place. It was built out over the harbor, rows of small tables with blue-and-white-checked table-cloths ranked along three platforms stepped up so everyone saw the view.

A stocky young black girl in a blue uniform and apron took them to a table on the lowest level, and handed them big menus. Then she brought ice water in fat tumblers, and stood beside the table waiting for them to decide what to order. The girl's hair had been straight-ened, then sculpted into a page-boy bob.

"I want some vegetables," Sara said.

"Asparagus is real good," the black girl said. "An' he does the zucchini nice, with butter an' herbs." She wore thick-lensed glasses with coral-orange plastic frames.

"O.K.," Sara said. "That's what I'll have."

"You want some fish? That's what they do here, sis."

"Yes. Oysters?"

"The belons are in." The black girl wrote it down. "A dozen of 'em? They're little."

"All right. And shrimp?"

"We have a special of breaded prawns—or you can have Bay shrimp, sautéed, and that comes with a vegetable, so you could just have the asparagus with that."

"Prawns. And you have fresh fruit?" Recreational eating. . . .

"We have a fruit salad—lots of fruit in that. Apples, oranges. Pineapple, too."

"Let me have that. And a big glass of milk. And can I have a carrot?"

"Wow," the black girl said, and wrote it down. "Don't see why not. I'll cut you up one, in little slices."

"I'll have the crabmeat salad, and coffee," Anne said. And when the black girl had left, "Sis, didn't you have anything to eat up there?"

"Too high for vegetables, except mostly potatoes, cabbage, and onions. And no fresh milk."

"Well, if you can eat it, I'll pay for it. Next lunch is definitely on you."

"Do you have a typewriter, Annie?"

"Yes, an old electric. In the den."

"All right if I use it?"

"Sure. —Letters, resumés?"

"Yes. . . ."

The daylight—bright gray, gilded occasionally with sunshine— poured in through wide plate-glass windows as if very soon the harbor's wake-sliced water would pour in after it, ferries and fishing boats steaming through. It was the largest space Sara'd seen since flying down, and she sat staring out into it, pleased with the sometimes sun's flashing from small waves—able to follow that glimmering path out across the harbor and beyond, where much bigger ships, made small by distance, sailed slowly out to the islands, out to sea.

Anne had parked in an underground garage, downtown. Then they'd walked up to the Market on the east side of the avenue, passing bookstores and small rug shops selling rich oriental carpets. Sara'd remembered the rug stores . . . found this all familiar, and was surprised the crowds of people didn't trouble her much—could hardly smell them, anymore. She found the best way was not to look into their faces as they approached. Watching the backs of those in front of her didn't bother her at all. From behind, these people had looked only odd, so many of them waddling duck-footed, as if they'd just learned to walk—as if they'd fall down, trying to run.

The Market had been crowded. There were several shabby men sitting on the curb across the street. One had a bottle. Another, a black man, was lying on the sidewalk up against a building, his pants slipped down, buttocks partially exposed. There were many more people shopping here, or come for their lunches, all walking around close enough to touch each other. It had been difficult not to look into their faces as they drifted among the fruit stands, bakeries, and seafood bars . . . butcher shops, stores selling kitchen appliances, pottery, and souvenirs. Sara'd stopped at a little newsstand, and while Anne waited, picked out three postcards—one of the Seattle skyline at night, for Mary Toby, one of downtown, for Pauline, and one of two pandas eating bamboo shoots, for Carla. It was surprising how much just three postcards cost.

People had been moving back and forth along the street, milling like a herd come to a river, so it was tiring trying to keep track of individuals. A surprising number were fat or looked as if there was something wrong with them. All part of an uneasy mob, made anxious by strangers jostling—and longing, Sara supposed, for smaller simpler family groups where they were known, and despite that, welcomed. Frightened alone, and uneasy in a crowd—so awkwardly balanced.

Sara had been hungry, and these people were such a herd, she'd thought of hunting. Easy to hunt, even easier to trap—any bright thing for bait, or the scent of pizza or woman's genitals rubbed on a post nearby. . . . She thought, if she were hunting, she wouldn't pick a fat one; they looked sick. She'd tried to see one worth putting down, cleaning and dressing out for maybe sixty or seventy pounds of good marbled meat. Guts for the dogs.

She could tell from the way the people moved, avoiding each other's gaze, staying a crowded little distance apart, that they'd scatter at the shot. Run this way, run that way, bleating—or hooting the way chimpanzees hooted when they were upset. They were such confused and awkward game, Sara had wondered how any city hunter could ever go hungry.

"What's funny?" Annie'd said.

"Nothing. . . ."

Now, in the bright restful harbor light, Sara looked across the table and saw in her sister's elegant face the beginning engravings of time. Small lines, now only indications, certain to deepen with years, to wear into her, begin to carve her away like ghost rivers etching her landscape into age—until, if she lived long enough, she looked like their mother.

"Well, what do you see?" Anne said, and sipped her ice water.

"How pretty you are."

"Bullshit. That was a very diagnostic look. Have I got lipstick on my teeth, or something?"

"No. Nothing, really."

"You were trying to see if I was going to look like Mom when I got old, right? And the reason I know that, is the first thing I used to do after I left her was look in a mirror. I couldn't wait to get to a mirror, check myself out. But I don't even bother, anymore."

"I look old already, so I don't have to worry about it."

"You do not look old, sis. You don't look old at all. Ageless and weathered—that's what you look like. The . . . uh . . . Georgia O'Keeffe look."

"Great. Thanks. . . ."

"And yes, you do need your hair cut. And anything else they can do for you, so you don't look quite so raised-by-wolves. You could go tomorrow, after you see the store. Want to see the store?"

"Yes, I do."

"Well then, we can make an appointment for you tomorrow—if they'll take you as an emergency case—and you can drive me to work and then go on to Solutions."

"I really don't want to drive your car, Annie."

"Oh, drive the goddamned thing. What else is it for? —Just, you know, be a little cautious. Those insurance assholes love to cancel their crappy policies."

Sara was thinking how to say she wouldn't drive the Mercedes . . . would much rather just take her time, use buses—when the black girl came with Anne's salad and Sara's oysters, sliced carrot, and fruit salad (with a red cherry on top), and her glass of milk.

"He's holdin' the prawns an' asparagus an' the side of zucchini so they goin' to keep warm for you."

"Thank you," Sara said, grateful as if the girl, daughter of country as hot as Alaska was cold, had brought her gifts.

"You wanted me to come, because you didn't want Mom telling you how to drive."

"Kevin, that's exactly right. You're really sharp. —What's that damn buzzing?"

"After you backed out and stopped? You put the parking brake back on." Kevin lounged in the passenger seat, bulky in yellow sweatshirt, gray jeans, and high-top purple-and-white sneakers. "Push the button on the brake."

The buzzing stopped, then started again.

"What the *hell?*"

"Seat belts," Kevin said, sighed at the effort, and tugged his around to buckle. "New cars, seat belts are automatic. This thing's three years old, now."

"I don't want to drive it, anyway." Sara buckled her seat belt, and carefully moved the transmission shifter from Park to Drive. The Mercedes didn't go anywhere.

"You got your foot on the brake?"

"No." Sara took her foot off the brake and put it on the accelerator. The station wagon started off too fast.

"You're going too fast."

"I know—just leave me alone for a minute." Sara lifted her foot off the accelerator, then pressed it down again, but lightly, and the Mercedes cruised around a mild curve past nearly identical big brick-and-cedar houses on either side—then the development's entrance . . . passed that, and continued on the same looping road lined with houses, the series of ponds behind those on the right . . . water darkening gray in gloaming.

Sara saw two small girls walking down the left side of the road toward her, and steered the station wagon over to the right, slowed down a little more. The sun had almost set, its fading copper light lightly glazing the car's left windows. The days seemed too long this far south, so early in the year.

She and Anne had come home from Penney's, found Kevin still out, "Trailing after that appalling McAllister kid," Anne had said. "Did I tell you about the mother—happy homemaker, moronically born again?" They'd phoned for an extra-large pizza with double cheese, mushrooms, ripe olives, ground beef, and pepperoni. "Ordering a pizza is the only sure way to get Kevin in before dark. Somehow, I think he senses a pizza—it would probably bring him back from the dead."

A small elderly man in a white jacket and little white paper cap had delivered the order, pale slender blue-veined wrists trembling with strain as he held the wide box out. Sara'd gone upstairs to get a twenty-dollar bill out of her purse, paid him, and tipped him two dollars. The old man had seemed to want to talk with Sara after that, stand out on the front steps and discuss the weather . . . how warm the days were becoming. Perhaps would have complained about traffic—he drove a very small white car with a pizza sign on top—but Anne had come out and thanked him, stepped back smiling, and closed the door. "Tipping a pizza delivery guy? Sis, get hold of yourself."

Kevin had come in after they'd started eating, said "Hi," and put a five-slice section of pie on a big plate, heated it in the microwave inset above the counter, then took a green can of 7-Up out of the refrigerator, and sat down at the island beside Sara.

The pie was gone quickly, Sara eating five slices, and Kevin his five. Anne had eaten two.

After the pizza, Sara'd asked Kevin to come ride with her.

"Me?" Kevin was still sitting, finishing his 7-Up. "No thanks, Mrs. Maher."

"Call me Sara."

"Sara. I don't want to go for a ride, O.K.?"

"Come on, I'm just going to drive around the development. I'm not going out in the street."

"Thanks, but no thanks."

"Kevin, do what your aunt asks you." Anne was folding the pizza carton small enough to fit in the trash can under the sink. "We're supposed to recycle this stuff, but I can never remember where cardboard goes. I think we're supposed to make little packages, tie them up. —*Kevin*."

"Hey—I don't *want* to. O.K.?"

"Kevin, just do it."

"Great." Kevin had finished his 7-Up, climbed off the counter stool, and followed Sara through to the garage. . . .

"That's it," Kevin said. "Second time we went all the way around. Mom's watching us out the kitchen window."

"I know. I saw her looking through the curtain."

"She's scared you're going to ding the car."

"Well, I'm not. I can drive—I just haven't driven for a while."

"Dad's got a new BMW, makes this look like shit. You going around *again*?"

"I'm going to practice starting a couple of times. And practice parking."

"Radical. . . ."

When night, pleasantly cooler, came down completely so nothing could be seen through the TV room's tall windows, Sara—avoiding looking at the news—got up off the couch and kissed Anne good-night. Then climbed the stairs, heard harsh music from Kevin's room down the hall, went into her own room and shut the door.

The paper bags from Penney's lay on the near bed, and Sara opened them in turn, took out two pairs of slacks, beige and charcoal gray, a medium-length skirt (light-gray wool) and three tailored blouses: a pale ivory, a chocolate brown, and one striped gray.

She took two folded pullover V-neck sweaters from a big bag—one sweater black, chain knit, the other natural white. Sara laid these out on the bed, disappointed with the black sweater. There'd been a dove-gray turtleneck she'd liked better, but Anne had kept after her to buy the turtleneck until Sara just couldn't do it. So now she was stuck with the black, which would at least go with the gray slacks and skirt.

She dumped four pairs of cotton panties and four bras, all white, out of another sack, along with three pairs of panty hose (one smoke, two flesh tone), and two new T-shirts (one white, one gray). A larger bag held a slate-gray exercise outfit, sweatpants and sweatshirt. "Always handy for super-casual," Anne had said, "—and you can come exercise with me."

Sara opened the shoe boxes, held each pair up to examine: black low-heel pumps (which had hurt her feet just trying them on, though they were her size). Dark tan loafers. Blue-and-gray New Balance running shoes; they were the only really comfortable ones.

She hung the skirt, slacks, and blouses in the closet, ranked the shoes on the closet floor. The sweaters went in the dresser's second drawer, underwear in the top. Then Sara went back to the bed and opened the last bag, unfolded the safari jacket and put it on. She stood looking at it in the long mirror on the closet door. Khaki. It looked all right with her jeans; the belt was nice. . . .

"One cocktail dress?" Anne had been standing beside the saleswoman, both of them staring at Sara in the beige slacks and tan loafers.

Sara'd said, "No."

"All right, all right. Not a cocktail dress, but some dress you could wear if you went out one evening. Maybe we'll go to a nice restaurant."

"No." Sara'd been surprised by how much the clothes had cost. It seemed ridiculous to be spending so much money, when jeans and sweatshirts would do. "I don't need a fancy dress."

"All right, you don't need a fancy dress—but wouldn't you like a fancy dress?"

"No."

"You don't want to just try Nordstrom's, maybe find something actually nice?"

"No."

"You're real fun, sis."

While they were in Penney's, walking out of Lingerie, Sara'd suggested they buy Helen a robe, so she wouldn't have to sit in the wheelchair in the hospital gown and blanket.

"I already bought her one, peach with white piping." Annie had stopped to look at a powder-blue suit jacket with matching miniskirt. "—She shit in it twice, and that was that." Annie took the suit off the rack, held it up to her front. "What do you think?"

"You'd look good in it."

Annie had sighed, and seemed tired of shopping. "If I were ten years younger, I'd look good in it. . . ."

Sara took off the safari jacket, and hung it in the closet. She wished she'd gotten the gray turtleneck, or at least something besides the black sweater. And she didn't have the excuse of not enough time; she'd made Annie impatient by staying so long in the dressing room. Had sat in there in her underwear, not looking at the clothes carefully at all, just happy to be away from the people in the store, away from all the clothes packed on both sides of the aisles. There was too much to choose from, too much for anybody to ever buy, and most of it badly made. It seemed to her people had gotten dumber in the last five years, to buy stuff like that at those prices. She'd sat in the dressing room until Annie came in after her.

Sara went to the dresser for her purse, searched through it, and found at the bottom—with forgotten tweezers and a Chap Stick—the small frayed clipping, an advertisement torn out of *Field and Stream* the year before, down in Billy Mitchell. *J. D. Banto, Guide and Outfitter . . . Crow Rapids, Montana.*

She sat on the near bed and picked up the phone, heard a dial tone, and punched in O, then the numbers from the ad. The operator sounded very young; Sara asked for time and charges, then waited while a phone rang in Montana.

"Hello. J. Banto Outfittin'." An older woman, with a Southern accent. Maybe Texan.

"Hello. I'm calling long distance; I'd like to speak to Mr. Banto."

The woman said, "Hang on," put the phone down with a clatter, and after a little while Sara heard it picked up.

"Banto. . . ."

"Mr. Banto? J. D. Banto?"

"You got him."

"Mr. Banto, I'm calling about your ad in *Field and Stream*—"

"I don't have no ad in *Field and Stream*."

"This was last year."

"Oh, right. O.K. What can I do you for?"

"Mr. Banto, I'm a woman, and—"

"I didn' think you were a guy, honey. Now, what's up?"

"Well, I've been in Alaska for several years, and I've been trapping . . . subsistence."

"Where in Alaska?"

"In the Brooks. We had a leased homestead."

"Past the Porcupine?"

"Yes, east of that. Up above the Kenana."

". . . Well, that case, I'd say 'subsistence' is the word."

"Yes."

"What's your name?"

"Oh, I'm sorry. Sara Maher."

"You callin' from Alaska, Ms. Maher?"

"Seattle."

"Well, welcome to civilization, if you want to call it that. What can I help you with?"

"I don't want help, Mr. Banto. I want a job."

"Oh, shit—pardon my French, honey. But let me guess—you want to wrangle, camp work an' so forth, and lead up to doin' some guidin' for elk or bear or cougar, an' so forth. Am I right or wrong?"

"I can do that, Mr. Banto. And I'm not lying—I can handle horses and dogs, any animal. I was raised on the Bow Tie, north of Drummond. I can ride and I can handle stock. And I'm a good camp cook, and I don't mean just rough cooking—I mean Dutch oven dinners, too."

"I'm sure. I'll just bet that's true."

"It is, Mr. Banto."

"Call me Jerry."

"Jerry . . . I'm Sara."

"Sara it is."

"It's true what I said, Jerry. I can wrangle stock and I can cook. I wouldn't lie about that. I mean it. And I can work harder than any hand you've ever seen, and I'd work for just grub and board until you were satisfied. And Mr.—and Jerry, I am a very good hunter."

"I don't doubt it."

"I've hunted to eat for several years. I know grazers—all kinds— and wolves, goats, and mountain sheep. I know . . . bears, very well."

"I don't doubt any of it, Sara."

"And I don't need comfort. I don't care about it. Weather doesn't mean much to me. I know that sounds foolish, but it's true."

"Anybody lived up in the Brooks a few years, I know that's true."

"—And I get along. I get along with everybody. I don't talk much, but I get along fine." Sara listened for Mr. Banto to say something, but he didn't. ". . . This is the most I've talked in a long time."

"O.K. now, Sara, just take it easy. See, the situation—"

"I guess I should tell you I'm not someone that's especially good-looking—you know, really pretty."

"Honey, listen . . . listen to me."

"I will, but I just want to say that you have probably never seen a hunter a lot better than I am. I'm a good shot, and I can find game."

"Darlin', I bet you can. I'd bet on it. An' if you'd called for a job a few years ago, I probably would have taken you up—give you a try, anyway, if you wanted to come out here."

"I can come right out. I know it sounds strange to say it, but I have a feeling it would be good working for you. That your family . . . that we'd like each other."

". . . Sara, I think we would have liked each other. Probably we could have worked together just fine, but honey, sad truth is I don't need another wrangler. Half the time now, we helicopter up into them mountains, or truck up, anyway—ride just a little way in. An' these days, it's mostly picture hunts. People come up with cameras and long lenses and all that. It's less an' less often people come with rifles—an' what huntin' there is, I got old friends need every trip they can get."

"I'd work for nothing."

"But that wouldn' be fair to these people out here, or to you, either. I know men guided an' hunted out here all their lives since they grew up, an' right now, today, they're happy if they get a family wants to go a day up an' a day back . . . take some pictures, have a picnic with food they're used to—food the kids'll eat, hot dogs an' Cokes—sleep out one night, an' then come back sittin' real heavy on the horses, complainin' all the way."

"I could do that work."

"No ma'am, I don't think you could."

"But some people still hunt."

"—An' most of them that do is old clients, already fixed up. What I'm tellin' you, Sara, is there isn't the business here to use you. Five, ten years ago, maybe. Not no more."

"I could work around the place. . . ."

"Sara, I got gran'kids workin' around this place. I got a horse-hand been with me for thirty years. If I knew of anybody hirin', anybody could use a person used to livin' rough an' makin' do, I'd phone 'em for you right this minute. But I don't know a one. The business is not that kind of a business, no more. We got swimmin' pools an' tennis courts out where I used to hunt cougars."

"O.K. . . . O.K. Then, I was thinking, what about sheepherding? I'm used to being alone, and I know animals. And I can handle things."

"Honey—it's Basques and Mexicans still doin' the herdin' out here. No way a rancher's goin' to hire some white woman to do that, sit out in the mountains half the year all alone except for a couple of dogs."

"But that would suit me. It would suit me just fine."

Mr. Banto laughed. He had an old man's squeaking laugh. "An' damn if I don't believe it—but isn't no other rancher goin' to believe it. Or take a chance on havin' trouble with his herders on your account, neither. I am sorry. . . ."

"O.K. All right. . . . Thank you very much for speaking with me, Mr. Banto."

"Jerry. It was a pleasure speakin' to you, Sara. I wish you an' me could have gone out in the old days. Would have covered them mountains like paint, I'll bet."

"Yes, we would have."

"You take care, now."

"Thanks again, Jerry," Sara said, and hung up the phone.

After a few moments, while she was still sitting there, the phone rang—and Sara thought Mr. Banto had changed his mind . . . had somehow gotten her number to return the call. But it was the operator, saying the call had cost four dollars and eighty-three cents.

Sara lay down on the bed coverlet as if she were going to cry, but had no intention of doing that. She closed her eyes to be less where she was, and after a while imagined herself at a campfire up in the Bitterroots. She was alone, she thought—then saw her mother sitting across the fire, its light bronzing her round pretty face, gilding hair already lighter than her daughter's. Helen Whaley was dressed as she used to be, going into town on the weekends when Sara was small—like a rodeo cowgirl, in jeans and buckskin boots, pearl-buttoned shirt and fringed buckskin jacket. When she'd dressed that way, it was as if she were making fun of the Bow Tie and ranching, working with cattle. "Playing Roy Rogers," she'd say.

Her mother seemed happy this evening, though—to be young again, well, and prettier than her daughter. She looked pleased with Sara, smiled at her across the fire, and appeared to have forgotten being in The Arbor . . . being sick, and old.

Sara imagined two elk steaks spitted on green willow sticks leaning against the fire's heat, hissing as they roasted. She'd squeezed drops of gall down the meat when her mother was checking the horses, then scraped rock salt onto the steaks before she spitted them. Sara could smell the elk steaks broiling, hear spatters of fat cracking in the coals. She'd shot the young bull low, just behind the shoulder. Put him down with that one shot.

Her mother sat staring off into the dark, wearing little white shell earrings Sara remembered.

Sara thought of asking if her mother was hungry, and Helen seemed to hear that before it was asked, turned to grin at Sara— opened her mouth wide and pretended to bite, to show how hungry she was. But her teeth were gone. She had only soft mottled gums, wet with mucus, in a mouth spotted as a sick trout's.

Sara leaned back from the fire, said "Don't," and woke herself saying it.

Relieved to be awake and have her mother gone, Sara got off the bed, undressed, folded her jeans and sweatshirt away, then took her underwear and socks into the bathroom. She brushed her teeth (avoiding the mirror), sat on the soft toilet seat to be rid of lunch, then took a shower—lingering, enjoying the hot water more this time. She soaped her panties, bra, and socks, then stomped on them under the shower's spray, humming, imitating the thudding rhythm the Koyukon women had danced to around the fur-draped pole. She turned and turned in the shower, stomping on her underwear, humming, then softly singing *"Yaaa . . . saaa . . . ho . . . ho . . ."* until she felt sick from the shower's heat, and turning and turning and turning.

10

"I simply do not understand you, Sara. I *mean* it." Anne, in a white denim apron over a maroon wool dress, was washing place mats at the sink. Kevin, sullen after Shredded Wheat and a banana, already gone to walk to school. "—It is just fucking *outrageous*. Strolling around on the goddamn roof buck naked? It is fucking outrageous!" Anne stepped an angry little two-step in oxblood high-heeled pumps. She was wearing a single strand of cultured pearls and small pearl-button earrings.

"I wasn't strolling. . . ."

"Don't think Kevin won't hear about this. Of course he'll hear about it. And that's just great; it's exactly what I need with Kevin, who's getting impossible, anyway—a goddamn aunt who's crazy as bat shit and is up on the roof naked!"

"I'm not crazy, Anne. I was just sleeping outside, and it was getting light, and I was coming in."

"*Outside?* You weren't outside; you were up on the fucking roof, for Betty Kass to look out her kitchen window over there first thing this morning—and guess what? Anne Rittman's older sister is up on the roof walking around with no clothes on. This is not that kind of neighborhood! *Believe* me." She rinsed the place mats one by one, shook water off them. "There are lots of kids in this neighborhood—the fact that you don't see them, the fact that they're all inside watching TV, doesn't mean they aren't here!" Anne dried the mats, stepped to the left of the sink, slid a drawer open and put them away.

"I'm sorry."

"I just thank God it was Betty Kass." Anne untied her apron, took it off. "—Thank *God*. When she called before breakfast, I thought . . . I just thought thank God it wasn't the Piersons, or those born-again assholes on the other side. It *could* have been. Any of them could have just looked across the pond—and there you were, apparently walking around up there looking at the goddamn sunrise. I mean— really, Sara—would it have killed you to wear a bathrobe? I mean . . . then I could have said, oh, you were just checking the roof for a little leak." Anne walked back to the laundry room, the apron bunched in her hand.

Sara sat at the island counter, looking at the last half of her blueberry muffin. She wanted it, but thought it would make Annie angrier to see her eating, as if she didn't care. She'd either have to eat it fast, or forget it.

Anne called from the laundry room. "Because I couldn't think of anything to say to Betty, it was such a surprise. And now," she came back into the kitchen, "—oh, it's so nice this hasn't hurt your appetite. Go ahead. Just stuff yourself. —And now, I'll have to call her back and pretend it's so funny, and you were checking a leak on the roof, and your bathrobe was in the washing machine and so forth. And she'll still think you're nuts."

"I won't do that again, Anne. I'm sorry."

"Well . . ." Anne came and sat down at the counter. "Well, don't look so abused. You're not a goddamned child. I already have one of those, and it's not working out. I really, really don't need another one. —What the hell were you doing out there? Sleeping on the roof, for Christ's sake . . ."

"I had trouble sleeping in the room."

"Oh, give me a break. What is this, the Jungle Book or something? Didn't you have a cabin up north? I mean, you didn't sleep in the goddamn trees, did you?"

"No. The room was just warm."

" 'The room was warm.' Look, sleep naked by the window, O.K.? Not *out* the window."

"All right."

"—And since I assume you don't have a bathrobe, I'll lend you an old one. It's blue, and too skimpy, but you're thinner and it'll fit fine."

"O.K."

"Thank you very much for your cooperation." Anne stood and picked up their plates. "You coming with me? Driving me to work?"

"O.K."

"I called Eleanor after Betty Kass's little bombshell—and believe me I didn't feel like doing you any favors—and Eleanor gave you an immediate appointment this morning as a special favor to me . . .

also since you're a fellow ex-Alaskan and so forth. She doesn't do things like that for everybody. So, after you drop me off, you can just walk up two blocks and you'll see Solutions on the left, beside the liquor store. You can pay for it, or tell her to put it on my account."

"I'll pay for it."

"You going to wear that?"

Sara looked down. She was wearing a clean white T-shirt, jeans, and her new blue running shoes. "I could put on my safari jacket. . . ."

"Why not, sis? That's what we bought it for. Go up and get it. You'll look very uptown. —I'll back the car out."

"O.K."

"I suppose," Anne said, "—this roof thing will seem funny, in a few years."

"That's right . . . that's all you have to do. Go right on Seventy-second, then right on Southeast Seventy-second, then left on Island Crest. Stay on this all the way to town—and just reverse it, going back. You're doing fine, sis, the brakes are a little soft—you have to start stopping early. I am damned if I'll spend a fortune to have them just look at the brakes. Then they'll say they're just the way they're supposed to be. —Red light."

"I see it."

"You really have to start stopping before that."

"All right."

"And use these seat belts." Anne demonstrated, plucking at the seat-belt strap across her breasts. "I mean it—that's one thing I always want you to do." She was wearing a long, belted maroon sweater, matching her dress.

"All right." Sara found it interesting to be driving somewhere. It was so effortless, like traveling in a dream. She turned the wheel slightly to the right just to feel the Mercedes begin to drift that way. ". . . And the bookstore's doing O.K.?" Then turned the wheel back.

"Well, Facets was a bookstore—could still politely be called one—but what it really is now is a crystal store, a New Age store."

"But people buy that stuff."

"Oh, hell yes they buy it. Know what I sell? The whole grim catalogue? Let's see . . . I've got books and pamphlets on astrology and vegetarianism, on Dianetics, past lives, somatics, Hellerwork, inner child nurturance, Reiki Healing, Grof holograph breathwork," Anne took a breath, as if in illustration, "—vitamin cancer therapy,

Kabala, tarot, rolfing, the Great Pyramid, massage—spiritual massage—and personal development, co-dependency, self-knowledge, self-understanding, self-love and recovery. . . ." She reached down to push the lighter knob in, then searched in her purse, found her cigarettes. "I have shelves full of New Age music tapes—doo-doo doodling, no rhythm or melody to upset anybody—and lots of thin little books full of the wisdom of various Hindu con artists and fake Tibetans. I've got five shelves on Wicca and the Great Mother and herbs. And I have crystals and stormolites and accretions and mineral chunks, all of which are browsed over," she lit her cigarette, reached to pull out the dash ashtray, "—are browsed over and occasionally bought by middle-class adults with oatmeal for brains . . . and probably with college degrees. Sociology, Humanistic Psychology, Transactional Counseling . . . Human Services. All that crap."

"I just keep going straight?"

"Keep going straight. —And it seemed to be a good idea when Connor and I were still together, and I wanted some independence. It was never fun to ask Connor for money; at no point in our marriage was that fun. It seemed like a good idea—make a few genteel not-too-demanding bucks with a quality bookstore, consistent with our being so upper middle class here at The Lakes. Unfortunately, people seem more and more interested in less and less quality. —You can go faster. . . . So, since the divorce, and it turned out I needed to make at least *some* money, I have gradually restocked with totally mindless shit." She tapped ashes from the cigarette into the ashtray. "And now I'm stuck with at least seeming to take it seriously. And believe me, that's getting harder and harder. Special sale days, yours truly is forced to actually dress the part, and can be seen strutting her stuff in a Peruvian poncho, Birkenstocks, a moonstone choker (fake), and no makeup. —Stop sign."

"I see it." Morning sunlight flashed into the windshield so Sara had to squint to see the road. The day was already too warm, certainly in the fifties, too early in the year.

"It's all I can do not to spit on their money when they pay out thirty, *forty* bucks for some piece of mining debris that cost me forty cents. It makes me . . . seasick. I would rather, believe me, I would rather deal with regular religious crap. I'd rather be selling crucifixes and plastic Virgin Marys—and there's an unbelievable tale; I never believed her story for a minute. But at least that stuff is *serious* nonsense."

"That's right."

"Now—O.K., we're coming into town, at least it's the strip and we call it town."

"All right."

"Drive a little slower."

"Annie, I'm going slow."

"All right. Facets is right up there in the next block; it's on this side of the street, just past the bank."

"O.K."

"Pull in right up there . . . one more . . . pull in up there. Any parking place alongside the store. They won't—they will not give me a designated parking place; don't ask me why."

"O.K."

"Fine. Sis, keep the keys. When you get your hair done, well . . . just go where you want. If you want to visit Mom again, go ahead, more power to you. You know how to get to The Arbor?"

"I think so. It's over past the University. Over the bridge, and go up I-Five to Forty-fifth?"

"Right."

"—And then just stay on that to Dixon?"

"Right."

"—And take a left."

"O.K. And there's a Seattle map in the driver's side pocket, anyway. But for God's sake, Sara, be careful. I cannot, I really cannot afford a big bump-up on the insurance. O.K.?"

"I'll be very careful."

"All right." Anne got out her side. "Lock it up."

Sara got out and locked it up.

"See? That locks the whole car. You don't have to push all the buttons down."

"Right."

"O.K. Come in and take a look at retard heaven. And please don't mention that vibrator stuff to Marie. She's just a kid and was very embarrassed, couldn't imagine 'why they picked on *me*. . . .' "

"I wouldn't mention it. Oh, Annie, I have a check I got for furs. It's for a thousand dollars."

"Is it good?"

"Oh, it's good. Bud's got a lot of money."

"O.K. Let me have it, and I'll take it to the bank this afternoon and deposit it, and give you the cash when you want." Anne pushed a glass door open (*Facets* printed on the glass in gold) and led inside. The store was narrow, with bare hardwood floors. Its walls were brick in every shade of weathered red, and the space (smelling of ashy incense) ran far back in a series of racks and display counters to the end of the building. "—I don't suppose you want to open a checking account with that?"

"No." The store was softly lit by rows of green shaded lamps hanging from a high, bone-white ceiling. Two women were standing together halfway down an aisle, looking through a book.

"Right. Well, please don't carry all that cash around in your purse. . . . Marie, I'd like you to meet my sister. Older sister, Sara, down from Alaska at last."

Marie, standing behind a counter to the right of the door, was looking through the cash-register drawer. She lifted her head, said a soft "Hi . . ." and stood gangling and frail, pale-gray eyes protected by glasses, long face dead white above a buttoned white blouse, long neck weighted with unbound hair thick and black as an Indian's.

"Problem?"

"No, Anne, no problem. I was looking for the key to lock the register."

"That's the old register. This one, there's no key."

"Oh . . . code. That's right."

"Why? You have to pee?"

"Yeah."

"Well, go pee. I'm here."

"Thanks. . . ." Marie drifted down the counter, out from behind it (she was wearing a pleated ankle-length skirt, dark-brown), then down the store's center aisle toward the back. She passed the two women—older, both gray-haired—now browsing at a tall display rack of mounted crystals. Marie walked like a model, erect, head up, placing her feet carefully, shoulders back.

"Not a mental giant." Anne walked behind the counter and shut the register drawer. "You know, sis, you could do this—take care of the store."

"Well, I don't—"

"Oh, of course—no wind in your hair and so forth and so on. I won't mention roofs. Well, look around, examine the depths to which mediocre minds are eager to sink." She slid a small plastic rack of charms (miniature pot-metal pyramids, ankhs, pentacles) farther down the counter. "I particularly recommend Swami Sockitooya on the second shelf over there." She pointed to white-painted wooden shelves ranked up and down the wall across the store. "—Little book with a dark red cover, just past the diet section. Dark red cover,

Swami's picture's on the back. He's picking his nose with his tongue."

"I had an appointment."

Eleanor, in a dark blue-flowered print, was a woman big as a big man, with a ruddy face that might have been a man's, but nicely made up and crowned with crisp auburn curls almost natural. "An appointment. . . . And you are?"

"Sara Maher."

"Umm . . . right. Anne Rittman's sister." Eleanor turned to her counter, opened a large black appointment book, and leafed through it.

It seemed to Sara Solutions was a pretty shop—nicer looking than Cut'n Up in Fairbanks—brightly lit, its paneled walls bleached white and decorated with framed charcoal drawings of classic hairdos. It smelled of dyes and chemicals for permanents, and was noisy, six dryers roaring, a pretty blond girl talking while she washed a woman's hair. The smells were worse than the noise, and Sara tried to stop breathing through her nose. Tried just breathing through her mouth, and that helped.

Eleanor found the current page, took a silver pen from a holder to make a note, and left the appointment book open. "You were up in Alaska, and you lost your husband."

"Yes."

"I said I'd do you, but my shampoo girl didn't come in, so I'm stuck with a client. We're all washing hair, today. Come on back. I'm going to let Frank work with you." Eleanor had wide shoulders; Sara, following, thought she must be a size fourteen at least. Maybe sixteen.

"Been down long?" Eleanor talked in the direction she was walking, as though Sara were in front of her.

"No, not long."

A woman peered out at them from under her dryer hood as they passed. Probably thought Sara was an emergency case.

"I fished out of Ketchikan with my old man for four years." Eleanor stopped to watch the young blonde shampooing.

"Did you?" Sara said. "Oh, that's great! I trapped. My husband and I trapped up in the Brooks."

"Thin trapping up there, isn't it?" And walked on, having made no comment to the shampooer.

"Yes, you have to cover much more territory that high. Don't you miss being up there?"

"I miss the hell out of the country, but I don't miss working that boat. Damn near killed the both of us. —O.K. This is Frank. He doesn't look it, but he knows hair, and you need some work. Frank— Mrs. Maher." And turned and lumbered lightly away, back toward the front of the shop.

Frank was tall and balding, had narrow black eyes and a big nose, and looked tough. He was dressed in blue denims and a blue cotton work shirt with the sleeves rolled up. There was a tattoo of a red-and-green parrot down to his right wrist, and long muscles in his forearms forced the veins up under his skin like thick cord. "That's puttin' it mildly," he said, staring at Sara's head. " 'Some work' is puttin' it mildly. What have you been doin' to that hair? You been cuttin' it, right? You cut that yourself."

"Yes, I did."

"You mean to have an off-wedge back there, or are we talkin' accident? Come on, sit down. Anne Rittman's sister, right?"

"Yes. I didn't mean to cut it that way," Sara said, and sat. The big padded chair was more comfortable than the Mercedes' seats—not so soft.

"That's a relief. An' what about the nails?"

"I . . . fell."

Frank stooped for a folded plastic sheet in a bottom cabinet, shook it open and draped her with it, tucked its transparency in at her sides, and fastened it at her neck. "I'm not talkin' about the two nails you lost. I'm talkin' about the raggedy dirty ones."

"They aren't dirty."

"Then they're so messed up they look dirty. People judge you by your nails, you know."

Sara said nothing, watched him slide open a drawer, select narrow-bladed scissors, a black rattail comb.

"—Nothin' to say?"

"What about?"

"About gettin' Jennifer to come do the nails. You know. . . ." he stepped behind her, ducked down to look at the back of her head, "—you know, it isn't a lot of use me givin' you a nice haircut, you go around lookin' like a longshore guy busted his nails on some coffee bags. Right?"

"I guess so."

"You guess so, huh?" A sudden flourish of the scissors, *snip snip snip.* It was so fast Sara couldn't tell what he was doing back there.

"I don't want too much off."

"Yeah? Well you are goin' to have some off, you want me to cut

this hair. You really butchered it, you know—an' there's plenty ladies would love to have hair this thick. Real healthy hair, but you
screwed it up. So, you want me to cut it, then let me cut it. I will—"
snip—"make it look good. Short, but good."

Sara sat looking into the big mirror in front of the chair, trying to
see what he was doing behind her.

"O.K.?" He was a smoker; Sara smelled cigarette smoke when he
talked.

"What?"

"O.K. do you trust me?" Scissors and comb poised over her head.

"All right."

Snip snip snip snip . . . all very rapid, the comb in his left hand, the
scissors in his right. "I see that look."

"What look?"

Snip snip. "The look. The 'What kind of weird guy is this to be
cuttin' hair?' look."

"No."

"Oh, yes. What kind of weird—" snip, comb comb comb—"weird
dude is this to be cuttin' hair?"

"I wasn't thinking that."

"Uh-oh. Now the nose is growin' for lyin'. An' you're like me—
you can't afford no more nose." Snip.

"But I wasn't thinking that."

"Oooh, that nose is goin' to be immense." Frank stepped farther
back behind her, slowly ducked to the right, then the left, staring at
her hair. "I want you to do me a favor."

"All right."

"I want you to let anybody—anybody—cut your hair next time.
But don't you do it."

"I didn't have anyone else to do it."

"Then leave it alone. Let it grow an' just tie it back. But don't cut
it—I'm beggin' you." He began to snip at the sides, above her ears.
He was doing it so quickly, Sara couldn't see him cut. He might have
just been pretending to cut.

"Really, I don't want it too short."

Frank didn't seem to pay any attention, didn't answer. She noticed his hands as he used the scissors and comb. He had large
hands. Big knuckles.

"—Really."

"Hey," he said, and stopped combing, cutting. "Listen, what you
want an' what your hair needs are two different things. You under-

stand? You got all the right in the world to do what you want. You don't want me to work on you, you just say so, no hard feelin's. But your hair's got rights, too. O.K.? It's got rights to look its absolute best. Do you agree with that?"

"I suppose so. . . ."

"O.K. An' if it's also O.K. with you I do the work, then just sit there an' let me an' your hair get together." *Comb, comb.* "Keepin' in mind I am not the person that wrecked your hair. You are that person. *I* am the person that's tryin' to salvage it." He flourished his scissors, took two snips of air for emphasis. " 'Cause what I am not—an' I got nothin' against 'em; some of 'em are aces—but what I am not is a gay guy just doin' some decoratin' here. For me, it's strictly a very serious profession, an' I spent years learnin' it, an' I know what I'm doin'." He ducked to her other side. *Snip snip snip snip.*

Sara watched Frank's face in reflection, harsh and intent . . . watched his large hands orbit her head, giving her such concentrated attention.

"Well?" *Snip snip snip.*

"Well what?"

"You decided on gettin' the nails done?"

"All right."

"No argument?" *Snip snip.*

"No argument."

"Now, you're gettin' smart." *Snip.*

"Jumping Jesus." Anne, standing beside Marie, rang up a sale to a stocky blond man wearing a thick white fisherman's sweater. She made change, and closed the cash-register drawer. Then she stepped down the counter to see better.

Sara turned her head left, then right. There was a display of small earrings on the countertop; a little square mirror, part of the display. Sara could see herself in the mirror. She looked like a woman surprised by her hair.

"Well, sis, they didn't leave you much—but it looks good. Really. It does look good. . . . It suits you."

"Sure."

"Hey, I mean it. It looks good. It's very trendy now, hair that short."

"Mmmm."

"I like it, Mrs. Maher." Marie, wrapping a small crystal pendant for the blond man. The man was listening to their conversation. Looking at Sara's hair.

Anne leaned back to better judge. "Sis, it really isn't bad. Don't you like it?"

"I don't think so; it's very short."

"Who did it?"

"Frank." Sara wished Annie would notice her fingernails. Jennifer had done a good job, buffed them and used a clear polish. Had put Band-Aids where the two nails were gone.

"Frank? Oh, God. . . . He's a madman, but he's really good. He did mine the time before. You know he's an ex-con?"

"No, I didn't." Sara put her right hand up on the counter so Annie might glance down, see how good the nails looked. But Annie didn't notice.

"Well, he is. Armed robbery. He learned to be a barber 'in the joint,' and fell in love with cutting hair. All Eleanor's ladies think he's a hoot."

"Well, he wouldn't listen."

"Hey, I like it," Marie said, surprisingly definite. She handed the blond man his small white box. "I think it's very spare."

The big man in gray tweed, the manager, wasn't in the office off The Arbor's reception room. A slender woman in a peach blouse and taupe business suit sat in there, working at a computer console. She looked up at Sara, smiled, got up and came out. Her hair, center-parted, iron-gray, fell almost to her shoulders. —The odor in the reception room wasn't of roses anymore; they'd changed the scented candle. Pine.

"Hi. Can I help you?"

"I'm Mrs. Whaley's daughter."

"Oh, Anne's sister—and you've visited already, haven't you? I'm Mrs. Todd, the assistant manager."

"Yes. Yesterday." Sara thought the woman was looking at her hair, thinking it was too short.

The corridor was lined either side, as it was before—the women and an occasional man watching Sara come toward them, watching as she passed, watching as she walked away. Or paying no heed at all, sitting with their heads fallen forward onto their chests, or sharply back, mouths gaping.

A different nurse than before was bending over a wheelchair, talking to a blue-gowned woman's small slumped bald head, an ear pale and crinkled as a little cabbage leaf.

The nurse wore no cap, only a white uniform with an LPN pin on its left lapel, and a white plastic name tag on the right, with "K. Ramsey" printed on it. When she straightened, having said what she wanted, the ear and its head lay still, made no acknowledgment. Sara was struck by how young the nurse—a sturdy brunette—looked, surrounded by such ruin. Her hair was cut almost as short as Sara's.

"I'm Mrs. Maher, Helen Whaley's daughter. And I wondered if I could ask you a question."

"Sure." Plump, and in her thirties at least, but here miraculously young and beautiful by contrast, the nurse stood beside the wheelchair, a flat red-and-white pack of Huggies baby wipes in her hand, interested in Sara's question.

"My sister heard from the doctor or the other nurse—Mrs. Solmssen?—that this sort of tumor my mother has could grow inside her head until it pushes her eyes out."

K. Ramsey seemed startled that Sara would say such a thing, would even think it. "That's so unusual," she said. "Mrs. Maher, almost always the patient expires before that would ever happen."

"But not always?"

"That would be *so* unusual." The nurse rested her right hand on the wheelchair's back handle, and began to gently roll the chair slightly forward, then back, then forward again, as if it were a baby carriage containing a restive child.

"But it could happen?"

"Well, I think you should talk with the doctor." The nurse seemed to feel Sara was odd to even ask about something so grotesque. Without looking down, she pulled a baby wipe out of the pack, held the damp napkin in her hand as if she were ready to clean the idea out of Sara's head. "—You know, check with him, rather than worry about something that might never happen."

"But it could?"

"Really, it's much more likely something else would happen first. O.K.? I mean we're talking about several months down the line, if that particular thing were ever going to happen at all, which it probably wouldn't." She stooped to mop casually at a small spatter of urine on the wheelchair's steel foot-rest. "Margaret," she said, to ankles bruised blue, "—we just had Rest Room, and you went and you didn't go. So now we'll take you back to your room and keep you there until next Rest Room. And if you don't cooperate, if you keep urinating whenever you feel like it, you are not coming back out in this hall at all." Then, straightening up, said to Sara, "Listen, why don't you go right on in. Your mom's in her room; and I think we had a little discomfort this morning. Just headache. . . ."

Helen Whaley, in a pale-yellow hospital gown, a light-brown blanket draped over her lap, crouched lower in her wheelchair than Sara remembered from the day before. She gripped the wheelchair's arms with blue-veined hands, looked up as Sara walked in, and stared.

"Airs . . . mesh," she said, taking a quick breath between the words.

"I just had it cut."

Her mother rolled her eyes as if a friend sat just beside her on the right, would take her point and be amused.

"I didn't want it this short."

Helen looked past her to the door, waiting.

"Anne's still at work. So, I came over."

"Catsaw . . ."

"What? I didn't understand, Mom." Sara took one of the small straight-back chairs from against the wall, brought it over to face her mother, and sat.

"Catsaw *right.*" Helen turned her head to gaze out the room's window at the stretch of lawn, evergreens.

"Oh . . . 'all right.' Good, because I just wanted to visit, spend some time with you." And when her mother turned to look at her, but didn't answer, Sara imagined the tumor (gristly lump, resting blood-red in blackness) peering out at her through Helen's eyes— and wondered if the tumor, made of brain cells, might not be intelligent, or at least conscious. Might be squatting deep inside her mother's head, feeling uncomfortable, restless, moving just a little, stretching as it grew—shoving against her mother's brain, crushing places, pushing blood vessels aside, not knowing how much that hurt. Not knowing it made her mother's speech waver between sense and nonsense. Sara thought of talking to the tumor (if it couldn't see her, it might hear), telling it what it was doing to her mother. It was benign, after all—might not be as savage, insane, as a malignant one. Maybe Helen's brain had already tried that—tried communicating with it, reasoning with it, and found it was just too dumb, too sloppy and disorganized to understand what it was doing. A fool. . . .

Her mother turned away, sat gazing out the window, looking worse in the yellow hospital gown than she had in the white one, last visit. And she was breathing in a noisy way—deliberately in . . . deliberately out—as if breathing were something she had to think to do, every time. Someone, perhaps the retarded girl, Carrie, had arranged the sparse gray wisps of hair, combed and fluffed them, then tied a narrow dark-blue ribbon to the sturdiest clump at the back, knotted a small drooping bow.

Beneath those occasional tufts and delicate down, her mother's scalp was blotched and mottled pink, a dog's skin in mange. And sliced across by the two flushed scars that met just beside the blue bow in an angry intersection.

"You have a headache, Mom?"

Sara's mother winced, as if to hear a headache mentioned would bring it on, then shook her head, 'No.'

"Well, is there something you'd like to eat? I could go get some ice cream, and we could both have some."

"Don' *wan'* it." Helen, speaking more clearly, seemed reluctant to turn from the window—as if that were the way death would be coming, through the back yard.

"Anything else? Something good to eat?"

Her mother turned from the window to stare at Sara with bright hazel eyes as direct as ever. Eyes out of place in a rotting head. "I can' tase . . . can not . . . *taste.*" She looked annoyed, harassed by these offerings.

Sara was afraid her mother was going to tell her to leave, so she stopped talking, stopped asking questions. She was sitting close enough to smell an odor of urine. Urine, baby powder, and something else, a faint sour odor she supposed was the sweat of medication. That smell, particularly, began to bother her, so she stood up and walked over to the window, looked out onto the lawn (the sun was out, had laid a long dark-green shadow beneath the hedge)—then, when she turned to walk back, stopped by the curtained bed against the wall. She hesitated, standing by the white cloth, glanced back and saw her mother watching her.

"You can look," Helen said, very clearly. "She won' bite."

Now, Sara didn't want to look . . . but found the curtains' separation, opened them a little, and said, "Hi" into a pale cave of white sheets mounded hugely, a light-gray open-weave blanket folded at the foot. Above those, an immense face rested on a small white pillow. The face was rounded as a moon, so wide its features were shrunk to the center and seemed too small. Its hair was elaborately curled blue-white, and the eyes were small black chips—Sara saw them reflecting the light.

"Hi," she said. "You O.K.?"

The face slowly put out a broad and coated tongue. The eyes remained the same.

"Do you want some water? Some juice?"

The face stayed still, its tongue sticking out, its eyes bright as a rodent's.

Sara smiled at the eyes, then leaned back and closed the curtains.

"Room . . . mate," Helen Whaley said, and chuckled with a soft clicking sound, amused by Sara's expression. Helen put out her tongue in imitation. Then she said, "Alaska."

"Yes." Sara sat down beside her mother again, and reached out to take her left hand and hold it, whether Helen wanted her to or not.

"Hubson . . . *hus*band killed. Eaten by . . . a bear?" At her question, Helen smiled.

"Yes. It sounds funny," Sara said. "But it wasn't."

"Not much funny," her mother said, speaking better and better, "—when you are *there*. If you are *not* there . . . most things funny."

"It was my fault," Sara said. And although she'd decided before not to say any more—her mother didn't need to hear it—she found she couldn't stop, it was so oddly pleasureful. "He would probably have lived. Or maybe, anyway. But I was too frightened to go for the rifle, so I just watched, and then I couldn't even watch. He loved me, and that was the last thing he knew, that I wasn't going to help him. That I was too much of a coward even to try." Sara drew in a breath the way her mother was drawing hers. "—I didn't care. I was just glad it wasn't me. I was happy, is the truth. I was more happy that it wasn't me than I was sorry it was him. And that's the truth." She thought of saying she felt the same way now about her mother and the tumor growing in her brain, but that was so bad she was able to stop herself, though the effort made her cry. "Oh, *Christ*," Sara said, let go of her mother's hand, stood and reached over to the night table for a Kleenex. She blew her nose. "I'm just terrified of everything."

Her mother was looking at her as if Sara was becoming more interesting to watch than the back yard through the window. "You all ri' . . . ?"

"I'm all right."

They sat for a while, silent, side by side, and Sara wondered if her mother was wishing to exchange bodies with her—they were almost touching. She imagined her mother slowly sifting out of her spoiling body . . . and slowly, slowly filtering into Sara's. Pushing, gently pushing to settle in, so Sara was able to cling only to her body's side—then not even that, but fell away to find herself in the wheelchair, shriveled and monstrous, staring out the window at green growing things, her head containing something strange.

Sara didn't doubt her mother would do that if she could—would then turn with what had been Sara's thin sharp-featured face, her narrow dark hunter's eyes, and say in the voice that had been Sara's, "I'm sorry, sweetheart. I love you—but not more than living."

Then they would stay sitting side by side, screams struggling to be first out of Sara's clotted throat, until, subsiding, she would imagine she'd been her mother all along, and had only dreamed her daughter's life. . . .

"Get sick to ah stomach."

"You get sick to your stomach?" Sara thought her mother was growing tired, weary of the visit, her speech beginning to suffer.

Decisive nod, the blue bow nodding also.

"Want me to talk to the doctor?"

" 'Edison. Ess 'edison."

"That's his name?"

"It ess *'edison.*"

"It's the medicine?"

"Yesss."

"Can they change it? I'll ask if they can change it to something that won't make you sick."

"Won' do it. Isn' any uh'r 'edison."

"They have to give you that?"

"Yesss." Her mother nodded, weary, apparently sorry to have brought the matter up, and the woman in the curtained bed against the wall grunted, grunted again, then farted.

Helen grinned a gummy grin, amused, and gestured that way with her right hand. "Com . . . pany," she said slowly. And Sara remembered very clearly a summer morning in Seattle, out in the backyard helping Helen garden. "Your father," her mother had said, staking her tomatoes, "—isn't even company." The tomatoes hadn't done well; not enough sun.

"Remember your garden, Mom? Tomatoes?"

Her mother made a face. "No . . . sun."

"Chard was O.K."

Helen considered. The chard had done pretty well, but not very well. "Bugs."

"We don't have them—didn't have trouble with them, up in the mountains. Mosquitoes, but not a lot of insects in the garden."

Helen looked an inquiry, apparently to save such difficult speech.

"What did we have?"

Nod.

"Cabbage, cauliflower—and onions, but just barely. Too short a summer, so high. Potatoes. . . ."

"F'owers?"

"Pansies and marigolds."

"Not . . . much."

"No. Mostly wildflowers up there. And they're really beautiful in the summer. Fireweed, wand lily—that's poison, but very pretty, and arnica, a beautiful rich yellow flower, and saxifrage. And forget-me-nots; they're very small up there, but they're a wonderful blue. Remember Daddy bringing us wildflowers? He'd swing down and pick them while he was riding."

"Could do tha' . . . anyway. Pick f'owers."

"Mom, Dad was a good rancher. He couldn't help the weather."

" 'A rancher.' Tha's funny." Annoyed, Helen spoke better, looked more formidable, more herself and less a thing. "Couldn' . . . fix a win'mill. Couldn' doctor cat'l—"

"Cattle?"

"Ri'. Cat'l. An' couldn' stan' up for . . . himself."

"I know he wasn't tough."

A smile. "You got tha' ri'." Helen Whaley turned her head to look out the window again, the subject of husband dismissed.

Sara heard, as if in answer to these mumbled insults, her father's call, when—tall, stoop-shouldered, his long horseface red with wind-burn and pleasure—he came stomping into the house on Bow Tie one winter evening, his red-plaid wool coat clotted with snow.

"Helen! Oh, *say* Helen!" Stomp stomp, snow powdering the hall's brown hooked rug. And a swift aside to Sara, who was playing with Peter by the fireplace. "Hi, Sarita—where's your sis?"

Her mother's answer, first from the kitchen . . . then nearer as she came down the hall in a long-skirted blue denim dress, her forehead oiled with sweat from the big stove's heat, her light-brown hair pulled back in a ponytail.

"Bad bull's sold, and heifers are bought."

"You sold Larry?"

"Sold that sucker," he took Sara's mother into his arms, "—for two thousand dollars to Bud Tate who really, *really* knows stock."

"Poor Bud," Helen Whaley said, and seemed to Sara perfectly content to stay in her lanky husband's arms—perfectly content, and so unlikely to become old, dreadful and dying, then to insult his memory.

For Sara, this old woman and that young woman were not the same person. They had diverged years before, time separating them more perfectly than strangerhood—only their cold humor kept in common. This dying woman offered nothing of her youthful self but her name and title as Sara's mother, Annie's mother. Had become only that—a remnant, and a duty.

Sara remembered playing with Peter—as if recalling her parents as they were had drawn other loved ones from the past—had brought Peter, a stuffed toy (never Annie's favorite), a large indeterminate terrier, his coat curly, a grimy white. And eternally sitting. Sewn and stuffed to sit, so that by day beside Sara, and at night resting in her bed, he sat even while lying on his side, brown button eyes shining softly by the night-light lamp—a pink plastic crescent moon, smiling beneath its small shade. . . . The kindness and patience of stuffed animals, their comfort so great Sara remembered Peter as fondly as any living dog she'd had, except for Dutchy. Patient and kind, so different from living animals and people—all active, occasionally foolish and contrary.

"Have . . . to pee."

"O.K. Let me help you?"

Helen considered that, then nodded.

Sara stood and went to the back of the wheelchair, tried to push it, and discovered its brake was on. Her mother clicked her tongue in annoyance, and reached down with a shriveled left arm to release the small lever. "Come *on*."

Sara pushed the chair carefully to the bathroom door, saw it would barely fit through, and eased it in. The bathroom was long and narrow with a small square frosted window at its end—its walls and ceiling painfully white, small floor tiles pale blue. Sara pulled the wheelchair back to the sink for room, leaned down and set the brake lever. She sidled past the chair to raise the toilet lid, then turned to face her mother, stooped to help her up.

"Carefu'. . . ."

"I'll be careful."

Sara bent into a bloom of odor—baby powder and staleness. Urine. Slid her arms under her mother's armpits (Helen's crumpled left cheek, soft as tissue paper, brushing hers), then slowly, gently lifted, feeling shallow gelatin in her grip, and beneath that looseness . . . small bones.

"*Carefu'.*"

"I am being careful." Lifted a little more, so her mother, almost upright, slumped to rest against her. Then, with Helen's wasted feet paddling weakly in pink slippers, held her up, turned her slowly to the left and set her gently down on the toilet.

Her mother sat annoyed, the yellow hospital gown still tucked beneath her.

"My dress," she said, very clearly.

"Just a minute." Sara bent, embraced Helen again (holding her breath against the smells), lifted slightly, then quickly put her left hand down to tug the cloth free.

"Owww. . . ."

"All right. All done."

Now, her mother sat frowning, ready to pee. Frowned more severely, and produced a sudden rush of urine splashing into the bowl. Gradually the frown became only preoccupation . . . then satisfaction.

"Do you need to do number two?" Sara was immediately sorry she'd put it that way, so stupidly childish—and was sorrier when she saw her mother's face.

"Don' you . . . *ever* talk . . . to me like that. Un'erstan'?"

"I'm sorry."

"You un'er*stan*'?"

"I said I was sorry. It was a stupid thing to say."

Her mother, frowning again, appeared to use her anger to produce another splash of urine, then said, " 'At's all," fumbled with her left hand for a fold of toilet tissue from the roll, and then sat waiting.

Sara waited as well, as if the situation might change in a moment or two—then, when it didn't, bent over her mother, put her left hand under Helen's armpit, lifted her a little up and to the side, took the toilet paper, and slid her right hand under her mother's buttock—withered, small, and oddly shaped—reached under and to the front, and gently wiped her dry. Then dropped the paper into the bowl, and let Helen down.

Her mother sat with her eyes closed, breathing noisily—then, when Sara thought she was starting to cry, began chuckling instead, sitting grinning, shaking on the toilet.

Sara was so surprised, she smiled . . . and, as the chuckling grew almost full, musical—became almost young Helen's laugh—began to laugh herself, and sat laughing along until she suddenly saw in her mother's flushed and furrowed face, desperate hazel eyes blurred with shame and terror. Helen being cut by her own accustomed bright weapon of mirth, like a favorite kitchen knife grown suddenly treacherous.

Sara stopped laughing, and caught her breath. "O.K. Let's get back into the chair, sweetheart," and that way released her mother to tears, meager shoulders shaking beneath the hospital gown's dull yellow.

Sara said, "Oh, Mom. . . ." Wished to glance away from that shriveled face, congested, snotty, running tears, but stayed facing her instead.

"—I'm so sorry." She gathered more toilet paper from the roll, gently mopped at Helen's face. "There," she said. "There. . . ."

"Oh," her mother said. "Oh, I'm . . . scared."

"Sweetheart," Sara said. "Come on . . . blow your nose." She hesitated to lift Helen into her chair so soon, and remind her of her weakness. Instead, she pulled the wheelchair closer, and sat in it herself. "We'll just stay here a minute."

They sat for a while face to face, then Sara's mother put out her right hand, palm up, as if she were offering something small, and Sara took the hand and held it.

After full dark that evening, Sara took down the window screen, climbed out onto the cedar shingles in Anne's bathrobe, and went on all fours up to the peak of the roof.

The stars were out, pale above the constellated lights of the city to the west.

Sara sat at the roof peak, looking out over The Lakes, the big houses crowded close, the ponds behind reflecting only suggestions of starlight beyond the streetlamps' glow.

She took deep breaths, then deeper, until her lungs ached with cool damp air. She sat watching the city for a while, then turned on the rough shakes to look southeast. There, more than fifty miles away, the pale mass of Mount Rainier rose from lesser mountains into the light of a rising crescent moon.

Sara sat watching the mountain, certain it would stay, and stay still—do nothing but be immense. She put her left arm out, curved to fit over Dutchy's shoulders if he'd been sitting beside her. She tensed the muscles of her arm as if against his furred flank, muscled ribs—tried to make him grunt, and breathed deeper to catch his odor on the air.

After a while, Sara climbed down the slope of the roof to her window, then into her room, and replaced the window screen. She stepped out into the hall, listened . . . heard no sounds, and went back inside to take her notebook out of the pack's side pocket. Then she went downstairs in the dark, the stair carpet pleasantly resilient beneath her bare feet. It was a relief not to have to see anyone, speak to anyone.

She walked through the living room into the den, turned on the small brass-shaded lamp on Annie's cherrywood desk, and found typing paper in the right-hand drawer. She rolled paper into the big old IBM Selectric, opened her notebook, propped it against a dictionary, and began to type her stories. She typed slowly at first, learning the machine, remembering how to touch-type. Then she speeded up. . . .

Hours later, naked in moonlight on her sleeping bag, Sara slept on the floor beneath her room's open window. She dreamed of something she forgot . . . and afterward dreamed that all things had come to an orange point. Then was wakened by a noise.

She lay noticing the footboard of the nearest bed looming alongside, and listened for that sound again. Something downstairs.

. . . Listened awhile, remembering her dream of everything drawing closer, then together into a point like a pencil's or colored crayon's, but much larger. Everything growing together so it made only one thing—everything certain all the time to draw together into a thick orange point. Sara thought of that, and had slid almost to sleep again when the noise—same as before—came softly up the stairs to knock against the bedroom door. An after-echo of a heavy wooden noise below.

Now she was awake, and sat up on the sleeping bag, then got to her feet and walked over to the bedroom door to listen. It seemed to Sara she was walking very lightly, too lightly to be heard by whatever made the noise.

She supposed it might be Anne, gone downstairs for some reason, slamming a door. Or Kevin, gone down for a snack. . . . Sara turned in streaming moonlight, found Anne's lent blue bathrobe over the back of a chair, and went to stand with the robe wrapped around her, listening at the door's moon-paneled white.

The sound came bumping up the stairs again; she could feel its movement in the smooth wood against her ear. The doorknob was cold, its roundness and chill waking her completely when she turned it, opened the door, and stepped into the hall. The carpet there was patterned with moonlight fallen through the stairwell windowpanes in rectangled colors, soft as dust.

The house was settled into sleep—its breathing only distant sounds of wood relaxing in ticks and easings too faint to differentiate . . . and an almost silent buzzing. Sara smelled a slight odor (sour as a wet dog's) drifting up the stairs, and supposed it rose from garbage under the kitchen sink, needing to be taken out, its smell wafting through the house's ventilators. She jumped a little as the noise whacked and thudded downstairs again—seemed to have jumped in anticipation, as if hearing it before she heard it.

There were no lights on, downstairs, no light below the moonlit landing. From there, the steps marched down into darkness. Sara doubted Anne was downstairs without light—doubted Kevin was, either. She wished she had the .44, wished the big Ruger was heavy in her hand.

There was another sound below. Something sliding, making the flooring sigh.

Sara thought of going back into her room, phoning for police. She imagined voices, the twirling red lights of squad cars parked along the drive. —An embarrassed Anne, apologizing to them. Kevin staring from the steps.

'Go downstairs, or go back to bed,' Sara whispered to herself, and heard the softest clicking sound below.

That sound decided her, and she went to the stairs and on down the first flight as lightly as if she were still dreaming, only the banister's coolness smoothly real beneath her right hand.

At the landing she paused, felt the stairs' carpeting softly rough beneath her feet, and saw how dark it was below. Smelled again that sour odor, and supposed a drunk might have broken in, come into the house through the Florida room in back . . . be stumbling around.

Sara went halfway down the second flight, stopped there, and said out loud, "You better get out of here!" And waited for any reply—perhaps from two tough boys come over to the island to steal TVs. But no one answered.

"—You better get your asses *out* of here! I called the police!"

So soft a silence, her words sank into it. She heard the entrance-hall clock below (that must know who waited there) only ticking, and wished she'd wakened Annie. It was Annie's house; she'd know better if anyone had broken in—and that would be more real and not so dreamlike. . . . Sara went on down the stairs to the entrance hall. She stood in darkness, barefoot on cold marble flooring, searched with her left hand for a wall switch, but felt only a twist of decorative trim. Light from the coach lamp outside glowed gold against the stained-glass window above the front door, but little light shone through.

She heard a soft chiming sound across the hall in the dining room, as if the tall cabinet had been brushed against, its glassware shifted.

"Kevin . . . ?"

In there, something heavier than Kevin made a floorboard creak.

Sara, tired of being frightened in what should have been a dream—feeling too tired to be tested this way—said, "Oh, *fuck you!*" She walked across the hall to the dining room doorway, reached alongside the door frame with her right hand . . . found a light switch where it should have been—and clicked it on to a sudden blasting roar, an explosion of sound that deafened her, shocked her still.

The bear stood upright, haloed in the light. Reared nine feet high, its fur's varied browns richer than the room, it stood swaying by Anne's fine long table. As it rocked a moment more side to side, flooring groaning beneath it, the great head just brushed the lusters of the chandelier, made soft music.

The grizzly toppled forward, fell to all fours with a house-shaking thud and came pacing at her, making the big room small. If she hadn't turned and run without thinking of turning and running, it would have had her.

Sara, purified of anything but flight, ran away through the dark house as if it were lit, ran too fast it seemed for anything to overtake her. Struck nothing as she ran, or if she did, didn't know it and wasn't slowed, the blue bathrobe streaming out behind her as a banner invisible in darkness. Nothing should have caught her, but the bear began to immediately, its odors of fur and rotted meat rolling out before it to announce what smashed after her not caring—shouldering a door frame splintering loose, ruining it and coming through in strength without measure while Sara dealt only in delicate speed. Squealing like a giant pig, the beast seemed to chase faster by destruction, riding its own noise of wreckage like wheels as it came crashing, so Sara felt it begin to catch her through the living room in shade and shadow, then break into the den just behind her in cascading glass from bashed French doors. It almost hooked her with a great attempting paw past the Florida-room door, then back up the corridor to the entrance hall again, its claws ripping carpet, then rattling, scraping swiftly over marble. She felt the warm approaching breeze of hurtling bulk at her back, heard snuffling grunts of effort.

Nothing should have caught her who running barely touched the floor, but the bear did in the entrance hall, even sliding slightly on smooth marble as it turned immense, straining the house's fabric, the noise of its pursuit following—and reaching into such poorly lit space, struck and hooked her left side, driving talons into her as if she were their accustomed sheath.

Sara, shaken in the air, began to scream but had no breath, penetrated so deeply between several ribs it was nearly pleasureful—felt entered within her what shouldn't be but still belonged, as if she'd needed that stroke of great claws forever, now had only fangs to wait for.

The bear placed her firmly down on the marble floor, heaved, hunched swiftly over her as she kicked only a little and tried to breathe, then bore with its weight so Sara felt bones break inside her, wished to say, "I'm dying . . ." to the bear—and sheltered by it, safe from any other trouble, felt its rich breath, the hot salt and wet of its slaver as it bent yawning to her face to bite.

Sara had just time to see, from beneath the perfect attention of the bear—see the stairwell lights flash on, and Annie, on the landing, stare down confounded, sorrowful, and safe.

Only then the bear's jaws closed, and after an instant when her skull sang with pressure, it broke so Sara could die into waking . . . woke . . . and lay, still living, in moonlight beneath an open window.

"That's all you're going to eat?"

"That's it. . . ." Kevin set his blue bowl aside, sat looking at a tangerine.

"Oatmeal is very good for you, Kevin—and you used to like it."

"Oh, yeah. Right. I really loved oatmeal." Kevin stood up, slid his black book bag off the island counter.

"Well, have the tangerine. They cost a fortune this time of year."

"Gee, I don't know if we can afford *tangerines*." Kevin grinned at Sara. "—So don't waste it, Mom. You eat it, O.K.?"

"Kevin—."

"I'm late for school." Kevin slung the book bag over his right shoulder and walked out of the kitchen. His oversized leather jacket (blue and red, with a large black eight-ball sewn on the back) looked big as a man's.

"He's growing up," Sara said.

"The hell he is." Anne, sitting beside her, reached over the counter for the tangerine. "—He's growing down. He's doing terribly in school. He did not used to be . . . he absolutely did not used to be such a pain."

"I think it goes with being thirteen."

"I don't believe that. I don't think that's a reason at all."

"Well, Annie, you let him get away with stuff."

"Oh, I 'let him get away with stuff.' " Anne peeled the tangerine. "And you'd know how to handle him, of course."

"I didn't say that."

"But you think so. All right, advise me. —And by the way, it hasn't escaped my notice that you are actually dressed *up*. Makes a difference, believe me—slacks look great."

"Thanks. . . ." Sara had tried on the beige slacks first, then decided on the gray slacks, new black shoes. The white sweater and the safari jacket.

"Is this just a tryout, sis—or a date, or what?"

"I just thought . . . I'd wear them."

"Good move. —And now, you were going to advise me about Kevin?"

"It's really not my business, Annie."

"No, go ahead. Advise me."

"I think it would be hard to raise any kid down here, and especially after a divorce."

"Oh, sure—civilization. Ruins 'em." Anne began to eat the tangerine, slice by slice, hardly chewing before she swallowed. "But up *there*—"

"Up there, Kevin'd have to work, or he wouldn't eat. He's too fat, anyway. It wouldn't hurt him to go hungry every now and then. Might teach him something."

"Thanks, sis. Very helpful—really."

"You don't think it would be good for Kevin to be in the mountains, where he couldn't sit on his butt for hours and watch TV? Where he'd have to read? And there's no garbagy fast food, and his clothes would be to keep him warm—not to show off to other kids? You don't think that would be good for him—to have to work, maybe work hard for what he wants?"

"Oh thanks, Rousseau—great suggestion." Anne ate another tangerine slice and wiped her mouth with a beige paper napkin. "If only it were that easy."

"I wouldn't let a dog behave the way you let Kevin behave with you. I think it's very bad for him to treat his mother like shit. And I think it's your fault for letting him do it, letting him get away with it."

"I really appreciate your advice," Anne said, finished the tangerine, wiped her mouth, and stood up. "—particularly since it's based on your own experience raising a child."

"I haven't raised any kids, but I've taught plenty—and I have raised a lot of pups. And I know what ruins them, and I know what makes them into fine dogs."

"Thank you for that comparison—Kevin and a dog. Let's just drop it, sis, before I lose my temper."

"You asked me."

"And I'm profoundly sorry I did. . . . You driving me to work?"

"If it's all right."

"Fine."

Sara had expected a different sort of room, paneled in dark wood, with bookshelves along the walls. But the Monroe Agency office was small, and looked like any business office. There were no books in it except for a few on Ms. Monroe's gray steel desk.

Ms. Monroe was older than Sara'd expected; she'd had a younger voice over the phone. She was in her fifties, at least—auburn hair (worn neatly up) lightening with gray—and had come around her desk elegant in a pale-green suit (its skirt wrinkled across the front), pale-yellow blouse and black shoes, to shake Sara's hand like a man, squeezing hard. Handshake over, she'd gone back behind her desk and sat down. There was a row of three framed pictures propped on the right side of the desktop facing her. Small pictures, all the same size; Sara couldn't see their fronts. . . . She wished she'd worn the gray skirt instead of the slacks.

"You see, Mrs. Maher, animal stories are a staple of children's books—but that doesn't mean just *any* animal stories."

"I know. But I'm very familiar—"

"And even when the material is right on the money—very professional and accomplished—even then, children's fiction is hard to sell, and pays very, *very* little."

"That's all right. I just thought that children would enjoy them. They're real stories. They're not all . . . nice. I heard stories like that up on the coast, from Eskimos. They aren't a sentimental people."

" 'Not nice. . . .' " Ms. Monroe had a face that used to be pretty—blue-eyed, long, its jaw a little heavy. Still attractive, but hazed with age in her office's cool light, obscured as if by cobwebs. " 'Not sentimental.' Well, we'll see, won't we? I'll be able to read them in a day or two. And you were a teacher?"

"Yes, a few years ago. Second and third grade." Seeing Ms. Monroe glance at her left hand, at the bandaged fingertips, Sara put that hand in her lap, covered it with the other.

"Unfortunately . . . unfortunately, that's not always an advantage. Many teachers are certain they know what children really like to read. And all too often, those teachers are dead wrong."

"I don't know if children will like reading my stories, but I think they'll remember them. I think they'll find them useful."

"All . . . right." Ms. Monroe stood up and Sara stood with her, thinking Ms. Monroe would come around the desk and shake hands again, but she didn't. " 'Not nice' . . . but memorable. And 'useful.' Well, we'll see, won't we? Why don't you call me . . . oh, late tomorrow. We're only a Seattle agency—not a *New York* agency—but we function very professionally. We don't play games. We get to the material, we get through it, and we tell the author our opinion, without any icing."

Sara said, "O.K."—wondering who the other person was to make up the "we"—then smiled and went out of the office and closed the door behind her. In the hall, she realized she'd forgotten to get copies made. Ms. Monroe had the only typed copy, the original. Sara thought of going back inside, offering to get the stories copied—then decided she'd look ridiculous. If something got lost, she could just retype it from the notebook. And she hadn't thanked the woman for seeing her, either—just smiled and walked out.

Sara didn't wait for the elevator; she found the fire door and went down the stairs, going down the steps faster and faster, as if she were leaving her stories like abandoned children, and they might know it and start crying after her.

On the street, a plump woman wearing a metallic-tan raincoat came walking toward her with a dog on a leash. Sara stood looking at the dog—it wasn't a breed she'd seen before. Very small, stocky, and covered with a soft fountain of amber fur, tail curled over its back. It looked a little like a Pekinese, but it wasn't. As they came up to her, Sara knelt on one knee, said "Hello," and held out her hand.

"Bainter isn't friendly," the woman said. She wore dark glasses, even with only pale sun shining.

The little dog had stopped to stare at Sara.

"Is that true?" Sara said to him. "Is that true—that you're not friendly?"

It seemed to be true. Bainter stared and trembled just short of a bark, or perhaps growling.

"What is he?"

"He's a Llasa." The plump woman seemed surprised Sara hadn't known it.

"First time I've seen one," Sara said. "He's wonderful," and reached out to the startled Bainter, picked him up as if they were the oldest friends, and stood to cuddle him.

The little dog lay in her arms, belly up, all dignity fled, and growled too late.

"Oh, no. Oh, no you don't. You don't get tough with me." Sara lifted Bainter to her face as if she were going to take a bite of him, and left him only cuteness for salvation. He struggled a little, then submitted to squeezing and conversation—was reduced to licking her ear.

"That's a first for that dog with a stranger," the woman said, apparently annoyed Bainter hadn't proved tougher.

"I miss mine," Sara said, inhaling Bainter, nuzzling him, crushing the essence of dog out of him, his useless leash dangling. He was left to lick for his life.

"Jesus, Bainter," the plump woman said.

Sara walked two blocks farther down the street, found a telephone booth, looked up the International House of Pancakes in its telephone book, and found one on Queen Anne North.

It took a long time to drive there because she got lost and couldn't find an entrance ramp for I-5. She talked to herself as she drove, pretended alternately to be Ms. Monroe—didn't let her get away with repeating "Not nice," and "Memorable," and "Useful," as if Sara were some idiot, making a fool of herself every time she opened her mouth.

"No, they are *not* nice. They are not the usual crap children have to read so adults will feel comfortable about them, and think they're not even people. As for being a teacher—I think we know more about kids than a fucking literary agent! And what the hell do you know about animals?"

"Well, I know about writing!" That's what Ms. Monroe would have said.

"Then talk about my writing when you've read it. Just don't give me all this preliminary take-charge shit!"

Ms. Monroe would have looked surprised then, not used to getting bit back. "Now, you wait just a minute—!"

"You don't even have any damn *books* in this office. What do you do in here? Sell stocks? Work on people's taxes?"

Ms. Monroe just sitting there.

Sara would have stood up, then. "Next time somebody comes in here with writing they've done, why don't you respect that, and wait until you've read it before you shoot your mouth off?"

Ms. Monroe, face red, and with nothing to say. . . .

Sara found a ramp onto I-5, went two exits and got off, headed east. She found the House of Pancakes at an intersection, pulled in and parked. It was pleasant being alone . . . not having Annie there, coming in to watch her eat.

The waitress was an elderly woman with big hips. Sara seemed to be seeing old people everywhere, people who used to be young, strong—as if age were a disease and was spreading. Too many memories making people sick, shriveling them up and killing them. As if that was what was happening to her mother—memories gathered into a knot in her brain, then coming alive and killing her.

"Can I get the big stack, and have them the strawberry pancakes?"

"Big stack—strawberry."

"And coffee."

"Regular?"

"Yes. And can I have eggs over easy?"

"Eggs over easy—bacon or sausage?"

"Can I have both?"

"Honey, you can have anything you want."

"You have cantaloupe . . . ?"

It was a long wait for the food. Sara sat in the big upholstered brown booth, looking out the window, watching people walk by. One of them, walking with two girls, was a boy Jack Joseph's age, with long hair in a ponytail. But he was a white boy, his hair reddish brown, and he was heavier than Jack Joseph. And not blind in one eye. . . .

Sara ate the eggs right away—ate them fast, so the pancakes wouldn't get cold. After she finished, she remembered she hadn't put salt or pepper on them. Then she ate the bacon and sausage. Bacon first.

She thought of using blueberry syrup on the pancakes, but decided the tastes of the berries would clash, and used the maple syrup instead. She cut down into the stack of pancakes—a soft uneven freckled brown, with occasional dark-red bits of strawberry—to make openings for the syrup to soak in, rather than have it just run off the sides. She smeared butter into those places, poured the maple syrup in . . . then poured more of it in slow circles over the top.

The pancakes looked so good, so rich that Sara sat admiring them for a few moments. Then she dug into them with her fork—she'd used so much syrup it oozed out, made a sort of pudding of the pancakes—ate that forkful, and decided to wait a little while between bites so they wouldn't blur into just one taste, but would stay separate, none wasted.

Even so, she ate too fast. It wasn't until her fourth bite she tasted a strawberry—soft, almost whole—in a big forkful of layered pancakes with syrup running off. She got some syrup on her chin, wiped her mouth with the paper napkin, and looked around to see if anyone was watching . . . thought she was making a pig of herself.

No one was watching her. Even so, she stopped eating for a little while, took the time to have some coffee. And when she began to eat again, she found it had been worth it to pause for the coffee, because the pancakes tasted new, almost as if she hadn't had any.

She ate at least half the stack, stopped and had more coffee, then used her spoon to scoop up the extra syrup on her plate. After that, eating more deliberately, she paid attention as she chewed each bite, to see if there was a piece of strawberry in it. She could taste strawberry flavor in the pancakes, but it was nice to get a piece of one of the berries.

As she came closer to finishing, Sara ate more and more slowly, each bite tasting better and better. She felt full, had felt full for some time, but that seemed to have nothing to do with eating. The last mouthful—a folded light-brown piece of pancake with syrup dripping through where it was torn a little, pierced by the fork—tasted as good as all the others had together. Her throat ached and tears came into her eyes, and she didn't chew and swallow it until it softened so there was almost no difference between pancake and syrup.

She had the slice of cantaloupe for dessert.

After her lunch, Sara felt better about driving Anne's car. Its upholstery seemed very much like the pancakes, a soft rich mottled brown. The pancakes and the car seemed to go together, and she drove the Mercedes the way she'd eaten lunch, starting fast from every light, then taking her time and enjoying it. Steering a little to the left . . . then a little to the right, just slightly, as she drove along. She missed the entrance to I-5 again, but didn't worry, the car was becoming so friendly.

She drove two blocks north, then took a cross street left and went down that until she saw I-5 ahead. Turning south, she drove along until she found an on-ramp. Sara thought Jack Joseph would enjoy driving the Mercedes; he'd enjoyed the snow-machine so much— probably liked all machines. And some machines were like dogs; they knew if you liked them.

She'd wait, and not call Ms. Monroe tomorrow as if she were worried and unsure and just had to know. She'd call day after tomorrow. It bothered her a little, the idea of Ms. Monroe reading her stories . . . poking her nose in where before it had only been the animals and Sara, alone together.

And she'd done the House of Pancakes. Wonderful, but she didn't need any more House of Pancakes, though it hadn't smelled as bad as most places since she'd come down. She was getting used to all the odors. People there hadn't bothered her, either; they weren't looking as strange today as they had, so fat and white. —Maybe Chinese food next time, with lots of vegetables. Mushrooms and bamboo shoots, and sweet-and-sour pork. Or pork chops, in some restaurant . . . pork chops and apple sauce. And next time, just tip 15 percent. That was all you were supposed to tip—not give a waitress two dollars and fifty cents, just because she was old.

11

"Hi." Marie was wearing a white peasant blouse, black jeans, and white athletic socks with sandals.

"Hi. Was business good today?"

"Oh, sure . . . oh, sure. Crystals and herbs. We sold just about all the brilliant-cut rose quartz we had. You know, in pendants."

"Good."

"And herb tea. —In little packages? People bought a ton of tea, the . . . uh . . . stuff for your kidneys. Vetch tea."

"Good. Is Annie here?"

"She's in back."

Sara walked through the store past two couples standing browsing at a bin labeled 'Wicca and Wishes.' Anne was kneeling on the floor against the right-side wall, surrounded by cardboard boxes.

". . . Well, sis, how was your morning? See Mom?" She was stocking the lowest wall shelf from a small open carton of books.

"No. I just drove around . . . had lunch."

"Skipped her, and I don't blame you. I tried the drop-in-every-day bit, and it got old very fast." Anne made a small stack of books, turned that on its side, and reached up to put it in place on the shelf.

"She was better yesterday—better than the first time. The nurse said she'd been having headaches, but I asked her if her head was hurting, and she said no. I think she just gets frightened."

"Terrified, is more like it. Sis, you know you have to be careful what you say, so she doesn't get more upset. I'm used to it; I know how to talk to her."

"I didn't upset her."

Anne finished a row of books, slid a thin brown steel bookend into place to hold the end of the row. The paperbacks were tall, with dark-blue binding. "Believe this? Christian Palmistry. 'See Christ's life directives in the palm of your hand. The secret signposts of a

Christian life. His own personal message to you—for you alone.' "

"Who writes all that stuff?"

"Clever people." Anne stood to place books on the next-higher shelf. "Listen, did you bring your exercise things?"

"Out in the car."

"All right. Your sweatpants and a T-shirt are O.K., but the running shoes are not what you should be using for aerobics—you ever done bench?"

"No. What's bench?" Sara bent to take a book from the carton, and leafed through it to the illustrations . . . looked at the palm of her right hand.

"It's a sort of narrow platform you step up and down on—do various steps on and off." Anne illustrated with a quick step forward, then back. "There're pairs of supports that go under it, and you can stack up anywhere from one to three pairs. Depends how much effort you want to put out." She fitted more books into place. "—Stepping up and down like that gives you more cardiovascular; it's more work than just jumping around. I suppose the running shoes will do. If you stay in town—the big 'if'—then we'll get you some cross-trainers."

Sara turned a page and looked at her palm again. Lifeline . . . the fainter line joining it. Separate line above. Under the illustration of a palm pattern similar to hers, there was a block of explanatory text— odd, in odd English. The Galilean rabbi Yeshua bar Yosep, having died and been restored to life by his father, an Iranian volcano god, had been so exalted that bite-and-sip-sized portions of his actual meat, bones, and blood—magically reconstituted after every tasting—remained eternally the refreshment of True Believers. And this magical Jew, having traveled dimensionally to examine Sara inside her mother's cervix, had then drawn a particular pattern on her fetal palm to warn her about storing up goods on earth, a far too lively plane.

Anne's health club was over in the city, one exit off the bridge. She took the exit faster than Sara would have, and had to use her brakes twice to slow down. The afternoon had become colder, grayer, tending to rain.

"I think you'll like this, sis. Well, maybe you won't, but it's good for you. You're just coming for this session—auditing, one time only, so you don't need to pay anything."

"O.K."

"And I suppose I was out of line, snapping at you about Kevin this morning. It's just that he's my kid, and I'm very touchy about criticism. I can criticize; I don't like anybody else doing it."

"I wasn't criticizing him."

"Oh, that's right—I was the one. The bad mother, too wimpy to raise a boy properly. Fabulous. . . ."

The Sound Body was upstairs in a tan stucco two-story building in a row of stores along Sherman Street. Sara, holding her running shoes, her sweatpants and gray T-shirt over her arm, could hear music with a quick thumping beat as she and Annie climbed the stairs, Annie a little ahead, carrying a small red gym bag.

There was a short hallway opening into a long loft space on the second floor—bigger than Sara had thought it would be, and bright with ceiling fluorescents and afternoon light from windows along its south side. There were two long rows of narrow gray plastic benches set out, spaced down the room. Each bench, about a yard long, had a rubber nonslip tread along its top, and most of them were resting almost a foot high on two pairs of square plastic supports the same color as the benches.

There were some people in the room already, most of them women, just standing talking, except for a young girl doing stretching exercises on the dark-blue carpet. There were only two men. One, gray-haired, lanky in a brown leotard—the other smaller, younger, in a sleeveless white top and white shorts.

The room's long north wall was mirrored floor to ceiling. Sara saw the people reflected there, the women in pretty exercise outfits: fancy T-shirts and leotards, or shiny spandex tights. None of them would be wearing just gray sweatpants and a gray T-shirt, except her.

"We change in here," Anne led to the right, into a narrow room with white-painted metal lockers. A woman was in there, long-haired and older, standing in black bra and panties. She was almost as thin as Sara, her sharp bones showing through soft freckled skin.

"Connie—my sister, Sara."

"Hi."

"Sis, our bathroom and showers are through there past the lockers; guys' are across the hall."

"Hey—what *about* it, people?" A big young woman stood in the doorway. Wide-shouldered, tanned, and tall—a nice-looking pug-nosed blonde in shiny green tights and a sleeveless white T-shirt top with red printing across it. THIS BODY WORKS. "Time's a-wastin'!" She glanced at Sara, who was just taking off her blouse.

"Judy—my sister, Sara."

"One-timer?" Judy wore her bright hair in braids, pinned up. Her shoulders, muscled as a man's, were round, smooth, tanned the shade of toast. Her eyes, china blue, their whites blue-white, were slightly bulged.

"Yes. She's just auditing."

"Done bench?" Judy was looking at Sara's body. Sara got into her T-shirt as quickly as she could.

"No."

"Well, we do two rows, so you set up in the back row behind me and a little to the right, and I'll keep an eye on you in the mirror." The blonde's voice was high-pitched for so big a girl. "—And start with just one level under your bench while you're learning the steps. If you can't handle that, go to no level—just the bench top. Any health problems?"

"No." Sara could smell Judy. She smelled of garlic.

"You'll have to sign a waiver, anyway."

"All right." Sara took her slacks off.

"And we work very hard in here, Sara. We do *not* wimp out. So, if it gets too tough for you, just march in place, or come in here so you won't disturb everybody's concentration. O.K.?"

"All right." Sara found an empty locker with hangers in it, and hung her slacks up.

Judy stood watching while Sara put on the gray sweatpants. "Not enough muscle mass," Judy said, turned and walked out. She moved, Sara thought, like a female black bear, but slighter, furless, and upright.

"The Sultana of Sweat," the older woman, Connie, said when Judy was gone.

"The Führer of Fitness . . ." Anne stood undressed for a moment, and Sara was startled by how beautiful her sister's body was in peach bra, peach panties—long-boned, softly muscled, her skin so pale, so fine-grained it seemed to contribute light. Anne reached behind her to unfasten her bra, took it off, then dug into her red zipper bag for a white cotton bra with wide support straps. Her breasts were bigger than Sara's, weighty, their nipples ruddy, still plump from suckling Kevin so many years before.

"Judy's a bitch." Anne bent slightly to settle her breasts into the white bra. "But she's a hellacious athlete. Champion aerobicizer, major weightlifter. . . ." And noticing Sara's glance, "Well, am I still a piece, or am I not?"

"I'd say you are."

"Good sister," Connie said, stood to look at herself in the locker-room mirror—white tights, an oversized pink T-shirt—and went out. The music was thumping louder from the exercise room. Sara heard Judy saying something to someone in her high hard voice.

"Now," Anne said, "—the Superwoman suit," reached into her zipper bag, and took out yellow floral calf-length tights, a matching sleeveless leotard. . . .

There was singing with the music, but only a rhythmical chorus, *"Tryyyin' . . . Tryyyin' . . ."* the syncopated beat running under the singing, and faster. Faster than Sara's heartbeat as she stepped up on the gray plastic bench, stepped as quickly back and off. They'd been stepping up and down, left foot then right foot, for some time. —A lot of stretching exercises first, then marching up and down the length of the room between the rows of benches. Then trotting up and down the room. Then running.

After that, they'd done 'grapevines'—facing front while they moved along sideways, legs alternately crossing in front and behind . . . then reversing the steps back down the room, pumping their arms up and down in rhythm while they did it. And now, just this stepping on and off the narrow bench, up and down in time to the music—crisscrossing their arms now, instead of pumping them up and down. On either side of Sara in the back row, Annie just to her left, the other people were stepping up and down to the music, rising and falling, their exercise shoes thudding on the benches almost in unison. Everyone was holding hand weights as they exercised—little iron dumbbells, a couple of pounds each.

It seemed to Sara there wasn't much to it, as exercise—maybe because her bench was only up on one level, one pair of platforms. Everyone else in class, except Judy, was using two pairs stacked under their benches. Judy was using three.

In front of Sara, to the left, Judy was leading the class from the middle of the first row—going up and down, on and off, calling the steps. Bouncing up and down on her high bench, glancing at people reflected in the mirrored wall in front of her.

Sara'd seen Judy watching her in the wall mirror at least twice, as if she expected her to fall in a faint or something . . . or just thought the gray T-shirt and sweatpants looked tacky.

The music's beat changed and Judy called out, *"Turn-step travel!"*— stepped up onto the right end of her bench with her right foot, stepped along it to the left, and swung away left and off. Then reversed direction—up with her left foot, stepped to her right, then away to the right and off the bench again. Keeping on the near side of the bench and swinging with those steps—up, step left, and off . . . up, step right, and off again. Swinging back and forth, up and off the bench, from side to side like the pendulum of a clock.

Sara stumbled once, then caught the steps and enjoyed them, liked half-circling up through the air, then down, pleased by the quickness of her feet. It didn't seem much effort, though.

"And *arms!*" Judy kept traveling, now pumped her arms up and down as she stepped on the bench, up and down as she stepped off, still traveling that fast-turning semicircle back and forth. Along her golden arms, heavy with smooth muscle, faint blond down picked up the room's bright fluorescents. Tanned under lights, Sara thought—or might have just come back from the South. California, Mexico. . . . "—I see some wimps not using full range of *motionnn!*"

Judy demonstrated full range of motion. She stepped up, swung and stepped off as if she were dancing, arms up as her feet went down, down as she stepped up again in counterpoint. A violent, balanced dance—swinging . . . swinging. . . .

Pleasant motion, it seemed to Sara, but not strenuous exercise. She wondered if Dutchy missed her, if he stood by his kennel in Frank Solokoff's yard and watched for her to come. The rest of the team would mourn her, but not so much. Lobo would miss her in his odd wolfish way—as much as he could miss anyone not his mother or his mate. And Vanilla would miss her, too, but not for long—only until the pups came.

"Step touch—step *touch!*" Judy had turned left side to the bench, from there stepped up onto it with her left foot, touched up with her right, then stepped down. Fast, faster than the traveling. "And *across!*" She stepped up onto the bench, and across and down off its other side—then up and back over and down, up and across and down—up-and-back-over and up-and-across, like stitching a fur.

"Marian . . ." Judy sang out over the music's ringing beat. "Oh, *Mariannn*, you are dweebing out on *meeee.*" Down past Annie on Sara's row, a woman said something, breathless—but Judy interrupted: "No excuses!" and was jumping, bounding up and over her bench and back again, her bare shoulders only glossed with sweat. She moved as if the music drove her, always a little faster. "A dweeb has *no* excuses . . . !"

Sara wondered if she should be sweating. She looked over at

Annie as she came back across the bench, and Annie was sweating. Sara went back and forth over the bench seven more times—then stopped and trotted over to the wall where the small square plastic platforms were stacked, picked up a pair, and came back to fit them under her bench, raise it to two levels.

When the bench was set, and she was up—had caught the rhythm again and was exercising—Sara saw Judy watching her in the mirror. She thought Judy might smile, seeing her working harder, but Judy didn't.

"*Straddle and Pli-oh! Pli-oh* left!" Calling that out, Judy straddled her bench facing to the left, and began to step on and off to either side very fast to the music's beat—left-foot right-foot, left-foot right-foot—only touching her white shoes' toes to the carpet each side, so she had to bound back and forth, back and forth, never still, supported each fast step only by the foot up on the bench. Left foot then right foot then left foot then right foot. Sara thought this was the best exercise yet; this was something that, if she kept it up long enough, would make her tired.

To her left, Annie said, "Jesus." Sara could smell a circus of odor in the room—sweat . . . many sweats, some sweet with perfume or powder, some sour. She could hear people panting as if they were running for their lives, feel the vibrations of their exercise up through the floor, up through her bench. They weren't stepping quite together, anymore. She felt odd to be moving so at ease, surrounded by such effort.

"*Pli-oh . . . right!*" And Judy—really light on her feet for so muscular a girl—spun around on her high bench so she straddled facing the opposite direction and shifted left side to right side with the music's beat—alternate supporting leg (left, then right) doing all the lifting, leaping, all the work, outside foot barely touching the carpet at each change.

Sara stopped exercising, went over to the wall—the music was so loud it hurt her ears—picked up another set of platforms, brought them back and slid them under her bench. Then she stepped up that much higher into the rhythm, left and right and left—liked that better. At least on three sets of platforms it was work, made the ankle she'd sprained slightly sore.

She looked into the mirror and saw Judy staring back at her—an unpleasant look, separate and still out of all her strenuous motion—as if Sara was doing the steps wrong somehow, doing something stupid. Judy stared at her, then looked away, called out, "Up-tempo! Move . . . Move . . . MOVE!" and began exercising faster, almost double time to the music's drumbeats.

"Christ. . . ." Anne, muttering on Sara's left, stumbled then recovered. "What about a little goddamn pause for water?"

Judy kept up that almost double-timing until Sara felt a little tired. Then she called, "Travel!" performing this step, too—swinging up onto the bench . . . swinging down and away—almost double time. She was very quick on her feet for such a big girl. Sara watched Judy's calf muscles knot and ease, smooth and brown and fat with power, lifting her up and over and down . . . then swinging to the other direction, up, over, and down, very quickly. Good balance.

It began to interest Sara, watching Judy move—move like an odd sort of animal, so solidly muscled. There was only the slightest heaviness as she stepped, as if—though not yet—there would be a time such bulky muscles worked a little against themselves. Sara wondered if Judy could run fifteen or twenty miles over snowed-in country without becoming too tired. . . .

"Well, fuck . . . this." Panting, Anne stopped traveling beside Sara. Instead, she just stood on the floor and marched in place in time to the music. She was out of breath, and Sara saw that one of the men and another woman to the left had also stopped working on and off their benches. They were marching in place, and Sara supposed they had to catch their breath—in poor condition for only an hour of exercise to bother them. Now, maybe a little more than an hour.

"Hustle off the left end!" And Judy began doing something new— stepping up onto the right end of her bench and turning there, stepping on and off very fast to the music's beat, until she'd turned a complete circle . . . then stepped off, over, and up onto the bench's other end, and did the same. It was a nice variation. Sara followed it, and enjoyed the turning around; it felt pleasant in the muscles of her back, tugged there as she turned, and seemed comfortable. It was harder to do than anything except the straddle steps—and done so quickly, fast as the music's fast drumbeats, it made her feel a little tired.

Then Judy changed the steps again, went back to simply stepping up and down, but still working her arms, and Sara saw that more of the class had stopped exercising. She thought maybe she should, too, because people were looking at her. —Then Judy glanced at Sara in the mirror, stepped off her bench and said something. She walked over to the wall, took the music tape out of the machine and put a different one in—then picked up another set of platforms, and came to put them under her bench so it was four levels high. Someone in the class said "Oh, wow. . . ."

As the new music started—synthesized piano and drum in a fast irregular beat—Judy marched in place. She stared at Sara in the mirror, and said, "Go for four?"

"*Sara* . . ." Anne said—and Sara realized Judy thought she'd been showing off all the time, raising her bench.

"I wasn't showing off," Sara said, and would have explained and said she didn't know anything about aerobics anyway, but Judy looked away from her and kept marching in place . . . waiting.

Everyone in the class had stopped exercising. They were watching Judy.

"Sis," Anne said over the music, "—let's just call it a day."

"This girl can kiss my ass," Sara said, and didn't care if anybody heard her—wanted Judy to hear. "I would have explained, but now she can just kiss my ass." And while Anne said something more into the music's rattle and thump, walked over to the side wall, got a fourth set of platforms, and slid them under her bench.

Judy looked into the mirror at Sara just once, then stepped up onto her high bench and began movements that were almost dancing to that music. Very fast dancing. And paying no attention to the class or anything else. Sara watched Judy for a moment, saw what she was doing—which was complicated, stepping up so high, triple-stepping, turning on the bench . . . then stepping (almost jumping) down and up and down again, arms stretching, pumping in rhythm. Then up, triple-stepping, turning in the other direction. It was intricate, but once Sara was up on her bench—so much higher—and moving, she was able to learn it pretty quickly.

Now, more and more pleased, a companion to the music, she stepped up and down—high, stretching steps—turned and jumped jumped jumped up and down, very fast, working at this strange sort of dancing as if she were running beside the sled, or hunting, trotting up across a mountainside to intercept a Dall sheep racing down the reverse. Sara gave up any worry to the music, felt she could outrun her own weariness, outrun her ankle's ache, and set herself to do it.

She exercised, watching the big girl working before her—smooth and tanned, her powerful legs packed with muscle, springy as any strong young animal's—and thought it would take a while to run her down.

Relaxed, Sara performed her exercise for that routine—then another Judy's mirrored reflection led her into—and some time after that into another . . . until she was dreaming, imagining she was dancing with the Indian women, dancing around the furred pole up to heaven. Dancing with the Koyukons as if she were one of them, and home.

She woke from this when the blond girl stumbled—tripped and recovered at once to continue stepping up, spinning, stepping to the side and down. It was a difficult pattern to follow, and Sara was surprised how tired her legs had become, how hard her heart was pounding. She heard people murmuring under the music, under the sound of her breathing—and looked at the big girl again, saw the weightier way she moved, saw the sweat running like liquid glass along her muscles. 'I can bring her down,' she thought, as if she were Lobo, or Lobo's wolf mother, and had her pack behind her.

As if the girl had heard the thought, or some odd sound, she glanced into the mirror, saw Sara, and moved even faster—whirling, stepping, leaping to the loud music as if she could move so fast forever.

But Sara was determined—or something in her, stronger and stranger, was determined—and although her legs were shaking and breaths burned, though her heart was beating so sharply it seemed to strike the bones of her chest, Sara knew no doubt. She thought if she died, Judy would look back and see her still following, following every step though dead. And that decided, Sara relaxed and moved easier . . . drifted again and began to dream she was running behind the team, running for pleasure up and up a slope of new snow through stands of spruce to train two big pups as wheelers—Vanilla's pups brought up from Frank Solokoff's.

She smelled the snow, heard the quick light jingle of harness—then heard a slamming sound as if the sled had struck something—and saw the big girl down.

Judy knelt beside her toppled bench, her hand weights lying on the carpet. It seemed to Sara she'd stepped wrong and the bench's left end had come off the platforms. Judy knelt there and tried to fix it . . . then slowly stood up, staggered and stayed standing, breathing in long whooping breaths as if she'd had her wind knocked out. Her face looked the way it would when she was old. Then she leaned forward and put her hands on her thighs, stayed braced that way, and looked up at Sara as if she were doing something terrible.

Sara kept exercising a little while longer. It seemed sad to stop

when she'd come so far, like ending a trip too soon for satisfaction—
and the music still going on, thundering. But when Judy turned her
head away, wouldn't look anymore, Sara slowly stopped . . . then
got down from her high bench. She felt too light—as if she'd float
away if she didn't walk carefully.

She put her weights down, went up to Judy and touched her right
shoulder, so solid, round, and tan, but trembling and wet with sweat
as she bent, braced and trying to take deep breaths.

"Too much muscle mass," Sara said, and Judy shrugged her hand
off, turned, tripped, then walked away down the room with everyone watching, got to the end of the room and bent to rest again—
then suddenly leaned farther over and vomited into a wastebasket.

"Oh, my God . . . oh, my *God!*" Anne in the driver's seat. "Judy
Van Zant barfing into the wastebasket! She will never, never live it
down!" She leaned over slowly, bound by her seat belt, and kissed
Sara on the cheek. "My big sister, my weird, skinny sister walked in
there out of the woods and ran that bitch *ragged*. She'll have to move.
Judy Van Zant is going to have to leave this town!"

"I'm tough on exercise girls. —In other circumstances, not so
tough." Sara's legs were aching. She bent forward against the seat
belt's unreeling to massage her calves. Her ankle hurt. "It wasn't
fair."

"Wasn't fair? That bitch has been bullying us for months! All for
our own good, of course. And then putting her bench up on *four*
levels."

"It wasn't fair to her. She hasn't . . . lived the way I have."

"Well, I loved it."

Sara sat back up, and saw a poodle as they drove by—a big smoke-
gray standard. An elderly man was walking him. She could see using
a dog like that for easy running, easy on the level. Could see why
some people had tried poodles out—smart, quick to learn. But no
good for hard hauling in high country. Legs too long. Backs too
short. . . . Anne turned left onto South East Seventieth, drove two
blocks. Then turned right into The Lakes, and along its street.

"Oh, shit. I don't believe it."

"What?"

"It's my fabulous ex—and what the hell is he doing here?"

A black BMW convertible, top down, was parked in the house's
driveway. Sara saw a man sitting behind the wheel, and recognized
Connor as they drove up alongside on the right. He was wearing a

gray tweed sports jacket and matching tweed cap with a bill, and looked fatter and more freckled than she'd remembered.

Anne got out her side and slammed the door shut. "What the hell are you doing here, Connor? It is not your day!"

"I know."

"And where's Miss Roundheels?"

"Not funny, Anne."

"You're so right. —And you're here this evening for what reason?"

"I had to come over to the Island anyway, and I just thought I'd drop by and see the kid—maybe take him out for a Coke. If it's a big problem, then we'll just forget it. I sent him in to shower and change. —Hi, Sara! It's wonderful to see you, sweetheart."

"Hi, Connor." Sara wanted to stay sitting in the Mercedes, but she got out.

"Back down from the wilderness. About Alan—I wish I'd met the guy. A rotten thing. . . ."

"Thanks."

"Connor, are you saying Kevin already thinks he's going?"

"And why the hell not, Anne? Do we continue this sort of warfare indefinitely? It is not good for the boy; it is not good for us. It's just silly."

"Oh, I'm so glad to hear you *say* that. Does this mean—could it mean that you're going to let me have some of the money you stole out of our so-called community property? Does this mean you intend to act like a man, as far as your responsibility to me and our son is concerned, rather than like a fat disgusting lying rat with red hair and freckles?"

"Not funny, Anne."

"You bet it isn't. —Balding, *used* to have red hair. . . . You have such unbelievable nerve coming here completely off the schedule and trying to take Kevin away while I'm gone. Isn't it too bad I got home in time to catch you? You could have had Kevin all to yourself; you could have left me a shitty little note. You could have Kevin— who has certainly not done his homework, yet—could have had him all to yourself all evening, and buy him a nice big cheeseburger and fries and a chocolate sundae and you both could talk about poor *Mom*, and what a pain she is."

"I don't talk about people behind their back—"

"Oh, you fucking liar!"

"Sara," Connor said, comfortable in the convertible, "—it's usually not this bad. Usually, we're fairly civilized."

"Right. You tell Sara all about it—poor victimized asshole and his impossible ex-wife. . . . Oh, wait a minute, I must be getting dense. Of *course*. Of course you have Miss Roundheels stashed away in some bar, nursing a beer—and probably giving blow jobs in the back—while you come here supposedly all alone, *such* a busy CPA, to have a hurried tender guy-to-guy visit with your son. Right? She's waiting for you?"

"That's ridiculous."

"Sis, you see that? See that lie just ooze out of him. It's like watching somebody go to the bathroom."

"For God's sake, Anne—"

"Oh, I've got a little reminder for you, Tiger." Anne walked away up the drive, and into the house.

"Isn't she something?" Connor said. "Still very attractive. . . ."

"Is she right about the money?"

"No. Well, only in a way." He turned a little in the car seat, to face her. There wasn't much room behind the wheel; he'd gained a lot of weight. "What she considers my crime about the money, involved knowing something about money besides how to spend it—and hiring a better lawyer. Anne's lawyer was one of those liberal losers; guy's known all over Seattle, sued Boeing a hundred times." Connor leaned over to open the convertible's passenger-side door. "Come on . . . sit down, and if you can stand it, I'll give you a quick summary of my side of this mess."

"That's all right."

"No, no. Come on, be a sport. I know you've heard Anne's side—now you have to hear mine. You're family, and that's the penalty you pay."

Sara got into the BMW and closed the door. It smelled almost the same as the Mercedes; they'd used a different cure on the leather. Connor leaned toward her and kissed her on the cheek. He smelled of after-shave, something citrus—smelled like grapefruit, but that couldn't be right.

"Hi, sister-in-law."

"Ex-sister-in-law," Sara said. "—Hi." Connor, seen so close, looked swollen as if life were cooking him, puffing him, singeing his hair ginger and spattering him with freckles. He was Kevin grown up—as if he'd made his son alone, with Anne having nothing to do with it.

"Now Sara, before I continue with my troubles, let me say again how sorry I was to hear you'd lost Alan. You're a sweetheart—a nut, but a sweetheart—and I felt terrible hearing about that. You were happy up there?"

"Yes."

"Then it was a damned tragedy. Are you all right? Really, are you all right?"

"I'm fine. I'm all right."

"And you're here to stay, or what?"

"Probably 'or what.' "

"Well . . . let me just tell you that *I* could have been hit by a bus and I doubt if Anne would have even realized it for several days. She'd just have come home on the third or fourth day—home from that ridiculous store—and finally realized there wasn't any lunch in the refrigerator. Did she tell you that I made her lunch? Every god-damned morning I would make her lunch." He shifted in the driver's seat, turning to face Sara more fully, the upholstery's leather squeaking softly at the friction. "—Chicken salad, tuna salad, egg salad. Really nice, very carefully prepared. A little chopped celery, tiny slices of green pepper mixed in. Just so she'd have a little love to-ken—and I'm still happy to call it that. Now, if I had been hit by that bus, then maybe, *maybe* in two or three days of coming home from that damned store for lunch, she would have noticed I hadn't left her anything, any of my little specialties to eat. Two or three days after I was dead, she might have noticed."

"She said you wanted her to have the store—something for her to do."

"Great. O.K. That's her story. —She asked me! She wanted to do something in the office. 'Please get serious,' is what I said. Something in the *office?* Sara—Hagerstrom, Rittman, and Brice is hanging on by its fingernails. You know what Chuck Hagerstrom would have said if I'd waltzed into his office and said, 'Oh, Chuck, Anne wants to come in and work. She's bored. She wants us to make up a job for her'? If I'd said that, I'd still be running, and Chuck would still be after me with that putter he plays with. And I wouldn't blame him."

"Well, then, that's why she wanted to open the store. Since she couldn't work with you."

"Sara, not exactly my idea. I said, 'Work in a store. Learn the business first.' That's what I said. I didn't say, 'Open a goddamned store; spend half the night there!' Did you know she let some witch-es—official witches—have a seminar there one afternoon? They served brownies with something in them—not pot, something that tasted like nothing I ever tasted. And that was Anne's notion of responsible behavior . . . reasonable merchandising."

"But you went, so it couldn't have been too weird. I remember you as being very un-weird, Connor."

"Listen, I went so it *wouldn't* be weird. And, speaking of merchandising, what Anne called bookkeeping was just bizarre, and I mean it, weirder than the witches. And she wouldn't—didn't want her *husband*, an experienced CPA, God forbid he should look at the books. Nooo, nononono. Not him! But talk about witchcraft—we're talking about single-entry 'This is how much lemonade I sold all afternoon, Mommy,' bookkeeping. If the IRS ever tries to audit that cockamamie little operation, it'll take years off their lives."

"I don't think Annie's a fool. I think she's probably a good businesswoman."

"Relax; I know she's not a fool. Don't you think I know why she did that? Do you think *I'm* a fool, Sara? She kept the books that way because it bothered the hell out of me!"

Sara started to say that was nonsense, then didn't.

"Um-hmm. Am I right? Yes? I notice you're not saying I'm wrong. We're talking here about a woman who has got to be in charge."

"Not true."

"It is true. You're her sister and you love her, but it's true."

"No. Not true."

"Listen. I'm her ex-husband, and I still love her. And it's true. For years . . . for *years*, part I played was the solid, limited, hard-working dull accountant with the mediocre education, married to Ms. Cultured Bright. And I . . . and Sara, I played my part. And I loved her. And I still love her, but I will no longer humiliate myself. Well, let me . . . let me be honest. I decided I could not eat any more shit—and please pardon my language there."

"Connor, this is really not my business."

"Listen—once in the family, always in the family. How are you getting along with Kevin?"

"She thinks you feed him too much, and she's right."

"Oh, she does? Let me tell you, you think I don't know Kevin overeats when I take him out? He's fucking famished, and it isn't for food—it's just for some plain ordinary hugging and caring and listening. That's the reason he eats. The boy eats when he's with me as if he was *starving*. What am I supposed to say to him? 'Kev, your mom loves you and I love you, so forget the goddamn lamb chops and apple pie and ice cream. Just sit there and have some salad and believe me, everything's going to be O.K.' Am I supposed to say that?"

"Why not say that?"

"Because it isn't true. Anne wants me to stop feeding rich things to Kevin when I see him—and I want her to present me with a son for those times who doesn't *need* to stuff himself with mashed potatoes as if he was dying of hunger. All right?"

"Connor—you want me to say something?"

"Yes, I really do."

"O.K. You schemed and took money that belongs to Annie. And you have another woman."

"—And it infuriates Anne, and it's not fair, and so forth and so forth. I know the way Anne talks about Lydia, and Anne is full of it. . . . Lydia is a very nice person. And no, she isn't a dummy that I can treat with the contempt Anne treated me. She's an intelligent, nice young woman, and she understands I do very difficult and demanding work—which is, believe me, what modern accountancy is. This city has become a goddamned snake pit of accounting firms—"

"Connor . . ."

"—We've always had Jewish accountants in town, and no problem. Very nice guys socially, gentlemen and so forth, but buzz saws in the *office*. You make a mistake, and they were right on it. Then— O.K.—last few years, we've gotten the Scotsmen down from Canada. Very hungry, and what they call accounting, frankly, a lot of people don't call accounting. Now—*now*—the Japanese are coming in. They finally figured out accounting is where it's at, after all the 'creative' horse manure is over. So, you're looking at a small firm of CPAs with all these kinds of really aggressive people breathing down our necks—people who don't know anything about a reasonable lunch hour, let alone leaving a little early, getting in some racquetball. Oh, nooo, nonono. Now, the game is work until you drop, and that was something Anne simply did not understand. Just didn't get the picture."

"She got the picture of Lydia."

"Well, you're a woman and you don't understand, and that's that. I had an affair with Lydia, and it developed into mutual affection and respect—"

"Oh, please."

"And—*and* I need it and I enjoy it. Anne treated me like a moron with a calculator up his ass long before that happened, and that was one of the reasons it happened, and I don't regret a bit of it. Period. And that's that." He settled deeper into the car's upholstery, ran both forefingers lightly around the wheel. His fingers were fat and rosy except where the knuckles dimpled paler.

"So, you're happier now?"

"You bet. I'm not saying it's perfect. What would I want if I could have the world—if I was emperor of the world? I'll tell you; I know just what I'd want. I'd want Anne back as my wife, loving me and respecting me for the work I do. And I'd want Lydia, too."

"Very grown up."

"Sara, I'm tired of being grown up. I was grown up for years, and it brought me nothing but fatigue and unhappiness. Listen, if I was going to live a thousand years, I'd stay with Anne until Kevin is grown and out on his own. But unfortunately—as you know better than anybody, right now—life is very very short. Maybe . . . maybe I'm supposed to just stay miserable for the rest of my life—but I won't do it. I am not going to do it. So, you just think of me as being a selfish shit. I don't care. Well, that's not true; of course I care. But I sure as hell don't care enough to sacrifice my pleasure in living. Period."

"Great for you, Connor. Doesn't seem to be working that well for Kevin. Your son's a mess."

"Thank you. Very complimentary."

"You know what I mean—and also, what about the money? Annie says you stole money from your joint property, and invested it with your friends and cheated her."

"That's absolutely right."

"You did that?"

"You bet." Connor looked pleased to have been asked. "But not in the way you're saying, not in that illegal way. Sara, what I did was, I took all those accounting skills Anne has been making fun of for fifteen years, and I put them to work—and her years of sarcastic bullshit cost her eighty-seven thousand dollars. Eighty-seven thousand, six hundred and twenty-three dollars and forty-one cents, as a matter of fact. And I will never admit I even said that to you. It was never said, period. Let Ms. Smart Ass learn what it means to really work for money, instead of living off her husband and making him feel like shit besides. Excuse my language, there. A little lesson in real life—it'll make a human being out of her."

"And what does cheating her make out of you, Connor? Because I think she still cares about you." Sara, looking past Connor—tired of looking at him—saw a big white-and-tan station wagon pull up into the driveway of the house across the street.

"Oh, no, she doesn't. She just wants me back in harness—that's where all that rage is coming from. She still can't believe it; she doesn't believe I'm able to lead a life without her." Connor smiled. Sara'd remembered his teeth; they were very even and white, the teeth of a handsomer man. "—But I *can* lead my own life. See this car? This car represents forty-two thousand, two hundred and sixty dollars and seventeen cents of that money we were talking about."

"Connor, I'm sorrier for you than I am for Annie. . . ." A man and woman, both very tall, had gotten out of the station wagon with two young boys—the adults unloading groceries from the back. Both the children were thin, looked tall for their ages. . . .

"That's because you're twice the woman your beautiful sister is ever going to be. —Oh, God, what now?"

Sara saw Anne coming down the driveway; she had a piece of typing paper in her hand. The paper seemed to have been folded and unfolded many times.

"What is it, Anne?" Connor said. "A writ?"

"It's something I had to dig up, *exhume* from a pile of soon-to-be trash. Something someone wrote to me once, with tears in his fat eyes." She stood at the passenger-side door and began to read from the paper. " 'Wildflowers—' "

"What the hell do you think you're doing?"

" 'Wildflowers,' " Anne read, much louder.

"Oh, my God."

" 'Brighter than roses, and a few more rare,
Their color relieves my landscape of care.
So, your beauty, Anne, decorates my life,
For I have a lovely wildflower of a wife.
Your blossoming breasts—' "

"That's it," Connor said. "—I'm gone." He started the BMW, and Sara got out.

" 'Your blossoming breasts . . . !' " Annie was shouting as he backed down the drive. Sara saw the people across the street standing watching, listening to her.

" 'Your blossoming breasts, whose nipples I suck—I SUCK!' " She ran down the drive after him. —" 'PROVIDE ME WITH THE HONEY OF LOVERS' LUCK!' "

Connor drove away.

". . . Teach that balding piece of shit to come sneaking around here when it isn't his day. You see that ridiculous cap?" Anne came back up the drive. "—The Whaley sisters are kicking ass this evening!"

Kevin, in black corduroy trousers and a white sweater layered over a red one, came out of the house and said, "Where's Dad?"

*   *   *

274

Next morning—its sunshine too mild, too cloud-broken to dry the night's damp—Sara dropped Anne off at Facets, then drove a block, parked, and went into Alpen-Land for more coffee and orange juice, and a heated cherry Danish with whipped butter. She was wearing her new black sweater with the dark-gray skirt, black pumps, and the safari jacket. It seemed to her she was as well dressed as any woman there. Better dressed than several. Except she needed a new purse. The big brown purse matched the jacket, but didn't match anything else.

After she ate, Sara used the coffee-shop phone and called Ms. Monroe at the agency. Her ankle ached slightly as she stood listening to the phone ring.

Ms. Monroe picked up on the fourth ring. "Sara Maher. . . . Yes, I have read your stories, Ms. Maher, and I have two things to say about them. —Would you rather come into the office?"

"No, this is all right," Sara said. She hadn't had to get dressed up, after all.

"Well, then—first, I enjoyed reading them, which is by no means always the case with material I'm given. And second, I see no market for them whatsoever." Ms. Monroe stopped talking, apparently waiting to see if Sara had anything to say.

"—I know of no publisher in the country who would be interested in animal stories, all of which end tragically. Too downbeat for children, too childish for adults. . . . Ms. Maher?"

"Yes."

"Now, all this is just my opinion, and if you don't agree with my judgment of your work, you could—you should—take it elsewhere."

"No, I think your judgment of my work is all right. I just hoped people would like the stories. I wanted children to read them, especially. They're so true . . . about what happens to animals that are odd. Different."

"Yes, of course—and I didn't say I didn't like them. I said I can't sell them."

"O.K."

"You know, you could send them to another agent. In New York, if you want. If you'll check this year's Writer's Market, you'll find some names—and I might be mistaken, and they might sell them for you."

"No, I think you're right."

"Very well. Would you like to pick these copies up, or should I send them to you?"

"I don't need those. I have everything written in my notebook."

". . . All right. I'm sorry I couldn't give you better news."

"That's O.K.," Sara said, and hung up. Then she went back to the café's counter and ordered another Danish—this one apricot—and hot chocolate with whipped cream. She took them to a small table at the end of a long display rack of imported candies, and sat there eating, drinking the hot chocolate, and pretended she was celebrating—that Ms. Monroe had said she wanted Sara to come to the office . . . and then told her in the office she wanted Sara to be her client. And was sending the stories to a publisher back East. She hadn't mentioned money, though—and Sara pretended within pretending, and thought she might get an advance. Five hundred dollars. Seven hundred and fifty. And she could see what the book should look like. The cover should be brown and blue, like the world. And the illustrations inside done in green and white, for the trees and snow. There shouldn't be any pictures at all of the animals the stories were about—only their paw prints in the snow, only disturbed spruce needles, little branches bent. There should only be pictures of the other animals, watching them.

Sara felt better pretending, while she was eating the Danish and drinking hot chocolate. But when she was finished and got up to go, having pretended only made her sadder.

A different nurse was on duty at The Arbor—another practical nurse, an Oriental woman who smiled pleasantly at Sara as she passed in the hall, carrying a small red-plastic tray of little paper medication cups, a jar of tablets. Her smile had revealed a gold tooth, upper right canine.

From the room's doorway, Sara saw her mother sitting by the window, gently rocking from side to side in her wheelchair. She was taking deep, snorting breaths.

"Mom?"

Helen stopped rocking, backed the chair around, and sat looking at Sara, breathing more quietly. Her right eye was nearly closed, as if she'd winked and forgotten to open the eye again afterward.

Sara went in and bent to kiss her. "You in pain, Mom?"

Her mother shrugged as if that was a question not worth answering, then sat more erect in her wheelchair, looking up at Sara with her right eyelid drooped almost shut.

Sara picked up one of the small straight-back chairs, put it beside her mother, and sat down. "Does your eye hurt you, Mom?"

That seemed to make Helen angry. "No, m'eye doesn' . . . hurt me. Does yoursss . . . hurt you?"

"I'm sorry," Sara said. "I know you must get tired of being asked these things."

"Damn ri'." Her mother cleared her throat. "Kevin doesn' . . . come."

"Well, Annie doesn't want him bothering you while you're feeling so bad."

"Ev'body believe tha', stan' on their head," her mother said, and quite clearly, "Too . . . fat."

"Kevin's too fat?" Sara glanced over at the curtained bed where the bloated woman lay. Wondered if that silent creature listened.

Helen nodded, and as if that motion had freed some small lever, her right eyelid slowly raised. The eye looked odd, its pupil so large the colored portion seemed black instead of hazel.

"Needs exercise," Sara said. "Needs something."

"Anne's fau'."

"I suppose."

"Evan jus' . . . like tha'."

"Dad?"

"Nev' . . . spank." Helen pronounced "spank" very crisply.

"He was gentle with us, Mom. I don't think that was bad."

Her mother pursed her lips, dubious—lips pouting, deeply gathered with no teeth beneath them.

"—Alan was gentle, too. If we'd had a child, I don't think he would have punished it that way."

"Two of a . . . kind," her mother said—then suddenly grunted and threw her head back as if someone had hit her in the face. The grunt had turned into a long indrawn breath—and, her head still held back, Helen stared at Sara as if it were she who was hurting her.

Sara sat in sudden cold. "Mom . . . ? Mom, should I get the nurse?"

Her mother then made an odd sound, a soft squealing, as if she were exerting some enormous effort. But when Sara stood up, Helen stopped that noise, said "No . . . no," and sat in her chair, head still held back, looking more frightened of having the nurse called than of her pain.

"Oh, Mom," Sara said, and leaned down to put her hand on Helen's forehead—then didn't, afraid she'd hurt her, shake the thing inside her mother's head and make her scream. "Please," Sara said, meaning for her mother to stop frightening her. And at this, a child's begging, her mother slowly straightened in the wheelchair, slowly sat up as if the pain were gone.

"Aw . . . ri'," she said. "Aw . . . over. . . ."

"Don't you want some medicine? They can give you a shot."

"Aw . . . over." And smiled a toothless smile up at Sara as if showing off, demonstrating what she could bear. "Sssit down."

Sara sat down, happy to have her mother instruct her, and stayed there watching Helen deal with her agony, address and bargain and struggle with it. Sara watched her mother's hands knot and unknot on the wheelchair's narrow arms, while slowly, methodically, she wrestled with the pain, slowly achieved the grip to hold it still—and nearer, a part of her, no longer a separate creature.

"Aw . . . ri'." Helen's face slowly relaxed into a frown. "—O.K."

"Oh, Mom . . ."

" 'Oh . . . Mom,' " her mother said in imitation. Then sat silent, slowly turned her head away to look out the room's window.

"The yard's so green," Sara said, and her mother slowly nodded. "Wouldn't you like a plant for your room? A begonia, or a little box of pansies? We could put them in the window."

"No," her mother said, and sat looking out into the yard. "Couldn' . . . care for."

"We'll water them for you. Annie and I'll take care of them. There's no reason you shouldn't have flowers, some pretty things."

"I don' *wan'* . . . pretty things." Saying that so clearly seemed to tire Helen, and Sara sat quiet, watching her mother, seeing how small she'd become.

Helen nodded as if agreeing with someone, nodded slowly again . . . and slid into dozing, her breath rattling softly in her throat.

Sara sat watching for a long while, listening to her mother's breathing . . . the random distant sounds outside the room, down the corridor. The woman in the curtained bed made no sound at all. Sara watched, felt she guarded her mother's sleep, and wished her gentle dreams.

After a while, Helen snorted, slept a little more, then snorted again and slowly opened her eyes. "Oh, my . . ." she said, and looked around the room as if to be sure what she suspected was so—her dream had been a dream, and this was not. She put her hands up to touch her fallen face, stroked it gently, then touched her scalp where her hair had been, gently traced her scars there with her fingertips. She put her hands down and sat for a moment with her eyes closed. Then she looked over at Sara, examined her, and said, "Have . . . to pee."

Sara stood up and went to the back of the chair, bent to release its brake, and wheeled it slowly, carefully through into the bathroom. Then she turned the chair, pulled it back a little way toward the sink, and stood there behind her mother, looking down at the balding scalp tufted with occasional gray, the scars marking mottled skin like a map of new country.

Her mother said, "Come . . . *on*," and Sara thought of the snow-shoe hare the team had injured, considered what she had to do, and put those things in order in her mind. She bent over the back of the wheelchair to hold Helen, hug her, kiss her pale temple. Then Sara slid her right arm up and around to fit the crook of her elbow to her mother's chin. She gripped her right wrist with her left hand for greater leverage—braced herself, yanked suddenly back—then twisted to the left hard as she could, grunting at the effort. She felt Helen's neck come swiftly to its stop—then pass it with so sharp a sudden crack that Sara hunched still, listening to see if anyone heard.

Her mother's feet began a quick jigging dance off the wheelchair's footrest, kicked a little in the air so her left slipper, pale pink, fell free on the bathroom floor. Sara smelled urine.

When the feet—left one bare, netted in blue veins—only stretched out, trembling as if seeking purchase somewhere else, Sara stooped, gripped the right armrest—lifted, heaved the loaded chair tilting over to the left . . . then half lowered it, half let it topple until it clattered thumping on its side, right wheel up and spinning, Helen slid halfway out into the doorway.

Sara bent to lift her mother's head, now floppily attached as a Raggedy Ann's, and propped it gently against the door frame. Then she stepped over and out of the bathroom, glanced down to see Helen's eyes half open, sleepy and remote. Sara held her hands up to see whether her mother, like the snowshoe hare, had spit blood on them. She saw no blood, and pausing only to pick up her purse, walked past the fat woman's silent curtained bed and out of the room, closing the door behind her. —Then she began to take deep breaths, and went down the corridor stepping so lightly, moving so slowly it seemed to her she was nearly swimming through the air. She drifted along between the double row of watchers and dreamers. Then, when she reached the doors to the reception room, hesitated before opening them—worried, she'd grown so light, that a wind might blow in from outside. A warm wet wind that would sweep her up and back down the corridor, blow her along the hall like paper, past palms and wheelchairs where the ruined people sat.

Sara felt she'd turned into two Saras—stronger together than she'd been alone—smiled at Mrs. Todd at the reception desk and walked on through, so alive she smiled again. But down the walk outside, she felt faint, and had to wander off onto the grass and lean against a tulip tree. She ducked a little under low branches to reach the trunk, and stood against it, pressing the side of her face against smooth bark. She whispered something to the tree, certain it would whisper nothing back.

She drove to the Safeway at Eastgate Mall; it was where Annie had said she shopped. Sara thought she might buy at least a few groceries, even if Annie didn't want her to. Some bacon, bagels. She'd missed bagels up in the country.

The Safeway was much bigger even than the market in Fairbanks, two or three times bigger. She felt better in the supermarket because of that, unnoticed, safe among its endless displays under bright flat light that shone sometimes white, sometimes pale yellow. There weren't many people shopping in the middle of the day.

Sara'd forgotten how much food the big stores held. She wandered amazed up and down each of eighteen long aisles stacked on either side with shelves of canned goods, jars, bottles and boxes of food in all sorts of colors and sizes. She saw endless things to eat—cookies, honey-roasted peanuts, ginger ale, salami (beef salami, Genoa, summer, low fat, and Jewish), artichoke hearts, mangoes, anchovy paste and Ritz crackers—things she'd dreamed of for years at odd hours. . . . Some nights, when she was still teaching at Inuviak, lying awake in her small corrugated-iron box, listening to the sea moaning, cracking its joints like a giant waking as the winter's ice began to give, she'd longed for marshmallows—and once wished for country ham (almost too salty to eat) and half an acorn squash, buttered and sprinkled with cinnamon, and a salad with bacon broken into it.

She'd wanted all these things from time to time—wanted them less in the mountains than she had by the sea—but wanted them all. And here they were, present and undesirable.

Sara felt much better walking down the long aisles, and was startled when the floor suddenly jolted beneath her feet. Jolted sharply to the right, so she almost tripped, then swung slowly back to the left, an uncertain motion—and suddenly farther left, so she stumbled.

She thought it was an earthquake—then saw a woman wheeling past her with a loaded basket-cart, saw the woman's two little boys trotting behind, both children small and blond, long-haired as girls, but with boys' tough blunt little faces. The floor was solid under those people—but not beneath her. It yanked almost out from under, and she staggered back and then to the side, feeling sick, and the floor rose up and lifted her a little way so she had to reach out to her left and hold a shelf for balance.

Then the floor dropped, and Sara fell to one knee with it, and stayed kneeling as it swung left—then left again so she bumped into the shelves there, nauseated, and had to close her eyes. She supposed people were watching her . . . though now the floor was still.

She heard wheels rolling behind her, and thought her mother might be coming in her chair—withered white arms pumping, pumping at the wheel rims, the scarred white balding head hanging loose on its broken neck, lolling across her chest from side to side as she labored after Sara, her smile sometimes visible.

Still kneeling, trying not to vomit, Sara was too frightened not to turn and look—and saw only a small man in a brown leather jacket pushing his cart down the aisle, looking to the right along high shelves of pasta as he passed.

As the man went by, she stayed kneeling, pretending to look at cans of peas on the lowest shelf, and didn't think she'd be able to get up until someone came to help her, and hear what she'd done to her mother.

She knelt there on one knee, reading the label on a medium can of garden peas. These were fancy-grade peas, and small. *Petit pois*—she remembered they were called that; she wasn't going crazy. These had been canned in Selby, Oklahoma. And a little bit of something had been added to them, but only a very small amount, to keep the peas green. Sara felt she could stay reading the label for a long time, because twice she forgot it after she read it and could start reading it all over again. She was worried someone might stop and ask her why she was crying—and thought if that happened, she'd say, "These were canned in my home town. I grew up in Selby; my mother died there, and that's why I'm crying. I was just reading the label—I was going to buy them—and then I saw they were canned out in the town I was born in. I knew they had a Del Monte plant, and I knew boys who worked out there in the summer. But I didn't know they canned peas. . . ."

If she said that, people would think she was a little strange, though not too bad, not someone who'd just done what she'd done.

But no sooner had Sara worked out that story, that explanation, than she forgot it, and knelt wondering what she would say if a store clerk came by and asked if she was all right. She tried to remember the story, and couldn't. . . . Something about a town. . . . Then she tried to make up a new story, and that was exhausting. She tried to put the can of peas back on the shelf and couldn't . . . so she lay down on her right side in the aisle, enjoying the coolness of the rubber tiles.

She supposed someone would stop and call for help when they saw her, and she would have no explanation but the truth, and that was no explanation at all. Two people crossed the aisle at the far end, but they didn't look her way. She hoped the people who did come and find her wouldn't have children with them. It would frighten little children to see a woman lying in the aisle holding a can of peas.

"Oh, help me," Sara said to herself, but she was unable to. If she felt better, she could have hauled herself up holding onto the store shelves, could have climbed them like the side of a mountain. She tried to think of someone to help her up—thought of Dutchy, who was so strong. "Oh, help me," she said aloud, and looked up the aisle to see if he was there. At first he wasn't . . . and then he was. He was standing in the center of the aisle yards away, staring at her. He didn't seem interested in the store, or the noise and odors of people he'd never known. He stared only at her, black-pupiled eyes blue as old ice, ears up and forward. His pinto coat looked deep and rich as chocolate cake with white frosting here and there.

Sara held out her hand, and Dutchy came to her, trotting, nails clicking over the floor—came right up to her so she smelled his scent of dog and snow. *"Hold,"* Sara said, reached up with her right hand and got her fingers under his harness . . . felt how warm his fur was as she got a grip. She still held the can of peas in her other hand—knew she should let that go. She pulled herself awkwardly partway up, embraced Dutchy, leaned on him hard, and managed to get to one knee. "Hike," she said. *"Hike."* And he spun and started away so strongly she slid across the floor three or four feet while she tried to get her feet under her—and as he lunged away, was hauled stumbling erect. She let go of his harness, staggered and stood swaying, trying to catch her breath . . . so much tireder now than when she'd run the exercise girl to vomiting.

"Good dog," Sara said, but Dutchy was gone.

She stayed standing, still holding the can of peas in her left hand, and looked away from the shelves of food, read no more labels. After a while, she was able to walk all the way to the front of the store, past people who seemed to see nothing wrong with her at all.

12

Λ

Anne was in the kitchen, washing red-tip lettuce, leaf by leaf, laying the wet leaves in the white-plastic dish drainer. She looked at Sara as she walked in, and Sara first thought drops of water had splashed on Annie's face, then saw she'd been crying.

"Where the hell have you been all day? They said you were in visiting Mom late this morning. Where the *hell* have you been?"

"I was; I visited her and then I went shopping for groceries—but I didn't get much. Then I just drove around." Sara put the small brown grocery bag on the counter.

"Drove around all afternoon. . . . Well, I hope you had a good visit with Mom, because while you were shopping—which you didn't have to do, which I've told you you don't have to do. You are a goddamn guest, you are my *sister*, for Christ's sake. —While you were out doing that, driving around in my car, they called me at the store and told me Mom fell over in her wheelchair again. She was apparently trying to go to the bathroom on her own to show she could do it—when she should have known better than to try—and the wheelchair went over and she hit her head on the door frame." Anne washed another lettuce leaf under the faucet, rubbed its wide pale-green base to clean bits of soil away. "She's dead."

"Dead . . . I'm sorry, Annie—"

"—And I'd really like to know what you've been saying to her, if you said something to upset her . . . because this eccentric act of yours is perfectly all right, but not if it means upsetting our mother so she tried to do something she couldn't do, knocked over her wheelchair and broke her neck! I'd just like to know what the hell you've been *telling* her. Did you tell her there isn't enough money to have her in there, have people take care of her?"

"I told her we loved her, that's all." Sara was surprised how well she was talking, but decided not to talk anymore unless she had to.

She looked down at the countertop beside the little grocery bag, and began to make first a coastline, then a country from the creamy slate-gray swirls in the material's surface. Certainly could be a country, with a coastline so sweeping, curved into a single beach. Inland would be more restful—prairie, stands of forest in low hills. Mule deer would be there—or that country's version of them—perhaps something like a camel, with slimmer legs and the pupils of their eyes slit like goats'. . . .

"Kevin was greeted by the news as soon as he got home from school, and he's upset—within reason, of course—not exactly prostrated. The fact of dying bothered him more than losing Mom. They weren't buddies." Anne washed another lettuce leaf. She'd washed six or seven and placed them in the white-plastic drainer. The red edges of the lettuce leaves made them look wilted, beginning to spoil. "—Sara, was Mom bad when you left her? Was she rocking back and forth?"

Sara answered from the countertop country, too far for blame. "She was doing that when I went in, but then she stopped. I think she was feeling better." These creatures—camel-goats—were tree browsers, hard to please with grass. It made it difficult to carry fodder when they were ridden far. Someone, an odd man as softly contoured as his country, might tell Sara you always travel with two of these animals, the second just to pack fodder. Blossoms—faded were O.K. Green shoots. Twigs, as long as their wood was tender.

Anne found a bad leaf, dropped it into the disposal. "First thing I thought, was maybe she did it the same as before—you know, rocking back and forth because of the pain. And you didn't say anything to upset her?"

"No, I didn't say anything to upset her."

"Well, something upset her. She went to the bathroom and didn't wait for help. —She could have just stayed and peed right in the damn chair! Everybody else in that goddamn morgue does it."

"I'm sorry." There were other countries in the countertop. Some less pleasant. . . .

"But not very, am I right? Not terribly sorry."

"I'm glad she's not frightened anymore, Annie. But I'm sorry we lost her. You lost her, especially."

"I didn't lose her 'especially.' " Anne turned on the faucet, ran water over another lettuce leaf. "She didn't give any more of a damn about me than she did about you. But she wasn't really that old, and it just seems very very unfair that such a strong person, such a *tough* woman, should be betrayed by some fucking little piece of meat that wouldn't stop growing. It's disgusting." She put the leaf into the plastic dish drainer. "I was over there and I was talking with that other nurse—what's her name, the Korean one—and the doctor'd been there and they'd already bundled Mom away downstairs. 'You don't want to see her now,' and so forth, and arranging for the cremation next week. Couvelier had a place he recommended. —They were all there. Big deal, not the usual just dying." Anne turned off the faucet. "I have a feeling they were a little worried we might sue the shit out of them—which I would dearly love to do, except I was the one who wanted them to take those cloth belts off her. After she knocked her chair over, they had Mom strapped in like the Frankenstein monster. Which, of course, makes this my fault to some extent."

"No, it isn't. —That's a lot of lettuce."

"So, we'll have a big salad. . . . And she was all right when you left? That halfwit, Carrie, took in the lunch tray and found Mom lying there in the bathroom. And why . . . why they have to hire a retard—I'm sorry, but a goddamn *retard* to clean up. 'Hire the handicapped.' For God's sake, it's supposed to be a quality place! Couldn't they at least have a black woman? And the roommate, that creature in the bed with the curtains—if she wasn't a grotesque vegetable she could have at least rung for help. My fault. My fault for ever letting them put that fucking human broccoli in there with Mom." Anne shook water off the last leaf, dried her hands on the dish towel. "It just meant she was all alone. That's what it meant." She opened the cabinet beneath the sink, hung the dish towel on its rack. "—And I notice you don't have much to say. 'Sorry we've lost her, glad she's gone.' It's easier for you, sis, coming through like a tourist."

"I know." It was more and more difficult to stay in the countertop country. Sara couldn't imagine enough to hold her there.

Anne tore a paper towel off the roll, then picked a lettuce leaf out of the dish drainer, and began patting it dry. "You missed the time, a morning it was of course pouring rain, when we were at the hospital—the *neuro*clinic, and the doctors told her. She didn't believe them and she wouldn't listen." Anne opened a cabinet above the counter, looked for something she didn't find, shut the cabinet door. "—Walked right out of the office. I had to go after her; I caught her in that ugly lobby, and sat with her and begged her to go back. And when we did, they showed her the scans and X rays (all that wonderful technical crap), and she told them they were wrong—period.

Trouble was her eyes—she needed new glasses, and that was why the headaches. Well, they just stood there, looking at her." Anne put the dry leaf down on the counter, picked up another wet one.

"Annie . . ." The countertop country was now no country at all.

"You missed that morning, and you missed a month later, when the two of us went to the University library to look up brain tumors. 'Just in case,' was what she said about *that* research. You know they have seven hundred and sixteen major entries on brain tumors? Thousands of mentions. . . . You missed all that. You did get to say good-bye, which I didn't get to do." Anne put down the leaf she was drying, walked up the counter, and stooped to open a lower cabinet. She took out a pink-plastic bucket with a round flat top; the top had a red knob handle at its rim. "—And if you'll forgive me for saying it, you don't really seem to give a damn."

"Annie, did you want her to live like that another year? Live until that thing maybe pushed her eyes out of her head?"

"Well, since you ask, no. I didn't want that—I just wanted her to live long enough to show some affection to me. I wanted to have a mother to lose, if you're so curious about what I wanted." She put the wet paper towel in the trash container under the sink. "I don't know why I always waste paper towels drying lettuce. . . ." She took the top off the pink-plastic bucket, put all the lettuce leaves in, fitted the top back on, and began turning the small red knob so the bucket's fittings whirred. "This is the only damn thing that works."

Anne turned the red knob for a while—comforted, it seemed to Sara, by the motion, the whirring sound—then turned the knob more and more slowly, sighed, and put the plastic bucket down. "I'm exhausted," she said, and went to the refrigerator, searched a short while and took out a big jar of low-calorie mayonnaise. Then she put the mayonnaise back, took out a smaller jar, marinara sauce. "We could have linguini instead of tuna salad."

"Annie, don't bother with that. Let's have tuna salad."

Anne came to the counter and opened the small grocery bag. "Sara, we don't eat canned peas. O.K.? We buy frozen peas. . . ."

"I really *really* do not want to eat this gerbil food."

"Just try it," Sara said.

"Thanks, but if you don't mind, I'll pass."

"You eat that salad, Kevin," Anne said, "—and be quiet. I've heard about enough out of you."

"Oh, hey, chill out."

"You shut your damn mouth. Don't you dare talk to me like that!" Anne stood up, pushed her stool aside. ". . . I'm tired and I'm going to bed," she said, and walked out of the kitchen.

"Kevin," Sara said, "—you need to learn when to be quiet."

"You see the way she looked at me?"

"I didn't pay any attention to it, and neither should you. Your grandmother just died and your Mom's upset and that's all there is to it."

"I don't care about the salad," Kevin said.

"I know you don't." Sara ate a piece of tomato.

"See the way she looked? Did you register that? That was a ton of hate. She hates Dad, and she hates me." He looked down at the salad on his plate. "There's eggs in this."

"A few slices of hard-boiled egg, that's all."

"And I don't like eggs and she knows it, too." He took a wheat roll out of the basket, broke it open, and began to butter it. "That's what all this health-food stuff is about, is trying to show like she really cares, and all the time she could care less." He hiccuped suddenly, and his face grew flushed as if he were going to cry, sitting bulky on the white-upholstered stool. His trousers were dark purple, his soccer shirt horizontally striped in yellow and white.

"Kevin, your mom loves you."

"Oh, right. Oh, absolutely. . . ."

"—She just doesn't *like* you. Why should she? You're not likable."

"*Hey.*" Kevin looked up from his buttered roll, startled as if by a sudden noise. "That isn't true."

"Kevin, how would you like to come up and stay with me in the mountains for a while?"

"In Alaska?" Kevin took a bite of the roll.

"That's right. You'd have to work very hard up there, but I think you'd learn to like it."

"Oh, man—is this for real?"

"Yes."

"Would I have to go?"

"No."

". . . I mean, thanks for the invitation, but you know—factually? That would not be the trip of my dreams, O.K.?"

"I just thought you might be getting tired of being a fat little asshole."

Kevin opened his mouth, but said nothing.

Sara ate some salad, chewed and swallowed. There was a lot of lettuce, not much tuna. "I'm sorry if that hurts you, Kevin, but you don't mind hurting your mother—so why should I mind hurting you?"

Kevin's face seemed sunburned. "And you're a drastic uggo!" He put down his buttered roll. "You're ugly as a fucking old witch!"

"I know I'm plain—"

"*Ugly.*"

"—And I was a coward, too. But that doesn't help you, Kevin." Sara took another bite of salad; there was some tuna with that.

"I don't want this," Kevin said, looking down at his dinner. "—And you're just weird, saying stuff to a kid." He picked up the buttered roll, but didn't eat any more of it.

"You're thirteen now, Kevin. That's old enough. I guess it depends what kind of person you want to grow up to be—a fat baby, complaining and eating and staring at TV?"

"Right, sure, that's all I do! And why don't you just shut up."

Sara drank some milk, then put the glass down. "If you do get sick of yourself, Kevin, when you're a little older, then I want you to remember what I'm saying, and come up and stay with me. Can you remember the name Kenana? It's a river in Alaska, up in the Brooks Range. *Kenana.* . . ." Sara ate some egg and another chunk of tomato, gave up on the tuna. Getting tuna was just luck; Anne had mixed it in in little pieces. "I live on the mountain where that river starts. You just go up the Yukon to Arctic City or Billy Mitchell—"

"Dork." Kevin got down from his stool, still holding the buttered roll, and started out of the kitchen.

"—Ask about me there; they'll tell you how to come up. Early fall is the easiest traveling."

"You," Kevin said at the kitchen door, "—are a queen geek," and left.

Sara sat alone at the island counter, drank her milk, and had a little more salad.

When she was finished, she got up, took the dishes over to the sink, rinsed them, and put them in the dishwasher—trying to rack them in their proper places the way Annie liked it done. Then she walked through the dining room and entrance hall, and up the stairs, each step's riser seeming a better and better friend . . . until she was at her door, hearing Kevin's painful music down the hall.

In her room, Sara stood and looked out the window for a while. She could see why her mother had liked doing that—looking from the inside out. Looking out into green distance, if only The Arbor's yard. Certainly better than looking from the outside in, finding out things you didn't want to know. Her mother'd known Sara was doing something terrible to her; had time to know that. Not time enough to understand why. . . .

Sara stood for a little longer, watching the last light fading outside. She could still see the far border of the pond behind the house. The rim of still water was the darkest, warmest gray. She imagined walking into the house in Montana all the years ago, her mother smoking Newports in the kitchen, standing at the stove—yellow-flowered apron over her blue work shirt and jeans—browning a pot roast in the biggest black-iron skillet. Bored, she would have glanced at Sara as she walked in, just up the half-mile from the highway after the school bus let her and Annie off. If it had rained that afternoon, they'd have splashed in puddles on the dirt road in their new rubber boots—hers yellow, Annie's red.

"Where's Annie?"

"Out back, with Blazer. . . . Mom, I know something now."

"Oh, good. Glad to hear it."

"Something serious."

"And what's that?" Turning the meat with two forks, examining the side revealed, turning the meat over again into soft sizzle.

"When I'm grown, and you're old and real sick? I'm going to kill you to stop you suffering."

Her mother smiled. "Why wait?" she said, and turned the meat again. . . .

Sara stood looking out the window until full dark, then went to the bedside table and picked up the phone. She dialed Alaska information for Fairbanks, then asked that operator for the number of the *Fairbanks Daily News-Miner* . . . and time and charges.

"*Daily News-Miner.* Night desk." It was a woman's voice. Young. Sara imagined her in a big room with fluorescent lights, rows of desks. Computers.

"I'd like to find out how much an ad would be."

"Let me give you Classified. . . ."

"Classified Advertising." Man's voice. "Can I help you?"

"Yes, I'd like to find out how much an ad would be. I want it to run for two weeks. And I can send you a certified check for the money."

"O.K. But we can't print unless we've received the check."

"All right."

". . . O.K. Give it to me. And please speak slowly."

"Should I write it out, send it instead?"

"Lady—if I don't know the length, I don't know what to charge you. We're used to taking ads over the phone, O.K.? Just speak slowly."

"But I don't want it to run for another month—not till April, sometime."

"That's fine. Send us the check, and a note with the date you want it to start—and we'll run it then."

"All right."

"Go ahead."

"O.K. . . . Wanted . . . *a strong healthy man experienced in placer sluicing and separating for gold . . . willing to assist a woman in hard work on a light-color stream . . . for a half share, subsistence, and expenses . . . One day's climb northeast above the headwaters of the Kenana River . . . Brooks Range. The man interested enough . . . will find the place. Bring rifle, clothes, and ammunition. Tools . . . provided.*"

"That's it?"

"That's it."

"I'll read it back if you want, but I got it."

"No, that's all right."

"That would be . . . a hundred thirty-six dollars for two weeks. Make the check out to the paper. And send it attention Classified Advertising. Put the date on there you want it to start running."

"All right. Thank you." Sara hung up, waited for time and charges—seven dollars and sixty-three cents—then got up and undressed to shower.

There had been only a sliver of the coral soap left, and that was gone. Annie'd brought up and unwrapped a new bar—Lily of the Valley—and left it in the stall's indented soap dish. Sara took a long shower, water very hot, to enjoy smelling this soap's lather—dark ivory, thick as heavy cream. She washed her hair with it.

When she turned the water off, got out of the stall to dry herself, Sara heard someone tapping at the room door. She wrapped the big towel around her, tucked a corner under her arm, and went to open it.

Anne was standing in the hall in a dark-green quilted bathrobe. "May I come in?"

"I thought you were going to go to sleep?"

"No, I'm not sleepy. I was, but I'm not. And I'd like to discuss your providing the perfect finish to this shitty day. Or were you already headed out onto the roof?"

"Come on in. You want to go out on the roof?"

"No, thanks. I have to live in this little luxury ghetto." Anne sat on the nearer bed. "I don't have the leeway you birds of passage do. —And yes, I know you're going. Kevin told me about your calling him a fat asshole, and then issuing your invitation. But before I get to that, which makes me very angry, let's deal with this disappearing act of yours."

"Well, I want to stay for the funeral, help any way I can—stay maybe two or three more weeks, until the end of the month. Then leave . . . if that's O.K."

"Well no, it's not O.K. You *should* stay and help out at the store. You *should* take some courses at the University. You should do *something* remotely civilized—even it's going out to Montana, if you want to play cowgirl or hunting guide or whatever."

"There's no work out in Montana."

"All right, then. Stay here and just grow up, sis. Do us both a favor."

"I don't like it down here, Annie."

"Oh, 'I don't like it down here, Annie.' Please do a little better than that."

"I don't want to spend my life down here. I don't like seeing so many strangers everywhere I go. It makes me uncomfortable."

"Then you're not a big-city person, that's all. So, don't settle in Seattle—sounds like a song, 'Don't Settle in Seattle.' Go live in the Cascades; they're very woodsy."

"I'm going back north."

"Unbelievable. . . ."

"Well, first to Fairbanks for a little while."

" 'To Fairbanks for a little while'—Oh, for Christ's *sake!*" Anne bounced on the bed. "What are you, Sara? Are you a slow learner, or what? You just got down here a week ago—and you looked like hell, and you were terrified. And now, you want to go trotting right on back?"

"Because leaving didn't help, and I'm *tired* of being terrified. —And I miss the dogs."

"Jumping Jesus."

"Annie, you're not listening. Being down here . . . being here is distasteful to me."

" 'Distasteful.' "

"How would you like to be locked in a monkey cage for the rest of your life? The noise and dirtiness, and the smell—and fighting for pieces of grapefruit and banana, and they never leave you alone—"

"Sara, for God's sake, don't you know this is all about Alan, and your not being some sort of heroine up there? Isn't guilt what this is all about?"

"No. I regret what I didn't do—but I was happier afterward, when he was gone. It was better alone."

"Very deep. Very deep bullshit, is what it sounds like to me."

"I do love you, Annie. And I'm sorry I have to leave."

"I know; you loved me since I was five, not before."

"—And I'd like to be with you, sometime. I'd like to see you. . . ."

"But only at the North Pole." Anne got up off the bed. "Which, I suppose, brings me to your insulting Kevin, calling him names and then issuing that invitation to go live with you."

"I told him the truth."

"Don't be so fucking arrogant! Who gave you permission to tell my son so . . . such hurtful truths? It's *my* job, you bitch!"

"You don't do your job."

". . . Listen, Sara, you're making me very angry, and now I am exhausted and I'm going to get some sleep. And if I were a man—and is there a sadder phrase for a woman to use than that?—if I were a man, I'd be tempted to kick your ass all the way back into that old-growth timber, not just for leaving us after a few fucking weeks after five years—but also for so very definitely putting me and my son into that 'monkey' category. That is frankly very difficult to forgive." She walked to the bedroom door, opened it, and said, "I wish you better luck up in paradise, than you've had so far," went out and closed the door behind her.

"Really . . . really, as far as I know, we are one of the last funeral homes in the area to make provision for viewing crematory events. And I think that's a shame. Even we couldn't do it, if Mr. Lacey hadn't had us grandfathered in."

Mr. Coughlin, stocky, bald, and neatly bearded—in his fifties at least—was wearing a beautiful dark-blue suit and matching vest. He smiled at Anne (the person paying), then smiled at Sara and seemed truly sad. "In a moment, in just a moment, you'll hear our music begin." He gestured, a neat small turn of his pale left hand, toward the room's side wall, curtained in blue even richer than his suit's. "Now, this is a natural process, and you may see details which some might find upsetting—but that is very unusual. Really, very unusual. We do have patrons who find it just impossible to view the cremation, and I think that's a little sad . . . because it is really really a beautiful process. I feel, we all feel here, that this last vision of brightness is worth it, to be able to see your loved one's entrance into light."

Sara was wearing her black pumps, and they still weren't comfortable. The gray wool skirt and striped gray blouse were all right, but Annie was better dressed for a funeral. Black business suit, white blouse, and pearls. Annie's eyes were swollen from recent crying, as if she'd lost more than Mom. . . . Sara heard music, or thought she did, then was sure as it grew louder. It was something classical, with a choir. It sounded like German music, very heavy, lots of serious voices.

Sara wished the curtain wouldn't open, but it did—pulled back on either side from a long low window. The window glass had darkened at the top and bottom, like the view window into an old oven. There was a narrow track, a kind of miniature railroad track, running across the space behind the window—and some sort of motorcycle chain running down the middle of that.

Sara didn't move closer to see better, and saw that Annie wasn't moving closer either.

For a while, nothing happened. Then the music grew louder, as if someone had turned the volume up. It was definitely German music, maybe Beethoven. The people were singing in German. And when the music was loudest, the motorcycle chain running down the tracks moved and got tighter, then kept moving along to the left.

Gas flames came on suddenly, as if someone had lit an old-fashioned stove behind the window—the flames in a blue row that turned yellow with blue tips and got brighter and brighter until Sara had to squint, looking into the light. She could hear the fire softly roaring behind the window glass, blazing from side to side, yellow light bright as sunshine pouring into the room. And through the brightness, Sara saw a long brown box—it looked like cardboard or plywood—come jolting along the tracks, and the end of it caught fire right away. She heard the thump as it caught, glanced at Annie, and saw her staring into the glare like a child into a fireplace, eyes wide and shining by reflection, mouth a little open in wonder.

Sara noticed Mr. Coughlin watching her, looking very sad, and supposed he was saying to himself, 'Well, I just finish warning them not to miss it, and here's this scrawny bitch about to do just that.' She turned so as not to disappoint him—and saw the box, on fire, jolt to a stop centered in the window. Then watched through searing brightness as it seethed and began to fold in upon itself, twisting, dissolving in flames. Sara stared into the heart of the light, trying to keep her mother some kind of company, but afraid to see her burning.

Something was moving in there, almost in time to the Germans' singing, disturbed by the heat as if by blowing wind. And Sara saw a stick with something at its end. Then only fire, so the fire became her friend. . . .

Anne was wearing the same clothes to say good-bye, as she'd worn weeks before to greet Sara at the airport. Same light-gray skirt and gray silk blouse. Same shoes and pumpkin-colored scarf, and long, loose, beautiful trench coat, pearl gray. Sara supposed she'd done it on purpose, had some reason—perhaps to show she was as happy to see Sara leave as she'd been to welcome her. There were more people at Sea-Tac this time; it was early in the evening. More people, but they didn't smell as they had then. Now, Sara could hardly smell them at all.

"Kevin was sorry he couldn't come to say good-bye—his friend Perry was coming over with some god-awful video, slaughtered teens. . . ." Anne slowed, walking alongside to the security gate, so Sara had to walk slower too, carrying her brown purse and a small soft-sided blue plaid suitcase—an old one of Annie's—with her new clothes in it. She'd checked the backpack through.

"Annie, I'll send the suitcase back from Fairbanks."

"Oh, please, do me a favor and keep the damn thing. It's a very old suitcase; I have no use for it. I suppose you'll be making a major J.C. Penney fashion statement up in Wolfjaw or wherever."

"Well, I'll leave the clothes at a friend's place down on the river. She likes pretty things; she'll keep them for me."

"—And, of course, you can wear them when you come down again."

"Yes."

"If you ever come down again." Anne stopped walking, so Sara had to stop, too.

"Annie, you know I meant what I said about having Kevin come up to stay with me. Not now, but maybe in a year or two. . . ."

"Sis, I assume that's a joke. Kevin doesn't even like you. You do realize that?"

"I don't like him, either. But I think it might be—"

"—The foundation of a good relationship and so forth. Well, I don't think so, so we'll just skip that little notion. I'd just as soon not get a phone call from that absurd Father Whoosis up there, to tell me

Kevin had gone the way your Alan went." Anne stood startled, as if someone just behind her had said it, someone she hadn't known was there. "—I'm sorry. Sara, I'm so sorry I *said* that." She put her right hand over her mouth, as if she might say it again, or something worse.

"That's all right."

"Oh, darling, I'm sorry. . . ."

"Really, it's all right. —You know, you wouldn't have to worry, Annie. I'd never let anything like that happen again."

"I'm sure you wouldn't—but I think we'll just forget about the wilderness experience, where Kevin's concerned. O.K.? He really wouldn't be interested."

"It would be such a good thing for him. . . ."

"I don't care." Anne, upset, took a quick small step left, then right, as if she were starting to dance, her hands making tentative winging motions. "—I don't care if it's the *best* thing for him! If it would make him into a rugged take-charge guy or whatever. I don't care; I'm not going to lend you my son!"

"O.K."

Anne sighed and stood still. There were some faint rain marks drying down the sleeves and collar of the pearl-gray coat. "I suppose we better admit this hasn't been the most wonderful visit of all time, with Mom dying—and you scooting back up to God knows where. But Sara, I'm still glad you came down. Even the trouble with Kevin—you got a chance to see us." She stepped forward and hugged Sara, kissed her very lightly on the cheek. She smelled of cloves—something like cloves in her perfume. "I think Connor was glad to see you, too—in the short time I gave him. That poem was so dreadful; but you know, I was always touched by it."

"It is a nice poem."

"Well . . ."

Sara saw that Anne didn't want to walk any farther with her—not through the security gate, then all the way out to wait for the plane to load.

"Want to say good-bye, Annie?"

"Would you mind, sis? I'm a hell of a lot better at greetings than farewells. I don't like people leaving me."

"I don't mind."

"So . . . good-bye." Anne leaned forward to kiss Sara again, and turned and walked away. Paused to call back, "I love you," then kept on, her beautiful coat swinging about her legs like a playful dog.

13

The Piper, an elderly Supercub, flew with a fine internal vibration, as if frightened at being airborne, and this made Sara sick.

She felt better looking out and down along the river—so broad (each meander taking miles), its ice glittering white beneath afternoon's bright slanting sun, and stippled green and brown by islands frozen in. She tugged the side window slightly open, so a little bitter air came thrumming into the sunny cabin, but it didn't help. She closed her eyes for a few moments as she rode, felt swiftly more nauseated, and opened them again to see—past the pilot's hands on the yoke, past a bloom of dazzle on the windshield's Plexiglas—far mountains, her mountains, ranging along the northern horizon, peaks snowy as deep winter's.

The pilot, Perez, had heavy hands, and heavy feet on the rudder pedals, so the Supercub slid and shifted as they flew, occasionally bucked up and down. Its engine, sounding desperate from takeoff to now, hurt Sara's ears. Her pack—jammed behind her with the small suitcase—bumped and nudged at her seat's back like a fat dog uneasy with flying, and made her uneasy, too. She closed her eyes again and took deep breaths of slipstream air. She felt like two people—one sick to her stomach, the other humming with pleasure at going home. Pleasure at being done with Fairbanks, too—the weeks spent waiting for other people's judgments.

Roy Perez—young, squat, and tough, his mustache luxuriant, his beard more fragile—had been filed to fly from Chancy to Eagle, but agreed on a fare of eighty dollars to detour north to Billy Mitchell. Perez smelled of high-octane gas and sweaty denim—and barely audible, sang a Ruth Pascoe ballad as they flew along. *"I'm fallin'* . . . *I'm fa-allin'* . . . *"* Sara thought it was an odd refrain for a pilot to be pleased with.

The rifle case tapped against some plastic in the cabin's short space behind them. Not hard enough to hurt the piece. Bud LeBeck had been angry at losing the Winchester. . . .

"I thought we had a deal. —Didn't we have a deal? I was goin' to keep that Model 70, an' I was goin' to sell off them other guns an' ammo in the duffle for you, once you weren't comin' back. Wasn't that our deal? Yes or no?" Bud—thin, unshaven, and tall, wearing a Padres baseball cap—had been sitting perched on his big brown-painted trading table, surrounded by bundles and heaps of fur, overhung by curtains and draperies of it, so he looked out as if from a cave of deep softness, colored gray and silver white, golden brown and darker warmer brown, rich as molasses.

"Bud, I'm sorry. But I am back, and I need the rifle."

"You don't need that rifle. I can trade you out a real solid Enfield .303—an' give you twenty-five bucks."

Sara had shaken her head, but worried that he was right, and that had been the deal and she was being unfair.

"Sara, what the hell is all this about the Winchester? Worried that bear's comin' down again this spring?"

"I don't care if she does."

"Um-hmm."

"What does that 'Um-hmm' mean, Bud?"

"It means I will give you fifty goddamn dollars on top of that Enfield, which is a real, real solid rifle."

"I don't want a .303."

"Well, for Christ's sake—"

"I'm sorry, Bud. But I need the Winchester back. I don't think that was the deal, anyway, that you were going to definitely get the Winchester no matter what, even if I decided not to sell my guns."

"The hell it wasn't—but all right, I don't give a fuck." He'd come down from his table, begun to pace back and forth, hampered by soft hanging tapestries of fur. "I should have written all that down. I suppose then you wouldn't think I was a liar."

"I know you're not a liar, Bud. It was just a misunderstanding. I probably misunderstood."

"Well, you sure as shit did."

"I'm sorry."

"Shit. . . . An' on top of that, you want to borrow a stake off me. Fifteen hundred goddamn *dollars*?"

"Well, I ordered hardware to be barged up to Billy after breakup. And I had the cash for most of it—but I still need enough to send a postal money order back, or they won't ship. And I have rice and Crisco and stuff coming up, too, and dog food."

"Don't you have a family? That's all I want to know. Why doesn't your family help you out with this? You want me to stake you on some gold sluicin' isn't goin' to bring in shit." While Bud paced, a hanging wolfskin had swung as if to caress his cheek, and was pushed aside. "I'd be happy to give you a little advance on furs, you get somebody strong up there to clear out them lines."

"I put an ad in for someone to come up and help work the creek."

"I *saw* that ad! I saw that damn fool ad last Sunday in the Fairbanks paper, an' damn if I didn't think it was you—'up over the Kenana.' " He'd reached out for the hanging wolfskin, seized it, shook it gently.

"I came up three weeks ago. I've been in Fairbanks, seeing some people."

"That homestead thing settled? —Only my business 'cause you're askin' to borrow stake-money."

"It's settled—and I filed a placer claim for Backache with the Bureau. I still have to mark it."

"Right, real dumb. Who you stay with in Fairbanks?" Stroking the wolfskin, combing his fingers through the fur.

"Karen Ismay."

"Well, that old lady's crazy as bat shit—cats had the bed an' you had the floor, right?"

"I didn't mind; she's always been nice to me."

"Crazy as bat shit. —Well, I saw that ad in there, and I said, 'Oh-oh, guess who's maybe comin' right back up to God's country. . . .' " Something about the hanging wolfskin, perhaps a drifting odor, had caught his full attention, and he'd stepped up to it, gathered it in, buried his face in its softness to smell it—and apparently found the cure satisfactory. "An' honey, I got to tell you, that ad. . . . That'll be the day, you get some dude go way up in those mountains, work his ass off for a year, get about one peanut-butter jar of color. Don't hold your breath."

"If nobody comes up, then I'll build a sluice myself, or Long-Tom boxes. Just take more time."

"—Like a year or two. An' don't you even *try* a Tom; takes three, four men to run one right. And I oughta know; I busted *my* butt, before I got smart. You need to sluice—simple sluicin', and good riffle-sticks runnin' Hungarian." Instructing, Bud had begun to pace again, back and forth in front of his trading table.

"Maybe."

"Hey—no 'maybe' about it. Do like I say, Sara, you want to do this shit at all—especially spendin' some of my money. An' run that box inch-and-a-half to a foot grade. Any deeper, you'll wash out; any less than that, you're goin' to be cleanin' riffles all day. . . . I hope you know just buildin' that shit is no joke—not even talkin' about shovelin' gravel, which is the real work. Few months after you start movin' gravel, then *maybe* I'll start seein' my money back."

"You can charge me interest."

"Damn right I'm goin' to charge you interest. I'll charge you ten percent."

"All right."

"That's ten percent a year." He'd stopped pacing.

"O.K."

"You're sayin' 'O.K.' now, but you just keep it in mind, pay-up time."

"I will, Bud . . . and I'm sorry about the Winchester. Why don't you take the little Ruger on account, for first payback on the loan? The Single-Six is very nice, and there's a magnum cylinder for it on the belt."

"Thanks, but I don't need a .22 pistol."

"Well, I don't need it either—it's a trapper's gun. And there're two boxes of solids with the belt and holster. That would make up for the rifle. . . ."

"All right, I'll take it. But it don't make up for the rifle. —You want the Winchester back? You got it back." Then, business concluded, he'd led the way into his narrow kitchen . . . begun to prepare sardine sandwiches with bought white bread, sliced onion, and Miracle Whip. The same pattern of linoleum covering the kitchen floor—large brown squares with smaller golden squares inside them—had been tacked up to cover the walls, except for a small window. Sara'd gone to the window to look out at the river, immensely wide, white, and silent, the lower fourth of a stupendous landscape rising from the river's ice to miles of dark green forest . . . then to serried mountains, snow and granite . . . then sky the shade of tool steel.

"An' if some fool does climb up there in the boonies to work on that creek," Bud had forked Miracle Whip onto the sardines emptied into a glazed brown bowl, and was mixing, mashing it all together, "—then you better write me a letter, send it when you go down to Billy Mitchell for your barge stuff after breakup. Ice should be bustin' down here in two, three weeks. Write me the dude's name an' what he looks like, an' I'll check him out—see you don't get some desperate pervert or a thief up there."

"I will. Thanks, Bud." There was something wrong with the brown bowl; it was lopsided. One of Terry's bowls from when she was doing ceramics.

"Don't thank me." Dealing out four bread slices, smearing the sardines-and-dressing on thick. "Just protectin' my investment. Kissin' that Winchester good-bye, an' it's my fault for not gettin' it in writin'. Damn if I shouldn't know better, doin' business with a woman." He'd dealt out four more slices, set each neatly down on a sardined partner, pressed them firmly into place to make four sandwiches. "—That bitch Terry damn sure should have taught me better."

"I didn't know you and Terry were having trouble, Bud. I thought you were getting along fine, since the new baby. I'm sorry."

"*Terry's* not havin' trouble—an' the *baby's* not havin' trouble. I'm the asshole's havin' the trouble. Well, never mind . . . I just pay the bills up here, that's all. I sure as shit wish *I* could go on down to Anchorage any fuckin' time I felt like it—hang around them Fourth Avenue bars. Shop in the goddamn mall an' charge any shit I wanted on my husband's credit card." He'd put two sandwiches on a paper plate, handed it over to Sara, gone to the refrigerator and took out two tall cans of Canadian beer.

"Well, write that down about the loan, Bud."

"Goddamn right I will." He'd popped both tops, passed her a beer. "I learned *my* fuckin' lesson. . . ."

The plane hit some knot of harder air—bucked, then settled steady, riding streaming wind clear as clear water, riding above the lazy curves of frozen river into a sky's light-blue burned white around the late season's sun. The tallest mountains, her mountains, stood sixty miles away, seeming to be brought no nearer by flying. Deep winter still rested in their peaks, white as feathers.

"You know," Sara said, raising her voice over the engine's, "—you know, I think you could set me down any time."

Perez glanced at her. Shouted "What's the matter? You paid to Billy Mitchell, and we're four, five miles downriver." He had no accent, except southwestern country.

"I'm feeling a little sick. I think I better walk on in. —I'd like to."

"Oh, shit. . . ." Perez shoved his yoke forward. "You sure?" The Supercub, as if it had heard about possible vomit in its cabin, slid steeply down, making Sara feel worse.

"I think it's better to let me off."

"All right, now—but I can't give you no money back, just coming in a few miles short."

"That's all right."

"I can't be refunding fare money."

"O.K. That's O.K."

"Long as that's all right with you."

"Fine. Just set me down when you find a place."

"Good fuckin' luck . . ." said apparently to himself as he banked the plane sharply to the left, and examined the stretch of river below while they bumped through the air—the river's late-season ice, nearer now, revealed grimy as a dirty sheet, and roughened here and there with slabs of broken floe twenty to thirty feet high. "Good fuckin' luck," Perez said, steered right, and descended farther. Sara stared out her side window, seeing only bad ice, and wished she'd just kept quiet and breathed deep up to Billy Mitchell. She could have vomited into her parka hood. . . .

The Piper flew down almost onto the river—vibrated, snarled over very rough ice, then banked right and settled so suddenly Sara was startled. It hit, bounced, then skidded, sliding a little sideways on its skis over ice somewhat smoother . . . only rippled in great slow waves that lifted the little plane, then settled it . . . then lifted it again.

Sara thought it would be too bad for her to have Perez land early, then vomit in his plane anyway. The Supercub slid—Perez stomping on his rudder pedals to keep it straight—and after a little while that seemed longer, shook, bumped, and stopped.

At once, Sara felt better. Felt fine . . . and like a fool for making the pilot come in short of the halfway decent strip the snow-machines would have left leveled on the river at Billy Mitchell.

"Sorry I made you set down."

"Shit, don't think a thing about it." Perez turned to smile at her. Quite handsome, if rough, when he smiled. "Better'n gettin' barfed on. . . ."

Sara got the small door open, climbed down, and reached up to accept her goods as Perez handed them down to her. Then she stood on the ice with the small suitcase, gun duffle, backpack and rifle case around her to watch Perez jockey the little plane . . . scooting this way and that, looking for a takeoff line. She thought he was probably a better driver than a pilot. He seemed more at home taxiing than flying.

Perez found his line after two tries, gunned the Piper's engine, and flew it away along the ice, its shadow sliding beside it, until the little plane jolted up and down, jolted again, then appeared to hop up into the air and stayed there.

Sara stood on a sunny prairie of ice, and waited until the plane was gone out of sight, its engine-noise out of sound, so she stood alone. She felt the frozen river's cold—more familiar, more reliable than any warmth—rise slowly through her boot-pacs' soles, slowly up into her bones . . . and stood still to let it come. Then she knelt to put her bare right hand down against the river, felt the ice's harsh texture—like sand and grains larger than sand—press against her palm . . . then gradually felt less and less, until her hand was chilled senseless as a stranger's. She stood and looked around her, saw no one and nothing but the river and those forested hills that rose to mountains from both its distant banks, and found herself at home.

She marched a mile upriver into a crystalline spring afternoon—the few grays fleeting as occasional clouds passed over and slanting sunshine fell blazing down again, flashed shimmering off the ice so the river became a mile-wide highway too bright to watch while she walked on it.

The pack was heavier than Sara'd remembered; the weeks south, the south's weather, had softened her. She'd left Seattle in warm rain . . . then been sheltered in Fairbanks.

The sunlight's dazzle off the ice rose and glittered around her so she squinted, nearly blind. But she didn't stop to unstrap her backpack and dig the snow goggles out of it—she didn't want them, preferred the brightness. Her duffle and rifle case, heavier than the suitcase in her other hand, pulled her out of balance—so after the first mile walking into this light, Sara stopped, unzipped the duffle and slid the sheathed shotgun out, checked its loads, then hung it down her back. The duffle that much lighter, the shotgun handier beside her pack, she walked along more easily, seeing well enough in a diamond world of gleam and sparkle to climb ice shelves when she could, skirt those propped higher. She breathed deeper and deeper as she went, until it seemed there was no longer any difference between her breathing and the air—that she held it only a moment, then let it go.

Barely seeing, she walked into the glare until it eased after another mile, when more clouds came over, and she saw distant ice dirty with dead trees frozen in. And soon saw branches and pieces of other trees the river had broken and swept away in spring the year before—and where, as she walked closer, the cleaner ice (refrozen after thaws) showed tracked with a winter's worth of animal pas- sage, paw prints of wolf and weasel, fox, a run of voles. . . . And in a drift of windblown snow, the double soft-whisked marks of an owl's wing tips, where he'd stooped out of starlight the night before, to lift a baby hare.

Tracked also with those, showing across windrows of snow, the long double ski-trails and center treads of snow-machines. Their last passage too recent to have drifted, or been blown away down the river. Sara saw no dog-team sign, but searching for it made her more anxious to see Dutchy—imagining a tragedy, that some ace freight- musher had come up the river early, happened to notice Dutchy— and Frank had sold him off. Or that Dutchy had pulled his chain staple out, and run.

For a moment, so strongly she yearned for Dutchy, Sara felt the same anticipation at seeing Alan—as if he must be where the dogs were—though this was only for an instant, before she recalled. She recalled as she trudged out of light and into a swift wilderness of shadows with gusting wind as high clouds went by, and after them, folding down onto the river in veils miles high, miles wide, a sifting fall of fine snow that fell like dust.

Sara stopped to take her airport wristwatch off—put it down on the river and left it there . . . then walked two miles farther on rougher ice. And when the snowfall drifted downstream, she trav- eled once more under sunshine in a haze of mirrored bright com- pounded light that rose around her, blurring her vision so she walked through riches of emptiness.

After those miles, she shaded dazzled eyes with her hand, and saw the familiar southern bend ahead that faced Billy Mitchell. She turned to the north bank to avoid walking so directly into the village . . . reached the bank past a small spruce-furred island, then climbed up off the river through bare cottonwoods and willow brush, then into spruce forest floored with old, layered snow. The snow here had been deeply thawed at least once; its crust lay glazed, and broke beneath her boots; the trees threw shadows that rested her burning eyes. Sara felt, if she came from a different direction than straight off the river, she might somehow blend into Billy Mitchell in an unre- markable way, so that Mary Toby would be less startled, Frank Solokoff less angry with her for returning after such definite fare- wells.

As the trees closed in—dumping sometimes, as she went beneath them, soft loads of snow sifting or thumping down—Sara looked left and right, a little worried about a bear, though it should be weeks, still, before they were out and working the river. But there'd been thaws, the spring was arriving; she could have told that without the snow crust, could have told it by the taste and odor of the air she breathed as she climbed a slowly rising slope, air tainted already with green and some smell of earth. Air no longer perfectly free of anything but itself and coldness.

She welcomed even her wariness, her fear of a bear, as certain notice of where she was. Here—and not in Seattle, or Fairbanks, or any place else but here.

Sara walked up through stands of spruce, the pack shifting slightly on her back, the duffle and suitcase swinging in her hands—and was pleased to notice herself tending just east enough to reach the ridge above Billy Mitchell, even through endless obscuring trees, some set close enough to touch with outspread hands. Her boots broke through into knee-deep snow often enough that Sara wished the snowshoes with her, instead of hanging in Mary Toby's shed.

Farther along, she found across the surface of the snow an ermine's prints—swift two by two, tiny, dented a little into the glaze—and stooped to follow them through close foliage, under the complicated shadows of the trees. Twenty feet away, or a little more, just past a narrow rough-barked trunk, the weasel had caught what he'd been chasing—had left behind four, five little puffs of fur whiter than the snow . . . and spots of red-brown blood, a single small hind foot, and a baby hare's startled head, its ears, shell pink, still childish. The owl's luck, and the weasel's, signaled early spring litters, the cyclical rise of hares. The numbers of lynx, marten and fox would rise with them for a year or two—rich trapping. . . .

Sara came out where she'd wanted to, at the crest of the ridge just above the village, and a hundred yards west of the graveyard.

She walked out of the forest and stood looking down the steep slope at the dog yard, its small shelters . . . at Frank Solokoff's mated plywood houses, blanketed with old snow, their roofs edged with rows of long icicles from several thaws. There were no lights on in the houses . . . only a shimmer of heat rising over the steel-pipe chimney. Sara supposed Frank and his boys were out hunting, or fishing through the ice upriver. She was ashamed of her relief, of hoping she might get all her business done—visit Mary Toby and gather her outfit and be gone—and wait for another time to talk to Frank. A little tired by even such an easy walk under only the pack's weight, the duffle and suitcase, she stood and felt her muscles rest, settle in the cool. A gentle wind was blowing up off the river, smelling slightly of engine exhaust, salmon, sewage and smoke.

A dog barked from below. —Kickapoo. If any had been sold off early, at least he was left.

Sara left the woods and started down the slope, digging her heels in, leaning a little back to balance the pack and luggage as she plunged down through deep snow.

Another dog barked, then a third. Dipsy . . . Fatso.

Sara came to a level, sank into deeper snow, and heard Doodle yelping just below her, saw him jumping up to his chain's limit to see what two-legs was coming so noisily down the hill.

They all began barking then, yodeling the chorus Sara knew.

She half stepped, half slid down to the row of doghouses, walked along past whirling, leaping dogs to the last small shelter, west in the row.

Dutchy hadn't barked, didn't bark now. He stood beside his little shed in the shadow of the hill and stared at her, watched her come.

"Hello," Sara said, and put down her baggage, slipped off the pack and shotgun.

Dutchy cocked his head, presented his right ear.

"Yes, it's me, Dutchy. It's *me*. . . ." And walked nearer.

Dutchy gave a sudden start, as if even with such notice, he was surprised. Then he trembled and slid down onto his belly, still staring at her, and began to whine.

"No, no, Dutchy-dog," Sara said, and trotted up to him, her boot-pacs noisy over the snow. "—It's me. I'm here. Everything's all right."

But Dutchy slowly turned on his back to present his white-furred belly to her, moaning.

"Oh, sweetheart," Sara said, and knelt—and Dutchy writhed suddenly onto his feet, charged into her and knocked her down, his heavy muzzle, cold nose burrowing . . . burrowing into her throat as if he wished to be able to open his jaws, tear her throat out and devour her. Make her permanently his, never to leave him again.

Sara lay beneath him as pleased as under a lover. And when Dutchy calmed—the rest of the team still clamoring—lay there longer, combing her fingers through the deep pinto coat (feeling the guard hairs already loosening for spring), and looking into his pale-blue eyes, their black pupils wide. His teeth still chattered faintly from nerves.

"What the hell are *you* doin' here?"

Sara turned her head and saw Charlie Solokoff, in striped paja-
mas, a brown bathrobe, and boots, standing in the snow by their
toolshed, staring at her. He had a rifle in his hands—a Ruger stainless with a scope sight.

"Hello, Charlie." She moved Dutchy aside, and got to her feet.

"I thought somethin' had come down botherin' the dogs."

"Just me."

"Well, shit. . . . What the hell are you doin' back? Tell you one
thing, Mrs. Maher; my dad isn' goin' to like it."

"Frank isn't here?"

"No, he's down at Ruby for a meetin'. —An' you're lucky. He isn'
goin' to like you comin' back up here . . . unless you're just visitin',
you know, stayin' in the village."

"I'm not visiting, Charlie."

Charlie Solokoff shook his big head. "Well, Dad isn' goin' to like
it, you goin' up on that mountain. You can take a bet on that."

Sara stooped to stroke Dutchy. "Did the dogs get some runs?"

"Oh, yeah. Dad took 'em out a few times—more'n a few. One
time, they threw the sled and knocked him off on a tree."

"He like them?"

"He said they was a show-off cheehacker team, for haulers, but I
guess he liked 'em. Liked 'em better after that Dutchy run him into
the tree. Daddy likes that Dutchy dog pretty good."

"You hear that?" Sara said to Dutchy, who looked up, listening
intently, as if only a little more attention might bring perfect under-
standing. "—Mister Solokoff thinks you're a good dog."

"Scared of him. That dog nearly took a hand off him, first time
out. Dad started likin' him right then. He didn' like him, he'd have
shot him."

"Where's Vanilla? She have her pups?"

"Had four—one died. Three left is good ones: two dogs an' a
bitch. They're all inside, in the shed."

"Well, I'll be taking my dogs, and I'm going to need my gear and
sled."

"Sled an' harness is over here; rest is still at Mary Toby's. Pop
didn' tell me to bring that stuff over here."

"And Charlie, I want you and your dad to have one of the pups
for your trouble."

"We don't want no pup. Only one Dad likes is that Dutchy."

"You hear that?" Sara said to Dutchy. "The team cost you anything, Charlie? Did the dog food last?"

"We didn' spend no money on 'em." Charlie stood watching while she went slow rounds across the yard, kneeling at each chain-post to embrace its dog. "Dad did like runnin' that team, though. Remind' him of old times. . . . An' none of my business, but what the hell you doin' back here?"

"Charlie," Sara said, "—I couldn't stay away."

"Oh, my good God *almighty*," Mary Toby said. "Oh, Lord, look here. . . ."

"Did you get my postcard?"

"I got it." Mary Toby, wearing a green corduroy dress that buttoned up the front, stood short and square in her doorway, a cigarette in a plump brown hand. The lenses of her reading glasses glowed rich orange with sunset. Sara supposed she'd been studying her Bible. "Seattle looks just like Anchorage—no difference I could see."

"It's bigger and warmer and wetter," Sara said.

"I suppose you want to come in."

"If it's no trouble."

"It ain't no trouble," Mary Toby said—and startled Sara by suddenly striding out onto the stoop and looking up at her more closely, as if to be certain she was who she seemed to be. Then turned and went back through her doorway, waited for Sara to kick the snow off her boot-pacs at the stoop, and come inside to set the duffle and suitcase down, unsling the shotgun and pack, and hang her parka on a hook in the entrance hall. The house smelled as it had smelled before, of cigarette smoke and woodsmoke and wet wool.

"Still carryin' that damn gun around," Mary Toby said, and led through to the kitchen. The TV was on in the living room, its sound turned off. There was no one else in the house.

"You want some tea?"

"Yes. It's good to see you, Mary." Sara pulled a chair out from the table, and sat down. It felt good to be off her feet—and better to be in Mary Toby's kitchen, no changes in all the weeks she'd been gone. The narrow kitchen smelled of curry. "What are you making?"

"I'm makin' Caribou Hindoostany," Mary Toby said, pumping to fill her teakettle. "Got the recipe off Denise Bower."

"Smells good."

"Better smell good, what that spice dust cost me. . . ." Mary Toby worked the sink's pump handle once more, topped her teakettle under the gush.

"Pauline and Carla still in the village?"

"No, they aren't—an' that child should be here. Pauline's gone to Fairbanks with Harris Willy, an' took Carla with her—an' he's noth-in'. He isn't goin' to do her any good at all." Mary Toby turned the propane stove's left burner to high, set the kettle on it.

"I got some new clothes down there—they're in the suitcase. I don't know where I'd wear them, up here."

"What did you get?" Mary took two of her blue-and-white china mugs down from little hooks in the tole-painted cupboard over the sink. Sara'd never seen her use her blue-and-white mugs—had assumed they were only for decoration.

"I got two pairs of slacks, and a skirt, pretty long. They're wearing any length they want—doesn't make any difference. There *is* no style. Skirt's gray. And I got two sweaters. I didn't like one—it's black. But I wore it and it looks O.K."

"You get some shoes?" Mary puffed on her cigarette, put it on the edge of the sink, and reached to take the sugar jar down from its shelf.

"A pair of black pumps—they are really uncomfortable—and some brown loafers, and running shoes."

"Well—you're goin' to *be* runnin' when Frank Solokoff gets back up here."

"I don't care," Sara said. "I'm glad to be back, and to see you."

"You haven't been gone that long to make a big deal out of it." Mary Toby packed her tea caddy with Red Rose. "I sure hope you don't want to be goin' back up that mountain. I don't know what the hell you're doin' here at all; it's real bad luck to be sayin' good-bye to somebody twice."

"I won't be saying good-bye again, except to go up to my place."

"No, you are not!" Mary threw her cigarette down into the sink, turned and glared at Sara as if she didn't like her at all. "—You can't go up there. You're *out* of there. You go up there, some of the men'll go up an' do somethin' . . . burn you out. An' that's the truth."

As if it had heard her, a snow-machine snarled suddenly, accelerating past the house . . . upslope.

"Mary, anybody tries to burn my place, and I'll shoot them. And if I'm away and they do that, then I'll hunt them right down those mountains. And any I get, I'll bury right there."

". . . You're tryin' to talk like a man, but you aren't a man. What are you goin' to do if Frank just calls the troopers on you? You don't have any right in the world to be on Native land no more. You goin' to start shootin' at Native police, at state troopers?"

"He won't call the troopers, Mary. I have a right to be on my place."

"You do not." Mary Toby went to her refrigerator, took out a small yellow-flowered pitcher of mixed powdered milk, and came to put that on the long kitchen table.

"Mary, I do have a right. Now, I do. I spent the last three weeks in Fairbanks, making sure I have a right. Ed Ostrander is a lawyer there, and he says I have a definite right. No question."

The kettle began a tentative breathy whistling, and Mary went to the stove to lift its lid, dangle the caddy in. "Isn't no lawyer goin' to say Porcupine's got to let a white woman stay on Koyukon land. An' that's that." She picked up a mug, pumped water to rinse it.

"I'm going to have a baby, Mary. It's Jack Joseph's."

Mary Toby dropped the china mug into her sink and broke it. "Oh, my *God*. . . ." She turned and stared at Sara, stricken—put her plump wet hands to her face.

"I'm sorry," Sara said. "Mary, I'm sorry; I shouldn't have told you like that." She stood up and went to Mary Toby and took hold of her wrists as if to pull her hands down to see her face. "I know it was a stupid thing to do—and I never even thought about a baby. I never thought about it, but it happened."

Mary Toby had nothing to say, and kept her hands up to her face even with Sara tugging at her.

"You stay away," Mary Toby said.

"No," Sara said, "I won't."

Mary Toby put her hands down, said, "You goddamn white people," took Sara by the arms and shook her back and forth, surprisingly strong. Then suddenly hugged Sara to her and held her hard. "Oh, my little girl," she said, though Sara was so much taller.

The dogs had been hard to harness, first day, hard to hold—rank from being chained almost two months with only the occasional runs Frank Solokoff had taken. Lobo had snarled and bared his teeth when Sara started to harness him, and she'd wrapped a quick loop of tug-line around his muzzle, yanked his right foreleg out from under him and shoved him down, fell on him, and lay there growling under her breath while he writhed beneath her, amazingly strong. He'd stopped struggling after a while, and lain cowed and still, pale black-dotted eyes half closed in submission. Sara had stayed resting on him a little longer, growling savagely, trying not to laugh, her face buried in the snowy fur at his throat, her teeth nipping at him there.

Then she'd gotten off him, gone to the chuck box at the sled, and taken out a piece of frozen chum salmon. She brought that back and knelt beside the half-wolf, feeding him by hand, comforting him in his humiliation.

At the sight of this irregular feeding, Fatso had uttered such yelps of longing that the others roused, so Sara had to take a piece of fish to each, and stroked and petted each—fed Dutchy last, and stroked him longest.

She'd taken the team out in early morning for shakedown runs across the river and back, working the dogs hard, settling them to harness. Then had eaten canned tomato soup, Caribou Hindoostany, and pilot bread for lunch . . . checked her outfit and lashings, kissed Mary Toby good-bye, and mushed back out across the river and kept going, singing a song she made up (half talk, half yelping) so the dogs yelped back, working into harness. The three pups—fat, black-and-white, and blue-eyed—were bundled, heads out, into a gunnysack perched swaying on the sled load. Very excited to be traveling, they'd yapped in chorus as the sled rocked, yawed, and slid rumbling-fast over crust ice melted, then frozen again. Sara had named the pups, but not the names she'd thought of in Seattle. Those didn't fit them. She called the males Trouble and Sneaks, the female, Easy.

The first day out, she'd sung her song to the team, run on under spring-season sun shining into evening, then shot a snowshoe hare for her dinner, and thought herself almost fully arrived. . . . On the second day, after the sled had hit a snow-buried log, she'd stopped to splint a broken stanchion, then run on beside the team exhausted and satisfied (sprained left wrist wrapped in her blue bandanna, knotted tight). She'd traveled at weary ease, as if that small hurt had been payment of final fare into the country.

That evening, Sara had chewed uncooked oatmeal for dinner, checked the dogs' feet and fed them, then walked out onto the miles-wide stretch of snow brilliantly orange under the sunset—no trees, nothing near her, nothing nearer than a mountain. She'd imagined Alan standing on the skyline ridge, watching, looking down at snow country too bright for ghosts. . . . As she stood, Sara's home had expanded around her, grown away into vacancies of snow and sky fenced only by spruce green, horizoned by rising steep and steeper slopes—the highest glittering with ice—slopes that rose so many miles away, the freezing air had seemed to rush softly past her, hurrying over her head, flooding to fill their spaces. The evening sky, clear of clouds above the sunset, had held trapped a pale daylight moon.

In the morning, when she'd roused at ease in Alan's sleeping bag (now smelling only of her), the country lay perfectly silent and cold— and its distances became still greater as she and her team traveled on, so she grew to keep her place in it. . . .

This third day mushing, very tired, not yet in condition, the team heaved up to Backache Creek in afternoon, and Sara—trotting along-side through thick snow, and out of breath—*whoa*'d them to camp before next day's reach around the mountain to home.

Backache was twice the water and fiercer than the homestead's Casual Creek. More small river than run, it brawled in summer, battering its way down a steeper bed. Falling so hard when not frozen—even now it loosed occasional swift overflow that foamed up light blue through ice cracks to go hissing down the mountain, hazed in frost, stirred and swirling past boulders.

Backache's far bank was the mountain's flank, drenched and ice-coated granite rising straight another thousand feet. The near bank was gentler, a steep slope down through drifts of snow, out of which the ruins of the last century's workings rose in black outline: remnants of storm-smashed sheds and narrow cold-crumbled pilings marching nearly to the frozen stream. There was nothing useful left; the hardware only rusted red ghosts of spikes and cleats, nails and hinges, that collapsed into powder when Sara touched them.

Downstream, dwarf willow (a few already beginning to bud) struggled up along the course, with poplar growing lower. Back away from the creek, a wide stand of black spruce stood—grown all staggering at different angles, drunken with frost heaves of autumns past. This stand had burned along its downhill rim years before, left good timber, but hard to haul up so steep a rise.

Sara explored the near bank, tacked her claim papers to stakes upstream and down, and found a good site for a small work cabin— then fed the dogs, turned in, and slept to the creek's chill presence, its ice-constricted creaking, until she woke in bright morning. . . . Before striking camp, she spent some time squatting at the stream bank, panning with a pie plate in a shallow wash of overflow—to find at last a few bright grains streaking dark sand across the bottom of the pan. Modest sign. . . .

Sara sat in sun on failing snow, high on the ridge east of the homestead cabin. She'd sat there on other occasional mornings, home from freighting supplies the day and a half over to the work-ings on Backache Creek. Seasoned sawed lumber (planks Alan had sawed and planed more than a year before), hardware, tools, food, dog food, baling wire, nail kegs, hinges, spikes, fine wire mesh, and angle irons. Rope, a coil of cable, block and tackle. . . . Everything needed to build a work cabin, and at least start on sluice supports, a shake box.

On each swing back down the long ridge to the home cabin, she'd expected to see the dogs' ears forward, hear growling to announce a stranger had come up, answering the newspaper ad. But the cabin always stood as empty as when, staggering weary, she'd first mushed the team down the ridge, so pleased to have come home. There'd been no sign of strangers on the place then, no smell of smoke, no tracks except visiting animals'. No human had been there. Only voles, jays, prints left by the same hopeful fox, still circling the high cache. And a small black bear early out of its winter den had been by, and broken the left shutter of the cabin's window—not being strong enough to smash both thick-barred shutters in, though claw marks were set deep into the window frame. . . . These animals' tracks and traces had been stepped into a snow just beginning to shallow, struck by two thaws at least, leaving only a week or two—perhaps three weeks, this high—to complete her freighting by sled. After that, when the high-mountain snow had failed, what was needed would travel on her back.

Each time, returning from the workings, Sara'd been disappointed to find no man arrived. But less and less disappointed, until she'd begun to wonder how to tell any stranger come up that she would like him to go back down.

Still, each afternoon she was home, she climbed the ridge once most chores were done, brought the Nikon binoculars and her notebook, and sat in the snow to write . . . pausing now and then to glass the country downslope, out across the meadow beyond Casual Creek—searching the homestead's landscape as if the act of looking might prevent an appearance. It seemed to her she didn't need the help, that she'd settled here now in some way equal to the country, and more powerful than she'd been, so she could alter what she didn't care for, or create what she did, as long as she was willing to spend whatever years and labor were necessary. . . .

Vanilla lay beside her on fragile snow half drifted over with spruce needles, her thick fur matted, shedding, and panted in the last of the long day's warmth. Forty-five degrees, by the afternoon.

Sara put the binoculars down, picked her notebook up—a new green ring-binder from Fairbanks—and reread her shortest story.

ONE FISH

A little while ago, a salmon with no name swam in the Pacific Ocean with a thousand other salmon.

This salmon had no name, and none of the other salmon in his school had a name, either. They only knew each other by the flashes of silver along their sides as they swam, and by the faintest odor each big fish left swimming so fast through the sea.

They swam through blue ocean as if they were fish-shaped birds flying through dark blue sky. They ate smaller fish when they found them—and when a shark or swordfish came drifting out of the distance, the whole school, a thousand silver salmon, turned together and swam away.

This was the life the salmon-with-no-name knew, and it didn't change until it changed. One morning, when the school was racing nearer the sea's surface, all thousand salmon suddenly turned another way as if someone had called them. All together, they angled slightly east to follow the path of the sun overhead, its light only light green, filtering down through the fathoms where they swam.

The school swung east, toward distant land, and the salmon-with-no-name swam with them.

They turned east again one night, when the sea was darker than darkness, and swam for many differences of sun to dark—swimming so fast, so deep, they hardly paused to hunt. Then they didn't hunt at all.

Sometime after that, the sea began very slowly to change its taste. It tasted less salty. It tasted of stone and was difficult to breathe. The salmon-with-no-name didn't like this new taste. And he didn't like having to swim harder in this strange water to swim as fast.

The farther and faster they traveled, the odder the water became, until it smelled of earth more than it smelled of salt and ocean.

The school was swimming into a steady current that blew like the wind from a place all stone and soil, so different from the richness of the sea.

The school swam faster, but the salmon-with-no-name swam slower . . . and slower. And soon he swam with the last of his school, among the last big gleaming silver-sided fish.

*Now they were swimming in water not the ocean's, but
the land's, fresh water, and the school swam faster still, flashing, flashing upriver through white water, not blue.*

*But one did not. The salmon-with-no-name swam slower
and slower, until he could see all the others above and ahead
of him—separate from him for the first time. A swift glittering city of great fish, a city that had been his—but now was
swimming away, fading away before him.*

*The salmon-with-no-name swam on for a little while in the
direction the others had gone. Then he slowed and slowed,
and stopped. He hung motionless in the depths where white
water turned to foam above him and turned to stones beneath.*

*When he swam again, it was out to sea—away from the
wind of strange no-salt water that blew from the land, away
from the smells of earth and stone. Away from all the others.
Then, he was the only salmon in the great Pacific Ocean who
swam alone.*

*He headed deeper into the ocean, swam fast and hunted
as if his thousand brothers and sisters still swam and hunted
with him, turning and turning through the sea like a great
swift fleet of silver. And he was pleased with this water's
taste.*

*Four changes of the sea's surface from sunlight to moon-
light went by as he swam alone, and he caught and ate three
small squid. After the fourth change, and near the surface
where the sea was glassy green, a swordfish came sliding out
of the light.*

*There was no school of salmon to see and signal warnings
to one another. There was only one salmon, swimming all
alone—and the swordfish came speeding, and struck him
from behind.*

Sara looked along the steep slopes past the meadow for a last time
before getting up to go down to cut some firewood, then work on the
sled—two uprights had broken on the basket, coming in the night
before. She put the binoculars in their case, stood, brushed snow off
her bottom, and walked back down toward the cabin, more and
more certain no one would be coming.

Vanilla padded after her, and the pups, playing in the dog yard,
came bumbling across the slope to their mother—but Vanilla growled
them off, tired of their prodding and suckling. It brought to Sara's

mind her own breasts, already sore in the mornings . . . but looking no different.

She hung the binoculars on the near peg in the dogtrot porch, then went back down the cabin steps and started across to the dog-yard shed for the splitting maul and Swede saw. The snow was sunstruck, gritty beneath her boot-pacs, already damaged by spring.

Sara noticed something on the mountain . . . looked more care-fully far up to the right on the mountain's shoulder, and saw a difference there, very small so much higher than the homestead—a mile and more higher. She stood still, staring, and saw three, four . . . five dots across a fall of light-gray scree. And, as she watched, the dots—pale, cream-colored—very slowly moved across that fall of rock, itself only incidental in the mountainside's immensity of snow-fields, stone, ice slides frozen in falling.

"Dall sheep," Sara said to Vanilla. " . . . Dall sheep." She saw her dogs fed with better than fish meal, smelled ghost mutton roasting—and turned and ran back toward the cabin, stooping, dodging, and stooping again to scoop the puppies up . . . and her arms full of their squirming, Vanilla trotting after, went up the steps into the cabin. She set the puppies down, slid her shotgun off her back and laid it on the bunk, then went out, shutting the dogs in.

Sara opened the dogtrot door, reached down the Winchester and slung it across her back—then bent to haul out the pack-board, un-buckled its canvas sack and substituted a coil of nylon line. She stepped into the porch to take a hammer hatchet from the tool shelf, picked up her rolled sleeping bag, and lashed both to the pack-board. Judging the binoculars unnecessary, she backed out of the dogtrot, checked the pockets of her old parka for gloves, matches, and her Clipit . . . and went down the steps, Vanilla whining through the cabin door behind her.

Sara walked to the right around the corner of the cabin, and up into deeper snow—walking fast, swinging along, checking the rifle's loads, 180-grain Silvertips, as she went.

There was no easier way to where she'd seen the mountain sheep—only directly up through steep timber to the tree line, a half-mile and a little more. Then right and up along the rock fall another half-mile. When she'd done that, in two or three hours, the sheep would have drifted on over the face ridge, and a mile or more around the mountain. There, with luck, they'd pause to graze lichen and last year's tundra grasses, exposed where wind had blown the snow streaming away.

Upslope from the cabin, Sara kept climbing, tending to the right above the dog yard, then farther right up a stretch steepening as she walked it—so that first she stepped erect, trudging through piled drifts . . . then fairly soon slowed and began to stoop as she mounted. A hundred yards on, she bent to the slope's rise, and from there clambered into trees growing on so steep a face that she tugged out her gloves, put them on, and commenced to climb hand over hand from small spruce to small spruce, going up on all fours.

She mounted through the trees as if they were only limbs growing from the mountain's trunk—the mountain a stone tree huge beyond measuring. Here, there were barely steps of rock and snow, held to the mountain's side themselves only by grace of crowding spruce. Sara climbed over white snow and gray stone, but up through green, hauling herself higher past endless branches, careful always to keep a grip while trying the next. Her left wrist, sprained mushing up from Billy Mitchell two weeks before, ached a little in reminder as she worked.

Her gloves tore after a while—and where they had, her hands were soon bleeding, chewed raw by the evergreens' rough bark, stung by frozen sap. But the cold as she climbed soon worked for her; she was able to let her hands be tools, chilled numb, cramped into hooks that fitted the small spruce trunks best. She used these senseless hands to hang from—forgot her fingers, and let the long muscles in her back do the hoisting. Those and her legs. Between them, they lifted her and lifted her—and if her back cramped, her legs worked harder. If her legs commenced to tremble, then her back bent, and hauled her up.

After a while, Sara rode herself as a passenger, no effort left to her at all. She rode herself and watched as she went higher—heard the spruce boughs slide past the slung rifle's barrel, heard the snow ledges creak and crumble beneath her boots. Heard herself desperate for air. And the less she was herself, the more she was herself, and happy.

All the while, she knew where the sheep were grazing—knew as if she were an early robin or winter jay flying above the trees, and saw the sheep moving so much higher, drifting . . . sliding east, slowly east as they grazed off the shoulder of the mountain. She knew where the sheep were without thinking about it anymore. And the less she thought, the more she knew.

Sara climbed up through trees past the morning and into afternoon—and then was startled to come to the end of them at timberline, where only the last scattered little spruce, ancient, dwarfed by suffering, grew from ice-spalled cracks, wind-hammered granite.

Here she stepped out into open air, and tried to flex her fingers. Waited, then tried again. And after a while, when they would bend at least a little, she stooped and went to all fours to crab sideways along a ledge of silver-blue stone, its edges frail enough to crack softly away beneath her boot-pacs, so she had to keep moving . . . moving to the right until she could scramble slowly up a pitch, watching her handholds, leaning in, leaning into the mountain so it might befriend her, hold her close. The coldness of its stone (perfectly remembering deep winter) radiated up under her, sandwiched her between that iciness and the heat of the sun on the back of her neck, her back where the rifle shifted, her buttocks and backs of her thighs as she climbed. . . .

When Sara reached a tundra flat, banked above with snow too painfully white to look at long, she stood staring to the right—and saw, watching vast stillness for movement, the last tiny distant dot of soft ivory as a Dall ewe followed her small flock up and over the midline ridge only half a mile higher.

The sun had swung down to shine in Sara's eyes by the time she reached that place, at the nearest boulder—one of five stones, sixty or seventy feet high, that stood along the ridgeline like soldiers. She and Alan had taken a full day, their first summer in the mountains, to climb this far. They'd disturbed the little marmots—silent now, as if Sara were a wolf, winter-starved, come trotting so high to hunt them. She and Alan had disturbed the little marmots here, so they scuttled and whistled in rage as the invaders settled to eat cold moose and sourdough biscuits—sitting in evening's shadow against this boulder's sun-heated granite to picnic, with summer's light still to last to midnight. They'd sat together in shade, and looked out into daylight and distance. . . . Later, a hawk's shadow had grown to an eagle's, and the eagle—a female, huge and dark bronze—had kited close enough overhead so they heard the slightest hiss and ruffle of wind through its plumage. The marmots had lain in perfect stillness and silence as it flew over, death's submissive subjects.

Sara crossed the ridge trotting, airy with altitude, and jogged down into a snowfield, regretting her snowshoes as she sank thigh-deep, had to slow and toil her way across. The snow, the depth and thickness of it, was what held her to the mountain for this stretch, only a thousand yards. She waded across at such an angle to the slope that during deeper steps, her left elbow trenched a small separate track beside her. To the right, the snowfield fell away to snow-fall, drifting steeply down and down to a blue-white vacancy . . . far beneath which commenced a landscape below.

But for fear of her voice starting the snow moving, or echoing over and back and forth to frighten the sheep farther along, Sara would have sung.

She reached the snowfield's edge, slowly climbed a wall of granite cracked up and down into angled pillars . . . and, once over that, sat for a while exhausted, cradling her hands, blood frozen to their torn gloves. Then she tucked her hands in under her parka, under her shirt to cuddle and warm them against her until, thawing, they hurt her more and more. From where she sat, Sara looked out across a peninsula of snowy tundra no more than six or seven hundred yards across to another rising wall of stone—this long buttress lifting sev-eral hundred feet, its black shadow sliding down and off the moun-tain—and saw her sheep grazing at its base.

When she could bend her fingers again, when they were only painful, Sara climbed down to the tundra, and trotted fifty yards or so, careful of her ankles among the thick tussocks. Then walked. . . . Then went on all fours, watching the sheep while they watched her from still so far away—pausing in feeding to see her, glancing up to find her almost always on all fours, and still. They noticed her sta-tionary at five hundred yards away. . . . Then four hundred, per-haps less. Then, after a while, closer.

Sara, so pleasantly weary small specks came swimming before her eyes, knelt in cold crunching shallow snow between two crowding tussocks brown with winterkill, and felt the early evening sun sting-ing her right wrist. She'd seen the flock's only ram, a young one—and that three of four ewes were pregnant, his winter duty done.

The ram was less than three hundred yards away and half-reared up, left foreleg bent as he stretched for some richer tuft at the gran-ite's base. Sara reached slowly back for her rifle, slid it slowly up and off her shoulder and brought it slowly around to cradle, twisting the strap around her left forearm for steadiness . . . lifted the leaf sight and snicked off the safety. Fitting the stock to her shoulder, she lowered her head to see the ram as the rifle saw it, and slowly squeezed the cold trigger to a terrific noise that cracked and rang across the mountain—and before the bullet reached him, knew the ram was dead.

The fifth and sixth trips to Backache, over spoiling snow, the team had hauled four five-gallon cans of kerosene, a second two-gallon can of Blazo, Visqueen—the rolled plastic sheeting heavy as a hard-wood log—and various tools: bucksaw, handsaws, auger, drill and bits, sledgehammer, adz, level, cord, a coil of light Dacron rope, dowel mallet, another gas lantern, and spare blades for the big plane—and food as well, to cache roped high between three white spruce. Burlap sacks of dog food (enough till they hauled the barge goods up), canned food, tea, rice, Crisco (the last of it), cornmeal, beans, honey, and peanut butter (the last of it). Cook kettle, tea-kettle, a pot and a pan, butcher knife, big spoon, small spoon, and a fork.

The sixth trip, almost all supplies hauled in (medicine box last), Sara had stayed on to work for two or three days—spring's generous sunlight lasting later into evening. She'd camped in a ragged clearing at the edge of the spruce stand and finished digging out the work cabin's foundation—ten feet square, and set well upslope of the old workings along the creek. She'd finished the foundation ditches the first day, and spent the second setting heavy stones into them to insulate the permafrost from the cabin's heat—big round creek stones chopped out of Backache's ice. Here, along the mountainside, the stream was already threaded through with spring overflow fleeting across, wearing the ice sheets away. . . .

Just before sunset the second day, Sara lugged the last south-wall stone up to the site, dropped it into the foundation ditch, stepped down to stomp it firmly onto rock-hard permafrost, then walked slowly around the cabin's foundations to be sure she'd made no mistake. After that, she quit work.

She put her parka on, sweat chilling her as the air grew colder toward night, and sat at her campfire to eat warmed peanut butter on pilot bread. . . . Then, finished, and stupid with fatigue, she got up and walked the circle around camp to check the dogs, say goodnight, loose only Dutchy to stay beside her. She came back to the ground-cloth and took off her boot-pacs, crawled into the sleeping bag, and slept through the shortening night and into morning with Dutchy lying close, his legs quivering now and then as he chased through his dreams. . . .

Sara woke to full morning light with her back hurting as if she'd fallen a distance. And when she got out of the sleeping bag and stood, was suddenly dizzy and almost sick enough to vomit, goose bumps running up her arms, her hands tingling. She went over to a tree and leaned against it, her eyes closed . . . and after a while, felt better.

It was a sunny day. Warmer, with no wind. Sara rebuilt the fire, went down to Backache for a pail of overflow for the dog pot, then set that to one side on the fire's stones. She dumped rice and frozen sheep guts in to boil. Then, tired of the smell of her clothes, she took them off and walked naked out of the spruces' shelter into bright sunshine and deeper snow, squatted to comb her fingers through it, lift handfuls to rub her body down. She reached for a pinch of snow to taste, and decided there were only days of traveling-snow left, even this high. Her breasts ached a little in the cold—ached just running with the dogs, now.

She stood and was kicking her way barefoot through snow back to the spruce stand, when several ptarmigan flew, their wings flashing far down the creek. Then, two more. Sara looked, saw nothing but poplars, the few small birches, willow greening along the bank. No breeze stirred the branches. . . . Past the creek's steep still-frozen run, farther down the mountainside, she saw nothing new through morning mist burning away in sunlight—only boulders, snow patches, a drift of granite scree slid down long ago, and the gray-green of tundra meadows draped over the slopes below.

She stood watching a while longer, her feet . . . legs growing numb with cold, and turned away just as Dutchy growled and came to stand beside her—so turned to look again and thought she saw a wolf, something not much larger than that, moving across the land-scape a mile down. Crows called, and Sara stood naked, shading her eyes with her hand, watching. She saw the wolf again—saw it mov-ing—then could see it was standing as it climbed, and was a man.

She walked back into the trees to her camp, brushed snow from her legs and feet with her dirty underwear, dug into her pack for clean panties and bra, and put them on. Then put on a fresh tan-and-white-plaid flannel shirt, and tugged her jeans on—not the cleanest pair. She sat on the tarp to get into fresh socks and her boot-pacs . . . Dutchy standing growling all the while. The team, chained to their trees, began to yelp.

Dressed, Sara dragged Dutchy to his tree and chained him. Then she checked the big Ruger's loads, slid the revolver down under her belt in the back, grip turned right for her reach, and walked back out into the snowfield. She stood waiting, chewing frozen strips of smoked mutton tough as green wood . . . and saw, far below, dwarf-willow branches shifting slightly in her direction along the creek's near bank, as if in slow succession the small trees were learning to walk—uprooting, taking only one or two tentative steps.

As Sara chewed and swallowed the last of her jerky, a man—still little with distance—came climbing upslope out of the willows. He carried a pack, had a rifle and snowshoes slung alongside it down his back. He wore a dark broad-brim hat and a blue parka.

A few minutes later, she could see he was climbing the way a young man climbed. And soon after that, saw a dark spot on his face that grew darker as he climbed nearer . . . and then, as he reached the crest, became a black patch over a blind left eye.

Sara was glad to see him, and sorry he'd come. She'd imagined many strangers. —Sorry he'd come, but since he had, she wished she'd put on her cleaner jeans, brushed clear a small reflecting surface on the creek's ice to look at herself in, that and combed her hair; it had grown much longer.

"Hey," Jack Joseph called to her. "You doin' O.K. up here?" He took off his hat and stood smiling in sunlight on the wind-packed snow just off the stream bank. Overalls, boots, a red wool shirt . . . and his torn old parka, hanging open. A lean boy, his skin the shade of light-cure leather.

"Doing O.K.," Sara said, and supposed her voice sounded strange to him. It sounded strange to her. "Patch looks good on that eye."

"Guys made me put it on, workin' the rig. Said a white eye was bad luck. Ghost eye." Jack Joseph stood in the snow as if expectant—Sara thought maybe he wanted her to go to him. Kiss him . . . something like that.

"They could be right. So, you've been up on the Slope?"

"Few weeks." He might have gained a little muscle working the rigs; looked tougher, but no older.

"You want some tea?"

"Tea'd be good, Mrs. Maher."

"Sara."

"—Sara."

She led up to her camp, saw him glance at the finished foundation, the tall tripod and block and tackle already raised and rigged to swing up logs to set for the cabin. He shrugged off his pack, snowshoes, and slung rifle—the same Remington carbine—and leaned them against a white spruce.

"Goin' to lift the logs with that?"

"Upper courses—you get the balance point and it's not hard. Haul it up off the ground, then I can swing it in where I want it—tie one end into place, swing the other end in." Sara shook her teakettle; it sloshed half full, and she hung it on the green stick crossed over the fire's coals. Then, to the side, where the dog pot grunted, beginning to boil, she fed the flames punk and broken branches to keep them high.

Jack Joseph hunkered on his heels across the fire, comfortable, long arms draped over his knees, hands hanging relaxed. His fine long fingers had been bruised, the nails blackened by oil field labor. He watched as she turned aside to dig out her tea tin, scoop the small caddy full, close it, lift the kettle's lid and drop the caddy in.

"How's the Slope, Jack?"

"It's all right. Good money." Jack Joseph looked into the fire, and didn't seem to have more to say about the Slope. ". . . You went on down to Seattle."

"Yes."

"Didn' stay long."

"I was in Fairbanks awhile, after I came up."

"Sure, I know that. —Didn' like Seattle?"

"No, I didn't like it. Too many people."

"Weird." Jack Joseph shifted slightly to his left, out of the fire's smoke.

Sara didn't know whether he meant her, or her coming back so soon after such a definite departure. Or only that too many people made for weirdness.

"You walk all the way up, Jack?"

"No, I got the machine down there a few miles. A day down there. Snow's pretty much had it."

Sara noticed his right eye, a rich dark brown with gold segments radiating from its pupil when he looked at her. A look more direct and brighter, she thought, for being from his only sighted eye. His other—she remembered white as a creek stone—was hidden now beneath the patch, unable to see even ghosts from there.

"—Reason I come up, my great-aunt Mary Toby told me about the kid."

"Well, she was right to tell you." The kettle began to murmur, and Sara turned to dig for her big aluminum cup—reached with a short piece of stick to tilt the kettle, and poured the cup full. "Honey?"

"I'll take some honey."

Sara handed the cup over, then opened the grub box, got out the big can of honey and passed it to him with the spoon.

"Old Frank is really pissed at you." Jack Joseph put a spoonful of honey into his tea, stirred it slowly.

"I have every legal right to keep that homestead on Porcupine Corporation land, and live there. I checked that out. In Fairbanks, up to the time I found out about the baby, they said I didn't have a very good case. But now I do—unless you want to say this isn't your child."

"I didn' say that."

"All right. And I have subsistence rights, too."

"An' he's mad you took the dogs. Gettin' to like those dogs."

"I offered to leave a pup with Charlie. . . ."

Jack Joseph drank his tea, hunkered as comfortably as if he sat in a chair. Sara could smell him, faintly, through the trembling air above the fire between them—dried salmon, gun oil, campfire smoke, and the light fine sweat of youth. She recalled those odors from their fucking, when he'd been on her . . . had been over and inside her. His sweat so smoky and sweet. She closed her eyes for a moment, saw the both of them sitting opposite across this small fire—and drew back in her vision until they were just visible in the mountain's landscape, tiny amid stone's gray, snow's white, and silver where the frozen creek lay down, already stained and running here and there with blue overflow. Sara drew farther and farther back, until she saw the two of them barely . . . then not quite, then not at all. Everything was mountains and the sky. . . .

She brought herself back to where they were, and regretted having to do it—then reached out over the fire's heat and put her hand on Jack Joseph's neck, just under his left ear, as if to reassure herself he was real. When she pulled her hand back, the boy stayed still, watching her.

"Excuse me," Sara said. Then, "How's Christine?"

"She's O.K. Says to say hello. —I figured I could stay up here, help you out."

"Well, thank you, but I don't think so. . . . There are three reasons I don't want you to stay up here, Jack Joseph. First, I'm too old for you, and you're too young for me."

"Bullshit."

"—Second, you're no gold miner. I'm going to be working all summer here, getting at least one sluice box built and set up. And working here through fall and early winter, too. I can dam a pond and keep breaking through the ice to get my flow; not let the ice get too thick. Then, just dig the gravel and sand to shake. There's almost enough overflow for sluicing, this steep a drop."

" 'Break through the ice. . . .' " Jack Joseph sipped his tea.

"—Work here early winter, then deep-winter back at the home-stead and come out to work here again in the spring. And I don't think you'd like digging channels and building sluice boxes and standing in cold water all day, every day. And panning when you're too tired to work the shake box."

"I can do it."

"You can do it—but you wouldn't want to do it. And pretty soon you'd pick a fight with me and quit, and then go back down to ride the river and fish, or go work up on the Slope with your friends."

"I wouldn't."

"Yes, you would. And third—the third reason is I don't want you up here, anyway. I don't want anybody up here in a personal way with me. Truth is, now I don't want someone to come up and help me work the creek. I really don't even want that."

"I heard about the ad you put in the paper."

"I thought that was a good idea, but now I don't. And I'm glad nobody's come up. I want to live here alone with the baby, and that's what I'm going to do. I'm happiest away from people."

Jack Joseph's eye grew narrower, darker. "I don't believe this shit—you goin' to have the kid up here all alone? *Hey,* this is my kid, too, lady."

"Yes, it is. And you're always welcome up here, Jack—or over on the homestead next winter. You come up and visit us, visit the baby any time you want."

"But not to stay, right?"

"No."

"It's just wrong. Just fuckin' ridiculous. . . ." Jack Joseph tossed the lees of his tea sideways, spattering into the snow, and Sara reached over through the fire's heat for the cup, tilted the kettle to pour some for herself.

"No, it isn't ridiculous. It's the way you feel about the river, Jack. That's the way I feel about up here—and we wouldn't get along."

Still hunkered down, staring at her. He looked better with the eye patch. Thin, handsome without the blind white eye visible. He'd tied his long black hair back with a short length of red knitting wool.

"—Coming up here was a man's thing to do, Jack Joseph, and I appreciate it." The tea was very hot; she blew gently into the cup to cool it.

"It's crazy, havin' a baby up here."

"I'll raise the baby up here—but I'm going down to Billy Mitchell to have it."

"An' supposin' the baby comes early? Then you're goin' to need some serious help on this goddamn mountain."

"Then I'll help myself. But that won't happen; I'll go down in plenty of time. I talked to the doctor in Fairbanks, and he said I was healthy, and it would be O.K."

"Don't you give me that crap. He said O.K. 'cause he figured you *livin'* down at Ruby or Eagle or maybe Fort Billy. I know no doctor said O.K. for you bein' up here—three, four goddamn days from anybody!"

"He said, O.K. And I also talked to a midwife, and I have two books about it, just in case."

"*Books . . .*"

"That's right." Sara was glad his pale eye was covered, that she didn't have to stand its stare. "And the women at the Fort gave me formula powder if I need it, and a fine-grinder and a big box of jars of strained food. And I brought up some diaper cloth."

Jack Joseph sighed like an older man. "An' supposin' the baby gets sick—or you get sick up here, or you get hurt. Then what's goin' to happen to the baby?"

"I'll take care of the baby. I won't get sick, and I won't get hurt. But if I do, I'll still take care of the baby."

"God *damn* it. . . ." Jack Joseph stood, went to the white spruce for his pack, snowshoes and rifle, then strolled away swinging them up onto his back—going as if a breeze had come up, was drifting him out of camp. No good-bye.

"Wait! Wait a minute, Jack. I have something for you."

"I don't want nothin' from you, bitch. Fuck you . . . !"

Sara supposed he was so angry because he was glad to be going.

"Wait a minute." She picked the sheathed shotgun up off the tarp, then went to reach into the cache sling, hauled down the possibles-sack, found the shell belt of birdshot alternating with sabot slugs—and two boxes of birdshot and a box of sabots. Also three boxes of Federal .44 magnum cartridges, 240 grain. "—*Here.*"

Jack Joseph was standing beside the creek, still facing down the mountain—appeared to be walking, standing still.

Sara carried the ammunition, shell belt and shotgun down, and handed them to him.

"I don't want this shit," he said.

"Take it." She was startled to see that Jack Joseph was crying. Tears in his good eye—perhaps behind the blind eye's patch as well. She didn't know what to say, so just drew the big Ruger from the back of her belt and handed the revolver to him, too. "—They're good guns, but I don't want them up here anymore. No ducks or geese settle this high; the eagles scare them. And if I want ptarmigan, I'll snare some."

Jack Joseph stood holding the guns. "I don't want 'em."

"Neither do I, and I'm tired of carrying them around."

"I said I don't want 'em. I don't want shit from you!"

"I'm giving you these guns, Jack Joseph. I don't need them up here. They're good guns for down on the river, but up here I don't need anything but the rifle."

Jack Joseph stood holding the ammunition, shotgun, shell belt and pistol, staring at her in an odd way. Probably thought she was crazy—had gone crazy in Seattle. He stood, decorated with guns. "I don't want 'em," he said, and held the pistol out to her as if it were some bright, heavy token of love, but Sara didn't take it back. "Let me stay a little while," he said. "I'll camp down the creek. You know, just till you get set."

"I am set, Jack."

. . . Sara watched Jack Joseph walk away downslope along the creek, pleased at his going—only slightly disappointed he hadn't been more stubborn. She saw by his posture—the way his back bore the burden of pack, snowshoes, and rifle, the sheathed shotgun and shell belt—that he'd tucked the big pistol into his belt on his left-side front, butt right.

He stepped along as even fishing Indians walked woods, as if at the very next stride, so relaxed, he might sink through the shallow drifts to his boot-tops, then deeper . . . deeper, and continue his journey half under the ground, as if his earth were soft as snow.

*   *   *

Sara woke in spring night's fleeting darkness, to the sound of rain. It pattered into the last of the snow on the cabin's roof, fell softly past the window.

"It's raining," Sara said to Alan, then woke completely and remembered he was dead. This was the first rain since she'd come back up; the first rain since before the first snow, nine months before. It seemed proper that rain had wakened her one of her last evenings at the homestead, rather than over at the workings—with Backache already cracked to thaw, the new cabin built, but for its roof . . . warm-weather labor already begun.

Sara lay in the wide bunk listening to the rain . . . an occasional clatter as an icicle melted free of the cabin's eaves. She listened for a while, figuring what more she might need around the mountain—how many backpacking trips would be required. Pots, pans, sourdough starter already gone—the shed's old barrel-stove already over (and just in time, sledded on the last of the useful snow). There were duplicate tools still to go . . . and food, the last of last fall's vegetables, sacks of tired cabbage, odd cauliflower, strange potatoes. The last sack of rice weighed one hundred pounds—would take her two full days to carry over, unless she broke the load up. . . . The pups murmured beneath the bunk, trying to suckle. Vanilla growled and shifted away from them. . . .

Dog noises woke her to bright morning—yelps, furious howls from the dog yard. Then Vanilla up and out from underneath the bunk, scattering her pups and roaring at the cabin door.

Sara, naked, climbed off the bunk—felt suddenly sick for a moment, and paused, standing, to take deep breaths . . . then felt better. She pulled on her jeans and green flannel shirt, then went to the door barefoot, opened it—and keeping Vanilla and the pups inside, slipped through to the steps. She thought it unlikely, these weeks late, that some man had come adventuring up to work Backache with her. . . .

There was nothing along the creek but morning sunshine, so every poplar branch, furred with green buds, was defined in windless light.

Sara stood on the cabin steps, watching, then sniffing the air for lightning fire on the mountain—unlikely after last night's rain. She went down the steps—the team still noisy over in the yard, Vanilla scratching at the cabin door behind her—and walked left to the cabin's corner, stepping to avoid the last snow patches. Looked upslope, and saw nothing but remnant snowfields higher, just below the ridge . . . the stand of sentinel spruce.

There was no smoke in the air besides the smolder of alder chunks from the cabin stove. None of the bitter flavor of burning forest. Sara walked on around to the back of the cabin, her feet chilled over cold moss, cold-furred spring grasses. There was nothing moving there but two robber jays scurry-flying along the ground, pecking at early insects. The birds paid no attention to her.

Vanilla thundered inside the cabin—Sara heard the pups squeaking with excitement, essaying barks. Bedlam from the dog yard.

She walked on around the cabin, saw the team leaping to their chain-ends across the slope. Dutchy, at the near stake, was standing silent, staring left across the cabin's front and on upslope, where the small creek bent around its high meadow's open ground to emerge and course downhill.

Sara stood at the front corner of the cabin and looked up to the left, where Dutchy was looking. She saw nothing moving in the trees, and nothing standing still—no man come packing up this late, and pausing to look the homestead over.

The dogs were making too much noise. Sara turned her head to call *"Shut up!"* to Vanilla—and when she turned back, looked high again and saw a bear walking down the ridge through the big trees, which looked smaller as it passed.

Sara stared as if watching magic. Her heart, to some music only it could hear, began a furious beat, so rapid she felt sick. The bear, very big—light brown in sun, darker brown in shadow—paced . . . drifted down between trees and among trees.

"It's not the same," Sara said to Alan or anyone. "It's a different animal." As it almost certainly was, and going . . . going on its way. Would be gone very soon, down the mountain. Had traveled the old bear trail high above the cabin—a different bear, though the same color. A different bear to have come down too soon for berries. And asking only to be let alone.

There was no reason to go after it. Certainly no reason to take the rifle down and go and see, when it was a different bear.

Sara walked up the cabin steps, opened the door carefully so as to keep Vanilla and the pups inside, slipped through the door and closed it. She intended to go feed the stove, slice mutton to fry for breakfast—hadn't intended to still be by the door, taking the Winchester down, dumping the light rounds on the cabin floor, working the bolt while she went to the canned-goods shelf for the box of two-hundred-grain solids, then fingering five free to load.

Stupid and unnecessary.

She remembered to close the cabin door on Vanilla, then ran down the steps—suddenly doubled to the right, out toward the dog yard to let Dutchy go, have him as her companion. Then felt that wasn't the thing to do, and turned again and ran down toward the creek. Barefoot, realized she was barefoot . . . running too fast to fall, the Winchester held up in her right hand.

Sara jumped half over the creek—splashed, dashing ice water—and was up and out the other bank, her left heel aching from hitting a rock. Felt she hadn't slowed, but was running faster and faster as the world grew more leisurely.

She bucked through the meadow brush and ran faster yet, splashing through shallow melt water here and there, the spring's mosquitoes (black wisps and smudges) rising, clouding to meet her. She ran so her running was a series of leaps, not wasting footfalls, and saw the bear again, only a reminder of its color passing through thicket four hundred yards left and higher. Moving fast—not knowing or not caring she was coming to it.

Sara saw the grizzly was following the creek upstream, along its wooded bend at the meadow's upper edge. She felt the meadow's slope rising under her feet—jumped damp berry bushes in her way, the rifle lifting her up and over—ran hard then ran harder, felt the winter's sharp stubble break beneath her feet as she went.

In the trees, she lost the bear, but ran on through the spruce toward water, ran until past rough trunks she saw sunshine sparkle, the creek dappling as its current moved.

Sara came out onto the near bank, oddly breathless but stronger all the same—a fast runner over slow earth—kicked through brush and saw the animal just across the stream and much bigger, ambling along that bank.

Sara stopped and yelled *"Heyyy!"* so harshly her throat hurt.

The grizzly, startled, spun neatly as a circus trick and stood eight or nine feet high to see her better. It seemed too big to be Alan's bear.

The creature's coat in sunlight was light cinnamon, rough with winter pelting—and now Sara saw, down the right side of its thick neck, an odd ruff of fur grown to lie reversed.

"God . . . oh God," she said, felt grateful beyond gratitude and swung the rifle lightly up, thumbed off the safety, and rested the sights on the sow bear's breast, high center. She smelled the animal on a mild breeze across the narrow water, smelled the harsh winter-denning odor.

The grizzly dropped suddenly to all fours and strode swiftly toward her, quickly bowlegged down into the creek, smashing shallow water, and snapped heavily at the air, fangs whack-whacking loud as ax strokes. She was bigger than being closer should have made her. Her eyes, the shade of honey and too small, too deeply set in that great head, stared at Sara completely, leaving nothing else to see. Sara shifted the rifle sights to the bear's right shoulder and commenced to take her shot.

She took up the trigger slack—and something came scrambling out of the brush across the creek so suddenly that Sara jerked the rifle that way and almost pulled the trigger as a bear cub, dark-furred and very small—newborn in winter—came scurrying from the brush to its mother.

The cub scuttled out into the creek's mild rapids—suddenly splashed to a stop, squealing in terror of Sara—and the mother wheeled to cuff it rolling to clear her way. But her cub came cringing back to her, soaked, crying, struggling over creek stones so the sow turned aside and hit her cub again, harder, to drive it away while Sara stood aiming, the rifle's sights shifting to keep track of the heaviest bone to break the grizzly down.

Wailing, the cub crawled out onto the far bank, and the sow— bright water flashing, splashing along beneath her—swayed back and forth, confused between her noisy young and Sara standing so close across.

It took too long to squeeze the trigger. Much too long, as if the rifle were reluctant to make such spiteful noise in a quiet morning. The cub was making noise enough.

Sara felt drunk with pleasure and possibility. It was difficult to breathe; time wouldn't pass to let her. She tried to take a breath as she leaned to put the rifle gently down on a drift of pebbles. It seemed improper to have the rifle between her and the bear. The grizzly swung back to stare at her, nearsighted. Sara began to breathe as if she never had before, so it surprised her. She stepped down into icy water and bent to find a stone—found one fist-sized, picked it up and drew back her arm. Shouted "Get *out!*" and threw it, just missed the animal's right side. Then bent to pick up another stone, smaller, smoother, dented at the back, and threw that and hit the bear's left foreleg, so it snorted and reared half-up, surprised.

"GET . . . OUT!"

Troubled more by shouting than by stones, the grizzly shifted uneasily, fell to all fours and dipped her snout into the water—shook her head from side to side, spraying water, making short rainbows of sunlight. Her cub yowled on the bank behind her.

Sara stooped for another stone, decided not, and walked deeper into the water—stood barefoot on slippery stones much nearer the bear, the shallow rapids splashing, soaking her trousers. She had no feeling in her feet. The cub was frantic, yelping like a puppy.

"You get out of here," Sara said to the grizzly, and looked at the animal with less and less interest, as if she'd seen all it had to show. She supposed some of the bear, some slab of muscle, some length of heavy white bone, was Alan.

"You heard me. . . ."

And the grizzly, more and more uneasy at the talking, grunted and suddenly wheeled massively left, turning on some odd point of balance—and splashing, dripping water, lunged hugely up and out its side of the creek. Strode slouching to nuzzle the cub. . . . Sara saw the bear's great paw prints over there, wet across a run of white pebbles. The grizzly grunted again, then shifted her direction as if in a wind, and walked swiftly away between trees that seemed to open and make an aisle for her—the cub, still whimpering, running after. . . .

Sara walked back out of the water, climbed the creek's bank, and bent to pick her rifle up. She snapped its safety on, and walked away through brush and stretches of ailing snow—her bare feet bruised, aching with cold—walked on out into the meadow and across it, hearing the continuing clamor of the dogs, their half-wild music. Her feet were hurting every step, the left foot worse. Mosquitoes came flying back to her in small soft clouds, as if relieved the bear was gone.

Sara crossed the creek downstream, below the cabin, climbed the slope and cabin steps and went inside . . . unloaded the 200-grains, loaded with 180s, and put the rifle up. She let the pups out, and kept Vanilla in. After she'd dried her feet, she pulled on thick wool socks and stood comfortably in those to start the cookstove fire, then re-heat yesterday's coffee, cut and fry two slices of mutton. . . . Had that for breakfast, and pilot bread with *kamamik* and honey.

Afterward, Sara went out to feed the dogs (ashamed to feed so late), her bruised feet tender in the boot-pacs. And decided, even starting almost midday, there was time to make distance to the work-ings with the sack of rice. Let the dogs travvy the last few planks . . . the sacks of vegetables, gardening tools and seed. Could come back in a few days, pick up the potted seeds already started.

As she walked across to the yard—the dogs calmer now, standing alert beside their little houses, watching her, eager for breakfast—

Sara saw two small windflowers just blossomed, petals cream-white, at the melting edge of snow along the slope. She thought of picking them, but didn't, and went on to the shed for the buckets and yoke . . . then walked down through willows to the creek for water.

The last ice left in that shade was so indefinite she could break it with her boot. Sara filled both buckets, yoked them, and set them down on the bank. Then she lifted her left hand, worked her wedding band free, stooped and reached down through running water to leave it lying bright among white stones forever, a gift to the country.